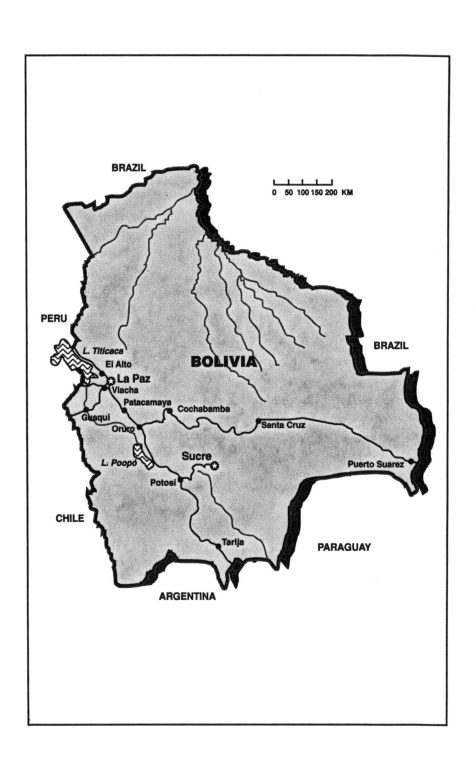

COUP!

A Novel

Alexander M. Grace

LYFORD
Books

This is a novel. The characters and organizations are an invention of the author, except where they can be identified historically, and are not intended to depict real persons or organizations. Any resemblance to actual persons, living or dead, is purely coincidental. Likewise, names, dialogue, and opinions expressed in the text are products of the author's imagination and should not be interpreted as real.

Copyright © 1991 by Alexander M. Grace

Lyford Books
Published by Presidio Press
505 B San Marin Drive, Suite 300
Novato, CA 94945-1340

All rights reserved. No part of this book may be reproduced or utilized in any form or by any means, electronic or mechanical, including photocopying, recording, or by any information storage and retrieval systems, without written permission from the Publisher. Inquiries should be addressed to Presidio Press, 505 B San Marin Drive Suite 300, Novato, CA 94945-1340

Library of Congress Cataloging-in-Publication Data

Grace, Alexander M. , 1951-
    Coup! : a novel / Alexander M. Grace
      p.   cm.
    ISBN 0-89141-418-5
    I. Title.
PS3557.R1164C68   1992
813' .54—dc20   91-26220
                                                      CIP

Typography by ProImage

Printed in the United States of America

This book is dedicated to my dear wife, who gave up her homeland, family, and life-long friends to follow me in my wanderings around the world, and who gave us three beautiful daughters to keep us company on the way. What a nice thing to do.

Glossary

The following brief glossary is meant as a quick reference for the reader, including military terminology, some specifically Bolivian expressions, and information that it would have been awkward to explain fully in the text of the novel.

Bolivia: Bolivia is a huge country, approximately the size of California and Texas combined, but with a population of only some eight million. Of this total, nearly two-thirds live in the uplands of the Andes in the western third of the country. The remainder live in the semitropical lowlands to the east, which gradually merge with the Amazon Basin.

Cadillac-Gage V-100: An American-made four-wheeled armored car. The Bolivian model is armed with a machinegun in the turret. It can also carry several infantrymen.

Cascavel: A six-wheeled Brazilian armored car, mounting a 90mm gun and one or two machineguns, and carrying a crew of three. It is designed for use in urban areas as well as in a traditional military role in open terrain. It is lightly armored but proof against small-arms fire and well protected against incendiary grenades. It is used by the Brazilian Army and has been widely sold throughout Latin America and the Middle East.

Cocaine: It takes several steps of chemical processing to produce cocaine hydrochloride, the substance actually used (or abused) as the recreational drug of choice of the 1980s, from coca leaf. The various processes separate the many alkaloids found in the leaf, of which cocaine is one. The first product is called coca paste, which is then processed into cocaine base, and finally into hydrochloride. The finished, pure cocaine HCL is subsequently diluted with other substances, both to increase its profitability by increasing volume and to diminish the effects that pure HCL has on the human body.

LAW-80: A British antitank missile. It is transportable and usable by a single infantryman. The unit is essentially a round of ammunition, and the firing tube is discarded after the missile has been fired. It has a range of five hundred meters and is reportedly capable of penetrating the frontal armor of most main battle tanks. It possesses a spotting rifle with a five-round capacity that fires tracer rounds to confirm proper aim.

Ministry of Interior: This institution, sometimes referred to in other Latin American countries as the Ministry of Government, is rather alien to the American experience. It handles what we would see as the roles of the Department of Justice, including the FBI, DEA, and the attorney general's office. It also controls the border police, immigration authorities, prisons, customs (usually), the secret service (that is, the protective agency for the president and other senior government officials), and the national police, which corresponds to both the state and local police forces in the United States. The ministry also runs what is generally termed the "secret police," or the internal and external intelligence and security agencies of the government. Consequently, the Ministry of Interior in Bolivia has a rather sinister reputation, being responsible for many "disappearances," torture, and other violations of the human rights of opponents of the regime in power at the time—perhaps not on the scale of Argentina, but proportionate to Bolivia's size a very bloody record indeed. During the dark days of the Garcia Meza dictatorship in the early 1980s the Ministry of Interior allegedly recruited murderers from the prisons themselves to serve as gunmen to help repress opposition to the regime. While the most serious human rights violations by the ministry seem to have occurred under military dictatorships, various civilian administrations have not been without similar, if less frequent, accusations of abuse, and there is the ever-present charge of narcotics-related corruption to which the ministry, as the principal law enforcement agency of the government, is particularly susceptible.

MOWAG: A Swiss-manufactured four-wheeled armored car carrying a crew of three. In the Bolivian service, it is armed only with a machine gun in the turret.

Regiment/battalion: The basic maneuver unit in the Bolivian Army is the regiment. With a strength of between 400 and 1,000 men, it corresponds most closely to a U.S. Army battalion, while a Bolivian battalion, at about 150 to 200 men, would compare to a largish company. There is nothing approaching a standard table of organization for a Bolivian regiment, as the significant difference in size implies. As is quite common in Third World armed forces, a disproportionate amount of the army's firepower is concentrated in a very small number of units, mostly located close to the capital city. This emphasizes the army's true primary role, not as the defender of the nation against external aggression, but as an arbiter of internal politics. While divisional organizations and nominal staffs exist, these are largely administrative entities, and it is the regimental commander who has actual control of the troops, one of the reasons that regimental commanders are constantly wooed by political power brokers both in uniform and out.

Steyr SK-105 Light Tank: This is the only tank-like vehicle in the Bolivian inventory, and is actually a lightly armored tank destroyer. It is made in Austria, possesses a 105mm main gun, and carries a crew of three. It is fully tracked.

UMOPAR: The Bolivian paramilitary narcotics police. This unit was formed in the mid-1980s with American support and training, in an attempt to give the police some armed muscle to deal with the increasingly well armed and violent traffickers of the Chapare and Santa Cruz areas. Trained in light infantry tactics and airmobile assault, the UMOPAR has been responsible for the arrest of many major narcotics traffickers at their well-protected and well-hidden ranches deep in the wilds of the northern Santa Cruz and Beni Departments, most notably Roberto Suarez Gomez, the former godfather of the Bolivian drug mafia, in the summer of 1988. Like other Bolivian police units, however, the UMOPAR has not been immune to charges of corruption.

Urutu: A six-wheeled Brazilian armored personnel carrier capable of transporting thirteen infantrymen and a driver. It is fully amphibious and capable of climbing over obstacles up to one meter high, using the independent walking-beam suspension of its six wheels. It has been widely sold outside Brazil in Latin America and in the Middle East.

Introduction

That the coup d'etat is a concept alien to the Anglo-Saxon way of life is best illustrated by the fact that there is no proper word in English for it. Of course one could construct a phrase to express the idea, such as "military takeover of the government," but that is not quite the same thing. The expression coup d'etat, or *golpe de estado* in Spanish, really refers to the rapid, violent seizure of power and correctly conveys the impression of a calculated assault on key governmental installations, institutions, and leaders. We are fortunate, in the Anglo-Saxon world, that we have been spared the personal experience of this phenomenon, but the headlines of the newspapers are regularly filled with accounts of these events in such places as Panama, the Philippines, Haiti, and indeed throughout the developing world. Furthermore, it should be noted that even in the "Western democracies" it has been less than thirty years since the last attempted coup in France and less than ten since the last attempt in Spain.

In my overseas experience with the State Department I have had the occasion to observe at first hand two coups and a number of more or less serious attempts, as well as several events that might very well have resulted in coups. The situation depicted in this book is, therefore, based on historical fact, although the actual events described are fictional.

The other element that forms the background to the plot is the narcotics trade in Latin America, another unpleasant element of life I have had the responsibility (I purposely avoid using the word "opportunity") to study up close. The American and the Latin American perspectives on this worldwide problem are very different and largely irreconcilable. The Americans see the source of the problem as one of supply and hold the opinion that endemic corruption in Latin America necessitates a strong American hand to keep the antidrug effort on the straight and narrow. The Latin Americans view the problem as one of consumption and strongly resent the implication that it is Latin American incompetence which prevents a solution when, as they point out, the U.S. government itself cannot prevent the massive cultivation of marijuana in California and Hawaii. They point out that while Americans invest money the Latin Americans invest lives, with hundreds of Colombian, Peruvian, and Bolivian policemen and soldiers dying each year in open combat with the narcotics mafia's private armies.

They are both right and both wrong. The drug problem is like a debilitating disease that affects both societies, albeit in different ways. While consumption of drugs destroys lives in the United States and Europe, the lure of easy money diverts Latin American efforts from more productive pursuits. The corruption spread by the drug mafia affects both worlds, gradually eroding the moral fabric of both societies and replacing it with something very dirty.

I have included this brief preface because both topics—military intervention in politics and the narcotics issue—tend to stir up strong feelings in many people. If in my handling of these subjects I can avoid pleasing anyone completely, I will be pretty much on the mark.

Alexander M. Grace

Prologue

Major Osorio lounged at his desk and watched through his open door with weary eyes as the two young lieutenants, Santander and Yanez, sometimes referred to by their colleagues as "Batman and Robin," came rushing through the outer office of the Criminal Investigations Division (DIC) of the Bolivian National Police in Cochabamba. They always seemed so eager, but naively clumsy. He had hoped that he could finish up the remaining few days of his assignment in Cochabamba without having to rein them in harshly before he moved to his next post in La Paz.

So far they had not managed to cause any real harm. It had been apparent from their performance at the Police Academy and their first tour together in the mining town of Potosi that they were idealists, unattracted by the lucrative offers of even the small-time graft available to policemen. Osorio knew from personal experience that a cop could augment his miserable salary by speeding up the endless process of getting people their driver's licenses or fixing traffic tickets. Then there was the ploy of providing extra protection to businesses and individuals who were able to pay for it. The possibilities were endless, even without managing one of the real gold-mine jobs in the narcotics police, called UMOPAR. Since these two wouldn't play that way, they had been purposely sidetracked here to the DIC, where they couldn't get in the way of the activities of the massive cocaine industry based in the nearby Chapare region, where much of Bolivia's coca crop grew. Still, they had followed up on stray leads related to narcotics several times, and only fast footwork on Osorio's part had diverted them so he was able to assign those cases to more experienced men who would do his bidding.

As the two tall young men burst into his office—without knocking, Osorio noted unamusedly—they were out of breath and looked excitedly at each other, wondering who should start. Osorio knew that this meant trouble.

Finally Yanez elbowed Santander in the ribs, and the latter started in. "Major, we have information about a major drug shipment leaving for the States tonight. Should we call the DEA man?"

"First of all," Osorio began in an exhausted and impatient tone of voice, "I think it's high time you two began to realize what fucking country you live in and work for. This is Bolivia, not the United States. We are a sovereign country, and we will enforce our own laws within our own borders. We do not need the fucking DEA to wipe our noses for us."

The two men hung their heads and pouted momentarily. Then Yanez chimed in. "We just thought, since the traffickers always seem to get wind of every case we hear about—"

"Just a fucking minute," Osorio said, rising halfway out of his chair. "You come in here with these 'cases' some imbecile on the street sticks in your ear, and just because we don't end up with a ton of cocaine on my desk you figure the 'traffickers got wind of it'? I'd watch my mouth if I were you," he said, pointing a finger at Yanez. "You come in here with shit, you get shit results. You put a good case to me, and we'll see what happens. Now, my second point is that I'm not about to make a fool of myself to the DEA or anyone else until I've heard everything you have to say."

Santander's face brightened a little. "Sure, Major. You see, I have a cousin who drives a gasoline truck for the YPFB [the Bolivian National Petroleum Corporation]. I was just at his house, and he was bitching that he was going to lose a thousand dollars that he had been offered to deliver a load of airplane fuel to a dirt airstrip about thirty kilometers this side of Villa Tunari tonight. See, my cousin fell off a ladder at home this morning and broke his leg, so he can't drive, and one of the other drivers is taking his place and his money."

Osorio sat back in his chair and let out a long sigh. This was serious. He knew the airstrip they were talking about and who worked out of it. He also knew that a clandestine delivery of fuel at night meant one thing, a drug shipment, and probably a large one, since only the larger shipments went out directly by airplane.

He rubbed his temples thoughtfully with his thumb and middle finger. "I'm sorry I blew up at you, boys," Osorio said in a low voice. "This changes everything. I think you do have something, and we're going to have to move on it fast."

"So," Yanez said eagerly, "are you going to call DEA or UMOPAR?"

"No," said Osorio. "I'm afraid you're right about not being able to trust anyone with this kind of information, and you shouldn't think that only Bolivian cops take drug money. I heard about a DEA agent in Mexico who retired after a few years and, coincidentally, married the daughter of one of the biggest heroin producers in the country. No, I think we should handle this ourselves. That way, if anything goes wrong we'll know that one of the three of us is bad."

The two young men looked at each other in some confusion. "But Major," Santander interjected, "if this is a big shipment, can the three of us handle the guards?"

"Getting a little nervous when it's not just locker-room talk, Santander?" Osorio chided him. "Just trust me. If three shotguns open up from the bushes all of a sudden, those druggies will head for the hills and look for other employment later. They're only in it for the money, and that's no good to them if they're dead. Even if the plane gets away we'll get its tail numbers, so it won't be going anyplace.

"Now I want you to draw three twelve-gauges and bring a jeep around to the front door. I'll be with you in a minute. We'll wait for the gas truck well out on the road to Villa Tunari. It shouldn't be hard to spot, and we'll tail it from there. If the driver is looking for a tail, it'll be at the start of his run. By then he'll have lost interest, and we can give him plenty of room, since we have a good idea where he's going."

Osorio waited for the two men to leave, jamming together in the doorway in their excitement. He watched them cross the outer office and head downstairs before he picked up the phone.

Santander and Yanez kept up a constant stream of conversation in the front seat of the jeep, parked off to one side of the highway in the gathering dusk. Osorio simply sat in the back, staring out at the passing trucks and cars without saying a word. Finally a large YPFB tanker truck rolled by, and all talking stopped in the jeep. They waited for a couple of cars to pass by and then pulled out onto the highway. The jeep was specially equipped for surveillance work and had a set of switches on the dash to turn the headlights on and off in various patterns. In the dark one set of headlights in the rear-view mirror looks pretty much like another, and Santander could change the apparent identity of the jeep in several different ways. On the highway, he had two full sets of headlights and parking lights blazing. When the tanker turned off onto a less-used rural road, he cut down to a single headlight and the parking lights, and as they neared what they assumed was the target area he dropped farther back and turned off all but a set of "blackout" lights that barely illuminated a few meters of dirt road ahead of them. The tanker was easy to follow from a distance due to a dangling red taillight, which jiggled wildly as the truck bounced along the road.

Suddenly Santander slammed on the brakes, throwing them all forward roughly. They were well off the highway now and had left the last farmers' huts behind as well. In the pale moonlight they could see the tanker truck halted at the far side of a clearing about two hundred meters away.

"We must be close," Santander said, turning off all of the jeep's lights and quietly backing up into the shadows of a clump of trees.

The three men climbed out of the jeep, and each checked his shotgun to see that a round was chambered. "You two skirt the edge of the clearing to the left, I'll go to the right," Osorio said. "Find the airstrip and come back here in ten minutes. Then we'll set up to cover the landing area and wait for the plane."

Santander and Yanez both nodded and moved off carefully, and Osorio stepped farther back into the shadows and watched them. His mouth was dry as he saw their dark forms slip silently through the knee-high grass of the clearing. Suddenly there were several gun flashes from the woodline behind the two men and the chatter of automatic weapons fire. Both of the figures went down, but then there was the boom and flash of a shotgun as at least one of them began to return fire. There was another boom and a flash from a different position, and Osorio's stomach churned as he watched the lone man skillfully firing and moving against overwhelming odds. Finally there was a sharp crack from another direction, probably a sniper with a night-vision scope, Osorio thought, and all firing ceased.

"It was a shame it had to come to this," a voice said from the darkness behind Osorio, and he jumped and turned in fright.

Even in the darkness he could make out the wiry frame of "Gusano" Murillo, and the moon shone off his gold-rimmed glasses.

"Yes," was all Osorio could think to respond.

"You did very well, Major," Murillo continued. "I'm accompanying this shipment myself, and although it isn't very large, only about forty kilos, it's meant as a test run for a much larger shipment next week. We'll be using a different landing strip then, so you'll have no trouble making a full report of this incident when you get back."

"What am I going to say?" Osorio asked, still unable to think clearly.

"Just tell them the truth about your subordinates' lead. Everything up to this point. Then you were ambushed. They were killed, and you just got away with your life to go for help. Of course, by the time you get back we'll be long gone."

Murillo stepped over to the parked jeep and fired a burst from a Czech-made machine pistol, spraying bullets across the windshield. "That should add credibility to your story."

"I suppose that will work," Osorio said quietly. "Thank you."

Murillo put a comradely arm around his shoulder. "It had to be done, my friend. You know we don't like this killing any more than you do, but those two just wouldn't take the easy way. It would have been so much better if they would have let us put their children through college, but they wanted it this way."

"Of course you're right, Gusano," Osorio said as he opened the jeep door and brushed the shattered glass off the seat, cutting his hand in the process. He put his hand to his mouth and sucked at the blood.

"That little cut will make it look even better," Murillo said, closing the jeep door for Osorio. "I'll be tied up with these two shipments for the next few days, but then I'll be in touch with you at your new job in La Paz . . . and you'll be seeing our gratitude for your work tonight the next time you check the balance at your Miami bank."

Osorio pulled away with just a nod.

Before dawn the next morning Murillo's twin-engined airplane had landed at a remote landing strip in central Florida, and his forty kilograms of cocaine hydrochloride had been secured in the spare-tire compartment of the Ford Fairlane he was now driving north on I–95 toward Jacksonville. Ordinarily he would have preferred to make the exchange of drugs for cash directly in Bolivia, where his organization had better control, but his employer had wanted him to scout out this new delivery route personally on the first deal. If it worked out to everyone's satisfaction the next and subsequent transactions would be handled in the old way.

There was virtually no traffic and a light drizzle cut visibility markedly, so Murillo was startled when the red light suddenly appeared in his rear-view mirror and a short blast from a police siren cut through the strains of the Julio Iglesias ballad playing on the stereo.

Murillo cursed and slammed the steering wheel with his palm. With no other traffic to gauge his speed by, he had let his foot rest too heavily on the accelerator, and he now saw that he had been doing over seventy-five miles per hour. The last thing he wanted right now was to blow the whole deal because of a stupid traffic stop. But his false Florida driver's license was in order, as was the registration for the car, and he spoke English as well as most of Florida's citizens, so there was every reason to believe that he could bluff his way through this. He pulled over, turned on the dome light of his car, and sat obediently with his hands on the wheel.

Had it not been for the bulletin they had just received about the robbery of a 7–11 store by a man driving a white Ford Fairlane, the two Florida state troopers would probably not have interrupted their cups of coffee to catch this speeder, not at 5:30 in the morning. They didn't know that the Ford involved in the robbery was already parked in a garage in Palatka, miles to the south, and they never would.

After checking the license plate the two troopers dismounted, one staying to the right rear of the suspect car while the other moved to the driver's window. They both looked carefully for the long-barreled shotgun reportedly used in the holdup, and watched the driver's movements. Neither of them noticed a dark blue sedan carrying four Latin males, which cruised by and took the next off-ramp, several hundred yards ahead. They also didn't notice it double back on the service road parallel to the highway.

Murillo cooperatively turned over his false license and registration to the officer, all the while apologizing for his excessive speed. You know, the deserted stretch of highway, the middle of nowhere, didn't realize how fast I was going, officer, I'll sign the ticket, just hate to see what it's going to do to my insurance rates next year, but it's my fault, no doubt about it.

Murillo tensed up when the trooper asked him to step out of the car and open the trunk. Of course there was nothing visible in the trunk, but it wasn't a good sign.

By then the blue sedan on the service road had driven slowly past the two stopped cars, separated from the highway only by a low chain-link fence and a grass strip. The troopers didn't notice that the three passengers bailed out of the moving car behind the cover of some roadside bushes about a hundred yards farther on.

Murillo walked slowly and popped the trunk, revealing its vacant interior. He smiled and spread his arms. However, these were experienced policemen, who were aware that trunks are almost never completely empty unless the car is new or rented, and this was neither. There were a couple of rags there, wedged to one side, and one of the troopers reached in to pull up the mat under which the spare would be located.

The distinctive sound of a pump shotgun having a round jacked into the chamber caused both policemen to freeze. They felt the cold steel of gun barrels at the backs of their necks as strong hands shoved them to the side of the road, took their guns, and forced them to lie prone. Their hands were cuffed behind their backs.

"They'll have called in my tags, so we'll have to transfer the stuff," Murillo said to one of the men, and two of them grabbed large plastic garbage bags, containing individual kilo sacks of cocaine, and shuffled through the grass toward the service road where the blue sedan now waited for them.

"You take the police car to the next exit and we'll all meet and ditch it and my car off the highway. We'll use your car from here on," he continued to the remaining man, who was covering the policemen with a folding-stock shotgun. "Give me that," he said, pointing to the gun.

The man hesitated a second, but complied. He heard the shotgun fire twice as he drove away.

It was an hour before another police unit found the abandoned patrol car and the white Ford. It was another thirty minutes before the bodies of the two troopers were found in the roadside grass. From the footprints in the dirt at the scene it was apparent that a number of suspects were involved. A massive manhunt was begun from the crime scene northward, but they had little to go on. Murillo, meanwhile, had turned back south and cut over to the west coast of Florida before crossing into Georgia and coming back to the delivery point in Nassau County in the northern tip of Florida, where the purchaser claimed to have connections and protection from the police. Twenty-four hours later Murillo, using another set of false documents, was back in Bolivia, and two million dollars had been deposited to an account in the Cayman Islands.

Chapter One

The man in the floppy straw hat emerged from the long hut in the treeline and squinted in the bright sunlight as he scanned the horizon. He wore a dirty blue guayabera shirt and pale grey slacks that, many years ago, probably belonged to a suit. From his shoulder dangled an Uzi submachinegun with an extra magazine attached with black electrician's tape to the one in the weapon.

He held the door of the hut open and shouted instructions to someone inside. Several barefoot campesinos shuffled out of the hut with armloads of brownish packages, each about the size and shape of a brick. They carried these to a roughly constructed wood table in the shade of the trees and dumped them haphazardly on its top before strolling over to a grassy patch in the shade, where they sat or lay down to rest.

The man in the straw hat then walked over to a shallow trench nearby, lined with plastic sheeting, where two other campesinos were busily pulling buckets full of a yellowish liquid out of a metal drum and pouring them into the trench. The man pointed to a large burlap sack. One of the campesinos left his bucket, dragged the sack to the edge of the trench, and poured a cascade of small green leaves into the pool of liquid. Both campesinos then stepped into the trench themselves, kicked at the pile of leaves to spread them evenly, and began to trudge up and down the trench, raising their bare legs high with each step like Italian peasants crushing wine grapes. After a few minutes the man in the straw hat said something to them and they climbed out of the trench and joined the others resting in the shade. The man took off his hat and used it to shade his eyes as he again scanned the horizon.

Several hundred yards away, at the crest of a small hillock covered with knee-high yellow grass, William Featherstone brought the field glasses down from his eyes and used the edge of his shirt to wipe the lenses clean of condensation and dust. He lay on his stomach next to another prone figure dressed in faded camouflage fatigues, like the borrowed set Featherstone wore. This man watched the hut through the built-in telescopic sight of a strange, short-barreled military assault rifle. It was apparent, however, from the deliberate way the man kept his finger off the trigger, that he was using the weapon only as an ad hoc telescope, having loaned his binoculars to Featherstone earlier.

"Well," Featherstone finally whispered, although there was no chance the men near the hut could hear them at this distance and above the incessant droning of thousands of unseen insects, "what does all this prove?"

The other man did not even raise his head from the rifle stock. "I promised you a surprise, didn't I? You wouldn't want to spoil it right at the most dramatic moment, would you?"

Featherstone sighed as he saw just the corner of a smile peek over the top of the rifle. He had learned that Bolivian navy Comdr. Juan Carlos Guerrero was not one to reveal information easily, and he found the smile out of place, as Guerrero was widely known as a humorless soldier, probably, thought Featherstone, of limited mental range, as he did not tell or apparently appreciate good jokes.

Featherstone swatted at something crawling on his face as he surveyed the scene for the hundredth time since sunrise over four hours before. The hut and Featherstone's position were on opposite sides of a long, narrow meadow of spiky yellow grass, separating dense patches of tropical forest. The meadow might be the bed of a dry river, and from the sandy soil, the bugs, the oppressive heat, and the humidity, Featherstone could imagine that they were in the Caribbean with a beach just around the next bend, rather than in the heart of the South American continent, hundreds of miles from the sea. He knew from his map briefing before this "field trip" that the muddy water of the sluggish Mamore River would be found somewhere beyond the hut, making its way slowly down to the Amazon and, eventually, to the sea.

Looking cautiously to his right and left, Featherstone could see other prone figures dressed as he was, also using their weapons' sights to watch the men across the way. He knew that still more of Guerrero's commandos were in the woods behind him, and that others were several kilometers to the rear with the jeeps they had ridden to this isolated hole.

As deputy chief of mission (DCM) of the American Embassy in La Paz, Bolivia, Featherstone had rather assumed his duties would be more limited to saying "Please pass the sweet and sour shrimp" at diplomatic receptions and making pompous demarches to the Bolivian Foreign Ministry on some mundane issue or other. He had been disabused of this notion shortly after his arrival several months before, when he learned that Ambassador Lance Pearson, a dilettante political appointee, reserved all of the even remotely entertaining or professionally important assignments for himself and left it to his DCM to deal with the Embassy Housing Board and to escort the wife of the occasional junketing congressman on shopping trips in search of alpaca sweaters and pewter.

Featherstone was nominally the embassy coordinator for narcotics matters, a vitally important function in a country such as Bolivia, one of the world's principal sources of cocaine, but Ambassador Pearson had limited Featherstone's job to writing lengthy biannual reports, to which Pearson affixed his own name, and chairing endless rounds of interminable meetings with the embassy's representatives from the Drug Enforcement Agency (DEA), the CIA, and the Defense Attache's Office (DAO). Right at this moment Pearson was accompanying a senior DEA officer to supervise a major antidrug operation that was so secret even Featherstone had not been informed of its precise nature.

Meanwhile, Commander Guerrero had been nagging his friend, the army attache, Lt. Col. Andrew Polsby, to have someone from the embassy visit his own counternarcotics operation here in the steaming Chapare region of Bolivia. No one in the embassy had taken much notice of Guerrero for weeks. After all, how much influence could a naval officer have in a landlocked country? Of course Featherstone was aware that Guerrero had a sound professional reputation, having commanded for five years the naval commando battalion, a two-hundred-man unit patterned after the American Navy's SEALs. According to Polsby these men were all jump-qualified paratroopers, trained in underwater demolition and experts in small-unit infantry tactics, not much inferior to the Green Berets themselves, which was some praise coming from Polsby, a former Special Forces officer himself. Polsby had told Featherstone how Guerrero had made a name for himself by taking his men out on "training missions" into the Chapare to blow up small cocaine laboratories, on the theory that this provided realistic experience for his men in tracking, infiltration, and demolition operations. Ambassador Pearson had hit upon this request as an opportune pretext to keep Featherstone occupied during the "big drug raid," which Pearson would then have to supervise himself.

Featherstone was thus occupied in bemoaning his fate when he almost dropped his binoculars, as the man in the straw hat suddenly leaped to his feet and started shouting and pointing in Featherstone's direction. All at once, several more armed men whom Featherstone had not noticed before appeared from around the hut and looked fixedly toward Featherstone's hillock. He could feel his heart pounding and he was certain that his constant fidgeting and slapping at insects, compared to Guerrero's utter stillness, had finally attracted the traffickers' attention. He looked at Guerrero, who had not moved, although Featherstone noticed that his smile had grown by at least two teeth.

The man in the straw hat shouted at the campesinos, two of whom jumped back into the trench and began to stomp purposefully up and down, while the others started to straighten out the piles of brick-sized packages on the table. Suddenly remembering something, the man in the straw hat quickly reached inside the hut door, withdrew a small backpack, and removed from it two wads of small papers, which he also tossed on the table. The papers had the reddish hue of Bolivian bank notes.

Featherstone had expected shooting and a charge by the traffickers at any moment, and this disjointed activity confused him, but his heart kept on pounding, so loudly now that he was sure it was audible to anyone within ten yards. All at once, he realized that it was not his heart at all but the throbbing of helicopter blades, as three large, dark-painted American Blackhawk helicopters roared over his head just above the tops of the trees behind him and headed down toward the hut. One helicopter dove straight at the hut and touched down within twenty yards of it, while the other two split up and swung around either side before touching down in the wind-whipped grass.

Even before the skids touched the ground armed men dressed in the yellow-beige uniforms of the UMOPAR (Bolivian Narcotics Police) were jumping to earth and racing for the hut, automatic rifles at the ready. They were joined by two men Featherstone recognized as DEA agents, although the orders were obviously being given by a Bolivian UMOPAR officer. The man in the straw hat watched this assault transfixed, and simply raised his hands, dropping his Uzi to the ground, as did the other armed men who had emerged from the treeline. The campesinos began to run in all directions, smashing into each other and into the trees, but were quickly rounded up by the UMOPAR men, who had encircled the camp.

As the UMOPAR officer and the DEA men checked out the contents of the table and the hut, two more helicopters swooped into the clearing, this time sleek Bell executive jobs. One immediately landed as near as possible to the hut, and a television camera crew jumped out: a cameraman, his assistant, a sound man, and what must have been the correspondent, wearing the obligatory khaki safari suit rather than the blue jeans and T-shirts of his crew. The other helicopter hovered over the clearing, near one of the Blackhawks, while the TV crew set up.

Featherstone assumed that the other helicopter was waiting for the police to declare the area secure, since it had been occupied by hostile men with automatic weapons just moments before, but it was the TV correspondent who waved to the helicopter, causing it to land. The doors of this aircraft did not open immediately, however, and the pilot quickly shut down his engine. When the rotors had finally stopped kicking up waves of dust and grass the side door of the helicopter opened and two men with mirrored sunglasses and clean white guayaberas stepped out, submachineguns pointed outward protectively. After them emerged two more familiar figures.

Newly elected Bolivian President Eduardo Boca del Rio climbed out just ahead of Ambassador Pearson. Apparently someone had prevailed upon them to remove their expensive suit coats, and both had opted for the campaigning-politician look, with loosened silk ties and sleeves rolled up to the elbows. Both instinctively stooped as they exited the copter, although the blades had long since stopped turning, and both also instinctively patted their carefully coiffed hair as they strode purposefully up the slight rise toward the hut, President Boca carefully explaining something and Ambassador Pearson gravely nodding.

"Now there's two of a one for you," Guerrero murmured. Featherstone had noticed that while Guerrero spoke superb English from having lived for some time in the States as a youngster, he had some trouble with idiomatic expressions.

The TV crew taped the two men walking to the hut and soberly examining the table. President Boca picked up one of the packages and showed it to Pearson while the UMOPAR officer made his report to the president, who graciously translated for Pearson, who did not speak Spanish. The policemen had taken a blanket from inside the hut and arranged on it the arms they had confiscated, about half a dozen automatic weapons, a couple of pistols, and some ammunition, which the president and the ambassador also inspected. The correspondent then came up to them and conducted a brief interview on the spot, at the end of which both men returned to their helicopter and swirled into the air in the direction of Cochabamba. The television helicopter followed suit a few moments later. Within the next twenty minutes the weapons and prisoners were loaded into one of the Blackhawks, the UMOPAR men heaved the stuff from the table back into the hut, tipped over the metal drum and several others found near the hut, torched the place, and then flew away themselves.

"Well, there you have it!" announced Guerrero triumphantly.

"Have what?" asked Featherstone. "It looked like a picture-perfect narcotics operation to me."

"Of course it was," said Guerrero, rolling over on his back and lacing his fingers behind his head. "Absolutely perfect. Except for one thing."

Featherstone sighed. Obviously, he was going to have to play straight man here. "What thing?"

"It was all make-believe. A real horse and pony show for your ambassador and the TV."

"That's *dog* and pony," Featherstone could not help saying. "I still don't see the problem. So they brought cameras to a bust. That's just good advertising, helps get the word out that the government is serious about tackling the drug lords." Actually, Featherstone didn't like the obvious grandstanding by the ambassador, but he wasn't sure that he just wasn't jealous of having been aced out of a spot on the six o'clock news.

"Bullfuck!" said Guerrero, apparently a little stung by Featherstone's correction. "You were here with us hours ago. You saw those guys dig the trench and pretend to be processing coca. You saw them load up that table with coca paste and then sit and wait for the helicopters. That one guy in charge even knew which way the copters were coming from. Hell, how do you think *I* found out about this supersecret operation? *Everybody* within a hundred miles of here knew about it weeks ago."

"Do you mean to tell me that somebody just threw away hundreds of thousands of dollars worth of coca paste and let those men get arrested just for show?" Featherstone rather hated to admit it, Guerrero being as obnoxious as he was, but this did all look a little strange.

"Are you kidding?" Guerrero asked, raising himself up on one elbow. "That's just pity cash for a trafficker. Operating costs. And don't worry about those poor guys going to jail. The campesinos will get a few days in jail, and the gunmen might even get a real sentence, but that's what they were paid for, and they won't suffer much. With money in our jails you can get yourself a nice little apartment, complete with stereo, TV, and even conjugal visits from your wife or any hooker you like. If you've got enough money you can get a "Saturday to Saturday" pass by renting a cop, who becomes your personal guard, and paying for his food while you walk the streets, go home, do whatever you want. You just check in at the prison every Saturday to pay up for the next week. You don't think you could find some poor slob in this country who would go for a deal like that?"

"Okay," said Featherstone, holding up his hands in surrender. "Suppose all of that's true. Why would someone go to that trouble?"

"So that you damn gringos can win the war on drugs and go home, just the way you won in Vietnam before you ran for the boats." Featherstone could see from the veins beginning to stick out at Guerrero's temples that this was a sore point, so he thought he'd let him say his piece and then get the hell out of there.

"This is just a little scene in the big picture. This will be repeated all over and for months. DEA will get a great 'body count' of drugs seized, some of which will be dummy stuff, like that shit down there, which was conveniently burned before it could be tested, some of which will be real stuff, which will find its way back out of the police evidence lockers into traffickers' hands, and some which will just be invested in the project. It's worth it if you guys start to feel good and eventually, the next time Congress is looking for someplace to cut the budget, well, hey, drug seizures are up, maybe we could cut the number of DEA agents, or Coast Guard patrols, or Customs officials at Miami International. But you don't have to believe me yet."

Thank you, thought Featherstone sarcastically.

"Tonight you'll come out with us, and maybe you'll see the difference between this operation and a real one."

"That's what I'm here for," Featherstone said, wishing sincerely that he were somewhere else for any reason.

The drive back to the commando battalion base camp was a long and bumpy ride for Featherstone, who hung on for dear life in the back of an open HUMMER vehicle as it raced along a dirt road through the thick tropical forest. As Guerrero had chosen to ride with several of his staff officers to go over the plans for that night's operation, Featherstone shared the vehicle of the leader of the "hit squad," as Guerrero had dubbed the fourteen-man teams into which his battalion was divided for tactical maneuvers, and which had provided security for their observation of the drug raid during the morning. Sublieutenant Alvaro Morales, or "Immorales," as the other junior officers called him due to his carefree bachelor life, was a handsome, trim twenty-year-old who was bubbling with enthusiasm about his unit and their work. If Featherstone had expected to have to worm information out of Morales he was sadly disappointed, as his primary problem during the two-hour drive was to try to turn the young man off.

"So," Featherstone shouted above the noise of the engine and the road, "how long have you been with Commander Guerrero?"

"Nearly a year," Morales answered proudly, "ever since I got out of the Academy. Do you have any idea how lucky I was to get this assignment? Every naval cadet at the Academy put in for it, and half of the army cadets were trying to pull strings to get a 'rotational' with Guerrero."

"What makes this post so popular?" Featherstone asked. "Frankly, if I were in your shoes, I think I'd rather be posted to La Paz, Santa Cruz, Cochabamba, any big city rather than out here in the middle of the jungle."

"There'll be time enough for that when I'm an old married man . . . sir," he added respectfully, not certain whether Featherstone had taken the "old" part personally. "Right now I don't want to spend my service time getting coffee for some admiral or typing in some office. For us, this is where the action is, and I wouldn't trade it for anything. Besides that, it's Guerrero himself who's the attraction. He's almost like a god to us younger officers coming out of the Academy. Do you know how he got his nickname, 'Coco'?" Morales asked.

"I think I heard it was short for crocodile," Featherstone guessed. "Something to do with being mean and nasty and living in the swamp."

"No, not even close," laughed Morales as he wiggled his rear end into a more comfortable position on the seat cushion and got a better purchase on the overhead straps to steady himself as he prepared for a long story.

"It goes back to his own days at the Academy. It's short for 'chocolates,' which is the slang term at the Academy for hazing. The senior classmen give out 'chocolates' to their 'favorites' at night. Now, you have to remember that the kind of hazing we got at the Academy is nothing like what you Americans would have at West Point or Annapolis. I'm talking about beatings with rubber hoses and broom handles. Every plebe class would lose a couple of kids who were literally beaten to death, not to mention those who went to the hospital or who just quit.

"Well," Morales took a deep breath, "Guerrero joined the Academy older than most of us. Most cadets start at seventeen, but he was nearly twenty."

"Why was that?" Featherstone asked, just to break up Morales' machinegun delivery.

"Well, he went to Vietnam first, of course. Didn't you know that?"

"No, I didn't," admitted Featherstone. "How did a Bolivian end up in Vietnam?"

"Well, that's another story. You see, his parents had a fair amount of money, for Bolivia. I think his father was some sort of engineer at the oilfields down south, but anyway he had put away money for Guerrero's education in the States. So they sent Guerrero, at the age of seventeen, to live with an aunt in Miami or somewhere and to go to the university there. But apparently Guerrero always wanted to be in the military, so, he just gets off the plane—this would have been in 1967 or so—and heads right for the U.S. Marine recruiting station. I guess in those days they were taking just about anyone dumb enough to walk in the door—no offense—no questions asked about visas, or green cards, or even age, and so off he goes to Vietnam. He went through the Marine recon course and ended up in the Battle of Hue during the Tet Offensive of 1968. Meanwhile, his parents were going nuts, pulling every string they knew of to get him out of the Marines and back to Bolivia, and they finally managed it the next year, but not before he had won himself a Silver Star and a bunch of other medals whose names I forget."

When Morales paused briefly for breath Featherstone made an effort to bend the tangent back toward the original topic. "Which leads to his being nicknamed 'Coco.' Right?"

"Oh, yeah," Morales laughed. "So, anyway, to make a long story short . . ."

Too late, thought Featherstone.

"His parents evidently resigned themselves to the idea that he wanted to wear a uniform, so they figured that it would be better to do it in Bolivia, where at least he would be close to home and where we didn't have a war on. So when he got into the Academy, a little older than most of his classmates, but with his combat experience, even though he never liked to talk about it, it made him a natural leader. This was way before my time, of course, but the story goes that he led some kind of underclassmen mutiny about the hazings and somehow got them informally banned for as long as he was a cadet and formally banned by the government later. What really makes the junior officers look up to him is that he didn't just oppose the hazings when he was on the receiving end, but he wouldn't let his own classmates do any of that when they were the upperclassmen either. That's something you don't see much of in our armed forces, I'm afraid."

Having completed his briefing of his staff officers, Guerrero lounged in the front passenger seat of his HUMMER with one foot braced against the dashboard while he tried to get some rest, even if actual sleep was out of the question. As he dozed his mind, too, drifted back to his days at the Colegio Militar in Irpavi, a suburb of La Paz where cadets from both the army and the navy undergo their introduction to military life.

At first it had seemed that he would have an easy time of it at the Academy. His experience in the American Marines gave him such valuable skills as being able to spit shine to a mirror finish anything that couldn't run faster than he could. Even the wealthier cadets, who could afford to bribe the enlisted men working at the Academy to do some of their work, could not hope to match him. And, naturally, he knew all about close-order drill and even the maintenance of the old Ml Garand rifles of World War II vintage that they used for training. He had confidently expected to be named to the highest rank in his class and to stay at the highest level achievable throughout his career.

However, he had calculated without the jealousy of some of the upperclassmen who, far from valuing his experience and maturity, envied it. Also, having been "raised" in the egalitarian atmosphere of Marine boot camp and then the even more earthy lifestyle of the "boonies" in Vietnam, he was not prepared for the petty carping of a horde of spoiled young men badgering and bullying him and his peers for no apparent military reason. But he soon realized that his was not the worst treatment to be meted out at the Academy.

One of his classmates, Cadet "Johnny" Quispe Mamani, was evidently the only fullblooded *indio* in his class, all of the others being either of European or mixed European and Indian ancestry. Quispe, however, was not only *indio* by heritage, he looked it and even spoke Spanish with a distinct Aymara accent. He tried hard to overcome the accent, but there was no disguising his dark leathery complexion, short sturdy build, high cheek bones and almost Oriental eyes. Although Bolivia had had its great revolution in 1952, ending many of the overt forms of persecution of the Indian population, which made up a sizeable majority in the rural parts of the country, in this closed environment at the Academy there were no rules other than those made by the upperclassmen after lights out. They did not believe Quispe belonged in their Academy or their army.

Quispe struggled at his studies, putting in much longer hours than the other cadets just to keep up, but he was making his way. This did not please some of the seniors, who, about two months after the start of Guerrero's first year, decided to make an example of Quispe.

Guerrero had just dropped off to sleep in his bunk when he heard the sound of scuffling and muffled screams coming from the hallway outside. He dropped silently to the floor, just as he had done more than once outside of Hue when Viet Cong sappers were inside the wire, and peeked through a crack in the door to see a number of hooded figures dragging a gagged Quispe toward the showers. Guerrero quickly pulled on his uniform jogging suit and grabbed a knit cap he had brought from the States. Using a pair of scissors to gouge out two eyeholes, he pulled the cap on over his whole head, terrorist style, and prepared to slip out of the room.

"Where are you going?" his bunkmate, Campos, asked, rubbing his eyes against the light from the hall.

"They've got Quispe, and I think they're going to kill him this time."

"If you know what's good for you, you'll mind your own business," the bunkmate warned.

"That's the problem," Guerrero laughed in a whisper. "I never did know what was good for me. You stay here, where you'll be safe," he added with mock concern.

Guerrero silently made his way along the hall to the closed door of the shower area. Stealing a look through the corner of the door's small window, he saw the back of a head, obviously of someone posted to guard the door, and beyond that the writhing body of Quispe. The hooded men had tied his hands together and his feet together and then hung him like a hammock between two rows of shower heads. They had positioned his face directly beneath one of the shower heads, and a stream of water was now gushing into his mouth, from which they had removed the gag, while they beat his exposed torso with leather truncheons. Each time he opened his mouth to scream in pain it filled with water. They were quickly drowning him.

Guerrero had never actually studied the martial arts, but in Marine boot camp he had been befriended by a big, muscular black man from Alabama, whose accent Guerrero never could understand but who had determined that Guerrero was "practically a nigger" and so a good guy. The Marine had taught the wiry Guerrero some fighting techniques that, he had claimed, had saved his life in fighting against the Ku Klux Klan. Guerrero thought that this was rather appropriate, what with the hoods and all, but he could not help wishing that his Marine buddy was with him now. Unfortunately, he had watched the man die in the street fighting in Hue in 1968.

Guerrero braced himself against the far wall of the hallway and launched a flying side kick at the edge of the door. The force of the blow on the back of his head from the door alone would have rendered the "guard" unconscious, but the momentum propelled him into the unforgiving tile surface of the urinals, and he would later wake up with a broken nose and jaw as well.

The crash of the door got the immediate attention of the other hooded men. There were four of them, and they turned, startled, to see what had happened.

"What the fuck are you doing with my *guagua**?" Guerrero roared, hoping that his voice would not choose that moment to crack. Without thinking, he had used the Quechua term for "baby" by which he jokingly referred to his younger classmates.

The four slowly turned, and Guerrero could imagine them smiling behind their hoods as they saw that he was alone. They advanced toward him with their truncheons casually held in their hands, leaving Quispe gasping and choking under the stream of water.

"*Well,*" one of them drawled in an obvious lowland, Santa Cruz accent, "I suppose we have enough chocolates to share with the nanny as well." Guerrero recognized the voice of Benitez, a particularly self-important senior with a reputation for cruelty.

---

* Pronounced "wa-wa"

Guerrero stood in a loose fighting stance in the center of the shower room, his left foot slightly advanced and his weight on his rear foot. One hand was open and held forward, while he held his other fist back, cocked at his waist. He stood still, letting two of the upperclassmen move around to either side of him while Benitez held back, letting the largest cadet move forward to confront Guerrero directly.

"This is a big mistake," Guerrero said.

"It sure is," snarled Benitez, "and you made it."

"No," answered Guerrero, with a confidence he did not feel. "You did. You should have brought more men."

The upperclassmen started to laugh, but their laughter was cut short as Guerrero pulled back his fist as if to strike the man in front of him, just as his left foot shot out sideways and smashed the knee of the man to his left. As the man crumpled to the floor, screaming in rage and pain, Guerrero recalled his black friend's lesson that most of the joints of the human body were made to bend one way only, and that forcing them in a different direction was a cause for immediate concern for the owner.

As the big man paused, unsure of whether to help his injured friend or to attack, Guerrero, now turned partially to his left, swung back around with his full force and weight, driving his elbow hard into the face of the man on his right. As the man staggered back Guerrero finished the job with a heel kick to the groin, dropping him as well.

The big man roared in anger and charged blindly forward, but Guerrero just tucked and rolled under him, sweeping his feet and sending him sprawling on the floor. Guerrero rolled neatly to his feet, facing Benitez. Terrified, Benitez lashed out with his truncheon, but Guerrero simply swayed backward, out of the way, and caught his hand as it passed, twisting the wrist and pulling the elbow straight, just as Guerrero's other hand thrust at the immobilized elbow, cracking it neatly. Guerrero finished the job with a blow to Benitez' kidneys and turned to face his final opponent, but the big man, now back on his feet, had no desire to try his luck again and turned to run.

He reached the door just as it burst open, catching him on the forehead and bouncing him off the wall behind him.

"Oops!" said Campos. "Just came to use the john." Guerrero smiled, and the two roommates shook hands. Together they lowered Quispe to the floor and untied him. Fortunately, the seniors had not had time to do major damage.

As they left the shower room with its human wreckage, Quispe supported between them, they saw a dozen pairs of heads duck back into the other rooms down the hall.

"You know they won't leave it at this," Campos said.

"Yes," admitted Guerrero. "And I don't suppose the hood fooled them any more than theirs fooled us." He raised his left arm, showing where the sleeve of his jogging suit had been pulled back almost to his elbow, revealing an elaborate tattoo of a dragon entwined around a Marine Corps anchor, a souvenir of a weekend pass in Danang which he remembered only vaguely himself. The tattoo was well known and widely admired. "I suspect that we will have company sooner or later."

"Maybe when they get out of the hospital," Campos laughed.

Quispe revived quickly, and, recognizing that a little matter like violating lights out would not count much after the events of that evening, the three spent the entire night talking, laughing, and finishing off a bottle of singari, a brandylike Bolivian liquor.

Although the next day was a hard one on all concerned, partly from lack of sleep, the tension that hummed through the classrooms and on the parade ground did not erupt. Several senior classmen were absent that day, and Benitez made an appearance only late in the afternoon, his right arm encased in plaster and held in a sling.

At about three o'clock the next morning a group of about a dozen men, all dressed in jogging suits and wearing hoods, crept silently down the stairs of the cadets' dormitory from the senior floor to the plebe floor. Someone had cut the circuit breaker for this floor at the main electrical panel, and the only illumination in the building was the pale light of a half moon that filtered in through the windows.

The group carefully counted the doorways from the end of the hall and stopped before the door to Guerrero's room, forming up on both sides. Each man carried a thick broom handle, cut to about two feet in length, and some also carried knives in their free hands. The door of the room was only pushed to, and the leader eased it open delicately, making sure not to hit his cast against the doorframe.

One by one the men slid into the room, some crouching by the lower bunk, others standing at full height around the upper. At the cry of "Now!" by the leader, a rain of blows poured onto the inert forms on each bunk, and Benitez gritted his teeth as he plunged his hunting knife deep into the center of the mass on the top bunk.

Suddenly the room was awash in the light of two powerful battery-powered lamps. Guerrero and Campos were squatting on top of the lockers that flanked the doorway. They immediately released the large painted rocks they held, which had formerly lined the Academy driveway, onto the heads and shoulders of the men below them, dropping two to the floor. From under the bottom bunk a muffled cry of triumph sounded as Quispe deftly fastened a pair of handcuffs to the ankles of two of the intruders, who tried to pull away in surprise, immediately lost their balance, and tumbled to the ground as well.

Now from the hallway came cries of surprise and pain, mixed with the savage bellowing of rampaging warriors. Other lights were now on in the hallway, and the intruders who had not found room to enter were submerged in a tide of more than fifty similarly clad figures, all wearing identifying white armbands. Guerrero and Campos leapt to the floor as Quispe rolled out from under the bunk, and while the latter two each struggled to disarm one assailant, Guerrero systematically disabled his opponents, working his way forward to Benitez, who was now cowering against the window, desperately seeking a way to open it.

He took a half-hearted slash at Guerrero with his knife, having realized that he had struck only at blankets and pillows piled on the beds, but Guerrero easily trapped his arm and held it, slowly applying pressure to the elbow as the dull thumping in the hall signalled the total victory of the plebes.

"You're finished here!" screamed Benitez. "You can't do this to upperclassmen. You have no right!"

"No, you're finished, Benitez," hissed Guerrero. "Find a different career. Get your daddy to send you to college or to give you a job on his cattle ranch, but you're out of the army as of now. Your friends can stay, but the word is out now that there will be no more hazing—period. If there is, I'll come and find the man responsible and cut his fucking heart out. They can kick me out of the Academy. They can even send me to jail, but that won't put the heart back in his chest, will it?" With his final word Guerrero gave a sudden jerk, and even Quispe and Campos could not help but wince at the loud crack, followed by an ear-piercing scream.

There was eventually an official investigation into the rash of accidents that had flooded the Academy infirmary with broken limbs, jaws, and general bruises, and it was duly determined that, as most of the injuries had occurred to upperclassmen, the situation involved a drinking party that had gotten out of hand. This was a manly thing for cadets to do, and as it was impossible to obtain any further information from any of the cadets, punishment was limited to the revoking of weekend passes for a month for the entire student body, and the matter was dropped. Benitez, who was confined to the hospital for several weeks while his arms healed, eventually dropped out of the Academy and did join his father in running their vast cattle ranch in the eastern lowlands. Guerrero, Campos, and Quispe all remained in the service, the latter two in the army, and Campos' tangential involvement with the "coup" at the Academy even permitted him a certain success in his career. Quispe's Indian blood still counted against him at each promotion, but his hard work and intelligence enabled him to hold various staff positions.

Guerrero, as a navy cadet, was largely protected by the interservice rivalry that pitted the small Navy High Command, which disposed only of some riverine units and a Marine battalion on Lake Titicaca, against the much larger army. Given Guerrero's unique experience and talents, the Navy High Command literally created the commando battalion for him in 1985. He had organized it, trained it, and led it ever since, ignoring the usual obligatory post rotations of other officers.

Guerrero was roughly awakened from his light sleep as he found himself suspended completely in space for some seconds while the HUMMER bounded over a particularly large pothole. When he finally came down, fortunately still inside the vehicle, he turned on the driver in a rage. The driver, whose face was a mass of green and black camouflage paint, stared back at the "old man" in terror. As unhappy as Guerrero was at his rude jolt, the sight of this bloodcurdling warrior looking at him with eyes the size of saucers, whites showing all the way around, and with his lower lip already starting to tremble, took all of the anger out of him.

"You got a date, son?" asked Guerrero calmly.

The commando only shook his head and started to stammer out some kind of apology.

"Well, in that case, let's slow down a little. It's always been my policy to try to keep casualties to a minimum during a road march."

The driver simply nodded, hunched over the wheel, and dropped the speed from a soft blur to a glacial crawl in an instant.

Chapter Two

Featherstone joined Guerrero and some of his staff officers for dinner at a "restaurant" in the small town of Villa Tunari, not far from the commando base camp. The establishment was basically a corrugated tin roof supported by large wooden posts around the edges, with a central core composed of what appeared to be a massive oven and some work tables, which comprised the kitchen. Picnic benches and tables were placed about under the roof but otherwise in the open air. A breeze had come up at nightfall, cooling the place pleasantly, but Featherstone had still found it prudent to switch to beer, as the commando officers were drinking, when he noticed that the beer seemed to attract fewer flying insects than the Coke he had originally ordered.

The rest of the town consisted of a few dozen cinderblock buildings with similar tin roofs. There was a dirt main street which became the highway where the houses ran out, without any appreciable change in width or durability. Other than that, there did not seem to be any plan to the place. Some of the buildings were painted in vibrant or pastel colors, not usually with all of the walls done in the same color, and some were not painted at all. The slightly warped strains of an old Olivia Newton John tape, obviously on a tape player with automatic reverse, had been droning on constantly for at least the two hours since the convoy had arrived in town, and Featherstone silently cursed the Duracell people for producing batteries that really did seem to last a "long, long time."

Featherstone could feel himself starting to fade. The shop talk among the officers did not interest him much, and he had been going since early the previous morning, when he had left his home in La Paz, put in a full day of work at the embassy, and caught the 1800 flight to Cochabamba, where at least he had spent a comfortable night at the Gran Hotel Cochabamba. He had been awakened before dawn, however, for the long drive out to the site of the "drug raid." After the ride back he had been taken on an unofficial visit to a small and technically legal coca farm near Villa Tunari. He still had their own raid to look forward to, followed by what promised to be an unmemorable night in the local hotel, another quick flight back to La Paz, and then still another full day's work at the office.

Pointing to the strange weapon leaned up against the bench at Guerrero's side, Featherstone asked its origin, more to keep himself awake than out of real curiosity.

With some pride Guerrero hefted the weapon, removed the magazine, and cleared the chamber, then passed it on to Featherstone. "It's a British Enfield 'Individual Weapon,' or IW for short. It's what they call a 'bull-pup' design. Although the overall length is only about thirty inches, it's a real rifle with a barrel just as long as your American M-16. They've just rearranged things, eliminating the stock and essentially starting the bolt mechanism right back at the butt plate, which gives the weapon a tighter radius of action. Better for handling inside vehicles or helicopters without sacrificing muzzle velocity, accuracy, or rate of fire, as you would with a submachinegun. There's another version with a longer barrel and a bipod mount, which functions as a light machinegun and which we have distributed, one per hit squad."

Featherstone certainly thought the rifle had an otherworldly, sci-fi look to it. It had a built-in four-power scope, and the ammunition magazine fitted into the body behind rather than in front of the pistol grip, as with the M-16. Featherstone also noticed that Guerrero always spoke Spanish with him when in front of his other officers, most of whom spoke little English. He made a mental note of this fact, as many Latins he had known would actually go out of their way to speak English in front of their uncomprehending compatriots, just to show off and fully aware that the non-English-speaker's natural reaction is to assume that he is being talked about, probably in an unflattering manner.

"How is it that you have English weapons with all of the American military aid coming in directed at the narcotics problem?" Featherstone asked.

"Actually," Guerrero replied, "you'll see a real mix of stuff in the Bolivian armed forces. We have Austrian tank destroyers, Brazilian armored cars, and most of the army has old Belgian FAL automatic rifles. There's a lot of American equipment coming in right now, but—and I hope you don't take this badly—I've found that if you want American equipment you have to take American advice and advisors with it."

Sensing a tense moment a-borning, Guerrero's executive officer, Lieutenant Duarte, chimed in, in an informative tone, "We were given the IWs by the British government as a sort of reward for a spectacular drug bust we did last year. It seems that a big British drug trafficker was coming to Bolivia to take personal delivery of a large shipment of cocaine. The police knew about it but were taking no action, so someone in the British Embassy happened to let slip the fact to Commander Guerrero. Since the delivery was to take place in our general area of operations we moved on it, rolled up the trafficker and nearly four hundred kilos of HCL, that's the processed cocaine," he added, assuming Featherstone's ignorance. Featherstone just smiled benignly and bade him continue.

"What made it particularly interesting," Duarte went on, "was that it was discovered that the British trafficker had made some nasty enemies along the way, and his shipment was laced with cyanide. If that stuff had reached England hundreds of people would have died, since we know that drug traffickers are not into recalling contaminated product for which they've already paid. The British government had been under some pressure from the U.S. to make a contribution to the drug war effort, so they singled us out for these weapons. They use standard NATO 5.56 rounds, so ammunition is no problem."

"That's fascinating," said Featherstone, not about to be put off. He turned immediately to Guerrero and asked, "So what's so bad about American advisors and advice? You know we have a lot of experience in fighting the narcotics trade worldwide. We only want to avoid every country's security forces having to reinvent the wheel."

"Well said," Guerrero laughed. "And very logical too. The trouble is that you may know more than we ever will about the drug trade worldwide, but you're in Bolivia now, and, if you'll pardon my saying so, you don't know shit about Bolivia. I don't blame the DEA guys," he added hastily, holding up his hands. "It would take more courage than I have to go into a drug bust with no arresting authority, sometimes even unarmed, and surrounded by local cops who might or might not be working for the other side. After what happened to that Camarena guy in Mexico, I'm very impressed that DEA can still find men willing to run that risk."

Featherstone nodded grimly at the mention of the DEA officer who had been kidnapped and tortured to death by Mexican drug traffickers some years earlier, allegedly with the active support of corrupt police officials. He was pleasantly surprised to see his own sober look reflected in the faces of the young officers seated around the table. He thought that he sensed a feeling of brotherhood between these young men and the DEA man, front-line soldiers in a life-and-death struggle almost unknown to the outside world.

Guerrero continued. "And I can't fault your superior sources of information, what with the scoop you can get from the international banking community and from satellite photography and radio and telephone intercepts. We could never match that. The problem is, and somebody said this about some totally different topic, 'You Americans know everything. The trouble is that you don't know anything else.' Some of your officers, from DEA or the CIA or the embassy, do try to learn our ways and our culture, but some come here without even being able to speak Spanish. How long do you think a Bolivian cop would last on the streets of Detroit? It wouldn't be so bad if you recognized the problem as even existing, but you Americans have the belief that with hard work and a positive attitude anything can be overcome, and I'm afraid it just isn't true."

Guerrero took his weapon back and reloaded it. "So, if you don't mind, I'll take the help I can get as long as I'm free to do things my own way. When the strings get too thick, I'll just do without, thank you. You'll notice that even the American HUMMERs we received from the Bolivian Army only when they embarrassingly found themselves with more American largesse than they could effectively use at one time."

Somewhere down the table one of the young officers, who had had at least his share of the beer, stood up and began the Bolivian national anthem. The others, including Featherstone, smiled greatly at the tension-breaker, stood, and joined in.

"Bolivians, good fortune has crowned our elections and desires . . ."

Featherstone could not help grinning at the look of surprise on the others' faces as he joined in the hymn. He had always made it a point, in the countries where he had been stationed, to learn the national anthem for those many official receptions when it was sung. On his first tour he had considered it a simple act of respect and courtesy, but he had later found that the benefit of impressing his local contacts far outweighed the few minutes' work it took to accomplish. It was only during his stay in Cuba that, as a matter of policy, he had refrained from following this procedure.

". . . that this land should be free, free!"

It was readily apparent that the Mormon Tabernacle Choir had nothing to worry about in terms of singing quality, but they more than made up for it in volume. Even the crew from the kitchen had joined in, with the heavyset proprietor in his dirty, sweaty tank top marking time dramatically with a large wooden spoon.

"Better to die free than live as slaves."

At the end of the first stanza several of the men began to sit, but Guerrero started up the second, staring fixedly at Featherstone, who simply raised his eyebrows and continued. The number of voices had been drastically reduced, as several of the officers were merely mouthing, looking from side to side, obviously unsure of the words. Just as in the States, thought Featherstone.

By the start of the third stanza only Featherstone and Guerrero were left, now trying to outdo each other in both loudness and longevity. At the end of the stanza Duarte, much to the relief of Featherstone, who didn't know whether another stanza even existed, broke in with a hearty round of applause, accompanied by warm back-slapping for Featherstone from the younger officer. Guerrero just smiled slyly and regained his seat, never breaking his gaze at Featherstone, which the latter returned.

After a filling dinner of *hochi* (a large rodent, denizen of the Amazon Basin), various river fish, and fried yucca and plantains, the group returned to the base camp to prepare for the night's raid. Guerrero explained that occasionally, to throw off the informants he knew the traffickers must have in the town, he would plan an operation after an apparent night of carousing by his officers. He believed that the negative effect of a couple of beers would be more than compensated for by the element of surprise they would thereby achieve.

Featherstone watched Guerrero and his officers paint their own faces and clean and prepare their weapons before giving minute direction to the troops in their preparations, conducting a detailed precombat inspection for half-full canteens, rattling gear, and dirty rifle barrels. He was impressed that of the two fourteen-man hit squads to participate in the operation, only two men had any deficiencies noted, and that all of these were corrected prior to move-out time. From his past experience in Latin America Featherstone knew that this level of attention to and participation with their men by officers was rare enough. He remembered accounts from the Falkland Islands/Malvinas War of 1982, when young Argentine conscripts died of exposure and malnutrition in their trenches while their officers sat warm and safe in Port Stanley, and when at least one young Argentine prisoner commented to a British captain that the Englishman was the first officer he had seen since disembarking on the island weeks before. Featherstone doubted that Guerrero would make a mistake like that.

After one of the NCOs had carefully painted Featherstone's face with camouflage sticks, turning him into something like the Creature from the Black Lagoon, Duarte insisted on taking a group photo, with Featherstone prominently posed in the center, hefting an old American M-60 machinegun with belts of ammunition hanging from his neck.

Guerrero then explained to Featherstone the workings of the "starlight" night-vision scope that he would lend to Featherstone to observe the evening's activities. He apologized that he didn't have anything more state-of-the-art, the American aid equals American advice conundrum again, and said that his men were trained to work in the dark, using only the slight aid provided by the magnifying scopes on their rifles. Featherstone was then treated to another bumpy HUMMER ride and a long trek through the dark jungle to a point where he could observe in safety, guarded by two commandos.

Featherstone braced himself against a large tree and scanned the clearing, several hundred meters wide, at the far end of which he could see several small huts. In the eerie green image produced in the starlight scope he could see the shadowy figures of several men spaced around the huts, all of whom appeared to be armed.

Finally the door to one of the huts opened, showing a lighted interior and releasing the rasping static of a radio. Several men ran from the hut with lighted torches and jogged along the length of the grassy clearing, pausing every twenty meters or so to light an oil drum. When they had marked out the makeshift landing strip there was sufficient light for Featherstone to put his scope away. Just then the distant sound of an airplane engine rose above the drone of jungle insects and the occasional night bird-calls.

He saw the plane make its first pass. A twin-engined private plane, possibly a Cessna, he thought. As the men on the ground fired two red flares into the sky, it circled around and came in for its landing. It touched down hard but kept rolling right up to the huts. The side door opened while the engines continued to rev, a jeep wheeled around from behind the huts to the side of the plane, and several dark figures began to load heavy sacks into the aircraft.

Featherstone picked up the scope again and focused on one of the guards standing in the shadows. Almost before he realized it, Featherstone saw another figure emerge from the surrounding jungle and swing something at the guard from behind, bringing him down in a heap. The new figure crouched again and moved toward the airplane. Featherstone scanned the whole scene and could see that all of the guards had now disappeared and that numerous shadows were closing in on the frenzied activity around the plane.

Suddenly someone fired a burst of automatic weapons fire into the air, bringing all motion to a stop. There were men all around the jeep now, pulling the loaders away. The pilot gunned his engine and started to roll, but two of the dark shadows had jumped into the airplane already. The sound of the motors eased and then died altogether.

Featherstone's guards signalled that it was clear to move forward, and all three made their way across the field past the burning oil drums, to where Guerrero had herded his collection of prisoners.

"Now *this* is what a real drug raid looks like," Guerrero trumpeted as his men heaved clear plastic bags of white powder off the plane. "This is cocaine HCL, not paste. The pilot and copilot are both Americans, and I think that your DEA office will recognize at least one of the men from inside the main hut there as having a warrant out for his arrest in the States. *That's* how you can tell the real thing from a put-up job. The trafficker who set up this delivery has lost his American connection and four hundred kilos, roughly speaking, of powder, approximately four million dollars worth at the local wholesale rate, five times that much wholesale once it's delivered in the States, and five times more after it's been stepped on and distributed on the street. Not even a drug trafficker can give up that much for appearance' sake."

"I'm impressed," admitted Featherstone, as Guerrero's men pulled the reloaded jeep off to a safe distance and then torched the airplane, sending a spectacular series of explosions and balls of fire into the night sky.

"Now what are you going to do?" asked Featherstone, once Guerrero had finished his work.

"Oh, we've called the UMOPAR to come and investigate this strange explosion in the jungle. They should be here by morning. We'll just leave the 'suspects' hog-tied here on the ground, and if some jungle animal or a swarm of army ants don't eat them first they will be taken into custody, tried, found innocent, and eventually released. Except for the Americans, who will be extradited back to the States, if there are any charges out on them. I suspect that this one Bolivian who is wanted by the DEA might prove a tougher nut to crack. You know how delicate these extradition cases are, but that's not my problem."

"And what will you do with the cocaine?"

"We'll drive that right into Cochabamba to have it tested, weighed, and turned in as evidence," Guerrero sighed. "I would be tempted to just destroy it here, but then there would be no proof that this wasn't just a load of talcum powder. There's always the risk that it will get 'lost' and back out onto the street, but there's plenty more where this came from anyway. Besides, the damage to the owner/trafficker has been done. He's lost it, and it would cost him almost as much to get it back from the police as it would to make more. The amusing thing about traffickers is, despite the huge amounts of money they take in, almost all of it profit, they're generally such idiots that they're always deep in debt. They use this shipment's money to pay for the drugs they sent out on the last shipment, and so on. And the kind of people they owe money to go in for debt renegotiation with a Black and Decker power drill. This guy's going to be scrambling."

"Do you know who this stuff belongs to?" Featherstone asked.

"Yes," Guerrero chuckled, "an old friend of mine from my Academy days." He would say no more.

Chapter Three

Behind the coy smile she showed to the well-dressed man across the table, Kelly Slater's mind was racing as she struggled with her decision. Of course she had already had nearly a week to think about it, and she had, but every time she thought she had definitely settled on a course of action some other argument had come to her head for the opposite one. But now she could postpone no longer. If she hemmed and hawed Alan might lose respect for her. After all, he was one of the few people she had ever known who treated her as an adult and an equal, even though he was a successful insurance executive in his early thirties and she a mere secretary of only twenty-two. No, it would be better to make a choice. If she refused politely he might have some argument held in reserve that would swing her over. If she accepted she would still have some time to back out if things got too heavy. So she swallowed and spoke.

"Alan," she said carefully, trying hard not to stammer, "I've been thinking about the trip thing . . ." Oh, great, she thought. That's brilliant. The trip *thing*. He's certainly going to be impressed with your choice of words. "Well," she continued, "I've thought it over and I'd like to take you up on your offer."

Alan's smile, already broad, grew even warmer as he reached across the table and took her hand in both of his. "That's great, Kelly. I was hoping you would. Don't worry about a thing. I'll make all of the reservations and preparations. All you have to do is put in for two weeks' vacation time and make sure your passport is in order. Oh, and don't forget your sunblock."

They both laughed quietly, and Kelly was certain that she had done the right thing. She shyly reached into her handbag and pulled out her blue passport. She had gotten one for the first time only last year, when she and another girl had taken a package cruise to Jamaica. She waved it delicately.

Alan took it and flipped to the page with the expiration date. Then he flipped through the other pages, finding only the one entry/exit stamp from Jamaica. Perfect, he thought.

"That's my girl," he said. "Always a step ahead of me."

Kelly was feeling better and better. Alan was so . . . so neat. He was head of accounting for the New York insurance firm for which Kelly had been working as a secretary for just over a year, after she had had the luck to be offered a transfer from the branch office in Des Moines, where she had grown up. She had felt lost in the big city for quite a while. Then she had been assigned to fill in as secretary in Alan's office for a few weeks when his regular secretary had been on maternity leave. The chemistry had worked right from the first, but Alan hadn't asked her out until after she had gone back to her regular post in personnel. He had said that dating someone in your own office was bad both for your personal life and for business. He was so mature!

When they had started dating, she was really hooked. Even though they both still "saw other people," she was convinced that the younger guys in the office could never measure up to this suave man who had introduced her to the nicer restaurants and clubs in town. Nothing too trendy, nothing too flashy, just the kind of places to prove that he knew his way around.

Of course, he hadn't exactly introduced her to cocaine. She had done marijuana occasionally in high school, where she had also learned that she couldn't hold her liquor. She had even done an occasional line of coke in the ladies' room of a disco. Even so, she had been more than a little surprised when Alan had offered her some at his apartment. He had explained to her that *everybody* did it in New York. Responsibly, of course. Never to excess. Never on a work night. Really, it was no worse than drinking, which she knew some of the executives with the firm did too much of, and during office hours too.

It had really shocked her when Alan had mentioned that one of the ways he was able to live so comfortably in the expensive community of Manhattan was by his sideline of distributing a little coke from time to time, just among his friends, of course. Then he had explained how, when he was in college, he had earned enough money to pay for his M.B.A. by making a trip all the way to Bolivia to pick up a whole kilo of coke, bringing it back, and selling it to his friends over more than a year. He had gone on to say that he had made two trips since then and really couldn't risk raising his profile any more, and he was wondering if she would be able to make a trip for him.

Before she had had a chance to turn him down cold—after all, other than the one cruise to Jamaica, on which she got deathly ill from the strange food, she had never set foot outside of the United States—he had spelled out how easy it would all be. They would travel together down to Rio for a short vacation, then on to some waterfalls on the border between Argentina and Brazil. From there he would return to Miami and she would go to Santa Cruz, Bolivia, wherever the hell that was. In Santa Cruz he had a friend who would meet her at the airport, put her up in a fancy hotel for two nights, and pass her the package (he never again referred to what the package contained) and get her on a morning flight to Miami. In Miami Alan would be waiting for her. He had a contact in Customs in Miami. All she had to do was wear a certain color of hair band and use the luggage he would provide, and she would be waved right through. Alan warned her that they sometimes had drug-sniffing dogs examine the checked baggage, so she would have the package in her carry-on bag, in which Alan would have prepared a hidden compartment. But, he added, the package would be wrapped in a special, sealed way that would prevent any scent of the powder escaping.

He even gave her advice on how to get through the out-going customs inspection in Bolivia. She was to wear a form-fitting minidress, which Alan would buy for her. She was very proud of her figure. He assured her that the simple little Bolivian peasant who would be the inspecting cop would be so busy drooling and blushing that he wouldn't even take his eyes off her as he inspected her bag. Once she got on the plane everything would be taken care of.

Then he hit her with the clincher. He said that a beautiful girl like her could probably always get what she wanted out of any man, but wouldn't it be better for her to have her own money and not to have to depend on anyone else? He was so liberal! With ten thousand dollars—tax free, he had added (he was an accountant, after all)—she could afford her own apartment instead of sharing with that tramp from reception who was always bringing strange men home at all hours. Maybe next year they could make another trip, maybe carrying twice the amount for twice the price. He had concluded his pitch by saying that this was strictly a business deal and that if she decided she was afraid, and he could understand that, he would still like to continue seeing her socially.

Kelly was not so sure about that last part. Here was a mature, serious, successful man who had taken her seriously enough to make these confessions and had trusted her enough to offer this chance. If she couldn't handle it, she suspected that in a city of the size and sophistication of New York he wouldn't have any trouble finding a girl who could. No, she had done the right thing. All she had to do now was trust in Alan and enjoy the trip.

After Alan dropped Kelly off at her apartment, walking her to the door but, as always on a work night, never beyond, he went back down to his car and drove to a bar on the East Side. Sitting at a booth along the wall was a familiar face. Alan smiled and gave a thumbs-up signal to the man as he strode across the room.

"It's a done deal," Alan said. "I've got us another mule. She's perfect. Purer than the driven snow and dumber than shit."

"That's great, Alan," the dealer said. "When will she be ready for the trip?"

"We're planning on the week after next, which would put her in Santa Cruz by the end of the month. I'll let you know the flight numbers and such when I've checked on the reservations. I think she's going to be very good. She'll probably do for two or three trips, if everything works out."

The dealer narrowed his eyes a little. He really didn't like dealing with amateurs. This wimp had certainly never done any time, never handled a gun. Of course, if he had he wouldn't be able to do what the dealer needed now. "But what if everything doesn't work out? Have you thought about that?"

"It's the same setup as before," Alan explained, a little put out that the dealer would question his preparations. "We split up at the Foz de Iguazu. She goes to Bolivia and I go to Miami. Her original ticket doesn't include Bolivia. We change that in Brazil. If she gets caught, my story is that we had a fight and I went on home. It looks like she took it into her own head to go into business for herself on the way back. No matter what she says, it's her word against mine, and all of the evidence is on my side."

"That sounds good," the man said. "I'll set things up from my end. Get me her photo, and I'll have her met at Viru Viru Airport in Santa Cruz and taken to the Los Tajibos Hotel for the delivery." The man took a sip of his drink and said, pensively, "You know, I was watching you at the restaurant earlier." Alan swallowed hard at this but tried not to show his concern. He was worried that he had not spotted the dealer there, and even more so that the dealer apparently didn't trust him very much. "She's really quite pretty, short chestnut hair, green eyes, and a knockout body. I think I might like a little piece of that myself . . . after the trip."

Alan let out a sigh of relief. Was that all this slimebag had on his mind? "Sure," he said expansively. "Help yourself. I'll be glad to set it up for you, maybe to celebrate her arrival with the stuff." He leaned closer, oddly conspiratorial now that mundane talk of drug smuggling was over and they could get down to more sensitive topics. "We're really talking a low-mileage item here, but she's eager to learn, if you know what I mean."

The dealer smiled and nodded that he certainly did.

Chapter Four

The Lloyd Aereo Boliviano Boeing 707 finally touched down at La Paz International Airport shortly after 1000 hours. As he descended the steps to the tarmac Featherstone was debating whether he would have time to drive all the way home to Calacoto to shower and change before returning to the office. He crossed to the terminal building with the shoving crowd of other passengers and was grateful that he did not have any luggage to reclaim, which would have meant a struggle with the formidable *cholitas*, the entrepreneurial peasant women who used the domestic flights to transport unknown quantities and sorts of contraband merchandise to sell in La Paz. He could already see them, short, stocky, and dark, dressed in their derby hats, colorful shawls, and multiple skirts, as they elbowed each other for strategic positions at the baggage claim area, even though it would be half an hour before the first bags appeared.

He crossed the interior hall of the small terminal and exited the other side, where taxis and private autos jockeyed for room at the passenger loading area. He scanned the area for the large American sedan that the embassy motor pool usually sent, or perhaps one of the bulletproof Chevy Blazers, but saw no familiar vehicles. After waiting a few minutes, shifting his overnight bag from one sore shoulder to the other and fighting off the advances of many aggressive taxi drivers, he went back into the terminal, found an unoccupied public telephone, and called the embassy.

The motor pool dispatcher was greatly distressed that no one had informed Sr. Featherstone that on specific orders of Ambassador Pearson himself all of the embassy vehicles had been reserved to deal with a Co-del (Congressional delegation) that was due in later that afternoon, so that none was available to pick him up at the airport. After thinking a moment the dispatcher, perhaps touched by Featherstone's expansive sighs, offered to drive up to the airport in his personal vehicle, but Featherstone merely thanked him and said that it would be quicker for him just to grab a taxi. Featherstone had ceased to be surprised by what appeared to be calculated efforts by the ambassador to irritate him, but as he could think of no earthly reason why Pearson would go to such lengths he put it down to unfortunate coincidence and his own imagination.

Featherstone picked an old but large Buick, which would at least give him room to stretch out in the back seat, rather than the more common Datsun taxis, settled on the price of the fare with the driver, and climbed into the taxi. They began the long drive down the four-lane highway that wound its way down from the airport, on the rim of the Altiplano plateau, into the valley in which La Paz was located, and Featherstone idly debated with himself whether the city was more attractive at night or in the daytime. During the day, of course, one had a spectacular view from the airport of the massive, snow-capped peaks of the Andes that surround La Paz: Illimari, Mururata, and others whose names he did not know. Below the snow line the stark, barren hillsides glowed in colors reminiscent of the American Southwest: purples, reds, oranges, and, above the mountains, the deep, burning blue of the sky, a color he had never seen anywhere else, a product of the city's twelve-thousand-foot altitude. On a moonlit night, however, you could see the gleam of the snows of Illimari under a thick dusting of stars, unobscured by pollution, and the multitude of tiny lights in the houses that climbed up the steep valley walls from the city's center appeared to be reflections of those stars in some vast, calm lake.

What one didn't see at night was the poverty of those same houses, the rough brick or adobe construction, or the dirty children playing in the dusty streets of the poorer neighborhoods lining the upper rim of the valley. One couldn't see the poor people, probably campesinos recently moved to the city in search of work, schools, and medical care, as they climbed up and down perilous steps in the steep mud walls of the valley, going and coming from distant jobs downtown. That took some of the magic out of the scenery.

Oh, well, Featherstone thought. No point in trying to go home now. He would take a quick shower in the embassy and change into the old suit he fortunately kept in his office against the day that a coup or a strike would cut the one main road from the city center down to the residential suburb of Calacoto where he lived. He hadn't needed it before now, but he was glad that his predecessor had advised him to take the precaution.

The taxi deposited him at the corner of Calle Mercado and Calle Colon, opposite the Banco Popular del Peru building in which the embassy was located, occupying the upper six floors of the eight-story building. He slipped slightly on the smooth cobblestones as he dashed across the street, narrowly escaping death beneath the wheels of a crowded bus, and weaved his way between the throngs of shoppers and businessmen, past the "ornamental" cement planters that protected the building from mad truck bombers, and into the embassy entrance. He nodded a greeting to the three Bolivian policemen who lounged in the featureless marble room, which contained only two elevators and a staircase, the only means of access to the embassy offices above. He swore under his breath as he saw the cardboard sign hanging from the elevator button, which indicated that he would have to climb seven flights of stairs before he could have the pleasure of getting to work.

He walked slowly now, saving his energy, and nodded again to the lone policeman who occupied the second floor landing, from which one could enter some of the bank's upper offices. He continued up the stairs and paused to catch his breath before entering the embassy reception area on the next floor. After a moment he straightened up a bit and entered the lobby area, showing his ID card to the Bolivian policeman and policewoman on duty by the metal detector, and waved at the receptionist and Marine security guard behind their bulletproof glass windows as the Marine buzzed him through the door. As he rounded the bulletproof barrier that separated the elevator that ran only between the ground floor and this lobby and the one that ran only from the lobby upward through the embassy floors, he was relieved to see the door slide open and several secretaries come out. Thank God! he thought as he jumped into the elevator to ride the rest of the way to his office on the sixth floor. Stepping out of the elevator, he waved casually to the ambassador's receptionist and the two Bolivian bodyguards who sat in the small vestibule in front of the elevators and worked the cipher lock to let him into the embassy's restricted office area.

After a shower and a middling meal in the embassy cafeteria, Featherstone felt better if not exactly good, and called his wife, Ann, before starting to work on his report. He told her of most of his misadventures on the trip, leaving out the drug raids, as he knew that she would not welcome the idea that he had been in the immediate proximity of loaded weapons again in what should be the twilight of an illustrious diplomatic career. The very problem of the missed ride at the airport was enough for Ann, however. While Featherstone had grown accustomed to rather shoddy treatment since his arrival, it made Ann coldly furious.

Ann thought Pearson was a pompous buffoon, who was using his post as a possible stepping-stone to a career in Congress, and that Featherstone was twice as intelligent, twice as qualified, twice as everything as the ambassador. She was very careful not to imply that she held her husband in any way to blame for the way he was treated, but Featherstone couldn't help but feel that it was somehow his fault. He knew that Ann was even more disappointed than he that he hadn't been offered an ambassadorship after his tour in Cuba. He had explained to her that being DCM in a tiny interest section did not lead directly to a chief of mission posting, no matter how well one did in his job, and that the appointment to the number two slot in La Paz was actually a significant promotion. But the truth was that he was too tired to talk about this just then, and he put her off by lying that someone was waiting for him and that he would be home for dinner.

Featherstone was having trouble keeping his eyes from rolling back in his head, and he had caught himself dozing off more than once, jerking his head back at the last minute before it came crashing down on the conference table. He looked around sheepishly to see if anyone had noticed. He was fairly certain that the CIA chief of station, Tom Evans, who smiled sympathetically at him from his corner seat, knew, and probably the DEA special agent in charge, Enrique Contreras, too. Ambassador Pearson was far too busy with the press attache, Lynn Monroe, working out the details of the press release that would detail the drug raid he had witnessed and that would form the basis of the message he would send back to Washington on the same subject.

"Okay," the ambassador said, leaning over his draft with a marker so that his nose almost touched the paper, "so we've got 120 kilos of paste, plus how many kilos of coca leaf?"

"Well," Contreras answered, "we estimated maybe a ton."

"Good," Pearson continued. "And how many kilos of paste would that have made if it were processed?"

"That's hard to estimate, because so much depends on the purity of the precursor chemicals, the skill of the chemist, and things like that."

Pearson looked up without raising his head from its position over the paper. "I don't care how *hard* it is, just do it for me, please."

"Maybe ten to twenty kilos more as an upper limit," said Contreras, knowing full well that the upper limit was exactly what was wanted.

"And how many kilos of paste could have been processed with all of the chemicals present at the site?"

"Let's say another hundred kilos," said Contreras, getting into the swing of things.

"Good, now how much would that be worth in terms of cocaine HCL?"

"Well, let's say that the paste could be turned into eighty to a hundred kilos of HCL, counting the potential product of the chemicals and everything. That would be about half a million dollars."

"No!" roared Pearson, glaring at Contreras now. "Not the value at the point of manufacture. How much would its street value be in the States, right to the consumer?"

"Oh," said Contreras, taken aback by the ambassador's outburst. "In that case, maybe about five million dollars or more, depending on how much it was stepped on prior to use."

"Thank you," said Pearson sarcastically, and then to Lynn. "Let's go with this: 'Over a hundred kilograms of cocaine hydrochloride or its equivalent with a street value of nearly ten million dollars.' "

Evans, Contreras, and Featherstone eyed each other silently. Featherstone had already briefed the CIA and DEA chiefs on his outing with Guerrero, as the ambassador had been "too busy" to see him earlier. Featherstone cleared his throat and pushed another copy of his report over to the ambassador's position.

"Excuse me, sir," he began. "But before you put the finishing touches on that message, I really think you should take a minute to read my report."

Pearson ignored Featherstone and continued talking to Monroe. "There! That's got it. You go ahead and get it typed up in final for the press and in cable format and have it back in my office before close of business."

When Monroe had left the room with her papers the ambassador sat back in his tall chair, which he had brought in especially, as it had a seat several inches higher than the others in the room and a back over a foot taller. He placed his hands on Featherstone's report, palms down, and slid it back across the table. "I *have* taken a minute to read your report, Bill, and, frankly, it was a minute wasted."

Featherstone set his jaw and waited for one of Pearson's famous dressings down, always best delivered in front of a large audience.

"I must say that I'm disappointed in you, Bill," Pearson continued. Featherstone supposed that he had taken a course somewhere in which they had suggested that the frequent use of the listener's name is a good tactic. "I'm sorry that you couldn't come with the president and me. I would have loved to have had you, to interpret for me." Gee, thanks, Featherstone thought. "But there wasn't room in the helicopter. That simple, nothing personal. And here you, the supposed professional, come up with this cock-and-bull story to try to discredit a significant antinarcotics operation. In your report you make the totally unfounded allegation that the DEA raid was a setup, a fraud, and yet in the same breath you insist that this other operation, run not by the police of this country but by some renegade soldier with no jurisdiction, was legitimate—just because he told you so."

Featherstone started to answer, but Pearson raised his finger, threatening Featherstone with it as with a gun, "I don't suppose it ever occurred to you that this Herrera fellow—"

"Guerrero, Comandante Guerrero," Featherstone corrected.

"Whatever!" groaned Pearson. "So, it never occurred to you that this Guerrero is working with some narcotics trafficker. Naturally, he could have found out about the DEA raid. After all, the Bolivian government's like a sieve, and he *is* a military officer. Then some trafficker friend of his gives him some inside skinny on a shipment being made by one of his competitors. Happens all the time. You should know that, and I think you do. The trouble is that you're so tied up in your personal bitterness at being second in command to a political appointee that you just shut your eyes to any other possible explanation."

Featherstone did not change his grim expression. He knew that Pearson was a blowhard and a glory hound. On the other hand, part of what he said was true, or might be. How did Featherstone know that Guerrero's raid wasn't just as much of a setup as Pearson's? And wasn't it also possible that he had ignored that possibility because he resented Pearson and would very much like to make him look like a fool?

"You're quite right, sir," Featherstone finally spit out between clenched teeth, "about Guerrero, I mean. We really don't know much about him. But that doesn't explain everything I saw at the site of the DEA raid."

"The matter's closed, Featherstone," Pearson said emphatically. "I'm willing to overlook your possible errors in judgement this time, but I'm not going to sit here and argue with my subordinates." Suddenly he softened his tone. It appeared that Pearson believed that he had the gift of irresistible persuasive capability. He did not. "Listen, Bill, we can make a fine team, all of us here," he grandly swept the room with his arm, taking in the tense faces of all of the embassy section chiefs. "But it has to be a team, and on a team there can be only one quarterback, and for better or worse it's me. I *need* you, your area knowledge, your language capability, but let's all start pushing from the same side of the door, and we'll all come up smelling like roses."

Featherstone just nodded silently, and Pearson smiled. "Good. I'm glad we got that settled," and he strode out of the room, followed by most of the other attendees, each of whom gave Featherstone a sad, pitying look on the way out.

Featherstone just sat there until he felt a hand on his shoulder. He looked up into the weathered face of Tom Evans.

"Hey, Bill, I know you've had a long day already, but how about if you invite a few of us over to your place for a few mixed metaphors?"

Featherstone chuckled at the reference to Pearson's famous speaking style. "What's up?"

"I just thought that maybe you, Contreras, Colonel Polsby, and I could huddle for a few minutes over a drink and talk about Guerrero. Regardless of what the boss might want right now, I think it's incumbent on us to explore this further."

Featherstone sighed. "You're always welcome for a drink, Tom. Just so long as you don't expect anything coherent on my part."

"Never did," he laughed. "See you later."

Featherstone slumped in the easy chair. One thing about La Paz, you couldn't complain about the housing, he thought as he stared at the high cathedral ceiling and wood-panelled fireplace in his living room. Contreras had just arrived and was fixing himself a drink at the bar. Evans and Polsby were already lounging on the couch, waiting for him. Ann had greeted everyone pleasantly enough and had set out chips and dip, but had then excused herself, more because she wasn't in the mood to face anyone than because she wanted to leave the men to their "boy talk."

"So, tell me what you know about Guerrero," Featherstone said to no one in particular.

"I'll go first, since I probably have the least to say," Evans started. "Guerrero has a reputation as being excruciatingly honest. His family had a little money, not a lot, but he very clearly lives within his means. That's very rare for a military type, especially one who operates in an area of drug activity.

"I can say this, I think, without giving anything away, because nothing came of it: We, that is the Agency, approached him some years ago, during the Garcia Meza pro-mafia dictatorship. He was in with a group of officers known as the 'generationalists' who were opposed to Garcia Meza, as we were, and we thought he might give us a window on their intentions. We set it up rather neatly, got an officer close to him at an athletic club he belonged to, made friends, and then pitched him. He politely told us to kiss his butt, thank you very much. He said that if he knew about a plot to overthrow Garcia Meza, we'd be the last people he would tell, because we can't keep secrets."

"Well, that says something for his IQ," sniped Featherstone, letting his general bad humor get the better of him.

Polsby jumped in before something even more untoward might be said. "I suppose you know about his Vietnam tour. Well, since he was commissioned in '73, I think, his attitude has kept him off the promotion fast track, but I have to say that he's about the best combat commander I've ever seen. He's created his own little army down in the Chapare, and they're really hot. From the enlisted men right up to his executive officer, everyone eats in the same mess, sleeps in the same ditches in the field. You may have noticed that even he carries a rifle, something you don't often see a Latino military type doing. All of his men are jump-qualified, and he's got about two hundred jumps logged himself.

"What's really weird is that they've let him do it. What seems to make it work is that he's navy. The army brass hates his guts, but the navy welcomes having a little extra muscle on the ground. He's even broken the conscript system. The Bolivian military is about eighty percent one-year conscripts, which doesn't make for much military expertise. Since they can only take a tiny percentage of the total eligible males every year, it's child's play for anyone with any kind of family connections to get out of the duty. So you end up with all of the conscripts being poor little campesinos, many of them illiterate. They love it. With three squares a day, a new suit of clothes, and a warm place to sleep, that's better than most of them had at home. What makes Guerrero's operation different is that his men re-up almost one hundred percent, officers and enlisted men alike. He treats the men right, doesn't cheat them on their pay or their rations, like some officers do, and even stands good for personal loans for them with his own money. Even after they get out, we hear that about fifty of his former troops have settled on farmland near his headquarters and that he brings them in for training once in awhile. He has the only real reserve program going in this country! He must be godfather to a thousand kids of his own men or of other young officers who worship his reputation. Everybody loves him."

"Not quite everybody," intoned Contreras. "There have been at least two attempts on his life in the past four years that I know of. The traffickers hate his guts. The local politicians hate his guts, and even the fucking crooks in the Ministry of Interior hate his guts."

Contreras took a sip of his drink and went on. "I heard a story about the Ministry of Interior. Since they're responsible for the police and the court system, especially the narcotics police and the internal security services, they've been heavily bought off by the narcotics mafia." Featherstone nodded. This was hardly news. "So one day these two slick Interior types show up at Guerrero's headquarters. This would have been a couple of years ago. You know the kind: aviator sunglasses, shiny suits, the works. They march into his office and plunk a fat envelope full of U.S. hundred-dollar bills down on his desk. Then they tell him there's plenty more where that came from if he would just quit blowing up fucking coke labs with his boys. Then they add, and this was their mistake, that if he doesn't knock it off they're going to kick his skinny butt all the way back to La Paz.

"So he stands up, sticks the envelope in his waistband, puts an arm around their shoulders, and walks them to the door. They think they've made a sale!" Contreras paused to choke down another drink between giggles. "So he takes them out on the little veranda there, facing the parade ground where about a dozen of his NCOs are standing around, and tells them that these two nice gentlemen from the Ministry of Interior are going to kick his skinny butt all the way back to La Paz and asks them what they think of the idea.

"Well, in about ten seconds these two thugs have been disarmed, stripped naked, and had the shit beaten out of them. The commandos then throw the clothes *and* the bribe money into their sleek Mercedes, plunk a wad of C-4 under the hood, blow the fucker to hell, and then make them walk all the way back to Cochabamba naked as jaybirds." Contreras obviously had wished to have done something similar more than once, from his enjoyment of the story. "His deal is that he put the word out that if any of his men are even scratched on one of their 'training missions,' he doesn't take any more prisoners. So the traffickers have to take him as an inherent risk of doing business and try to stay out of his area of operations whenever they can."

Contreras then grew serious. "I have to admit that the raid the ambassador went on, which was purely an UMOPAR operation by the way, was probably a setup arranged either by the government alone or with the cooperation of drug traffickers, but I can't say that officially. I can't prove it. When it comes right down to it, DEA here has to do what Washington wants, and what Washington wants is powder on the table. It's fucking Vietnam body counts all over again. Everything from manning levels to budgets to promotions are calculated in terms of how many 'labs' we destroy, so every trench we fill in or every barrel of acetone we kick over becomes a lab; or in volume of drugs seized, so anything that even smells like cocaine automatically becomes pure hydrochloride ready for market. That's just the way it is.

"What I *can* say is that what the ambassador said about how Guerrero might have found out about the delivery he busted up is dead wrong. I'm not going to say this in front of the ambassador, because I frankly don't trust him to keep his mouth shut, but Guerrero has a first-class intelligence network in the Chapare among the campesinos. Sure, the campesinos grow coca, which is perfectly legal, by the way, and they take the traffickers' money, but they don't trust them or like them. Traffickers can pay half of what they promised or take the crop and pay nothing at all, if the mood strikes them. If a campesino puts a bunch of sticks or pebbles in the middle of a bale of leaves to raise the weight a bit, and they do with a lot of their regular produce, a trafficker will come back and cut his legs off. If a trafficker, or more likely, one of his lowest gunmen, takes a fancy to a campesino's daughter, well he takes her.

"Guerrero treats the people right. He's built a small clinic where his medics treat people for free. He's built a little school where his officers take turns teaching both kids and adults how to read and do arithmetic. He's even been known, and this is just rumor mind you, to track down and kick the shit out of a trafficker who leans too heavily on one of 'his' campesinos. He doesn't hassle them. He doesn't shake them down. So they talk to him. My guess is that he learned the old 'hearts and minds' lesson real well in the 'Nam."

"So," Featherstone concluded, "what you're all saying is that this does not sound like the kind of guy who would be a stooge for some trafficker, knocking off his opposition?"

All three heads nodded vigorously. Featherstone pursed his lips. "Colonel, could you arrange for Guerrero to stop in and visit me, very unofficially, next time he passes through La Paz? I think this is a man worth getting to know better."

"You got it, boss," the colonel saluted smartly.

"One other thing," Contreras added as they headed for the door. "One of the guys that was picked up on Guerrero's operation is wanted in the States. His name is Francisco "Gusano" Murillo. He's reportedly one of the right-hand men to Lazaro Benitez, probably the biggest trafficker in Santa Cruz."

"Can we get him extradited to the States?" Featherstone asked.

"That's the interesting part," Contreras continued. "He's a trafficker in his own right and all that, but he's wanted in Florida for killing two state troopers in cold blood. They apparently pulled him over on I-95, thinking he was a robbery suspect, when he was transporting some coke. They didn't know he had a follow-car full of thugs who came up and overpowered the two cops. They disarmed them and cuffed them, but then Murillo offed them himself, execution style, just out of nastiness. One of the thugs later got arrested for something else and spilled the whole thing. We've got a better case for extradition with him than with any other trafficker who's ever been picked up. There's no way the government can deny us this one, and with what he's got in his head we could trace the movement of every ounce of coke Benitez produces from the bush to the men's room at Studio 54."

"Keep me posted on the government's response," Featherstone said. "You know how memos sometimes seem to bypass my desk." Contreras smiled sympathetically and patted Featherstone on the back as he went out the door.

After his guests left, Featherstone slowly climbed the stairs and dressed for bed. He did this as quietly as he could, but in La Paz, where the temperature drops sharply as soon as the sun goes down, one does not go to sleep without donning the mandatory flannel nightwear.

Ann didn't move and waited for him to get into bed before she spoke. "Bill?"

"I'm sorry, honey. I tried not to wake you."

"I wasn't sleeping. I just enjoy listening to you stubbing your toes in the dark." She turned toward him, and in the light from the hallway he could see that she was smiling, at least on the outside.

"Any chance of our just cutting our losses and getting the hell out of Dodge City?" she asked.

"I've given it a lot of thought in the last twenty-four hours," he said. "Do you think we should?"

"I don't know," she sighed, lying back down on her pillow and staring at the ceiling. "Heaven knows that there are enough medevacs from this place that we could cook up something if we had to."

"That's true," Featherstone said. "It just sticks in my throat that I should be forced to do something I really don't want to do by some plastic clown with a nice haircut." He raised himself up on one elbow and looked at her. "There are so many good people here, both Bolivians and Americans, doing such important work, that I hate to leave them to the likes of *Lance*." He said the ambassador's name with as greasy a tone as possible.

"Then we stay," she said flatly. "Our tour will be up in eighteen months or so, and that's the end of it. If you quit when you don't want to you're going to have to live with it for a lot longer than that."

"I suppose you're right," he sighed with relief. He didn't know what he had done to deserve her, but it seemed that flowers and dinner on their anniversary wasn't exactly just compensation.

"Just promise me one thing," she added. He expected something about taking care of himself, but she continued, "If that sleazy bastard gives you half a chance, I want you to bring me a nice big piece of him."

Featherstone had been awfully tired when he climbed the stairs to the bedroom, but after all, tomorrow was Saturday.

Chapter Five

They used to call it "*Dia de la Raza,*" but then someone started to ask just which race it was whose superiority they were celebrating. If it was the Spanish race, then where did that leave Bolivia's Indian majority? And if it was the American Indian race, then how come they celebrated it in Spain? So Bolivia, like many other Latin American countries, had opted to change the emphasis of October twelfth to the discovery of America and to leave it at that.

In any case, it was a good enough excuse for a holiday, and on this twelfth of October evening the reception hall of the Gran Hotel Cochabamba was ablaze with lights and alive with hanging crepe-paper decorations prepared by some of the wives of the commando battalion's officers and NCOs. It was an elegant old hotel, meaning that the rooms weren't much but they were clean. However, one could get a fine meal of local culinary specialties in the restaurant, and there were attractive gardens all around the rambling pink-and-white Spanish colonial structure.

Guerrero relaxed in his chair on the edge of the dance floor, watching the younger couples enthusiastically going through the paces of the traditional dance, the *cueca*. In the *cueca,* the partners face each other from about two or three meters apart and dance forward and back to the lively music. Each waves a white handkerchief over the head, or at any other height, as they meet in the center, circle each other, and resume their original positions. The men are as gallant as can be, while the women are alternately flirtatious and coy. At a given pause in the piece the free-style portion begins, and the men vie with each other to perform the most original and acrobatic *zapateo* (a taplike dance movement).

Guerrero was always pleased to see these young people, all very fashionably dressed, all of whom knew the latest American dances and who had their record and tape libraries at home filled with the likes of Madonna and Billy Idol, still fully enjoying the traditional dances. It gave him faith that the Americans had not totally corrupted his people with their fast-food, disposable plastic culture. It was not as if the Americans actually *had* a culture, of course. Their music was either hillbilly picking and strumming or it was really either African or Latin American. The only way Americans could aspire to true culture was to learn European classics. There was no taking away from American technology, industry, and democracy, but when it came to things of the heart there was always something lacking.

He wished Marisol were here. It was over a decade since her death, and he still missed her. She had never lived with him in the Chapare, where he had been stationed for nearly five years, and yet he half expected to find her waiting when he came home at the end of the day. She had been so beautiful, a typical Tarijena girl, with fair skin, long dark hair, and dark green eyes. He had never understood how it was that she, of all people, had been able to look beyond his unattractive face, pock-marked by juvenile skin disease and ill-formed in any case, and to find something worthwhile.

He had certainly done everything in his power to win her over. He had used the traditional approach. In those days, although the custom had been lost somewhat since, it was still fashionable for the better families of La Paz to go to church late Sunday morning on the Prado. This was the one flat part of the city, with two lanes of traffic in each direction separated by a central mall area with broad sidewalks, shrubbery, and fountains. The men would usually opt out of church altogether and sit drinking coffee or beer at one of the sidewalk cafes along the Prado while the women and children went to worship. After church the women would sit together on the benches in the central mall while the younger children ran and played around them.

But Sunday on the Prado was really for the young adults. In those days it was still the custom for the girls, usually in groups of two or three, to stroll around the Prado (it was only about three city blocks long) counter-clockwise, while the young men, also in groups of two or three for mutual protection, would stroll in the opposite direction. Eye contact could thus hardly be avoided, and if all went well, on the third or fourth circuit, one would find couples, walking side by side or even arm in arm. The mothers and aunts would then have the opportunity to size up the match and give discreet approval or disapproval as the situation demanded.

That was how he had met Marisol. He and Campos were the usual team on his side, Quispe generally preferring to stay back and study or to catch a bus up to the Altiplano to visit his family on weekends. Marisol had been attending the Universidad Mayor de San Andres in La Paz, studying medicine, and her father had arranged a transfer with his company to La Paz in order to permit her to continue to live at home with them.

On Sundays like those he never regretted having gone to the Academy. The cadets were always resplendent in their dress uniforms, grey for the army, white for the navy, with their short ceremonial swords at their sides. The rows of American combat ribbons that Guerrero was permitted to display set him apart from the rest, although he doubted that Marisol ever really noticed them. He saw her walking with another girl on one pass and was interested. On the next, she was standing talking to a couple of young men, and civilians no less, but he noticed her watching him as he passed. On the third round she and her friend were unaccompanied, so he and Campos made their move. There had been a brief clash, as Campos had apparently assigned himself Marisol as well, but one hard look from Guerrero had told Campos that this was not a subject for debate.

After a couple of turns together around the Prado they stopped to be introduced to Marisol's mother and grandmother, who were seated opposite the church. After a whispered conversation between Marisol and her mother, Guerrero had been invited to tea that afternoon, after which he would be permitted to take Marisol to an early movie and then back home, as the next day was a school day.

Tea was tense. The mother apparently liked Guerrero, and the grandmother spent the twenty or thirty hours that the meal seemed to last doting on him and filling his plate with pastries and his cup with tea faster than he could empty them. The father, however, obviously disapproved of the military on general grounds. He sat and glowered at Guerrero across the table the whole time, saying a total of perhaps eight words, most of which had to do with passing things around the table. Guerrero sweated profusely despite the cool La Paz temperature, and he could feel his high uniform collar gradually strangling him.

He was too traumatized to take much advantage of the movie interlude and kicked himself all the way back to the Academy, down in the lower suburb of Irpavi, for saying hardly anything the whole time. In an uncharacteristic burst of romanticism he grabbed Campos and Quispe, who had just returned from El Alto, and his guitar, and commandeered a taxi, an exceptional level of profligacy for Guerrero, for the ride up to Marisol's house in Miraflores.

It was dark by this time, and they stood in the street facing the blank walls of the gardens of the homes that ran up and down the street. Standing on the opposite side of the street they could just see the windows of the upper floor of Marisol's house, and they began to serenade her. With Guerrero and Campos singing to Guerrero's guitar and Quispe playing his *sampona* (Pan pipes), they may not have been good, but no one could have faulted them for lack of volume or ardor. One by one, windows opened at various houses nearby. Old ladies smiled sweetly and girls giggled, half hiding behind their curtains. It was not for some time that Marisol's window opened, and then it was her father who appeared, not Marisol. He still wore the same sour expression as earlier, and Guerrero began to wonder if he had any other. After a couple of songs, each loudly applauded by the neighbors, the street door opened and the maid came out to invite the gentlemen in for refreshments. Guerrero knew he had won!

They had been married shortly after his graduation from the Academy. Until then it had been like a fairy tale, but now the reality of life began to close in on them. He was posted to a remote garrison in the Amazon Basin and quartered in a simple thatched-roof hut, with no glass in the windows and no running water. Guerrero regretted having dragged Marisol out of the university for a life like this, sharing his squalor as the wife of an underpaid junior officer, and now he understood his father-in-law's opposition to his daughter marrying a military man. Still, they survived and were happy, both at this post and the next two, which were virtually identical. Marisol had not completed her medical studies, which she hoped to resume if they were ever posted back to a city with a university, but she knew enough to do volunteer work, helping the itinerant doctors occasionally sent around by the Ministry of Health.

It was unfortunate that the regional doctor had been at the other extreme of his area when Marisol's time to give birth came. There was a local midwife, of course, who had assisted in hundreds of births, and if everything had been routine nothing bad would have happened. But Marisol was a delicate girl and she had been weakened by a bout with amoebas, which hit everyone sooner or later in the tropics. One of the village women had come running for him when she went into labor, and his commander had lent him his jeep. When he arrived he could tell that things were not right from the look on the midwife's face. He forced his way in against the midwife's objections, and at least had the satisfaction of holding Marisol's hand, her thin little hand, as she died. In those conditions there had been no hope of saving the baby, a little boy, either. Marisol's father never spoke to him again and would cross the street if they happened to encounter each other in La Paz. Guerrero didn't blame him a bit.

For some months after Marisol's death Guerrero had sunk into an unrelieved depression. He didn't drink or stop his work, but he was like a robot and spoke to no one outside his official functions. Then, suddenly, as he was sitting in his little office or riding in a patrol boat on the river, and he closed his eyes, and she would be with him, comforting him. He thought at first that he was losing his mind, what was left of it, but he heard no voices, saw no apparitions. He just realized that the love they had shared still lived within him. If he had a decision to make he knew in his heart what she would have told him to do. She had been so much smarter than he, able to see right through the most complicated issues to the basic question. He knew that he would never love another woman, but he would not be bitter. He had had something most people never experience, and he had been very lucky. And then he had his new family, his *guaguas*, to take care of.

Now he sat at the edge of the dance floor, smiling to himself, when the fiancée of young Morales grabbed his hand and dragged him out onto the floor as another *cueca* was starting. He stood up ramrod straight for a moment and looked around him, and the young woman thought for a moment that she had made a terrible mistake. Without changing his serious expression, Guerrero slowly reached into the inside pocket of his jacket and, with a flourish, whipped out a white handkerchief, waved it around his head, and began to dance, to the riotous applause of the crowd. He would match his *zapateo* to that of any of these young puppies any day, and besides, as he danced he usually looked at the floor and could imagine that he was still dancing with Marisol, as he had done at so many other twelfth of October dances.

The party broke up before midnight, so Morales and his fiancée decided to go to a disco, as they had their dancing shoes on. It was a typical Bolivian disco, different from its American counterparts in that only couples were admitted. While this might appear to be a handicap to the disco's primary social function, that of aiding in procreation, one found that the numerous cafes around town would be filled on a Friday, Saturday, or holiday evening with tables of young men and women looking for partners to go dancing with. It was the same process as in the U.S., just begun rather earlier in the evening. In a moment Morales had staked out a table, ordered drinks, and then whisked his fiancée off to the dance floor for some more modern rhythms.

Federico "Kiko" Soares did not worry about finding a date before going to a disco. His father, Paolo, a Brazilian-born rancher, was also one of the major cocaine traffickers in Bolivia, and it would be a brave doorman who would turn away his son and his two husky bodyguards under any circumstances. Kiko had done this sort of thing many times. Usually his expensive clothes and gold jewelry told a girl all she needed to know, and more than one would excuse herself from her current escort to visit the ladies' room and end up at Kiko's table, leaving the poor slob sitting across the room with two half-finished drinks. Sometimes Kiko had to take more forceful methods, actually cutting in on a particularly attractive girl, but he had yet to meet a man who would confront his bodyguards to protect a casual date, who probably welcomed the improvement in any case.

Kiko was feeling exceptionally lucky tonight. This might have had something to do with the impressive amount of cocaine and liquor he had already consumed that evening, but Kiko was a handsome, well-dressed, rich young man, so luck had very little to do with it. He walked casually into the disco as if he owned the place, which he could have done had he wanted, his bodyguards brusquely making way for him with their meaty arms. He put out his hand and the bartender slapped a drink into it without being asked. Kiko had been here before. Kiko loved this part of his life. He never carried money or credit cards or ID. The local merchants knew that someone would be around the next day to pay generously for anything he bought or used, and if someone wasn't, well, it would be best just to keep quiet about it.

He had been watching one girl whirling around the dance floor since he entered. She was wearing a modest but beautiful white dress and her shoulder-length brown hair swung around her head like a halo. Great legs, he thought, as her skirt flipped up on a turn. She would do very nicely for tonight.

Kiko strode confidently onto the floor, while couples gladly moved as far out of his way as possible. He came up behind Morales, smiling all the while, and shoved him out of the way, catching him off balance and sending him crashing into a nearby table. He then struck a dance pose out of "Saturday Night Fever" and began to dance, as Morales' fiancée stood, terrified.

Morales moved far too fast for the bodyguards, who were still across the room. He was on his feet in an instant. He spun Kiko around and caught him with a blow to the solar plexus. As the startled young prince doubled over in pain Morales grabbed his head and shoved downward, his knee swinging up into Kiko's face. The force of the blow lifted Kiko off his feet and sent him flying backwards.

The bodyguards came rushing across the room now. The older one, out of the corner of the eye, saw his junior partner reaching for the automatic pistol stuck in the rear of his waistband, but he caught the man's hand and made a signal to cool it. No one, he knew, wore their hair *that* short except the military, and he didn't want to have the death of a soldier on his head, in front of dozens of witnesses. He remembered his first *patrón*, Jose Abraham Baptista, the first real godfather of the Santa Cruz drug mafia, who had allegedly financed the Garcia Meza coup d'etat in 1980. Baptista had gone around after the coup mouthing off that he had made this government and that if they didn't give him the recognition he deserved he would kick that fat general out on his butt and put another one in his place. Then one morning a Toyota Land Cruiser full of men with *very* short haircuts had met Baptista coming out of his house and had put nearly a hundred bullets into him. And *he* was the godfather! The army wouldn't lose much sleep over offing a couple of simple gunmen. No, thank you very much. A little slapping around would be more than sufficient. Then they would get their young charge the hell out of there, and the boss would likely reward them handsomely for their wisdom and presence of mind.

The bodyguards moved ponderously across the floor as the other dancers scampered for cover. Morales was very proud of his black belt in Tai Kwan Do, and he was now bouncing lightly from one foot to the other, after shoving his fiancée in the direction of the door and telling her to go get the police. He was not very worried, and he didn't expect much help from the police anyway, but it would get her out of the place to somewhere safe while he dealt with things here.

Morales had also seen the younger man start to reach for something and the older one stop him, so he decided to deal with the more unpredictable threat first. He quickly spun around, and for a fraction of a second the bodyguards thought that he had wisely chosen to run for it, but Morales was merely getting up momentum, and brought his right foot arcing around, striking the younger man with his heel just at the temple, sending him spinning into the wall. Without losing a beat Morales then brought his right foot down and shifted his weight to it. He then kicked upward with his left foot, which lifted his whole body off the ground, enabling him then to kick with his right, straight into the face of the onrushing bodyguard, knocking him on his back.

The older bodyguard was down but not out, and was struggling to his feet when he saw Kiko, his nose covered in blood, fumbling with an ankle holster. Before he could say or do anything, Kiko had raised his weapon, a small .45, and fired once, twice, three times. The first round went wild and struck a waitress, who screamed and collapsed as the bullet pierced her leg. The other two tore through the back of Morales' jacket and plunged out his chest. The bodyguard stared in horror at the look of shock on Morales' face as he staggered and fell atop him. The bodyguard knew the man was dead before he hit the floor, and kicked and shoved to get out from under him. Then he snatched the gun out of Kiko's hand and stuck it in his own pocket, grabbed Kiko's arm with one hand and his gradually recovering partner with the other, and rushed out of the place.

The funeral was held in La Paz, where Morales' father, Gen. Rene Morales, commander of the 1st Division, lived. The young Morales would be buried not in the cramped cemetery in the upper city but in the nice one, with open grassy spaces still reserved, in the crowded, narrow valley below the city, on the way to the suburbs of Obrajes and Calacoto. It was a grey, cold day in La Paz, unusual for that time of year, but it suited the mood.

All the top brass of the armed forces were present, and Guerrero had come up with some of his staff and the members of Morales' hit squad, who both formed the firing squad for the salute and served as pallbearers. Featherstone was there along with Lieutenant Colonel Polsby, both to represent the embassy and because Featherstone remembered the talkative young man fondly.

The ceremony was short and elegant. Navy Commander, Adm. Wellington Barco said a few words, as General Morales could not bring himself to speak without his voice cracking with emotion. When it was over Featherstone expressed his condolences to the family and to Guerrero, whose face was an icy mask of pain and anger. Featherstone had seen

Guerrero walk up to the casket, place his hand gently on it and mouth the words, "*mí guagua*." To Featherstone Guerrero had said only, "Well, I expect I'll see you at the trial."

But Featherstone touched his arm and said, "Perhaps you could find time for a talk while you're here in La Paz. I know that this is not a very opportune moment, but there are some rather important matters I think we should discuss sooner rather than later."

Guerrero looked at Featherstone for a moment with a quizzical look in his eye, and then glanced at his watch. "All right. It's only 10:00 A.M. Let's meet at the Cafe La Gaita on Calle Potosi in an hour. You know the place?"

"Yes," answered Featherstone. "It's very near the embassy."

"Good," was all Guerrero answered as he walked off.

There had been no lack of witnesses to the crime, chief among them Morales' fiancée, who had paused at the door of the disco to look back in time to see her lover murdered. An inquest had been called for the coming week, and Guerrero had let it be known that he would brook no acts of individual revenge by his men and that he had complete faith that justice would be done.

As the guests filed out of the cemetery they passed the line of vehicles belonging to the senior military officers. General Morales was standing next to his dark blue Mercedes, nodding solemnly to the departing friends and family members. When Guerrero reached the general, the latter stuck out his hand, undoubtedly expecting some words of comfort or expression of honor at having served with his son. Instead, Guerrero turned his stony gaze on him and rendered a proper salute. Guerrero's eyes shot back and forth from the tear-stained cheeks of the older man to the shiny new vehicle that undoubtedly cost ten times the general's annual salary, and the general knew that Guerrero was silently asking where the money came from, if not, directly or indirectly, from his son's murderers. When the general had returned the salute, Guerrero continued on his way, only muttering, half under his breath, "Nice car, my general."

Chapter Six

Two large, beige American sedans with darkened windows turned off Avenida 6 de Agosto, cut brusquely across the oncoming traffic, and turned left, stopping at the gate to the garage entry of the official residence of President Boca del Rio. There they waited, blocking traffic, while the military police guards rolled aside the heavy iron gate to let them enter.

Sergeant Robles, whose military police battalion had its barracks directly across the street from the presidential residence, frowned as the cars gunned their engines impatiently and then roared into the parking area. Robles had recognized the cars as belonging to the Ministry of Interior and was aware that only senior officials used the ones with the darkened windows, but he could tell that the passengers were not government officials, and he spat on the ground as the cars cleared the gate. He and his men stood watching as the cars disappeared into the parking garage, confirming his suspicion. Official visitors would have dismounted in the courtyard and gone in the main entrance. No, these were visitors no one wanted noted, and that meant only one thing to Robles.

Inside the garage, out of sight of the military guards at the gate, a Ministry of Interior security man quickly opened the rear door of the first car, and Lazaro Benitez climbed out, followed by Paolo Soares. Although both vehicles were driven by regular Ministry of Interior security personnel, the six bodyguards who accompanied them were Benitez' and Soares' own men, and these escorted the two drug lords into President Boca's house.

Boca rose and strode to the door as Benitez and Soares entered his living room.

"Manco and Paolo," he gushed, shaking each of their hands with both of his. "How good to see you, come in and sit down." Benitez had been given the nickname "Manco" years ago. This ordinarily referred to one-armed men, who are common in Bolivia, thanks to a favorite test of the Bolivian miners' bravery, which is to see who can hold a stick of dynamite with a burning fuse the longest. The winners very often earn the name Manco. Benitez had both of his arms; the name apparently derived from an injury he suffered to his arms in his youth, but he did not like to talk about the episode and it had been years since anyone had had the nerve to ask him for details.

The president and his guests sat, as one of the Ministry of Interior men poured out small cups of rich coffee, using china with the Bolivian presidential seal embossed in gold. "We're not here just for a social visit, Mr. President," Benitez said curtly. He had a way of making Boca's title sound like a rather low insult. "There are two very important items of business that we have to discuss immediately."

"Of course, Manco," the president nodded gravely. "What can I do for you?"

Benitez really didn't like to deal with Boca personally. He much preferred to have his henchmen arrange to make the large deposits to foreign bank accounts that filled the coffers of the president's party or went into his own pocket. Benitez hardly cared which. Underlings could ordinarily be trusted with passing messages and instructions, but even that was only rarely necessary, as Boca knew that the money would continue to come and he would continue to be president only so long as Benitez' trafficking operations were not seriously interfered with by the police. Benitez was more than willing to contribute an occasional small shipment of cocaine, or preferably unprocessed coca paste, to make the UMOPAR look good to the Americans, so long as the costs left an acceptable margin of profit. However, he did not want any miscommunication now, and it was worthwhile for him occasionally to take the measure of the man he had helped into the Palacio Quemado, as the Bolivian equivalent of the White House is called.

"The first matter is actually fairly easily dealt with, although it is of the greatest importance," Benitez continued, seeing that he had Boca's full attention. "It concerns the unfortunate accident involving Paolo's son, Kiko."

"Ah, yes," Boca said, already starting to sweat, despite the cool La Paz temperature. "The shooting. Very tragic."

"The *accident*," Benitez emphasized, "has placed in danger Kiko's very life, and we want to be assured that everything that can be done is being done to ensure that he has a *fair* trial."

"I just want you to understand," Soares interjected, "that we're not talking about some slimy pistolero who might have to do six months in a cell that's nicer than the hovel he usually lives in. We're talking about my own son here."

"Of course, Paolo," Boca said, patting Soares' knee and swallowing hard. "Of course you realize that the fact that the dead man—"

"The assailant," Benitez corrected.

"Yes, the assailant . . . well, the problem is that the fact that he was a military man makes this a much more ticklish problem for all of us. The military are furious and they want blood. They don't care who might have been at fault. You have to understand the terrible pressure that I'm under—"

Benitez closed his eyes and raised his hand, bringing Boca's pleading to a halt. "I understand one thing. We are two of your party's most *loyal* supporters, and we expect a certain amount of loyalty in return. I'm sure you're also aware that we are not without influence in certain military circles as well, so I really don't think you have much to worry about if you simply try to do us a little favor."

"Yes, Manco, of course you're right. I'll do everything I can. Now what was the other matter?"

"I think you are aware that my friend Gusano Murillo was arrested recently in a totally illegal operation. An operation that was run not by the constitutionally designated police authorities but by that fucking savage Guerrero, who seems to think that the Chapare is his own personal fief, where he can do whatever the hell he wants."

"Yes, Manco," Boca was nodding furiously, wringing his hands at the same time. "You don't know how many times I've had the navy commander in here on the carpet about his inexcusable, violent behavior. But, I don't know if you're aware that the Americans have now gotten mixed up in this thing. They have an international warrant out for Murillo, for *murder,* Manco. They want us to extradite him to the States, and my legal advisors tell me we don't have a leg to stand on."

Benitez hurled his coffee cup, still full of steaming liquid, at the president. One of the Ministry of Interior men stepped forward, but he stopped when all six of the bodyguards reached for their ill-concealed weapons. Benitez stood up and paced back and forth furiously as Boca trembled and wiped his face and shirt with a napkin with the presidential seal embroidered on the corner.

"You listen to me, you sorry excuse for a man!" he roared. "It has cost my organization millions of dollars to place you in this house and this job. We had some very lean years after Garcia Meza was kicked out nearly a decade ago. That line of civilian presidents that followed him would rather play the great statesmen, doing their best to ruin the one really profitable industry that Bolivia has, just to please the Americans. *Our* people don't do cocaine. The fucking Americans do. Let them worry about it, and we'll just worry about what to do with their money. You're the fucking *president of Bolivia*. The Americans can't do anything to you that you don't let them do. Stand up to them! Be a man! If they want to cut off aid, let them! I spend more on socks than they give Bolivia in aid, I'll take care of everything."

"But, Manco," Boca groaned, "I know that your people make a great deal of money, and we certainly are grateful, in the party, for your donations, but you traffickers have been talking about paying off Bolivia's foreign debt for years, and you never actually do. Of course," he added hastily, realizing from Benitez' cold look that he had gone too far, "I understand that you have many expenses, and there's always the risk of doing your business, what with fucking American aircraft carriers prowling in the Caribbean, looking for your planes and boats—"

"Understand *this*!" Benitez screamed, bringing his face within inches of Boca's. "You say you don't have a leg to stand on? Well, you better get up off your butt and earn your keep, or I'll show you what it's like not to have a leg to stand on. You got that?"

Without waiting for an answer, Benitez and Soares swept out of the room, followed by their bodyguards, who kept a cautious eye on the Ministry of Interior men until they were out the door. They climbed into the sedans and squealed out of the garage.

Robles saw them coming but was intentionally slow about opening the gate. The more furious the car horns' honking became the slower he went. "Go ahead," he thought. "Come on out of those bulletproof toilets and pull a gun. There's nothing I'd like more than to scrag a few dopeheads." But finally the gate opened enough to permit the cars to leave, and they sped into the flow of traffic without making even a pretense of looking.

"Well," Benitez sighed, as he settled back in the car seat and turned to Soares. "It looks like it's up to us. That fucking faggot is too scared to shit without the Americans' permission."

"It's a shame," agreed Soares. "I really thought we had finally found someone we could work with."

"Yeah, we'll deal with him later. Right now our first priority is to take care of your boy," he said, patting Soares' arm. "Then I think the same method will work with Gusano, but if it doesn't I have another plan in mind that might actually let that shit Boca do the right thing for us and maybe even come out of it looking like a real nationalist."

"Since when do you care about Boca's image?"

"Since it occurred to me that he needs to be replaced," Benitez smiled. "You see, if he dies when he's doing what the Americans tell him to do, he's just a dead man. If he dies when he's doing something the Americans don't want, then he's a national martyr, undoubtedly killed by the CIA."

"Undoubtedly," Soares and Benitez laughed.

Guerrero had neatly nipped off the pointed end of his *saltena,* a spicy Bolivian meat turnover baked in a hard pastry shell and filled with meat juices, and began gingerly sucking out the steaming juice. He saw, with a mixture of fascination and horror, that Featherstone was examining his own *saltena* from every possible angle. Having decided on a direction of attack, Featherstone was about to take a large bite when Guerrero held up his hand.

"Excuse me," he said in a soft voice, "but I strongly suggest that you use the spoon and eat it off the plate."

Featherstone resented Guerrero's arrogance. "I've eaten these before, you know," he lied. "I think I can deal with it."

"Suit yourself," Guerrero said. His smile broadened as Featherstone bit into his *saltena* and sent a rivulet of boiling meat juice cascading down his hand, over his wrist, and somewhere up his sleeve. He dropped the *saltena* on the plate with a mumbled curse.

"You Americans," chuckled Guerrero. "You think you can take everything by storm." He held up his own half-finished *saltena* and turned it slowly in the air. "A *saltena* is like life. You have to take it step by step. You Americans tend to bite into them like a sandwich, and this squeezes the insides out and all over the place. You have to nibble away a bit of the crust and drink the juice, then gradually work your way through it, and you don't spill a drop." He demonstrated. "I really think I should look into a career in philosophy."

"Yeah, don't quit your day job," Featherstone grumbled as he vainly tried to mop his hand and arm with the tiny triangles of what appeared to be ordinary typing paper that passed for napkins in the cafe. He finally dug into his coat pocket and found an old kleenex, which did much better.

"Now that the *saltena*-eating lesson is over," Guerrero continued, "you said that you had something important to talk about."

"Yes," said Featherstone. "I'd like to hear more about your antinarcotics activities. It seems that the arrest you made of this Murillo character has already caused quite a stir."

"What you really want to know," Guerrero said, starting on his second *saltena*, "is whether I'm for real and whether I'm actually working for the mafia too."

Featherstone looked up, embarrassed at Guerrero's frankness. "Well, yes, actually."

"Fair enough. The answer is: you'll never know. You can prove that a man is corrupt easily enough. Just take a look at his bank account, his house, his car. Could he pay for it with his salary? If not, you've got your man."

"Unless he won the lottery like the Minister of Interior did recently," Featherstone added.

Guerrero threw his head back and laughed. "Huerta, that crook? Let me explain to you how the national lottery works."

"You mean it's rigged?"

"No, the lottery itself is as honest as any. But haven't you ever noticed that the winners of the really big jackpots, you know, a hundred thousand dollars or more, are always people you've heard of? Either they're government officials, or policemen, or military officers, or reputed drug traffickers. What the mafia does is they buy off the guy or girl at the lottery office who answers the telephone. Then when a big winner calls in, instead of informing the lottery people, this person calls his mafia boss with the winner's name and phone number. Then the mafia calls the winner up and congratulates him on his good fortune. Then they offer him, say $105,000 for his $100,000 ticket. Naturally this poor slob jumps at the chance and sells his ticket, not that he ever had any real choice, of course. So then, the mafia has $100,000 in perfectly clean money for the bargain price of $5,000. They can give this ticket to any official they want to bribe, and the official not only gets the money, but he can flaunt it as much as he wants. 'Sure I've got a BMW, I won the lottery. Didn't you see my picture in the papers?' It's a great scam."

"Oh," said Featherstone humbly. So much for the in-depth briefing he had received in Washington on the ins and outs of the narcotics business.

"Getting back to my own case," Guerrero continued. "You can check out my financial situation and find that it isn't very impressive. I can live comfortably partly because of my folks having some money, but then again I could just be a more careful sort of crook." Guerrero shook his head. "It's really difficult for me to talk seriously with you Americans about the drug problem, because you people just aren't serious about it yourselves."

"Now wait a minute," Featherstone objected. "We may not have all the answers either, but we're certainly putting our money where our mouth is. We've got programs going. We've got people on the ground risking their lives. Don't tell me we're not serious."

"Sure," Guerrero continued undisturbed. "You spend money like water, but let's look at *your* side of the problem. How much demand for cocaine do you think there would be if anyone in the States who got caught with half an ounce had to serve a guaranteed sentence of six months in the county jail, rooming with a big, hairy guy named Bubba. You wouldn't even have to enforce it everywhere, all the time, just often enough for the risk to be there, to make people think twice before taking dope. But, no, you've decided that personal use is about as serious as a minor traffic violation, because the personal users are your own people, educated people, singers, actors, congressmen, lawyers. You make a big deal about how bad our judicial system is, because it's corrupt. Okay, it's corrupt. I'm very sorry. The only difference, though, between yours and ours is that here you pay your money straight to the judge, and in the States you pay it to some fancy lawyer who gets you off just the same."

"Well, yes, that's the American judicial system for you—"

Guerrero cut back in, his temper rising. "And let's talk a little about extradition, shall we? We arrest a Bolivian trafficker here; you insist that we extradite him to the States because he would get off scot-free in our judicial system. True enough. It's a pretty strong insult, but it happens to be true. Then, when some snot-nosed American yuppie comes down here and tries to score his own stash and we arrest him, you insist that we extradite him to the States too, because he would suffer in our jails and wouldn't get out so soon. You can't have it both ways."

"Fine," said Featherstone. "I can't argue with you, because you're right. Neither of us makes the laws, but maybe we can make a difference. I've seen you in action, and I've checked around a little on my own, and I think you're straight. All I want is for you to trust me enough to let me help you, officially if I can, unofficially if necessary. Just tell me what's going on, and I'll do my best to see that the information gets to the right people."

"I should apologize for flying off the hamper," Guerrero said. "I'm not in a very good mood today. My only question is whether you can deal with your own ambassador. From where I sit it seems like he's buying President Boca's show hook, line, and simper."

"That's 'sinker'," Featherstone corrected. "And I'm afraid it's true, but there are ways of seeing that people in Washington hear the truth. I can only promise to do my best."

"That'll have to be good enough," Guerrero said. "It wouldn't do, though, for us to be seen together too regularly. If I have anything for you, I'll get to you somehow."

Featherstone bowed his head for a moment and then raised it again. "So, fine, that explains who's really to blame for the drug problem, in your opinion. My question is, why do you care? I mean, why don't you just go with the flow like so many others? Even if you don't want to take cocaine money, why don't you just find a purely military niche for yourself where you can do your own thing without having to worry about the narcotics business at all? Plenty of honest soldiers have done that in Latin America, Southeast Asia, the Middle East. If it's really America's problem, that would seem to be the logical thing to do."

Guerrero shook his head slowly. "Don't misjudge me. I've had an American 'experience,' but I'm still a Bolivian soldier born and bred. I'd like to see our military and our country organized along American lines with all the good things that should bring, but that just isn't going to happen. Since that's the case, I have to hitch my wagon to the military's star, and I don't like what's happening in that regard.

"Time was when nothing moved in this country unless the military gave its okay. There have been other big-time players, like the miners and the big landowners. We got rid of the landowners in the 1952 revolution. Other groups have come and gone, like the various political parties, but we could deal with them, compete with them, and usually win. Now, I don't like the way the military has made its career around kicking out one government after another, but for long periods we managed to stay out of politics pretty much, just sort of holding a veto if we needed it.

"That's changed with the mafia. They totally eclipsed all the other players, and now they're coming after us. They *bought* a coup in 1980 and left the military to pay the check afterward, and they can do it again whenever they want. They have so much money, tens of millions of dollars, that we just can't compete with them, and I don't like that. Like most other officers, I could learn to live with losing our veto to some legally and fairly elected government that could turn this country around and make something of it, but I'll be damned if I'm going to knuckle under to a bunch of slimebags like these traffickers."

"So you go out and blow up cocaine labs for fun," Featherstone chided him.

"I do what I can," Guerrero smiled shyly. "I know it isn't much, but it's sort of a protest. And, like they say, violence never solved anything, but it sure makes me feel a hell of a lot better."

Chapter Seven

It had been a long flight from New York to Rio de Janeiro, but Kelly had been pleased to note that Alan had gotten them first class seats. It had been quite a difference from the only other plane trip in her life, flying down to Florida for that Caribbean cruise, where she had been in the most tourist of tourist class. Being served champagne while waiting for the plane to take off and later being served dinner on real china, with real cutlery, instead of the plastic dishes and forks the poor people back in tourist class were using. Now this was the way to live!

Rio had been fantastic, from the fabulous room at the Sheraton with its view of the sea, to the hotel's private beach, to the trips they took to Sugar Loaf and all around the city. They had even been taken on a trip to a jewelry factory, kindly offered by one of the owners of the many jewelry shops located along Copacabana Beach. Alan had haggled about the price, but he had finally bought her a small opal ring, nothing too flashy, just right for the level of their relationship.

The whole city seemed to live on the beach, and she had been shocked at the almost total nudity. She had thought her own bikini daring enough, but the local girls went totally topless and with a G-string that could be identified only if it happened to be a bright color. She had been pleased to note that despite the distractions Alan never ogled the other girls, and appeared to have eyes for her only. She assumed that if he were normal he probably took a look now and then from behind his sunglasses, but it was his discretion in doing so that marked him as a truly mature man.

After Rio, they had taken a domestic Varig flight to the Foz de Iguazu. Naturally, Kelly had never heard of the place before, and was more than a little frightened when Alan told her it was out in the jungle somewhere. She had held his hand tightly on the ride from the small airport to the hotel in the "taxi" that was actually a Toyota jeep. When they arrived, however, she had been relieved to see that Alan again knew exactly what he was talking about. The hotel was in the style of an old Spanish hacienda as it may well have been at one time. It was located right next to the huge series of falls, hundreds of feet high and maybe a mile wide. Alan had pointed out to her the modernistic hotel on the Argentine side of the falls, and she had readily agreed that the classier, old-fashioned Brazilian hotel was by far the better choice.

It had been just before they were due to leave from Iguazu, Alan to fly back straight to Miami and Kelly to continue on to Santa Cruz, Bolivia, to do their business, that he told her of the change in plans. Instead of taking delivery in Santa Cruz she was to go to Santa Cruz and spend a couple of days just lounging around the hotel pool. Then she was to take a short flight to La Paz, receive the merchandise, and fly to Miami from there. At first Kelly had been very leery about changes in what was supposed to have been a perfect plan, and at this late stage in the game, too. However, Alan convinced her that it was the best decision. He said that she would still be met and "protected" while she was in Santa Cruz, but that the organization he dealt with had recently developed better connections with the customs police in La Paz, so her departure from the country would be more secure from there.

Kelly had thought briefly about abandoning the whole scheme, but she really couldn't do it. Alan was so great. Here she had accepted this very expensive trip already, along with the occasional gifts he had bought her, and she couldn't just back out of the deal when her turn to perform came. She was still terrified about having to travel alone in a strange country, even without having to transport drugs as part of the arrangement. Just the trip was enough to scare her. But she knew that if she did something as juvenile as reneging on her promise that would be the last she would see of Alan, and she already had some hopes that what they had started would last long beyond this one trip and this one deal. She had even scripted out in her mind how she had half decided to graciously refuse to accept the money for making this trip, once they were safely back in the States. She was already thinking of the $10,000 as a nest egg for "their" future.

She couldn't say yet that she absolutely loved Alan. He was mature and sweet and all that, and he certainly did his share in bed without making her feel like some stupid "boy toy" like the one football player she had been foolish enough to date in high school. But this was the closest thing to real, adult love that she had ever experienced, and if it was going to fall through she couldn't let it be because of some conscious act on her part. No, she had concluded, she would have to go through with the arrangement . . . for both of them.

The day before Alan was to see her off at the airport he had gone over the contact instructions with her one more time. In Santa Cruz she would be met by a man named Pablo who would be able to recognize her. She didn't ask how, because Alan had all of these things planned out. Pablo would call her by name and drive her to the Los Tajibos Hotel, where she would spend the next two nights, and would pick her up to take her back to the airport for the flight to La Paz.

In La Paz, she would be met by another man named Pablo, a different man, though, who would also know what she looked like. He would take her to the Hotel Plaza, where she would spend the night. At some time after eight that evening a man would visit her room and deliver the package. He would place it in her carry-on bag himself, and she was not to touch the package or to open her bag again until after they had arrived in Miami. Alan had explained that this was to prevent any trace of cocaine powder from somehow getting on her hands and attracting one of the sniffer dogs that sometimes worked the airports. She would keep whatever stuff she needed for the trip in her shoulder bag.

The next day, after checking out from the hotel, she would be picked up by the second Pablo and driven to the airport. Alan had bought her a tight silk minidress to wear for the trip. Although it was not going to be comfortable, he said that the distraction of her face and figure would keep any suspicious policemen at the airport from paying attention to her baggage. Alan said that someone would be watching her until the plane actually left and would step in if there were any problems. He assured her that people "with connections" were involved and that they could fix anything that went wrong. So far, Alan hadn't been wrong about anything on the trip, so she had to trust him this once more.

Chapter Eight

The morning after the meeting between Benitez, Soares, and President Boca, a motorcycle messenger rang the street bell of a stately house in a residential neighborhood of Cochabamba. The maid ran across the garden to the gate and received the thick envelope addressed to Dr. Juan Sebastian Moro, a judge in the local criminal court. She giggled coquettishly as the messenger touched the brim of his helmet, then scampered back into the house, where she delivered the envelope to Dr. Moro in his study.

Moro opened the envelope, not finding any return address to indicate its origin, and glanced at the contents. The coffee cup in his hand began to tremble and the hot liquid spilled onto his fingers and onto the rug, but Moro did not notice. Inside the envelope were a dozen large, glossy, black-and-white photographs, obviously taken within the last twenty-four hours. Several were of his own automobile, a couple of his wife shopping at the nearby market, and several more were interior shots of rooms of his own house. The one that he continued to grasp in his shaking hand as the blood rushed from his face was of his twelve-year-old daughter leaving her school in company with some girlfriends. In each photograph in which a member of his family appeared someone had drawn, in bright red grease pencil, a circle with a cross inscribed within it, like the crosshairs of a telescopic sight. Moro stared at the one of his daughter, the junction of the cross meeting over one of her eyes. The only other item in the envelope was a news clipping referring to the Soares shooting case, which Moro would be hearing that afternoon. The message was clear enough.

That afternoon Moro sat in his courtroom, dressed in his robes and surrounded, he knew, by dozens of policemen in and around the building, but he felt naked and defenseless. A black cloud of dread had hung over Moro all day, but he began to sense a means of relieving that dread as the prosecution called witness after witness in the case. Of the fifteen individuals who had made depositions after the shooting to the effect that the young Soares had shot the unarmed Morales in cold blood in the course of a fistfight on the dance floor, virtually all of them now were either unable to remember anything concretely at all or were under the impression that Morales, too, had had a gun, which must have been removed in the chaos following the shooting.

Of all the witnesses only Morales' fiancée had stuck by her story that Morales had been unarmed, that Soares and his bodyguards had started the fight, and that Soares had subsequently shot Morales to death as she watched from the doorway of the disco. However, the distraught young woman had been unable to give more than a few moments' worth of testimony at a time without breaking down in tears or beginning to scream "Murderer! murderer!" at Soares, who sat neatly dressed in the sort of clothes a high school student would wear when meeting his girlfriend's parents for the first time, shaking his head in innocent disbelief and denial. In the light of the evidence Moro had little trouble agreeing with the defense attorney that a murder case could hardly be based on the hysterical testimony of an emotionally deranged woman, especially when it conflicted with sworn declarations by several other witnesses, including that of one of Soares' bodyguards, who was a former police officer himself. Since the prosecution could offer no further evidence, Moro declared the charges dismissed, although he delivered a lengthy speech deploring the kind of establishment that served liquor to young people obviously lacking in the maturity to handle the substance, which was the ultimate cause of this tragedy.

Soares rose and embraced his attorneys and his bodyguards, who hustled him out the door of the hall. In the back of the room Moro saw a stocky man in an expensive suit, who wore sunglasses despite the fact that the courtroom was not very well lit. As soon as the verdict was announced the man had stood quietly, made an almost imperceptible nod of the head to the judge, and left the room. Moro had felt a great weight lift from his shoulders when the man left.

After the journalists, attorneys, and other observers had finally left the hall Moro rose to leave on wobbling legs. He looked back across the empty benches and saw one man still sitting against the back wall. The man was wearing military camouflage fatigues, and his dark eyes held Moro in a death grip. Moro had never seen such a mixture of hatred and disgust on a man's face before. But so be it, thought Moro as he entered his chambers. He recognized Guerrero's face from his occasional appearances in the local press and knew that he was not a man to be trifled with. But he also knew that Guerrero was not a man who would go after women and children. If he wants me, Moro thought, he's welcome to me. At least my family is safe now.

At the same time the envelope was being delivered to Moro's house in Cochabamba another motorcycle messenger was pulling up to a wrought-iron gate in Sucre, where the Bolivian Supreme Court sits. Beyond lay an enticing view of a spacious garden and a house built in the traditional Spanish colonial style typical of Sucre. As the messenger leaned on the buzzer a short, balding man approached him from behind, walking a Doberman on a leash. The man tapped the messenger on the shoulder, and the messenger explained that he had a delivery for Dr. Esteban Linares Vasco, Minister of the Bolivian Supreme Court, at this address. The balding man identified himself as Dr. Linares, took the envelope, and asked the messenger to wait in case there was an answer to go back.

For some reason the messenger became nervous, and was about to mount his motorcycle and ride off when a pair of policemen rounded the corner not ten yards distant, greeted the minister, and stopped to chat. The messenger decided to wait. Linares opened the envelope and glanced at the contents, then began to laugh.

"Yes, there will be an answer," he said to the messenger. He showed the photographs to the two policemen, who suddenly became very serious, and then he spat on the photographs, replaced them in the envelope, closed the flap, and handed it back to the messenger. "Take this back to whomever gave it to you, and tell them to go to Hell."

The two policemen suggested that they take the messenger in for questioning, but Linares held up his hand. "No, gentlemen, this one is just what he appears, a messenger. I've seen dozens like him in my time. Let him work for us for a change."

At that the messenger leaped upon his motorcycle and roared off down the dusty street.

In a car parked two blocks away a man had been observing the scene through a small telescope, which he concealed in a cupped hand. When the messenger had left he raised a radio to his mouth, said a few words, and then drove off.

Just after lunch that afternoon Linares was preparing the materials he would take to the extradition hearing for the Murillo case, which he would decide that day. As he filled his old leather briefcase, Rosario, his wife of thirty years, came storming into his small home office.

"That thief that we paid over 500 pesos at the garage didn't do anything to my car. I just tried to start it and nothing. And now I have to go to the church for the ladies' club meeting, and how am I going to get there?" Linares knew his wife only too well, and he was grateful that he would not be in the mechanic's shoes when Rosario got ahold of him. In order to avoid the possibility of bloodshed he held up his own car keys and dangled them in front of her flashing eyes.

"You can take my car, dear," he said soothingly. "They're sending a vehicle for me from the court anyway for this afternoon. Maybe you can pick me up there later, and we'll stop for tea on the way home."

Rosario took the keys from him with a mild snort, pecked him on the cheek, and marched off, murmuring something about the mechanic's mother, if he had one. Linares smiled and returned to his preparations.

Rosario walked through the kitchen, shouting some last-minute instructions to the maid, and out to where their two aging cars were parked side by side in the carport. She climbed into her husband's car, squeezing a little behind the steering wheel, as she was not as slim as she once had been, started the engine, and honked the horn for the gardener to run and open the gate. The gardener knew better than to keep the señora waiting, and he dropped his rake and sprinted across the lawn to swing the tall iron gates wide.

When she saw the gardener in her rear-view mirror Rosario let out the clutch and the car began to roll backward out of the carport. As it did so, however, a tube of mercury, which had been placed inside the hubcap of the right rear wheel of the car, turned from vertical to horizontal as the wheel moved, thus completing an electrical circuit that connected a pair of household batteries to a block of plastic explosive wedged around the wheel rim, not far from the gas tank. Although the movement of the wheel cut the circuit again in a fraction of a second, that was all the time that was necessary to activate the electrical detonator, which ignited the explosive. The car was lifted completely off the ground and hurled against the wall of the house before it crashed back to the ground.

As the man who had constructed the bomb was a professional, he had also included a large amount of steel wool around the explosive. The force of an explosion often blows nearly all of the air away from the point of ignition, so if one wants to start a fire as well as an explosion one adds steel wool, the superheated particles of which remain to ignite any flammable substance when fresh air rushes back in. With mist now spreading from the ruptured gasoline tank, a fireball immediately engulfed the Linares' car.

Inside the house, Linares was knocked flat by the force of the explosion, and by the time he had raised himself on his hands and knees his mind had cleared enough for him to realize what had happened. He crawled for a few feet, then managed to pull himself up, using a bookcase for support, and stagger to the kitchen. There he found the maid bleeding from a cut on her forehead caused by flying glass from the window, but otherwise unhurt. He passed her and opened the door to the carport, only to be faced with a wall of flame.

He turned and ran now, out through the living room and out the front door of the house. The gardener had been unhurt by the blast and was staring helplessly at the fire, which had now consumed both of the automobiles and the garage. Linares grabbed the man by the shoulders, shook him, and screamed at him to go and call the police and fire department. When he had gone Linares looked down at his feet and found his wife's glasses, or at least the frames, twisted by the force of the explosion. He knelt beside them, clenched his fists to his head, and bellowed.

On a rise several blocks from the Linares home a man next to a public phone had been watching with binoculars and had seen the column of black smoke rise from the house. He stepped up to the phone and made a brief call, hung up the phone, and walked away, smiling.

Later that afternoon Francisco Murillo lounged at the defendant's table in the courtroom in the Supreme Court Building in Sucre. He talked in stage whispers with his attorneys and winked repeatedly at the young female court reporter, who put on her coldest professional face in return. The session was already half an hour late in starting, and the buzz from the visitors' gallery was growing increasingly loud.

Suddenly the door to the judge's chambers opened and Dr. Linares strode into the room. He was not wearing his judicial robes, his dark suit had a torn sleeve, his tie was missing, and his collar was open. His forehead and one cheek were smeared with soot, and one could clearly see the tracks where his tears had washed away the grime.

The hum of conversation turned briefly into a roar until Linares' gavel brought the room to utter stillness. Murillo and his lawyers had suddenly become very serious and attentive.

Linares began to speak in a deep, sonorous voice, which was quiet but reached every corner of the hall. "I have given this case careful consideration in light of the Constitution of the Republic of Bolivia. While I had prepared extensive legal arguments for my decision, I see no reason at this time to delay the proceedings, and we will turn immediately to the ruling of this court.

"FRANCISCO MURILLO," he called out loudly, and Murillo stood uncertainly at his place, "this court has determined that, based on the evidence presented to it by the government of the United States of America, it is not only legally possible for the Bolivian government to agree to the request for extradition submitted by the United States, it is the plain duty of Bolivia as a civilized country to comply with this request."

The noise of voices began to rise again, but Linares cut them off as he continued to speak. "That is the legal decision of this court. It is my personal view that, since the state of Florida, which will be trying your case in the United States, recognizes the death penalty, *if* you are found guilty as charged for the crime committed, I would find it gratifying to learn that you had indeed been executed. My only regret in this case is that the Bolivian judicial system is not in a position to exact this penalty for the crimes you have certainly committed on our soil, but I have unlimited faith in the fairness and firmness of the American judicial system to deal with this situation." With that he banged his gavel again and marched out of the room as the journalists in the gallery elbowed each other, each trying to get out the front door and to a telephone first. Enrique Contreras sat back in his chair in the gallery, folded his hands behind his head, and smiled at the ceiling.

Chapter Nine

The large, warehouselike structure at the navy commando battalion base camp consisted only of a cement floor, a high, angled roof, and simple walls, all made of corrugated metal. It served variously as a vehicle maintenance area during the rainy season, for storage of bulky items, and as an occasional gymnasium. This evening it served as an impromptu assembly hall and was filled with the nearly 250 men of the battalion. The troops were seated cross-legged on the floor by squads with the officers sitting in folding chairs along the walls. At the front of the hall a makeshift speaking platform had been constructed of several loading pallets placed one on top of the other and topped with a sheet of plywood.

There was a low hum of conversation in the hall as the men waited for Guerrero's arrival. The news of the release of Soares had just been broadcast over the radio, and there was a sullen tension in the air. The dull murmuring was immediately replaced with the stamping of boots and scraping of chairs when the men leaped to attention, as a grim-faced Guerrero strode into the building, flanked by an equally sober Duarte. Guerrero hopped onto the platform and Duarte stood at parade rest next to it, facing the troops with his jaw set. Guerrero gave the command for the men to stand at ease and stood still himself, observing them for several long moments as if he were evaluating them to see if they were up to some test.

Guerrero had no public address system, but years of addressing assembled troops had strengthened his lungs and there was not a sound in the hall as every man strained to hear his words. "Gentlemen," he began, "a serious decision has been thrust upon us, one which no military man should ever have to make, but we will have to make it now. That decision is whether our first duty as soldiers is to the government which has been elected to administer the nation and to the officials it has appointed or to the nation itself, which exists beyond the reach of party politics and personalities. In the best of times we can serve the latter by serving the former faithfully. At some point, however, the actions of the government and of the men they place in positions of authority are such that we cannot be true to the nation by continuing to follow their orders. Such a time has come now.

"We have lost a dear brother. The death of one of our number is something every soldier must come to terms with in his own way. It is a part of our profession. Death in a training accident or at the hands of an enemy of the nation is a risk every man takes when he first puts on his uniform. Death at the hands of criminal scum is not something a civilized people should have to tolerate. But all societies have their criminals, and it is for this reason that the police and courts have been created. When those institutions fail to function, it is a sign that the society is in decay. When those institutions serve the interests of the criminal elements themselves, it is a sign that the true power in the nation has passed from the hands of the people and voters to the hands of those who feed on the corruption of our society and who drink the blood of innocent people around the world.

"We know this to be the case in our country today. We know that Lieutenant Morales was murdered. We know who did it. We also know that he will walk free because of the power of the narcotics mafia and weakness of our current government. Since we know these things, if we take no action we are, in effect, condoning them, and we will be as guilty of Morales' murder as the animal who pulled the trigger, and as guilty of the liberation of the killer as the judges and lawyers and politicians who take the traffickers' bribes. I cannot live with that shame. I have called you together, my dear friends and colleagues, to announce my personal decision to do everything in my power to bring down the government that has made this state of affairs possible, cost what it may. I do not have the right to order you to join me, but I ask you now whether you will do so of your own free will."

The walls of the flimsy structure shook with the roar from over two hundred throats. It was an animal noise, not individual voices. The men of Morales' own squad rushed forward, tears streaming down their faces, their fighting knives raised in clenched fists, and they knelt before the platform, all shouting together.

Occasionally, a single voice would rise above the others: "Give us blood, Coco!" one shouted. No one but his own Academy classmates ever used Guerrero's nickname in his presence, but this was not a time for protocol. "You lead us. We'll follow you into Hell!" cried another. "*Viva Guerrero!*" finally won out over the other words and noises, gradually replaced by a rhythmic chanting of "*Viva! Viva! Viva!*"

Guerrero stood like a statue, staring at the far wall of the building as the men crowded around the platform. After a long moment he held out his hands for silence, and the noise gradually died down.

"Thank you, my sons," he said quietly. "Frankly, I expected nothing less from you. But this is a serious step I am asking you to take. When you are dismissed, I will see the group commanders and my staff in my office. I want all of the rest of you to return to your quarters and think about what we are about to undertake. This will not be a palace revolution of the kind for which our country is unfortunately so famous. We will be outnumbered and outgunned, and if we are to triumph it will only be after hard fighting, possibly against our own brothers in uniform who will follow the orders of their superiors, no matter how false. We must be ready for both deaths in our own ranks and the responsibility of deaths of other Bolivians. This is not a matter to be decided in the heat of the moment. I have taken much time in making my decision, and I want you to take time in making yours. Those of you who do not want to join us should leave the base by tomorrow morning's assembly. We will carry you as being on leave until after the operation is over, one way or another, and no one will think any the less of you for your choice. Now, go with God."

Duarte snapped to attention and called the formation, which was now hardly more than a mob, to do the same. As he did so, as if a switch had been thrown, all talking stopped, and the simultaneous stamping of hundreds of boots on the cement floor of the hall showed that the men had all gone ramrod-straight in an instant. Guerrero turned and left the hall, followed by his officers, before the sergeant major dismissed the men, who quickly broke into small, talkative groups. Duarte, who was the last officer to leave the hall, heard the most typical comment from an infantryman somewhere behind him. "About fucking time! Now let's go and kick some trafficker butt."

Guerrero led the way into the two-story building that served as the battalion headquarters. In the large central room that housed the battalion's small office staff the desks had been moved against the walls, and the center of the room was now occupied by a large sheet of plywood supported by sawhorses. A blackboard had been set against the far wall.

Guerrero took his position next to the blackboard as the officers filed into the room. They could see that the makeshift plywood table was covered with a large map of the city of La Paz and its immediate vicinity. Resting on an easel next to the blackboard was another map of the whole of Bolivia.

Besides Guerrero and Duarte, who entered last and closed the office door behind him, were the commanders of the four combat groups into which the battalion was divided and the four members of Guerrero's staff: his S-1 (Personnel), Sublieutenant "Chino" Takagi; the S-2 (Intelligence), Sublieutenant Daniel Rivera; the S-3 (Operations), Sublieutenant Victor Yanez; and the S-4 (Logistics), Sublieutenant Walter Ochoa.

Rather than using the standard company and platoon structure of an infantry or marine unit, Guerrero had organized his battalion in self-contained commando teams, or "hit squads," as he called them, each of fourteen men. Each of the three regular combat groups contained four such teams and the fourth, or support group, contained specialists in antitank weaponry, demolitions, and mortars. The primary weakness of the unit was its light armament, basically only the personal assault rifles of the men plus a few automatic weapons, a couple of heavy machineguns and recoilless rifles mounted on HUMMER vehicles, three small 60mm mortars, and about two dozen British LAW-80 light antitank weapons. Its great strength was the expertise and training of its men, far exceeding that achieved in any other Bolivian military unit, as those were composed mostly of short-term conscripts.

The first person to speak was Lt. Bernardo Vasquez, commander of the group to which Morales had belonged. He walked up to the table, examined the map for a moment, and then said, "Commander, I don't think it's necessary for me to declare that I'm ready right now to go out and die to avenge young Morales. I rather had in mind, though, that we were going to hit some of the fucking traffickers themselves. Kill them and their bodyguards and anybody else who got in the way until we were killed ourselves. That I can understand. What I don't really see is how the two hundred of us can possibly overthrow the government. The army has over twenty thousand men, and we have to assume that the traffickers have covered themselves well enough—they certainly have the money to do it—that the army will fight to keep these scumbags in power. So what will that get us?"

Guerrero clasped his hands behind his back and rocked slowly on the balls of his feet and his heels, then said in calm, measured tones, "That's a fair question and deserves a fair answer. Actually, the odds, on the surface, are even worse than you suggest. The army has nearly twenty-two thousand men in uniform at the moment, and the air force and navy have another four thousand men each. At this moment the only people we have supporting our *golpe* are within two hundred meters of this room. That puts us at a disadvantage of about a hundred to one. That's why I've called this preliminary meeting, to outline to you the prospects as pragmatically as I can, and to let you each decide whether you want to participate. It will then depend on the ten of us to come up with a plan that will make it work."

Guerrero began to pace back and forth slowly in front of the map of Bolivia. "I know that none of you have ever taken part in a real shooting *golpe*. I haven't either for that matter, although I was involved in the planning of one which would have driven Garcia Meza from power if he had not resigned when it became apparent that he had lost the support of the majority of the officers of the armed forces. That is the way most of the *golpes* in this country have gone in the past, and that is just what we cannot count on this time. We will never be able to win over enough large-unit commanders to convince the government and the rest of the army high command that resistance is useless. We will have to work at a lower level, among the junior officers who have not been bought off by the mafia and who, hopefully, feel the same way we do. Unfortunately, this will have to be done very discreetly, and we will not be able to test our handiwork except in an armed confrontation with loyalist units. At that point, if we have done our job well, the enemy will crack at the first blow and the neutral units, which will probably be in a majority, will swing over quickly to the winning side. In either case, it will all be decided within twenty-four to forty-eight hours."

The officers looked at each other with curious expressions, but no one spoke as yet. Guerrero continued. "First of all, let me explain that the odds aren't really as bad as they seem. In 1961 there was a coup in South Korea. Out of an army of over six hundred thousand men, only about twenty-five hundred were directly involved, and it worked. The trick of a *golpe* is that you hit the enemy at his weak points, just as we are trained to do as commandos."

Guerrero moved over to the map of Bolivia and pointed with his finger. "As I said before, it will all be decided within forty-eight hours at the outside. Therefore, only those units which can reach the battle within that time from a standing start are of interest. By seizing the centers of communication and moving with speed and stealth we can eat up a good portion of that time before most of the army is even aware of what is going on. Therefore, we can largely discount the units stationed in the north and east along the Brazilian border or in the south along the Argentine border. In fact, because of the mountainous terrain and poor roads, we can pretty much forget about anything outside of the triangle formed by Cochabamba in the east, Potosi in the south, and Lake Titicaca in the northwest, as well as troops assigned to noncombat formations. The exceptions to this are both based near Santa Cruz: the 'Manchego' Ranger Regiment, which is airmobile, and the air force's fighters. That already cuts the odds down a great deal."

One of the other group commanders, Lt. Andres Kolkowicz, the son of Polish immigrants, raised his hand nervously. "Correct me if I'm wrong, sir, but isn't the bulk of the army's firepower still contained within that triangle?"

Guerrero wagged his finger in the air as if to ask their patience. "I was getting to that. My point is that we are definitely not up against the entire armed forces of the nation at all. The number of troops that will play a role will only be five thousand to six thousand men maximum."

"Oh, so we're only outnumbered twenty to one," laughed Yanez. "Now that's more like it." The others joined in by chuckling half-heartedly.

Guerrero just smiled. "One stem at a time, my son," he cautioned. He turned toward the blackboard and began to write the names of regiments well known to all of the men present.

"Now that we have the scale of the forces that will be involved in view, in this kind of warfare we next have to determine who will be on which side."

The officers turned and began to nod in agreement to each other. Perhaps the old man hadn't lost his mind completely after all. When he had finished, he had written the following:

"Colorados" Infantry Regiment
"Ingavi" Mechanized Infantry Regiment
"Calama" Armored Regiment

"Tarapaca" Armored Cavalry Regiment
"Lanza" Armored Cavalry Regiment
Marine Infantry Battalion
Military Police Battalion
Colegio Militar cadets
"Manchego" Ranger Battalion (Santa Cruz)
Army headquarters troops
Air Force Fighter Command (Santa Cruz)
Air Force headquarters troops
National Police

"These, gentlemen," he said when he had finished, "are the units that matter in any *golpe* scenario, other than ourselves, of course. Our first goal will be to win some of these units over to our side, to help us to seize key installations and individuals. That will be essentially my task alone. Our second goal will be to neutralize others of these units, those we cannot win over absolutely, to prevent them from being able to intervene effectively in the battle. That will be the job of the planning staff. The third and final goal will be to engage in combat those units which cannot either be converted outright or neutralized, and render them *hors de combat* through shock action and maneuver. That will be the task of all of you present and your men."

The officers continued to study the list and the map silently, and Guerrero could tell that he had not yet convinced them of the feasibility of the undertaking. Finally, another group commander, Lt. Marcelo Zuniga, raised his hand, as if in a high school classroom, and waited for Guerrero to call on him.

"Would it be too soon to ask which of the units on the list you expect to be with us instead of against us?"

Guerrero nodded. "Another fair question. Yes, it is too early to be certain about much, and I don't want to promise anything I can't deliver, but I can be pretty sure about a couple of them. First, I think you'll agree that the Marine battalion at Lake Titicaca will go with us, if only because this is a navy-led operation, and they know that if the army crushes us they will be assumed to be part of it whether they are or not. Naturally, we're not talking about U.S. Marines here," a couple of the younger officers' eyes rolled skyward, remembering Guerrero's own stint with the Yankee jarheads and wondering just how objective a judge he would likely be in this case. "Our Marines are just conscript infantry like all the rest, really just another light infantry battalion, but a move by them toward La Paz and the airport at El Alto would keep the air force worried and force a diversion of enemy forces to meet the threat.

"Next, my periodic courses given at the Academy and my own reputation there should be enough to win the cadets over to our side." This statement was met with assorted groans from officers who had themselves left the Academy only a year or two before. Guerrero leaned on the map table and stared at them for emphasis. "Before you start scoffing, let's remember that these kids have had ten times the training that the conscripts will have had. They're really a tight, professional infantry battalion, and a large one, at nearly a thousand strong, right inside La Paz itself. They've been the key to more than one coup in our history too.

"Lastly, there's the police."

Some of the officers could no longer hold in their anger. The support group commander, Lt. Agusto Martinez, finally exploded, "The Marines, a handful of kids, and now the bought-off and half-assed cops. These are our allies? I'd just as soon go it alone!" His comments were met with enthusiastic nodding all around the table.

Before Guerrero could answer, Duarte, who had been sitting quietly and listening, slammed his hand on the table and shouted at Martinez, "The trouble with you, Martinez, is that you just don't know what the fuck you're talking about. We're not talking about taking on the Russian Army rolling across northern Germany. What we need is speed, secrecy, and a little manpower to seize the jugular of the country. If we can do it fast enough and completely enough there won't be any fighting at all. And who better than the police? For most of the targets we need to hit, they're already there, and nobody is going to raise an eyebrow at a couple of carloads of cops driving anywhere in town, but you sure as Hell turn heads when it's a truckload of infantry. Half of the coups that fail do so when suspicious troop movements are spotted before the plotters are ready to strike. That gives the loyalists time to move on them first. If you just don't have the balls for it, why don't you just say so?"

Guerrero interposed himself before any more hot words could be exchanged. "Excuse me, gentlemen, but before you draw knives and get blood all over my nice new map, let me say that you're both right. Lieutenant Duarte is correct when he says that the police more than make up, in convenient positioning and knowledge of the terrain and installations we intend to seize, for their lack of heavy weaponry. Lieutenant Martinez also happens to be right when he questions whether the police, who have been most completely infiltrated by the drug mafia, could be trusted to support our operation.

"The answer to Lieutenant Martinez' objection is that there are policemen and then there are policemen. The ones who have been bought off tend to a large extent to work directly in the narcotics field or in areas like this one, where the traffickers center their activities. There is also the Special Security Service of the Ministry of Interior, which has been converted since the current government took office into a gang of hired thugs, paid more or less directly by the mafia. However, that's only a minority of the national police, and a very small minority of those stationed in La Paz, where our primary targets are located. Most of the police resent the traffickers' influence in this country as much as we do, and many of them have lost friends killed for doing their job too well or too honestly. There's a counterterrorist unit in La Paz, and riot police, and roving patrols, all of which could come in very handy, if not for facing down the armored cars of the 'Tarapaca,' then at least for seizing secondary targets and watching our backs." Martinez and Duarte both eased back away from each other, and Martinez stuck out his lower lip and nodded as he pondered the idea.

"That's about all I can offer for now. I'll be leaving in the morning to work on trimming down the column of enemy units and, hopefully, adding something with a little more meat on it to ours. In the meanwhile I want you group commanders to work with your men on street-fighting tactics. We're going to need it. But I also want you to see that they get plenty of rest. When things start to happen, they'll happen fast, and there won't be much sleep to be had by anybody. And that includes you, too. I don't need some foggy lieutenant reading his map upside down and sending his men off to storm Illimari instead of the airport. I want the staff officers to begin working out the logistical details of the skeleton of a plan which I will leave with them tonight. Lastly, let me repeat to you, now that we're here alone, that I meant what I said about wanting you to think seriously about whether you're in this or not. When and if we roll out of here on my orders alone, we will have broken the most solemn vow of a military officer, that of obedience. I have no right to demand that of you. If you come with me, it must be because you would go with or without me. Every man, of every rank, must make that decision after, as we say, consulting with his pillow. You group commanders are now dismissed."

Guerrero turned, walked into his small office in the back of the headquarters building, and shut the door quietly. The other officers began to walk out the door and Martinez stopped, turned to Duarte, and extended his hand.

"Only brothers can talk to each other that way without meaning harm," Duarte said as he shook the outstretched hand and clapped Martinez on the back with the other. "Do you suppose a beer would be out of place at a time like this?"

"I don't even know where I left my manual on 'Coup Protocol'," Martinez laughed, as they walked out into the courtyard together.

Chapter Ten

Sergeant Robles spat on the ground again as the beige sedans with the darkened windows rolled into the presidential garage in La Paz.

Benitez was alone this time, but his usual entourage of bodyguards escorted him, as he climbed out of his car and marched into the president's home. Again Boca greeted him warmly, although he knew that Benitez would be in a bad mood because of the outcome of the Murillo trial. And yet Benitez did not begin to scream or throw things. Instead he sat down in one of the Victorian easy chairs in the living room and waited for Boca to do the same.

"Manco," the president began, "you don't know how sorry I am about the way the Murillo trial turned out. Naturally, I'm delighted that the Soares boy got off, but that was a much easier case."

Benitez looked at the president as if he were looking at a dog, and not a favored dog either, and he talked to him in that tone of voice one uses with pets. "Sr. Presidente, the Soares boy got off because I got him off—I! Murillo failed to get off because I failed. You are no more to blame for the Murillo case than you are to be thanked for the Soares one, because you have done nothing. You have proved to be less than a man of your word and to be worth far less than my organization has paid you over the years."

"But you're wrong, Manco," the president pleaded. "I did everything in my power to help. I talked to the judges and the prosecuting lawyers personally. My men over at the Ministry of Interior were working night and day to dig up something, anything in their pasts to use against them, to force them to cooperate, but it was useless. I was surprised that Moro changed his mind at the last minute, but that Linares character was unshakeable."

Benitez had finally had enough. He leaned forward and snapped, "Would you stop your whimpering, you fool? Moro changed his mind because my people got to him in a way he could understand. Linares ... well, yes, he was unshakeable, even though we certainly shook him hard enough. That was a miscalculation on my part. But let's get one thing perfectly clear. You haven't done shit for me! Now I want to see some performance, and to make it simple I'm going to spell out for you exactly what you will do and when you will do it."

Benitez' face was very close to that of the president now, and he made every effort to spit as he spoke. "Fortunately for you, all is not lost. If Murillo is taken to the United States he will be tried, not just for murder, but for killing two policemen. That tends to make the Americans mad, and Florida has the death penalty, you know. Of course, I don't particularly care if they execute Murillo, I never much cared for him anyway. But they don't really want Murillo. They want me And to get me they're more than capable of offering Murillo the chance to live out his stinking life in prison. He knows all there is to know about my operations, all the way from the bank accounts I use to my tactics for smuggling drugs into the States and into Europe, and the men who have agreed for one reason or another to cooperate with me. And *you*, my friend, head that very distinguished list."

Boca was mopping his brow with his trembling hand and wiping the sweat on the leg of his pants. "Surely, Manco, there must be some way of keeping him from talking ..."

Benitez just smirked. "Do you mean to suggest that I have my trusted colleague ... killed?" Boca just wrung his hands and continued to sweat. "Of course I could have him killed. There's nothing easier to have done in prison. Either here or in the States. The trouble is that I then run into a problem of credibility, you know. A man in my position, just like yourself, for all my power I have to rely on the loyalty and devotion of others, and to earn that loyalty I have to show that I support my friends. Now, if Murillo were to talk no one would question my having him killed. That would be a simple act of revenge, and everyone can understand that. However, if Murillo talks, then it's too late, and killing him won't do me any good, other than making me feel a lot better inside."

Boca had removed his glasses, which he needed very much but wore only when out of the public eye. They had steamed up badly, but he could find nothing to wipe them on. Benitez smiled and pulled a silk handkerchief from his pocket to hand graciously to the president.

"Thank you, Manco, thank you," the president said quietly. "So what can we do then, Manco? About Murillo, I mean."

"That's where you come in, my friend," said Benitez, patting Boca on the knee gently. "You are going to save the day."

"But what can I do?"

"Don't worry," Benitez soothed. "I'll take care of most of it myself. All you really have to do is give a couple of simple orders through Minister of Interior Huerta. He's a very cooperative man, after all. And they're orders which will actually save Bolivian lives. No problem there, right? Then, you get to play the great humanitarian. You will have to issue a presidential decree not only refusing extradition of Murillo but granting him a full pardon."

"But what about the Americans? They'll scream bloody murder!"

"Funny you should use that expression, Sr. President," Benitez said, smiling even more broadly. "I suspect the Americans will be screaming quite a bit by that time, and more than one of them will be rather bloody as well."

"I'm sorry, Manco," Boca whined. "I just don't understand."

"You will when you've heard my plan. You see, you will be forced to release Murillo in order to save the American hostages."

"What hostages?" Boca gasped. He could feel his head reeling. He wished he could just walk out of that office, go to the airport, and fly off to live quietly in some far-away land with his family. Why on earth had he ever gotten into this? Being president wasn't worth it. He didn't want to hear the rest of Benitez' story, but he had no choice now.

"Why, at the American Embassy. You see, four days from today terrorists from the Peruvian Sendero Luminoso will seize the American Embassy here in La Paz. Among their various demands will be the release of a number of 'political prisoners,' of whom Murillo will be one, as a victim of Yankee imperialism, to be sure."

"And what will I have to do?"

"First, you will, or the Ministry of Interior will, actually, facilitate the entry of the terrorists into the country from Peru and help them gain access to the embassy. Then, when the embassy has been taken and the demands are made, you will immediately agree to the terms in order to avoid further loss of life. Hell, the Americans might actually be pressuring you to do just that by that time." Benitez sat back in his chair, as cool as if he had just sold a used car at substantially above blue-book value.

The president sat, his head bowed, and he seemed to have aged ten years since Benitez entered the room. He laced and unlaced his fingers for a long moment. Finally he said, "I suppose that would be the best way to handle the situation."

"Of course it would!" Benitez assured him.

"Are you certain that there would be no more bloodshed than absolutely necessary?"

"That's part of your job," Benitez explained. "One of the things Huerta will do is to pull the police guards off the embassy, discreetly of course, thereby letting the terrorists gain a good foothold. Once the Americans can see that they're in an impossible position, they'll cave in quickly enough. They did it in Tehran and again in Tripoli and Islamabad. Their Marine guards are just there for show. You can see from history that they never fire, even in self-defense. And you needn't worry about the Sendero Luminoso men. They're professionals. They work closely with my Peruvian colleagues. Of course, they can be tough as nails when it's necessary, but they know exactly how much force is required. This operation will be a tremendous political coup for them, too, so their hearts are really in it. We're all very excited about this."

Boca sank back into his chair, unable to raise his head. "Very well, Manco. You make the arrangements and just give me the details of what you want done and when."

"That's the spirit, boss," Benitez said loudly, clapping Boca on the shoulder. Boca did not rise to see him out, and Benitez did not miss him.

Holy shit! Robles almost said out loud. Ordinarily the military police guards were not allowed into the house itself, their area of responsibility being the exterior perimeter of the grounds. However, Robles had a relationship with one of the housekeepers, and she frequently invited him into the kitchen for a snack of one sort or another. He had been standing near the door to the living room eating a sweetcake when he overheard Benitez' plan.

Robles put down the unfinished cake and stepped very quietly toward the garden door. He did not start breathing again until he was well outside.

"What's the matter, Sergeant?" one of his men asked. "You don't look very well. Did she really run you ragged?" the man laughed.

"Shut the Hell up!" Robles answered curtly, and the man just raised his eyebrows and turned away. What was he going to do now? Whom could he tell? If he picked the wrong person and told someone who was in with the traffickers, he'd end up dead before he knew what hit him. No, he would have to think about this for awhile. In any case, it looked as though he had a few days' grace.

Chapter Eleven

Guerrero left early the next morning for the western highlands of Bolivia. One of his men drove him to the outskirts of Cochabamba by back roads and dropped him off before dawn. From there he would take one of the large, crowded, intercity buses in the direction of La Paz, so as not to attract the attention of the Ministry of Interior agents who worked at the various airports. Guerrero wore civilian clothes, different enough from his habitual uniform to camouflage him at a distance, but ordinary enough that someone who did recognize him would not suspect him of trying to wear a disguise. With a felt hat to hide his balding head and break up his profile, sunglasses, which he rarely wore, against the bright sun of the Altiplano, and a well-used windbreaker and jeans borrowed from a friend, he fit in well with the mass of humanity jammed aboard the *flota* as it pulled out of the bus depot and began the long trip to La Paz. The drive would take all day, but the meetings he had to conduct were better done at night in any case, and a few hours to think without interruption would do him no harm. As the bus lurched onto the highway amid gaily colored trucks piled high with produce from the rich Cochabamba Valley and with the inevitable campesino "tourist class" passengers riding on top, he wedged himself up against the bus window and appeared to go to sleep, but his mind was racing.

After making one preliminary stop on the road to La Paz, Guerrero's bus finally arrived at the central depot just after dark. He could have found a communal taxi only with difficulty at that hour, as people were fighting for space on anything that would carry them home. In any event, after over eight hours on the bus he didn't mind stretching his legs a bit, and his destination was downhill. He strode down the main avenue of the city, which changes its name every four or five blocks, past the San Francisco Cathedral and its plaza, and down the length of the Prado, where he gave himself the luxury of strolling down the center of the mall area, imagining he had Marisol on his arm once more. When he reached the Plaza del Estudiante he scolded himself for his frivolity and turned off onto a side street. Although La Paz is a city of over one million people, it is strictly divided into working-class and business areas, and the "people who matter" are tightly concentrated in the strip of office buildings along the Prado and its extensions. It would not do for him to be recognized in the city when he had no official purpose in being there.

Taking his own advice, he now climbed several blocks up a steep street to permit him to avoid the Plaza Aboroa, where both the Ministry of Defense and the U.S. ambassador's residence are located. Then he swung back down again until he reached the house he sought in San Jorge. As he came down the street he could see the conscript soldier standing guard at the garage gate, a typical perquisite of high rank, so he kept on walking, rounded the corner on which the house stood, and stopped out of sight. He quickly took off his jacket and tossed it and the small cloth overnight bag he carried on top of the seven-foot wall that surrounded the garden, grabbed hold of the top of the wall, and acrobatically hoisted himself up. While the jacket protected him from most of the broken glass embedded in the top of the wall, he still managed to get a few cuts on his fingers and knees. But in a second he had dropped noiselessly to the ground below.

He walked upright and purposefully around the back of the house and past the chubby maid who was scrubbing clothes at an outdoor laundry sink next to the kitchen door. He wished her good evening as he shot past her into the house, and all she could do was follow him, drying her hands on her apron, a look of astonishment on her face.

General Morales had just sat down to dinner when Guerrero appeared at the kitchen door. Morales looked up and saw the grim face Guerrero wore, and knew why he had come.

"General, Sra. Morales," Guerrero said politely, doffing his cap as he did so, "I'm terribly sorry to burst in on you like this—"

Morales didn't let him finish. "Not at all, Commander. Won't you join us for dinner?"

"I'm afraid that I really can't stay, sir," Guerrero apologized.

"Of course. My dear," Morales said to his wife, whose eyes had already begun to fill with tears as the sight of Guerrero's face brought back memories of her lost son and of the funeral, "please excuse us. Go on with your dinner. The maid can heat mine up again later." His wife and his fourteen-year-old daughter just nodded as Morales arose and guided Guerrero into his study.

As they entered the room that Guerrero had visited often enough before as a young officer and in which he had received the general's stern admonition to take good care of his son but to toughen him up as well, Guerrero grabbed two high-backed antique chairs and placed them facing each other in front of the aged record player. He selected a record at random, making sure, however, that it had singing on it, and started the music. While it was highly unlikely that any of the local talent had the expertise or the interest to bug the room, Guerrero did not want a servant to overhear what they had to say either. When he sat down the general was already seated, forearms resting on his knees, waiting.

"I've come for your support," Guerrero said flatly.

"Who's with you and when do you plan to move?" Morales asked.

"I've got my own men . . . and now you, sir," Guerrero said, looking the older man straight in the eyes.

Morales shook his head slowly. "And that's all? Maybe I misjudged you. I half expected you to come in here with a plan to overthrow the government, but I see now that you are just going to go out and shoot up some traffickers."

"You were right the first time, General," Guerrero said. "President Boca is just as guilty for your son's death as if he pulled the trigger. He and his cronies have permitted the country to decay to such a point that young punks like the Soares kid can go around killing our officers and get off scot-free. We'll go after the traffickers too, but only after we've pulled the plant up by the roots."

"Well, then, I think you're going to need more than two hundred men, even yours, Commander."

Guerrero did not smile at the backhanded compliment. He just went on, "General, you know the coup game better than I do. What we need is a name, a well-known, respected, general officer to stand up for our movement before anyone will sign on with us. You are that first step."

"You're right, of course," Morales admitted. "*If* I go with you, and I'm not decided on this yet, I'm certain that I could bring along Admiral Barco and the navy command, just by pointing out that this is your show. I imagine I could also swing the Academy cadets, having been commandant of the Academy until just last year. Having your name to trade on would also help matters. Those youngsters are tired of having people sneer at them and call them 'narco cadets' on the Prado. No decent family would let their daughter go out with the average cadet these days." Guerrero could see the corners of Morales's mouth turning sharply downward as he spoke.

"But even that's not enough," Morales continued. "You need to get some of the 'five horsemen' or it will still be a massacre." Morales was referring to the commanders of the five key regiments in and around La Paz, who could either make or break a coup at their whim, the commanders of the regiments "Calama," "Tarapaca," "Lanza," "Ingavi," and "Colorados." It was reputed that they even had a special communications net, totally enciphered, among themselves, bypassing the army and division commands. Among them they possessed virtually all of the army's armored fighting vehicles, and their troops had the most modern weaponry in the armed forces.

"That has occurred to me," Guerrero answered. "What would you say if I said that I could bring over the 'Colorados' and had a means of neutralizing the 'Calama' in Patacamaya?"

"Now we're getting somewhere!" Morales said with enthusiasm. He was rubbing each of his forearms with the opposite hand in a rhythmic motion, and Guerrero could see that he was staring at a framed picture of his son on a bookshelf. A neat black ribbon had been tied carefully to one corner of the frame. "If push came to shove, I could bring in the military police battalion. I'm the godfather of the commander's son, and he's been a protégé of mine since he left the Academy. It's hardly more than a company, really, only about 150 men, but they guard the Palacio Quemado and the Chamber of Deputies along with the honor guard from the 'Colorados,' and their barracks is right across the street from the president's house. But that's still not enough. The 'Tarapaca' from Viacha alone could cut through us like a hot knife through butter, and if they linked up with the 'Lanza' coming from Guaqui and drove into the city to meet the 'Ingavi' at the army general headquarters . . ." Morales shivered theatrically. "No, to pull off a coup you have to have overwhelming force. That way no one stands in your way, and there's no bloodshed."

"That's the problem, sir," Guerrero said in a grave tone. "There's no way we can bring in enough commanders to make this a walkover. Word would inevitably get out, and trafficker money would buy them off as fast as we could convince them. No, we're going to have to get dirty on this one. I know that the military has tried at all costs to avoid situations where you have troops facing off against each other. Failure to prevent that was how the Spanish Civil War started, and no one wants that, but we're going to have to drive hard in the other direction. Instead of going out of our way to avoid a fight, we've got to prepare for the one everyone else is trying to avoid. That way, with a sharp, hard blow, we'll smash them at the first go, while they still think that it's just a show. They'll be out there lining up on the fifty-yard line with their pads and helmets, and we'll be there with guns and knives."

"You spent too much time in the States," Morales said, and he smiled, briefly, for the first time in a long while. "Do you really think you can pull it off, son?"

Now it was Guerrero's turn to smile. "You'll have to trust me. There are a couple of other cards I have up my sleeve, but I'm not sure about them yet. So, can I use your name?"

Morales reached out and shook Guerrero's hand firmly. "Let's do it! I'll get busy this very night, and I'll deliver the men I promised. Then it will be your job to put it all together. When do you plan to move?"

"Within the week. Time wouldn't ordinarily be a factor for us, but once the ball starts rolling every day brings another chance of a leak, and then it's all over."

"I'll be ready," Morales said, rising as Guerrero started for the door.

Guerrero paused in the doorway and turned to the general. "I'll see myself out," he said as he winced at the thought of scrambling over the glass again. "Oh, and General?" he groped for the words, "I'm sorry about what I said at the funeral. It was wrong of me."

"No, son," Morales said, patting Guerrero on the shoulder. "You were right. By the way, I sold the car and gave the money to the Church. I never thought I'd find the air fresher on one of those buses filled with *cholitas*, but somehow I do."

Guerrero found himself walking more and more quickly now, even though he was going uphill, no easy feat at that altitude. The aches in his muscles from the long bus ride had worked themselves out, but his new energy had more to do with the fact that things were coming along. His next meeting was in a bar well across town, above the stadium in the Villa Fatima area, a working-class district where most of the streets, once one got off the main avenue, were unpaved. He took two different buses to get to the general area and covered the last couple of hundred yards on foot, weaving through the still-thick crowds of shoppers on the avenue and then winding through the narrow streets, flanked with houses made of undecorated brick and cement blocks, obviously built to no known construction code, until he saw the hand-painted sign over the low doorway he was seeking.

The interior was poorly lit. A short bar hugged the back wall, and the floor was covered with a scattering of small wooden tables at which workers were drinking massive bottles of Taquina beer after a hard day's work. There was tinny dance music coming over a radio and the noise of raucous conversation filled the room, which would make casual eavesdropping difficult indeed.

His two guests were already there, seated at a table away from the door. Both of the men wore rumpled civilian clothing, although one was Police Captain Luis Venegas, commander of the small American-trained counterterrorist squad, and the other was Campos, now Lieutenant Colonel Campos of the "Colorados" Infantry Regiment. They were already well into their first beers, and Guerrero noted that another bottle sat on the table with the cap half pried off.

"Hey," he greeted Campos, slapping him hard on the back, "where's your red suit?" Guerrero was referring to the smart red jackets and kepis worn by the "Colorados" guards of honor at the Palacio Quemado, Bolivia's equivalent of the Coldstream Guards at Buckingham Palace. The uniforms were patterned after those worn by that regiment at the Battle of Tacna in the disastrous War of the Pacific against Chile in 1879. Guerrero had never really understood why that uniform had been chosen to preserve rather than one from the War of Independence, which at least had a victorious outcome, but tradition was tradition.

"I've got it out in the car, if you'd like me to go put it on," Campos teased.

"No, I guess what you have on is rather more discreet." He turned to Venegas. "Thank you for coming, Captain. I was more than a little surprised to find that you two knew each other so well."

"Oh, yes," Venegas said, carefully pouring Guerrero's beer. He held the glass at a sharp angle to prevent the low air pressure at this altitude from creating a head of foam that would fill most of the glass. "We've trained together frequently, what with the colonel practically running the 'Colorados' all by himself, and me with the responsibility of pulling his cookies out of the fire if there were ever any kind of terrorist attack on the palace. Let's just say that we're fully aware of each other's shortcomings." Both men laughed, and Guerrero was relieved to see that this was obviously not the first time they had been out drinking together.

Suddenly Campos became serious. "As much as I enjoy seeing my old classmate, this is probably not a social visit, since this is not the place I would have picked for one. From your phone call I assume you have something to say that you do not want to see in the papers tomorrow morning. Now, what is it?"

Both men leaned closer, trying hard not to look conspiratorial. "I think you have already guessed. I am planning a *golpe* to overthrow the government which has permitted the traffickers to take charge of this country and to kill military officers—and policemen—" he added, nodding to Venegas, "at will. I have the support of General Morales, and he and Admiral Barco will form the core of a junta which will call new elections after the garbage has been swept away." Guerrero stopped and took a long drink from his glass.

"That's a fine theory, Coco," Campos said. "Naturally, I would like to know who else is coming to this party."

"My battalion, of course," Guerrero said slowly, hoping to make his forces seem more numerous by taking more time to list them. "We also have, or will have, the military police battalion and the Corps of Cadets from Irpavi. The navy will also support me, so there will be the Marines from the Lake as well."

Campos stared at Guerrero with wide eyes and made a rotating motion with his open fingers. ". . . AAAND? Don't tell me that's all you've got."

"I was rather hoping that I could count on you gentlemen."

Venegas slammed his glass down on the table. "Fuck it! I'm in. I moved over to counterterrorism to try to get away from the drug business, but I still have to attend too goddamn many funerals of my friends who didn't get out in time. Worse than that, I'm sick of losing friends, not to bullets, but to dollars. Some old pal of mine suddenly can afford a four-bedroom house in Calacoto, a BMW, and can send his kids to school in the States, but we all know that he's making the same money as I am. The difference is that he's done six months or a year with UMOPAR or in some other post in either Santa Cruz or Cochabamba, where he was worth paying off. I know it, and he knows that I know it, so, pretty soon he stops inviting us over and stops visiting me. It's less embarrassing that way.

"Not that I really blame them, actually," Venegas said sadly. "The truth is that I had to get away from it because I knew that sooner or later I'd be bought myself. What are you supposed to do? An officer who makes maybe $400 American a month, with a wife and kids to support, gets an offer of $10,000 for doing nothing. Just looking the other way. They even sweeten the deal for you by giving you information on some other trafficker so you can make a bust and look good, just so long as you leave your patron's business alone. On top of that you know that if you don't take the money the best you can hope for is that the traffickers will use their pull with the politicians to get you transferred to where you can't do them any harm. At the worst, you get a bullet in the back of your head. And even if you did keep your job and didn't take the money, how much good could you do alone, knowing that half of the other guys on the force might already be on the take?"

Venegas hung his head, shaking it from side to side, then he looked Guerrero hard in the eye. "If you swear to me that you're going after the traffickers' balls, you can count on me and the forty men of my SWAT team. You've trained with us too, so you know that on our own turf, here in the city, we can kick anybody's butt, including those schoolgirls of yours from out in the jungle. And to make it more interesting, I think I can swing the riot police company. That's two hundred more men, and they're tough little bastards in their own right. They don't have the weaponry or tactics to stand up to the 'Tarapaca,' but they give a coup a certain air of legitimacy, don't you think?" he said, twirling his hand in the air in a cavalier fashion. "They can serve to stand guard publicly at places you've already taken. Gives the man in the street the idea that things are really under control. And if you get stuck in any really nasty house-to-house, having a few guys around who are good with shotguns and tear gas might not be such a bad thing."

Guerrero smiled and gave a thumbs-up signal to Venegas, but Venegas reached over and grabbed his forearm with a strong, calloused hand. "Just one thing. If you *don't* plan to go after the traffickers, if this is just another scam to put some different scumbag in power, you'd better plan to kill me before I find out, because I'll come after you myself."

Guerrero nodded gravely at Venegas and then turned to Campos, who was rubbing his chin pensively. "Now, what's this I hear about your running the 'Colorados' practically single-handed?"

Campos smiled. "You slimy bastard. You won't get my regiment by just flattering my vanity. So, tell me, what's in it for me?"

Guerrero had a sinking feeling in his stomach. He knew that the commanders of the key regiments around La Paz could make demands of huge sums of money on whatever government was in power, if that government wanted to remain in power. He thought he knew Campos as well as he knew himself, but they had spent little time together in the last few years, being stationed hundreds of miles apart, and he now feared that his friend had changed. Even if Guerrero could find financial support for his coup and buy Campos off, a man who would act for money would turn around and betray him for more money, and the traffickers had all the money in the world. His mind was racing. If Campos was crooked, not only was the plan dead in the water, but he would be too, literally, as soon as Campos talked to the right people. He searched his soul and asked himself if he could kill his friend for this cause. Just as he decided that he couldn't, that he would take his chances on Campos' discretion no matter what, Campos spoke.

"What I mean is, if you're coming after me, that means you don't have my boss. If you're using Morales as the figurehead, that means you don't have the army commander. That tells me that there are going to be a lot of personnel changes, 'come the revolution,' and I was just wondering. You know how much I've always hated walking. Well, I just thought that I'd always wanted to command the 'Tarapaca' Armored Regiment. Do you think I could have that? . . . Assuming that we win, of course."

Guerrero let out a long sigh of relief. "If that's all that's worrying you, I can assure you that you will have your own personal tank, after the coup. And as to your reasoning, it's not that I don't have anybody else in the army with me. It's just that I knew how hurt you'd be if I didn't come to my oldest and dearest friend first."

"Be that as it may," Campos laughed, "I take it that we can count on polite objections being raised by the other four regiments near the city."

Guerrero shook his head. "If things go according to plan, we won't have to face them all at once. We should be able to eliminate the 'Ingavi' at general headquarters before they know what hit them. Then, if the 'Tarapaca,' which is the closest unit, comes in on the run, it will be alone with very little infantry support, and we should be able to deal with them. If they wait for the 'Lanza' and the 'Calama,' that will give us six to eight extra hours to get ready for them."

"At which time they will clean our clocks," Campos noted.

"Not necessarily," Guerrero disagreed. "I have a couple of things in the works that will delay the arrival of both of those regiments, and might even prevent them from coming at all. In the meanwhile, every hour that we hold out means that more units are likely to pick us for the winner and declare support. I also have another iron in the fire which might make time work for us even more, but I can't promise anything on that yet. Now, the big question is: are you in or are you out?"

Campos started rubbing his chin again. "Gee! Ten-to-one odds against us, not counting the tanks; distinct possibility of a violent death, all in exchange for something I would probably get in six months' time anyway by just sitting on my duff? That's awful hard to pass up. Let's do it!"

The radio, which had been switched to a sports broadcast, suddenly announced a goal in a local soccer match, and the cheering of the bar's patrons drowned out the small celebration at the little table near the wall.

It was nearly midnight when Guerrero left for his final meeting. He let Venegas drive him as far as the Parque Triangular, but he chose to walk from there because by that time the buses had ceased to run and the streets were virtually deserted of taxis and other vehicles. He chose a circuitous route through Alto Obrajes, first climbing a steep ridge to pass through the residential area, which paralleled the main road down to the Calacoto suburbs but still occupied a high plateau, overlooking the road. Guerrero still did not wish to run the risk of having another "friend" happen by on that one well-travelled road, offer him a lift, and then begin to wonder what he was doing in La Paz at all.

The longer route took him nearly two hours, but he arrived at the sacristy door of the small church in Obrajes itself just at the appointed time. He knocked and Padre Tomas, a middle-aged Irish priest who had been living and working in Bolivia for over a decade, opened the door, first a crack to identify the caller, then wider to let him in, before carefully closing and barring the door behind him.

"I might have known that even though I've yet to see you at mass, you'd not miss a skulking meeting like this, Juan Carlos," Padre Tomas scolded as they shook hands.

"With any luck, Father," Guerrero answered, "this won't last nearly as long as one of your sermons."

The priest led the way through several back rooms and halls behind the church itself until they came to a small room normally used to teach the catechism to young pupils. The walls had pin-ups of religious scenes cut from some book, and a large wooden crucifix hung over the blackboard. A simple wooden table, which would have served as the teacher's desk, was at the front of the room, and seated at it was an elderly man wearing a heavy llama-wool sweater and a tattered cloth hat. He had not shaved for a day or two.

Although the man dressed very much in the style of the workers of the Altiplano, one could tell from his face and delicate hands that he did his work with his mind, in an office, and not with a pick and shovel down in the galleries of the tin mines around Potosi and Oruro. Unlike Guerrero, or Campos and Venegas earlier, however, his was not a disguise for the evening. Joaquin Leon Palma always wore these clothes, never wore a suit and tie, and always seemed to have a stubble of dark beard, even when speaking before the Chamber of Deputies or on television. Actually, he dressed this way especially when he was to appear on television or before the legislature, because it was the trademark of his position as president of the Bolivian Workers' Central (COB), the principal union, of which the well-organized and volatile tin miners formed the hard core, and it would not be good for his image as a leader of the working class for him to dress like the lawyer he had been trained to be.

The man regarded Guerrero through the thick, round lenses of his glasses, through a plume of bluish cigarette smoke, and squinted. Guerrero could not tell whether the curl of his lips, in which his stubby cigarette dangled precariously, was a smile or a sneer. As Leon occupied the one regular chair in the room, the priest and Guerrero pulled up two of the small, one-piece desk/chairs of the students and sat on the table parts.

"Thank you for coming at such short notice and at such a late hour," Guerrero said.

"How could I refuse?" Leon asked. "Usually when a soldier wants to see me late at night it's because he's kicked in my door and wants to drag me off for questioning. A polite invitation is a change in tactics which I certainly wanted to encourage." His lip curled again, and Guerrero simply nodded as the labor leader staked out his ideological turf.

"It's funny you should mention the kicking in of doors," Guerrero said after a pause. "That's exactly what I've asked you both here to talk about."

"No, let me guess," Leon interrupted. "You've been passed over for promotion once too often, so you've decided to launch a *golpe*. Then you find out that you don't have the military muscle to pull it off, so you've come to me to convince my miners to support you, to put their bare chests in front of the machineguns of the 'Tarapaca' so that you can be a general. It's been done before, my friend."

Guerrero smiled tensely. He had expected this kind of abrasive attitude, as Leon was famous for it in his dealings with the government and with business. "That's not quite the case, Doctor," he said, using Leon's academic title, which he could see pleased the little man no end. "You're right in that I'm going to launch a coup, and I won't try to convince you of my motives, although, in my case, I would become an admiral, not a general, since I'm in the navy. You're also right in that this is going to be a minority coup, not one of the typical palace revolutions. We're going to have to fight against long odds, but you're wrong in one important respect. That is that I'm not asking the miners to get out in front of this one. What I'm here for is to tell you of my plans, and to ask you if your miners will want to jump on the bandwagon *after* we've gotten underway."

"Let me guess again," said Leon with the same cynical tone. "You're going to clean house in the government, drive out all of the corrupt politicians, call for new elections, and bring an era of peace and prosperity to the land. I can save you some time. You can go to the library and dig out the declarations of the leaders of the last twenty coups this country has had, just change the names and dates, and there you go!"

"We're not going to get anywhere with baiting each other," Padre Tomas interjected. "Let's hear the man out and then decide what's best for ourselves and for the country." Although Padre Tomas was not Bolivian by birth, he had wholeheartedly adopted the country as his own. What's more, he had dedicated his life to the defense of the poor and oppressed, intentionally turning down assignments to the richer parishes in favor of working-class districts. During the hard years of military government during the 1970s and early 1980s he had placed his own life at risk by volunteering to visit the hundreds of political prisoners, whether they were Catholics or not, making himself a witness as to their location and physical condition to attempt to prevent their "disappearance" later on. Since more than one priest had "disappeared" in Latin America during those years, there had been a distinct possibility that a priest with this kind of embarrassing knowledge would join them, but his selfless piety and compassion had earned him a following at all levels of Bolivian society, and he had survived to become something of a legend, particularly among the leftist students and workers whose lives he had helped to save.

"Thank you, Father," Guerrero continued. "What I am proposing is not only to clean the country of the narcotics traffickers who are sucking the lifeblood out of our people and to remove the particular politicians, policemen, and military officers they have purchased with their filthy money, but to make this the last coup in Bolivian history."

This last statement caused even Leon to sit up and raise his eyebrows. Padre Tomas smiled and said, "Now *that* will be a neat trick, *if* you can do it. Now, how do you plan to accomplish that?"

Guerrero leaned closer to the table and was pleased to see that the other two men involuntarily did so as well. He knew that he had their undivided attention. "This will be the last coup because, after it is successful, there will be no more army."

The two listeners sat in stunned silence for a moment, and then Leon let out a burst of air in what might have been intended as a laugh. "You don't expect us to believe that, do you?"

"Yes, I do," Guerrero said calmly. "And I'll tell you why. Our armed forces have served no purpose during the past half century other than to fight against our own people. We do not have an army that could put up more than token resistance if we were invaded by any one of our neighbors, and our air force would do no more than provide some exciting target practice for the advanced jets possessed by the other countries around us. Peru, Chile, Argentina, Brazil, any one of them could roll right over us in the blink of an eye. I expect we'd do better against Paraguay, but their army is so small that it's insane to maintain a military to defend ourselves against a neighbor which couldn't possibly conquer us."

Guerrero paused, wishing that he had a beer, but he supposed that this was not the place for even social drinking. "So what are we wasting our money on every year? We have a national conscript army because of the theory that this would make the armed forces more responsive to the will of the people, but this hasn't stopped those same conscripts from gunning their brothers down in the streets whenever their professional officers ordered them to. I suppose that the army has served something of a role in building the nation, teaching illiterate recruits to read and write and bringing men together from all over this large country, but there must be more cost-effective ways of doing this than by buying jet aircraft and tanks which we'll never use against a foreign invader."

He paused again and was satisfied that Leon had no pat comeback this time. "What I propose to do is to disband the army, navy, and air force and sell off or scrap all of the fighter aircraft of the air force and all but a handful of the armored vehicles of the army. We would do away with conscription altogether and keep only a cadre of two or three thousand paramilitary troops, who would be moved over to the Ministry of Interior to protect against the formation of interior guerrilla movements like the Sendero Luminoso in Peru. The Ministry of Defense would be disbanded, and virtually all of the installations of the military would be either converted to low-cost public housing, schools, or similar uses. To attract a good selection of men for the new defense force, I would double salaries across the board, but the overall portion of the budget now being spent on the military would be slashed by more than half, the difference going to social welfare projects."

Leon was frowning deeply, but it was no longer a frown of animosity, rather of curiosity. "What makes you think you can get even a handful of army officers to back you in this scheme? Won't they want to protect their own jobs, to say nothing of the great military institution? Allende in Chile was killed for a lot less than what you're proposing."

"You have to remember that this is a minority coup. The small percentage of officers who will make this coup will all pass over to the new defense force. The ones on the losing side won't have much to say about it. Once they don't have any weapons anymore they'll just be another bunch of unemployed bums and will go off to visit their Swiss bank accounts or will find other means of earning a living. What we will have to avoid studiously is drastically upturning society while this change settles in, so that no significant element of the population turns against us while our defenses are down."

The priest raised another question. "But even if you cut the armed forces back to a couple of thousand men, will that be a guarantee against a future coup? You know that in some of the African countries, they only have armies of a couple of hundred men, and they still have coups every other day."

"There's a big difference here in that those countries are the size of a large postage stamp, where Bolivia is the size of California and Texas combined, bigger than most of Western Europe put together. With the size consideration *and*," he added, "the existence of the armed and nasty miners, a couple of thousand men, even working in perfect harmony, would be hard put to pacify this country against any kind of popular resistance."

"So what exactly do you want the miners to do?" Leon asked. He was now thinking ahead, seeing himself as a minister in the new government and the hero of the labor movement.

"All I want is for the miners, and the students, and the workers to be ready. I can't have the whole country aware of the date and time of the coup, but, when they hear that we've taken La Paz, I want people out in the streets in support of what we've done, and I want the miners to pull their rifles out from under their beds and head for the city, as they traditionally do in times of unrest anyway, and put some pressure on anyone who is still resisting. If things go according to plan, the bloodshed will all be over by then. If not, they should go back home and pretend it never happened."

"So," Padre Tomas concluded, "you're offering us a big chunk of the defense budget and removing the army as a player in the political game in exchange for a little public support after the fact?"

"I hope to be able to offer you a good deal more than that, when the time comes," Guerrero added, "but that will depend upon a certain amount of luck, and I don't like to promise what I can't be sure of delivering."

Leon and the priest looked at each other. Leon was the first to speak. "*If* your coup succeeds, the miners won't be far behind you. Just be sure you don't disappoint them. They have no sense of humor at all."

"Neither do I," said Guerrero grimly.

Chapter Twelve

When Guerrero threw open the door of the commando battalion headquarters building, he found his staff and the group commanders hunched over maps and piles of papers, struggling to put together a plan for the coup. Guerrero had taken the time to stop by his quarters for a quick shower and shave and to change back into his camouflaged fatigues. It was already darkening outside, and he had hardly slept during the day-long bus ride back to the Chapare, but he could not afford to sleep until he had provided his officers with the information they would need to fine-tune the attack plan.

"Well, is it good news or bad news?" asked Duarte, putting down his pencil.

Guerrero smiled, paused, and gave a firm thumbs-up signal, to the cheers of the tired men in the room. He pulled a chair up to the table with the large map of La Paz and environs on it.

"Okay," he began. "Here's what we've got. We have the Marines and the Academy, as I expected, and General Morales and Admiral Barco will give us the horsepower we need to attract other units. More importantly, we have the 'Colorados,' the military police battalion, and the counterterrorist and riot police units of the police, which will help give us some muscle on the ground. We can also, I think, discount the participation of the 'Calama,' if the arrangements I made hold." Guerrero reached over and circled the name of each unit on the blackboard that was committed to the coup, and put a star next to the name of the 'Calama.'

"Now, I'm going to give you your group assignments and then I'm going to catch some sleep. I want you all to get at least six hours sleep tonight as well and then be prepared to brief me and your subordinate leaders first thing in the morning. I want to be ready to move in forty-eight hours if necessary."

"We've called in our 'reservists,'" announced Takagi. "That gives us three full fourteen-man teams extra, one assigned to each combat group."

"Good," said Guerrero approvingly. "We'll need them. Now let me give out your assignments and explain what the other allied units will be doing." He stretched over the map of La Paz, using a pencil as a pointer.

"First of all, Lieutenant Vasquez' Group A will handle the peripheral tasks—"

"Excuse me, sir," interrupted Vasquez. "You know that Morales was one of my men. If it's all the same to you, I would like to request that my group have a central assignment in this operation."

Guerrero turned on the younger man, and said in a low, rumbling voice, "You will take the assignments I give you, and you will perform them to perfection. I have no time for macho attitudes or personal pride. If you can't handle that, take off your officers' insignia right now, and you can serve as an infantryman. What's it going to be, Lieutenant?"

Vasquez stiffened at this unexpected assault. "Whatever you say, sir. I just—"

Guerrero raised his hand and cut Vasquez' explanation off. "I understand your feeling, Vasquez, and you'll have to trust me that you'll get your fill of vengeance and then some. In fact, once I explain your additional tasks, I think you'll be more than satisfied.

"Now, getting back to the operation. Vasquez, you will send one of your teams, reinforced with about thirty Marines who should be joining us on the night of the attack, to hit the military airfield on the east side of Santa Cruz. This will be the single most important action of the opening phase of the coup. Your mission will be to disable or destroy all of the air force fighters based there, as well as the transport aircraft, and to crater the runway to prevent its use for at least forty-eight hours. A second team will hit the international airport at Viru Viru on the other side of town, with the sole mission of cratering the runway and knocking out the airport control tower. They will have to avoid contact as much as possible with the security forces at the airport and break off as soon as they complete the mission. As soon as they have completed that task they will split into two squads, one going to the television station and the other to the radio transmitter, where they will destroy the facilities before breaking off. Your third team will take up a position outside the barracks of the 'Manchego' Ranger Regiment in Montero," he indicated a point just north of the city of Santa Cruz.

"This whole operation will center on keeping the 'Manchego' out of the fight in La Paz. If they can't fly out they're dead in the water, but we have to buy time for the units at the two airfields to do their work. As soon as the Rangers get word of what is going on in La Paz, or if an alarm is raised from either of the airfields, they'll mount up in trucks and head either for one or the other. If we can mount a successful ambush just as they clear the perimeter of their base, even if it's with only fourteen men against nearly five hundred, that will force them to deploy, search the area, which our men will have already left, and then slow their advance to a crawl, waiting and watching for another ambush which will never come. If we're really lucky, the sight of a few burning truckloads of Rangers just might give them a reason to sit this one out altogether."

Guerrero paused intentionally, studying the map as he let the thought of killing fellow soldiers sink in. After a moment he looked up and faced the men, who were all staring at him wide-eyed. "You might as well get used to the idea," he said calmly. "This is going to be bloody, no two ways about it. And the bloodier we make it at the outset the more likely it will be that the other side will call it a day. If we go in for half measures now, they'll think that by pushing a little harder or holding on a little longer they can win. *That's* what will drive the body count up. If anyone is going to have a problem with that, I suggest they bow out now." No one moved.

"Very well. Vasquez, you will hold your remaining two teams in reserve for another job which I will explain to you privately.

"Zuniga, your Group B will have the primary task of pacifying the city of La Paz proper. The key target there will be silencing the 'Ingavi' 4th Cavalry Regiment at the army general headquarters and seizing that location. Most of the mop-up work in the city, capturing key individuals and buildings, we can leave to the police and to the military police battalion. You will be supported in your assault by the cadets from the Academy, but I will have to rely on you to spearhead the attack. The other troops will be good enough for laying down a base of fire and, hopefully, cowing the 'Ingavi' into surrender, but four of your teams will have the job of getting into the headquarters area and raising enough Hell to take the fight out of the defenders. Remember that if the 'Ingavi' doesn't fall within the first couple of hours the game is up. You will hold one team in reserve under my personal command for a separate mission which I will pass on later."

The officers were frantically taking notes on their small notepads, doubled over their work like schoolboys the day before a big test. Guerrero continued. "Lastly, Lieutenants Kolkowicz and Martinez, your Group C and Support Group will have the toughest job of all. You will send one team, reinforced with an antitank section from the support group, to back up the Marines who will be coming down from the lake to cut off the advance of the 'Lanza' Cavalry from Guaqui. If your men can knock out a few of their APCs, I think the raw firepower of the Marines might well convince the 'Lanza' to back off. A second team, supported by the 60mm mortar section, will hit the air force base at El Alto. They have a couple of A-37 attack jets stationed there which must be destroyed, and you should try to damage both the civilian runway at the airport opposite the base as well as the military one. That way, even if the 'Manchego' from Santa Cruz manages to get airborne, they will have nowhere to land close to the action and will have to divert to Cochabamba, which will cost them time.

"Your team of reservists, reinforced by a squad of riot police, will have the job of taking and *holding* the television and radio repeater station at the edge of the Altiplano plateau. I can't overemphasize the importance of this task. While I don't expect there to be much initial resistance or a quick reaction by the other side, once they realize what's going on they will hit that place with everything they have, if they're smart. Your job will be to hold out while we are broadcasting our messages to the whole country from the television and radio stations in the city. When you can't hold any longer your men will destroy the facilities and exfiltrate back to our positions."

Guerrero paused and took a deep breath. "That leaves you two teams, plus the remaining antitank sections of the support group to begin preparing defenses against our biggest threat, the 'Tarapaca' Armored Regiment, which will be barrelling down the highway from Viacha. You can set one team to cover the old airport road, but since that winds this way and that through the working-class neighborhoods all the way up to El Alto, I doubt that they'll even try that at first. The rest of your force should concentrate on setting up an ambush on the airport highway itself. It's four lanes wide, and while it winds along the rim of the valley it's the fastest way for vehicles to make it to the center of town. Fortunately, it also offers long, clear fields of fire, pretty much away from most of the civilian residential areas."

Kolkowicz raised his hand. "If we have a few hours time I think we could blast some kind of antitank ditch across the highway and pile the debris on the downhill side to form an additional barrier, maybe pile some burned-out autos there too. There are plenty of spots where there's a steep cliff wall on the left-hand side of the road as you're coming down the hill, and a sharp drop-off on the right. If we cover the barrier with fire, it should hold."

Guerrero shook his head. "There's no point in trying to set up barriers, because the Brazilian Cascavels and Urutus of the 'Tarapaca' have walking-beam suspension systems on their wheels which permit them to climb barriers of up to a meter in height. We also can't bother with trying to shoot out their tires, since they can run for a hundred kilometers on flat ones, and you know that that's about four times farther than the distance from El Alto to the Plaza Murillo. Since the Brazilians built them especially for antisubversive street fighting, they're tough to knock out with Molotov cocktails or other homemade incendiaries. Our only hope is to go for clean antiarmor kills with the LAW-80s, keep their infantry cover pinned down with small-arms fire, and hope they run out of enthusiasm before we run out of LAWs.

"Unfortunately, until they split the old 'Tarapaca' into the new one plus the 'Calama,' it was designed specifically as a coup breaker. The other regiments had nothing that could really deal with tanks, so as long as the commander of the 'Tarapaca' remained loyal to the government the regime was safe. If the 'Tarapaca' went over to the plotters, the incumbent president just quietly packed his bags and headed for the airport. What gives us a chance of pulling this off is that there hasn't been a successful uprising since the revolution of 1952 which didn't either have the support of the 'Tarapaca' or at least its guaranteed neutrality. I'm banking on them knowing that we haven't even approached the tankers, and therefore not taking us seriously until it's too late."

Guerrero could see the sweat rolling down the face of young Kolkowicz and guessed it was not entirely due to the humidity. "Now, I don't expect you to hold off—" he consulted a sheet of notepaper he took from his shirt pocket, "—twenty-four Cascavels, twenty-four Urutus, twenty-four other armored cars, and upwards of four hundred men forever with your fourteen or so. As soon as the team at the airport is finished they will drop back and reinforce you. You will also have at least one company from the 'Colorados' from the start to give your positions some depth, and as Zuniga's men finish up in the city they'll be shuttled up to your position to reinforce you.

"The big question will be how fast the 'Tarapaca' reacts. If we can keep them in the dark for a couple of hours we've already got a big leg up. Even after they get word of the coup they should take some time to mount up and form up for a coordinated advance, which will also give us time. If they choose to wait for either the 'Calama,' which we know isn't coming, or the 'Lanza,' which might not show up either, they're dead meat. I suspect, however, that, at some time after about H-plus-four hours, we can expect a visit from the cavalry, and we will have to be ready."

Guerrero paused while the pencils of his subordinates raced across their pages. "I will give the specific tasks of the reserve teams tomorrow. Keep the men at their urban combat training, and Kolkowicz would probably be well advised to focus on antiarmor tactics. Make sure the weapons are clean and equipment checked. This is going to be a 'come-as-you-are' war, so go ahead and issue a dozen full ammo clips and four grenades to each man, plus two days' rations and two canteens of water. I'll talk to Ochoa later about what kind of transport we'll need for him to lay on and where I want it to be and when. For now, I'll leave you gentlemen with that little project to think about, and go catch some shuteye." Guerrero rose, causing the others to rise in unison with him, and headed for the door. He paused there for a moment and said, "I don't suppose I need to add that if there are any deficiencies in the precombat inspection the man responsible and his immediate superiors will wish they only had to face up to a Cascavel. Good night, gentlemen."

Guerrero walked quickly away from the headquarters building toward his own quarters. He had always hated commanders who he knew hung around outside doorways, hoping to catch bits of commentary by their subordinates about their performance. He also knew that junior officers were very much aware of this habit and never made significant comments until a full five minutes after the commander left. So there was no point in wasting his time there.

Silence reigned inside the headquarters as the junior officers diligently finished their notes and checked locations on the various maps posted around the room. Finally, Kolkowicz spoke up, "I can't fucking believe it! I'm going to go up against the 'Tarapaca' with one lousy team?"

Duarte didn't look up from the tablet he was writing on. "If the team's lousy, it's your fault. Are you telling me you can't *handle* a few dozen armored vehicles?"

"Don't worry, brother," Zuniga laughed. "Just as soon as I get finished kicking 'Ingavi' butt I'll come along and bail you out too."

"Or maybe, since we've got the police on our side," added Rivera, the battalion intelligence officer, "we could just put a traffic cop up on the highway and direct the tanks over a cliff as they come into town."

Duarte was glad to hear the men laughing. If they had been dead serious, then there would be cause to worry. Not that he wasn't worrying already.

Chapter Thirteen

Kelly felt light-headed as she descended the steps of the Lloyd Aereo Boliviano jet at the El Alto airport. She had been told to expect this because of the altitude of La Paz, but she suspected that the feeling had more to do with the fact that the end of her trip was finally approaching and that she would soon conclude the deal for which she had been waiting so long.

She really wasn't so worried anymore. So far everything had gone exactly as Alan had said it would. She had been met by a very nice little man who called himself Pablo, although that probably wasn't his real name, at the airport in Santa Cruz. He had driven her all around town, pointing out the few sights, and then to the luxurious Hotel Los Tajibos, where a room had been waiting for her. She had spent a couple of very pleasant days lounging by the pool, fending off the persistent mosquitoes, who pretty much kept their distance once she remembered to put on her insect repellent, and the even more persistent young Romeos around the pool, for whom an effective repellent had not yet been found. Still, she had to admit that she had rather enjoyed their attention and their flowery compliments. Even when they didn't speak English she could tell from their tone that they were complimenting her, and she could only hope that they weren't being too gross about it.

At the appointed time Pablo had reappeared, driven her back out to the airport, and stood faithfully by until her plane had departed. She now walked slowly toward the terminal, partly to let her swimming head settle down, and partly to let the press of people in the doorway thin out. As she didn't have any baggage to claim she was in no hurry, and she figured that by staying apart from the crowd it would be easier for her new Pablo to spot her. The sunlight was so bright that she wished she could have put on her sunglasses, but her green eyes were part of the recognition pattern, as Alan had called it, so she just had to squint and keep moving through the thin, cold air toward the terminal.

She passed through the double doors and into the passenger waiting area, scanning the crowd of travellers and the people who had come to see them off, hoping for a look of recognition. Suddenly she felt something. In Santa Cruz, the first Pablo had politely presented himself in front of her, bowed slightly, and introduced himself. Now she felt an arm slip around her waist and smelled an overpowering odor of both perspiration and cheap cologne. She turned quickly, pulling away at the same time, and stared into the face of a stocky man, at least a head shorter than she was, smiling a lewd smile that revealed a gap in his upper teeth.

"Hey, baby," the man said in heavily accented English, "don't you have a little kiss for Uncle Pablo?"

She pushed him away roughly. "Hey, yourself! This is strictly business, remember? Keep your hands off of me."

Pablo put up his hands defensively and made a mocking, hurt, face. "Sure, baby. I'm just trying to make this look good, you know? Come on, the car's out this way."

He made an exaggeratedly gallant sweep of his arm and she walked briskly out the front of the terminal, although she had to swat his hand away twice more as he touched her waist, ostensibly to guide her in the right direction. He held open the front door of a late-model Toyota Celica, took her bags, and tossed them into the back seat. Kelly sat pressed as far over to the door as possible during the long ride down from the airport, worried to death that they would both die in a car wreck, as Pablo spent most of the time leering at her and not watching the road; on more than one occasion his hand missed the gear shift and came to rest on her knee.

"Hey, lighten up, baby," Pablo said after she had brushed his hand away yet again. "You won't be leaving with the merchandise until tomorrow, and the nights in La Paz can get very cold and lonely." He smiled a gap-toothed smile at her while weaving in and out of traffic at the same time.

"I've never been *that* lonely, thanks," she retorted, staring out the window and fuming. This was going to be a long twenty-four hours, she could tell. And you can bet that she'd tell the man who brought the package tomorrow all about this creep, and Alan would hear about this too. This guy would be looking for a new job before long. It was bad enough that she had to travel half way around the world, risking everything to do this job. She shouldn't have to put up with this guy's advances too.

Then she realized just how lonely and scared she really felt. On the plane coming in she had been toying with the idea of making another trip eventually, thinking about what she could do with $20,000 instead of just $10,000. Everything had gone so smoothly up to that point that it seemed like no effort at all. Now all the fears she had originally forced from her mind when Alan had made the proposition to her came flooding back. What if she were caught, here in a foreign country, with drugs. Sure, Alan had promised that their connections could get her off, but how fast? And the fact of the matter would be that she would be guilty as Hell. Even if they got her out of jail, wouldn't the arrest go on her record? What if she lost her job back home? What would her parents say? Oh, why had she gotten into this mess?

Her thoughts had kept her from enjoying or even noticing the scenery as they entered the city, until the car finally pulled up in front of a tall, modernistic building situated along a broad avenue with a kind of narrow park down the middle of it. Pablo reached across her to open the passenger door, making no effort to avoid rubbing up against her breasts.

"Here's your hotel, baby," he said, his face pressed close to hers. She couldn't identify all of the spices on his breath from what had obviously been a fulsome lunch, but she thought she might pass out. "You can walk around town, if you like, and then have dinner in either of the two hotel restaurants. The package will be delivered to your room at about ten o'clock tonight. Make sure you're there—and *alone*." He leered at her, and she pushed her way out of the car, retrieved her bags, and marched up the steps to the revolving door. Just as she reached the attentive doorman who stood ready to turn it for her, she realized that she had not heard the car pull away from the curb. She turned and saw Pablo leaning way out the passenger window, from which vantage point he had been ogling every movement of her body as she ascended the steps. A shiver ran through her as she hurried inside.

After that welcome she certainly didn't feel like taking in the sights. She had to admit, however, that the hotel was nice, and the view from her room of the snow-capped mountains was breathtaking. She just rested on the bed for awhile, then checked through the one bag in which the package was to be carried, taking out all of her things and leaving the false bottom exposed. She left the clothes she wouldn't be needing anymore stacked neatly next to it for the man to replace once the package was hidden. Then she went upstairs to the rooftop restaurant.

The elegant maître d'hôtel escorted her to a table near the windows, and she was entranced by the view. It was dark outside now, and the twinkling lights of the houses climbed up to the darkening blue dome of the sky along the walls of the steep, narrow valley in which the city was located. She could see the bright yellow lights of what she guessed must be the airport highway as it snaked along the edge of the Altiplano plateau then plunged into the valley, clinging to the steep valley walls, cliffs really, from which it had been cut, leaving a sheer wall of rock and mud on one side, a precipice on the other. She was sorry now that she had missed the view from the airport side, and she made up her mind to ask the man tonight to supply someone else to drive her to the airport the next day. As she thought again of the second Pablo, her skin began to crawl.

After a fine dinner, which, if she was figuring the exchange rate correctly, cost only the equivalent of about ten dollars, she went back down to her room to wait. She tried the TV, but all of the programs were in Spanish, not surprisingly, and she regretted that she had not taken the desk clerk up on his offer of the pay-for-view movie in English. She had already seen it, but now the company of English-speaking voices would have been welcome.

There was a soft knock at the door. She glanced at her watch. It was just after ten. This must be him. She hurried across the room and flung open the door. There, smiling his gap-toothed smile, his hair slicked back with a fresh coat of grease, was the second Pablo.

"Surprise, surprise, baby," he said enthusiastically, beaming up at her and then letting his eyes travel the length of her body and back. "I'm the man with the goodies after all."

He brushed past her into the room, swinging an attache case from one hand. He walked over to the table where her bag stood ready. Kelly stayed by the open door, watching him.

"All *spread out* and ready for me, I see," he laughed, nodding after a pause at the case. "Oh, I think you'd better shut the door—and put on the chain. We definitely don't want to be disturbed. Do we?"

As she silently shut the door and attached the chain, Pablo gently laid his attache case on the table next to her bag and opened the lid. From his pocket he pulled a pair of surgical gloves and slipped them on, not without some effort, over his chubby fingers. Then he pried up the false bottom of her bag with the point of a switchblade, which he had also taken from his coat pocket, and took a large plastic-coated package from his case. Kelly could see that it enclosed some kind of yellow paper envelope and consisted of several layers of clear plastic around it. It was just the shape of her bag and fit snugly into the hidden cavity. With the package inserted, Pablo removed his gloves, putting them back in his pocket, then replaced the false bottom and filled the bag with her clothes before closing it carefully.

When Kelly had seen Pablo draw the switchblade she had been grateful that she had not had to bring the money to pay for the drugs herself. Alan had explained that the drugs would be paid for when she got on the aircraft the next day, by a direct wire transfer between banks in another part of the world. All very sophisticated. She didn't have any doubt that someone like the second Pablo wouldn't bat an eye at slitting her throat and keeping both the money and the drugs. Well, at least that was over with, and now all she had to do was wait until tomorrow, although she was disappointed that there would be no higher authority here to whom she could report the conduct of this Pablo. That would have to wait until she saw Alan again.

Pablo closed his own case and put away his knife, but instead of heading for the door he reached into his other coat pocket and pulled out a small white plastic bag. "Now it's time for us to celebrate. How about it, baby?"

Kelly had advanced across the room to watch what Pablo was doing, but now she shrank back. "No, thanks! You've done what you came for. Now get out. I'll find my own way to the airport tomorrow."

Pablo tilted his head and stuck out his lower lip in mock sorrow, putting the small package back in his pocket. Then, suddenly, with a speed she would not have expected from such a portly man, he was across the room and had flung her on the bed, with him on top of her. She struggled with him, but he had her arms pinned to her side.

"I'll scream," she gasped as he nuzzled her neck with his stubbly face.

"Sure," he said in a deep, panting voice, "and when the police get here you can tell them how your cocaine connection got fresh with you. I'd be interested to hear you explain that."

He pressed his lips against hers and tried to force his tongue into her mouth, but she bit down hard. He yelped quietly, and moved his face down to her breasts, nuzzling them. Then he moved his hand down to pull up her skirt, but that freed one of Kelly's hands. She was glad then that she had not cut her fingernails. She pulled her hand free and dug her nails deep into his cheek, clawing at his face with all her might.

Now it was Pablo who screamed and jumped off the bed. He put his hand up to his face and stared in horror at the blood on it. "All right, you bitch!" he hissed. "You find your way to the airport." He grabbed his attache case and stormed toward the door. "And tell that faggot Alan that he'll never get another ounce of coke out of this country!" Pablo fumbled with the chain and finally got the door open, slamming it after him.

As soon as he was out of the room Kelly flew off the bed and pressed herself against the door, fastening the chain and turning the deadbolt latch. Then she staggered into the bathroom and threw up.

In the elevator Pablo dabbed at his cheek with a soiled handkerchief. "That bitch!" he muttered, half out loud, to the consternation of the well-dressed couple who were riding down from the hotel restaurant. The man pressed the button for another floor, and they got off as soon as the elevator stopped. Oblivious to them, Pablo stayed in the elevator and rode it down to the level of the coffee shop. There he got off and stomped straight to a bank of public phones, put in a coin, and waited for his party to answer.

"Hi," he said at last. "It's me. Yeah, I've got some information for you. There's a shipment of coke going out on the flight to Miami tomorrow afternoon. In the carry-on bag of an American girl. Travelling alone. Age, in the early twenties; short brown hair, green eyes. Yeah, very tasty. I want the stuff back. You can have her and whatever you can squeeze out of her folks back home. You know the drill. Okay, okay! Half of the stuff for me, but then you split whatever cash you get if her folks try to buy her out of here. Deal!"

Pablo hung up the phone with a smug smile on his face and headed out into the night. The cool air stung the wounds on his cheek, but he didn't mind so much anymore. He'd been hurt worse than that in his life. He'd have to stop by the prison and visit his little friend sometime to see how she was holding up after playing hostess to half the narcotics cops in town. She should have been nicer to me, he thought, and he headed off to a whorehouse he knew of where he could act out his fantasies.

Chapter Fourteen

Earlier that morning, as Kelly had been preparing to depart Santa Cruz, Guerrero arose early. He spent the day going over the detailed plans his officers and staff had made the night before. The noon mess was even noisier than usual, as the men went through the age-old ritual of building up their courage for the coming fight by making light of the risks, boasting of their valor, and disparaging the enemy. The officers were somewhat quieter, being better informed of the risks they were actually running, but the mood was still generally positive. Guerrero was feeling very pleased with himself for his selection of these young men and the state of readiness to which his training had brought them.

That afternoon he watched as the teams ran through their urban combat drills at the site of a small, abandoned food-processing plant near the base that the local municipal authorities permitted the battalion to use for training. The men moved quickly, deftly, each team acting as part of a larger organism, each one knowing where the others would be without having to look. If the job they had to do couldn't be done with these men, Guerrero thought, then it couldn't be done at all.

As he watched one of the last teams conduct a live-fire drill, Duarte's HUMMER came roaring up to his position, skidding to a stop in a spray of gravel and dirt. Duarte hopped out, accompanied by two men in civilian clothes. Guerrero recognized the first as Captain Venegas, the police counterterrorist specialist from La Paz. The other he didn't recognize but, from his short hair and stiff bearing, Guerrero assumed that he was military.

Duarte rushed up to Guerrero and said, close to his ear, "These men have come from La Paz with some important news that they'll only tell to you personally. I know Venegas, so I thought it would be all right to bring them here."

"You did the right thing, Lieutenant," Guerrero assured him. Then he walked over to where Venegas and the other man were waiting by the HUMMER and shook Venegas' hand. The other man snapped rigidly to attention and executed a smart salute, which Guerrero returned.

"This is Sergeant Robles, of the military police battalion," Venegas said. "He's the reason we're here now."

Guerrero led the men over to an area where the partial foundations of some ruined buildings gave them a place to sit, removed from where the troops were training.

Venegas started, "It was last night that we brought the military police commander on board, and fortunately for us he briefed Sergeant Robles here, who will be in charge of the gate detail at the presidential residence tomorrow night. Robles was in full agreement with our plans and motives, of course," he said, nodding to the sergeant, and Guerrero smiled and nodded in answer. "But when he had been told, Robles came out with this story he had heard a couple of days earlier but hadn't known who to tell about it."

"Excuse me, sir," interrupted Robles. "It wasn't exactly a 'story' I heard. I was there myself."

"Well, then, tell us in your own words, Sergeant," Guerrero offered, trying to put the obviously nervous man at his ease.

"Well, sir," Robles stammered, "It's like this. You see, I have this, well, arrangement with one of the housekeepers at the president's house. I know that I'm not supposed to go into the house itself. My post is out by the gate, but on my break, when it's rainy or cold, she sometimes lets me into the kitchen . . . to warm up, sort of . . . you understand?"

"Perfectly," Guerrero smiled. "Now go on with your report."

"Yes, sir. You see, the other day this Benitez character paid another visit on President Boca—"

"*Another* visit?" Guerrero asked. "Are you talking about Lazaro Benitez, the drug trafficker? Does he visit president Boca often?"

"Well, sir, not really all that often," Robles answered, still unsure of himself and wishing that he had just kept his mouth shut, as a good sergeant should know to do. "Usually about once a month, but more often recently. Sometimes it's other people, from the same line of work, if you know what I mean. But, anyway, Benitez was there, and I happened to be in the kitchen. I wasn't eavesdropping, mind you!" he added hastily. "I was just having a quick cup of tea and a sweetcake, and I really couldn't help overhearing. Benitez was yelling a blue streak at the president and it, well, it sort of caught my attention, so I eased closer to the door. That's when I heard it."

"Get to the point, Sergeant," Guerrero said impatiently.

"Yes, sir. Benitez said that he was very upset that this Murillo fellow didn't get let off at the court and that he didn't want him extradited to the States. President Boca said that it couldn't be helped, and Benitez said that he would take care of the hard part. He said that he was bringing in some Sendero Luminoso guerrillas from Peru who would take the American Embassy by assault and hold the Americans hostage. Then President Boca would have to release Murillo to get them freed, and the Americans couldn't hold the government responsible." Robles hung his head. "And President Boca agreed."

"Son of a bitch!" growled Duarte. "That slimy bastard's going to be the first one up against the wall!"

"That's enough of that, Lieutenant," snapped Guerrero. "Now, Sergeant, when is all this supposed to happen?"

"It was to have been four days from then. That would be tomorrow sometime."

"Good!" said Guerrero. He first patted the sergeant on the shoulder and said, "Thank you, Sergeant. This information is of vital importance. You've undoubtedly saved a lot of lives by telling us this."

Robles straightened up with pride and discreetly rose to wait over by the HUMMER.

"We don't know what time tomorrow the terrorists are going to hit, but I would suspect that it will be late in the day. Not so late that no one will be in the embassy, but probably not first thing in the morning either," Guerrero surmised. He turned first to Venegas. "You need to get back to La Paz as quickly as you can. I was going to hold your men in reserve, but their first priority now is going to be the defeat of the Senderista terrorists. If the government is in on this we can't just surround the building with cops, since someone in authority would just pull them off. What we have to do is somehow reinforce the security discreetly, just until the coup goes down that night. Then, of course, we can come down on them like a ton of bricks. I had planned for us to be ready to move tomorrow night in any case, but hadn't set the hour, just in case some last-minute delays came up. Now we *have* to move tomorrow night."

Guerrero then spoke to both Venegas and Duarte. "I'm going to La

Paz myself tonight. I've got a contact in the American Embassy whom I will have to warn about the terrorist attack. What I want you to do, Venegas, is tell the people in La Paz that the coup comes off tomorrow night at 2330 hours. I prefer to avoid midnight, because people get confused as to which day you really meant. Duarte, you're in charge here. You carry out the plans we laid out whether I come back in time or not."

"Wait a minute," said Duarte. "You're talking like you don't expect to make it back. Don't you want to take some men with you, if there's some kind of danger?"

"No," Guerrero said, "I'm just being careful. I could be hung up by something as simple as a bad landing gear on a Lloyd jet on the way back. I don't want the plan screwed up just because I'm not there in person at the right moment. There is the chance that I'll get picked up. There always has been that chance. In that case, having a couple of men with me wouldn't change anything. You just go ahead and do what you've been trained to do."

Duarte frowned pensively, "Just the same, if you don't come back, I have a pretty good idea where you'd be, and we'll come looking for you."

"Thank you, my friend," said Guerrero warmly. "But not unless the goals of the plan won't be affected by it. Although I am reminded of that scene from the movie 'Butch Cassidy and the Sundance Kid' where Paul Newman is going to have this duel and he tells Robert Redford off to one side, 'I don't want to sound like a bad sport, but if the other guy wins, kill him.'" The three men laughed, but Guerrero could see a hardness behind Duarte's eyes that he had not seen before. He would pity the man Duarte blamed for his chief's death. That made Guerrero feel rather warm inside. Guerrero did take the precaution of talking with Venegas quietly as Duarte made arrangements for Guerrero's trip to La Paz. Guerrero accepted a small item from Venegas and slipped it carefully into his pocket.

There would be no time for a discreet and leisurely bus ride up to La Paz now, so Guerrero had one of his "reservists" from the area drive him in to Cochabamba airport in his private vehicle. He waited in the car while the man purchased a round-trip ticket, using his own identity card to meet local regulations, and then rushed through the airport just as the plane was boarding. Although he wore civilian clothes, which he hoped would prevent the casual observer from recognizing him, Guerrero made no effort to disguise himself, praying that even if he were noticed among the press of passengers he would not attract any particular attention, or that a report of his trip to La Paz would not be delivered until it was too late to interfere with the operation.

He arrived in La Paz after dark, went straight to the taxi rank, and took a cab down into the city, taking advantage of the ride for one last survey of the terrain over which his men would be fighting in little more than twenty-four hours. He left the cab at the lower end of the suburb of Obrajes and walked briskly away from the main avenue into the unlit side streets. There was virtually no pedestrian traffic at this hour in this residential neighborhood, and Guerrero was as certain as he could be that he had not been followed, although he could not be sure that he had not been spotted at the airport and a watch arranged for him on his return trip. He rounded a corner and saw the garden wall of the house he was seeking. A Toyota jeep happened to be parked near the wall, half pulled up onto the sidewalk to leave room for cars to pass in the narrow street, and he used it as a ladder to climb to the top of the wall, stepping gingerly over the razor stripping on the top and dropping lightly into the garden below. He walked quietly through the garden and came to the large sliding glass doors that opened onto the terrace on one side and the living room on the other. A man with salt-and-pepper hair and a neatly trimmed beard lounged on the sofa and a woman with shoulder-length blonde hair rested gently against his side as they watched the news on TV. There was a feeble fire in the fireplace. Too little oxygen for a roaring fire, Guerrero thought. The man had his shoes off, his stocking feet propped up on the coffee table. It was such a tranquil scene that Guerrero almost hated to disturb them. Almost, but not quite.

Guerrero saw that the sliding door was fixed only with one of those simple latches the doors come with. He easily wedged the blade of his survival knife between the door and the frame and silently popped the catch. The man and woman turned suddenly when they heard the door slide open behind them.

"Good evening, Mr. Featherstone," Guerrero said quietly. "I'm sorry to drop in on you unannounced, but there is an important and a rather discreet matter that we have to discuss, and I'm afraid it can't wait until normal business hours."

"That's quite all right, Commander," Featherstone said, once he had recovered his composure. "Ann, this is Commander Guerrero, the man I was telling you about from my visit to the Chapare."

"Oh yes," Ann said, nervously extending her hand, and wondering whether that was the right thing to do with a man who had just committed breaking and entering. "Pleased to meet you."

Guerrero took her hand gently, clicked his heels, and inclined his head in a formalized peck that prudently touched only his own thumb and not her skin.

"Ah, yes, well," Ann stammered. "I'll just make myself useful out in the kitchen. Would you care for some coffee, Commander?"

"That would be wonderful, Mrs. Featherstone," Guerrero said graciously, and he watched as she left the room before he and Featherstone sat on the couch and began to talk.

"I'm glad you came to see me, Commander," Featherstone started. "Our people in the embassy, the ones who deal with such things, have said that there are rumors of an impending coup d'etat. I was wondering if you had heard anything about that."

"Well," Guerrero said, smiling knowingly, "that's a safe thing for your intelligence people to report periodically, since it's very usually true here in Bolivia. It's like reporting that there's going to be a strike next week. You might miss on the exact timing, but with the average Bolivian government having a life span of only eight months, over the whole of our history, it's a safe bet. Of course, some governments last their full term, and we haven't had a real coup for about a decade, but that just means that we're overdue."

Featherstone frowned slightly. "Shall I put that down as a 'no comment,' then?"

"Well, that's not really what I came to talk to you about," Guerrero continued, ignoring the question. "A piece of information has come to my attention which affects your embassy directly."

Featherstone took a renewed interest and leaned a little forward.

"It has been reported to me that Lazaro Benitez, the drug czar of Santa Cruz, has contracted with the Sendero Luminoso to send a team of terrorists here to seize your embassy and hold the people in it hostage in exchange for the release of Francisco Murillo, to prevent his extradition to the U.S. The attack is scheduled to take place sometime tomorrow."

Featherstone took a deep breath. "May I ask where you obtained this information?"

"I can only say that it was from a reliable source who got it at first hand."

"Thank you, Commander," Featherstone said. "I'll advise our ambassador, and we'll inform the Ministry of Interior, being careful to leave your name out of it, if you like, and make sure that the terrorists get wrapped up before they can cause any trouble."

"Yes," Guerrero said. "I would prefer it if you kept my name out of it, but I'm afraid that's only half of the story. The other half is that this attack is being conducted with the full knowledge and cooperation of President Boca and the Ministry of Interior. I'm afraid you won't get much support from that quarter."

Featherstone's mouth dropped open. "Surely you're not serious. The president himself knows about this and approves?"

"I'm not certain that you fully understand the kind of power that the narcotics mafia can exercise when they have something specific they want to go after. They can't conquer a country or run a government outright, although they tried hard enough during the Garcia Meza regime. But they found out that they don't need to. They can get what they want by just putting on the pressure very hard when their vital interests are at stake. The Murillo case is one of those times. Of course there is no proof of the government's involvement, none that I could lay out for you here on the coffee table, no satellite photographs or telephone tap transcripts, just my word. I just thought you ought to know."

"Well, yes, thank you," Featherstone mumbled. "It's still very hard to believe. And I'm not sure just what we can do in that case."

"All I can suggest is that you look out for yourselves. The only other thing I can tell you is that if the attack does take place you won't be alone for long. If the terrorists don't take control in the first few minutes, every second they can be denied will bring you closer to safety. That's all I can say for now."

Guerrero rose and quickly headed for the door. "You'll make my excuses to your wife, won't you? I'm afraid I really can't stay for coffee."

Before Featherstone could answer Guerrero had slipped out into the night and vanished. Ann was standing at the top of the steps leading from the kitchen when he turned around, the coffee tray in her hands. "I heard it all," she said. "I expect that we'll be needing this coffee ourselves."

Featherstone was already reaching for the phone. "I expect you're right, love. The first thing I want you to do in the morning is to run, don't walk, to the airport and get yourself on a flight out of the country. Lima, Santiago, it doesn't much matter where to, just away from here for a couple of days. Guerrero said that the target was the embassy, but he might have been mistaken. Our residences could be targeted, and I'd rather that you missed out on the excitement."

Ann had set the tray down, and now she pressed the telephone cradle button on the telephone, cutting off his call. "What's that quaint American expression you have? 'Kiss my butt?' Yes, that's it. Now you listen to me, William Featherstone," she said, grabbing his ear and twisting it very hard in the best tradition of the British school matrons she had been raised with. "I have been the good little diplomatic wife for many, many years now, and more than once I have let you shuttle me and the children off to safety while you stayed on to write your silly little telegrams so that people in Washington would have something interesting to talk about over their coffee and doughnuts in the morning. Well, I'm giving you fair warning now that those days are over, my dear. The children are grown and gone now, and it's just you and me. I let you chase me out of Cuba when the going got rough, and I want you to know that I lived through Hell, not knowing from one minute to the next whether you were alive or dead, and there were a lot of those minutes before you came back. I promised myself then that I'd never go through that again. I'm here now, and I'm going to be with you *at the embassy* tomorrow, whether you like it or not. If something is going to happen, it's going to happen to both of us. Is that quite clear?"

Featherstone's face was contorted in pain and she added another twist to her grip on his ear. "Yes, yes, okay, you Limey bastard!" he finally gasped. She let him go and kissed him lightly on the forehead as he rubbed his sore ear.

"That's a good boy. Now I'll just run upstairs and pack us a little bag of extra clothes, some food, and a couple of good books, just in case we have to sit out a siege." With that she tripped off up the stairs as contented as if preparing for an afternoon picnic.

Featherstone was not pleased about this turn of events. He would have felt less, well, encumbered, if she were safely out of the way in Miami or Chile, but, on the other hand, she had always been a tremendous source of support for him, and he knew that he could use all he could get at this moment.

He put the telephone receiver up to his good ear and dialed the ambassador's number. After getting his grudging acceptance of an emergency meeting of the Country Team, the heads of the various embassy sections, at the residence in an hour, he called the other embassy officials and then set out himself on the drive up to the city.

Featherstone paused when he had finished his briefing. Lieutenant Colonel Polsby and Tom Evans looked grim, and Enrique Contreras of DEA was gnashing his teeth like a madman. Ambassador Pearson simply held his head in one hand, and all were silent, waiting for his reaction.

"Thank you, Mr. Featherstone," the ambassador said without raising his head. "You know? I was aware of this political appointee–career foreign service rivalry long before I was given this post, but, and I'll be frank with you, I always assumed that it really was a case of the professionals, who really knew what they were doing overseas, resenting the presence of well-meaning amateurs like myself who just happen to have an in with the current administration. Of course, on the other side, I knew that we political appointees can do some good, precisely because of our connections, being able to get the president's or some congressman's ear on an aid bill where one of the Foggy Bottom boys would have been out in the cold." Featherstone knew that this wasn't going to be good. "I am, therefore, more than a little amazed that you, Bill, the long-time professional diplomat here, could have swallowed such a large ration of bullshit without question. I can only conclude that your jealousy of my close personal relationship with President Boca has so clouded your judgement that you are willing to grasp at any straw to try to muddy those waters. I am *not,* I repeat *not,* going to go to the government with this sorry tale, and I am not going to poison the well in Washington, where, as you know, Congress is about to vote an additional ten million dollars in aid money for the fight against narcotics trafficking for Bolivia."

Tom Evans raised a finger, "But, sir, we always have to look at the worst case scenario and prepare for it—"

Pearson cut him off with an icy look. "What I want to know from *you* is whether the Agency, either here or in any other country, has any information to support this cock-and-bull story?"

"Well, no, sir, we haven't, but in terrorist cases the chances of having real advance warning like this—"

Pearson cut him off again. "Thank you. That answers my question. Now, does anyone else have any corroborating information?"

The others present were busy examining their shoes.

"Good!" crowed Pearson. "That's what I thought. The one thing that

Mr. Featherstone has failed to mention to us is the source of his information. I, however, don't need to ask. It's that Guerrero asshole, isn't it?"

Featherstone just looked at him stonily. "It would appear that I have nothing else to contribute to this meeting."

"You don't need to tell me," Pearson continued. "We've been getting rumors of a coup, an effort to send this country back into the military dictatorship that it has managed to avoid for nearly ten years. Now we get this wild story smearing the Boca administration, and whom do we get it from? Mr. Featherstone. And who is Mr. Featherstone's great confidential contact, the one who has tried to smear the Boca administration before? Guerrero. I don't know about you *professionals*," he said with malicious emphasis, "but I can certainly put two and two together when I see them. Guerrero is the one behind the coup, or at least he's in with them, and *that* is what I plan to tell the Minister of Interior in the morning. Now, thank you gentlemen, and good night!"

As the guests filed slowly out of the residence and down to the street outside, Polsby, Contreras, and Evans caught up with Featherstone. Polsby was the first to speak. "It *was* Guerrero, wasn't it?"

"I can't say," Featherstone sighed, "and it looks like it wouldn't make any difference. I'll begin packing my things as soon as I can draft up an elegant-sounding letter of resignation. They don't pay me enough money to put up with this."

"That's certainly a mature attitude, Bill," Evans said. "That doesn't, however, answer the problem of what the Hell we're supposed to do tomorrow if there's going to be a war at the office."

"Well," Featherstone said, "I don't suppose that Pearson will allow anything which resembles increased security measures. The only thing you might do is to tell your staffs, very discreetly, that tomorrow would be a good day to take off, and maybe take an extra long lunch yourselves. I plan to be at the embassy because I've been in hostage situations before and I just might be able to save some lives in spite of that imbecile in there." He jerked his head back toward the large white house at the top of the drive.

"The one thing that I was told that I didn't mention in there," Featherstone continued, "was that, if something did happen, we wouldn't be alone for long, and if we could hold out, help would be on the way. From where I don't know."

Chapter Fifteen

Guerrero had not originally planned to travel to La Paz at all again before the coup and he decided to take advantage of his presence there to fine-tune the plans for the coup with Campos and General Morales. Once he had finished this chore he headed again for the airport by bus. He waited at a coffee shop near the entrance to the airport until just before the 1230 flight to Cochabamba, and then took a taxi to cover the remaining mile or so of unoccupied flatland that separated the buildings of Villa Satellite and the terminal itself. He moved quickly through the terminal, paid his airport tax at the booth just as the flight was being called, and joined the mob of people pressing their way forward. It was always like this on the domestic flights, as seating wasn't assigned and everyone absolutely *had* to get on first.

Guerrero finally worked his way up to the gate and handed his ticket to the stewardess, who seemed to look at him with unusual interest. Guerrero figured for a moment that perhaps he hadn't lost all his boyish charm. She handed him back the stub and the boarding pass, and he broke free into the crisp air outside the terminal. He half turned when he heard a murmur of discontent from behind him as the terminal door clicked shut, but strong hands had seized his arms from behind. There were at least two men, and two more came striding up to him. They wore expensive suits and dark glasses, what amounted to a uniform among the State Security Service (SSE) thugs of the Ministry of Interior. One of the men facing him had his hand conspicuously inserted inside his suit coat.

"Commander Guerrero?" one of the men asked politely.

"Yes," Guerrero answered. "What's this all about?"

"You'll have to come with us, sir," the man answered. A beige sedan with darkened windows swept up to the terminal door and the men behind him began to push Guerrero forward toward the open rear door.

"I'm a military officer," Guerrero protested, although he knew it was in vain. "If there are some legal charges against me, they must be handled by the military police and a military tribunal."

"There are no charges, sir," the man insisted, still very politely. "We only have a few questions to ask you at the Ministry. I assure you that it won't take long and that we'll drive you back to the airport to permit you to catch the next flight." By now they were at the car. Guerrero knew there was no point in arguing, but he braced himself in the doorway, prepared to make the thugs work for their pay. Just then something heavy and blunt struck him on the back of his head, and he did not remember anything more.

Guerrero awoke suddenly when someone tossed a bucket of water into his face. He recognized the pale green paint of the walls of the basement of the Ministry of Interior. He was in one of the small, ten-by-ten-foot rooms with thick doors and walls where interrogations were conducted. He was sitting in a hard wooden chair. His hands were cuffed beneath the seat of the chair, just behind where his feet were tied to its legs. He found himself staring at the smiling face of Paco Venetti, the head of the Bolivian Narcotics Police.

"Good morning, Coco," Venetti said. "I'm so glad you could make it. This would have been a very dull party without you." Venetti laughed at his own wit.

"Rumor has it that you've been planning a little coup. Something about cleaning out all of the corrupt pigs who have been ruining this country. Well, it looks like things aren't going to work out quite that way." Venetti pretended to scratch his left ear with his right hand and then suddenly lashed out at Guerrero, striking him with the back of the hand, snapping his head around. Guerrero coughed and spat blood onto the floor.

"It took you a long time to wake up, but you're going to wish you never had. Now, who else is in on the coup with you?" Guerrero glanced at the gold Rolex on Venetti's wrist. It was just after three o'clock. Guerrero let out a sigh. This was going to be a long, long afternoon and evening.

Kelly had had no trouble getting a cab to the airport. The kind doorman had even negotiated the price of the ride for her, much to the displeasure of the driver, and had told her how much to pay, tip included, as none of the taxis had meters. She had just over two hours to get to the airport and make her 6:00 P.M. flight to Miami. She had seriously considered discarding the package and the false-bottomed bag with it, but she had finally decided that she had come so far and gone through so much that it would be foolish to come away empty-handed after all.

She was wearing the tight minidress Alan had picked out for her, and she was sitting as demurely as possible in the back seat of the cab, hoping that the driver's sudden interest in the rear-view mirror would not result in their deaths as he finally pulled out of the afternoon traffic of the downtown area and onto the broad expanse of the airport highway. Still, it was almost over, she thought.

At the airport she paid the driver what the doorman had suggested, plus a couple of dollars' worth of local currency. That pleased the driver greatly, and he wished her a good trip. At least that's what she assumed he said, but from the look in his eyes she decided that it was better that she not know precisely. She fought off the attentions of several baggage handlers in blue overalls, who very much wanted to help her with her two small bags, then checked in at the international counter and then retired to the airport coffee shop until her flight was called.

She took her time, waiting for the press of the more impatient passengers at the immigration booth to thin out, just as Alan had instructed her. On the way she stopped at one of the airport shops and bought a box of coca-leaf tea bags. Alan had also suggested this. As the coca-leaf tea was perfectly legal, she would wedge it into an outside pocket of the bag with the package, and, if a sniffer dog did happen by and show an interest in her luggage, she could voluntarily produce the tea and offer to turn it in if there were a problem. Between this ingenuousness and her beauty, the customs inspector would undoubtedly just laugh it off and let her go.

The line was finally clear, and she walked up and turned in her passport, smiling coyly at the shy immigration officer, who stamped it without looking at the page. Things were working perfectly. He waved her through graciously, and she came to the customs inspection station at the entrance to the international waiting area. She placed her two bags on the inspection counter and had to bend over, ever so far, to unzip the one safe bag first. Then, having attracted the young inspector's undivided attention, she did the same for the other bag, smiling all the while.

Just as the young man was about to help her close the bags, having recoiled in horror as his hands came in contact with the lacy, silky underwear with which the bag containing the package was filled, another, older officer came up. He wore a short khaki flight jacket and dark glasses, although, Kelly noticed that the hall was poorly lit. He carried a riding crop with which he brushed the regular inspector aside, and he bent over her bags.

"Good evening," he said in passable English, and the smile on his face gave Kelly the same feeling she had had at her last encounter with Pablo number two. He twirled his riding crop deftly between his fingers and placed the end of it on the counter, just next to her bag, marking the height of the top of the bag with his finger. He then inserted the stick into the bag itself, noting that there remained a gap of over an inch between where his fingers grasped the crop and the top of the bag.

He gave a curt command to the young inspector, who quickly began emptying clothes onto the counter. Kelly's mouth felt dry, and she began to tremble as the new inspector, still smiling, opened a Swiss Army knife, pried up the corner of the concealment compartment, peered under it, and told the younger man to replace the clothes. For one brief moment Kelly thought that Alan's preparations were going to work after all, that the man was going to let her through, but instead of waving her on, he zipped up the bag, took it in his hand, and said, "Would you please follow me, Miss?"

On wobbling legs, Kelly followed him into a small room to the side of the immigration office. She was conscious that all of the other passengers in the hall were watching her with open mouths, and she knew that they would be talking about the big drug bust on their way home. The officer carefully put her bags on the floor and directed her to a small bench in the corner. Almost immediately a stocky woman, dressed in a khaki uniform that barely fitted her, entered the room. The officer told Kelly to take off all of her clothing, that the female officer was going to conduct a body cavity search. He then left the room and closed the door. The policewoman stood with her arms folded, frowning as Kelly slowly began to undress. The tears that had been welling up in her eyes but which she had been blinking back now began to flow freely. The policewoman was not impressed.

After the humiliating experience of the body search, Kelly, dressed again, was handcuffed and escorted out to a waiting police car and forced into the back seat. As the car drove away from the airport, heading for the highway into town again, she could see her airplane, the only foreign one on the airstrip, taxiing out onto the runway for the flight home. She began to cry again.

The police car finally pulled up to a two-story building surrounded by a high brick wall, with police guards posted all around. Kelly was taken from the car and escorted into the building and down a flight of stairs to the basement. The smiling officer led the way, pausing to knock at one heavy door with a small window in it. The door was opened from within, and Kelly could see a heavyset man, wearing khaki police uniform pants but stripped to his sleeveless T-shirt, leaning over another man who was tied to a chair, bleeding from numerous cuts and bruises around his head.

"Colonel Venetti," the smiling officer announced. "We have that little surprise you ordered from the airport, and as you can see she's everything they promised."

Venetti was panting heavily from his exertions as he took a long look at Kelly, who had pressed herself against the far wall of the hallway. Guerrero raised his head slightly, and he could see the figure of a slender girl through the doorway with the one eye that had not swollen shut.

"No one else has had her yet?" Venetti asked, putting his leather sap on the table and taking off his pistol belt as well.

"No, sir," assured the officer. "As you ordered."

"Good, take her into the next room." Venetti turned to Guerrero and lifted his chin roughly. "I'll be back in just a little while, Coco. This night is really just getting better and better, isn't it?"

Guerrero let his head loll back and remained motionless as Venetti left the room, leaving the door ajar.

Kelly found herself sitting on a narrow steel bed, staring at the thick door that had been closed on her. After a moment it opened, and the heavy man from the other room came in, wiping the sweat from his brow with a towel. "I understand there was a little misunderstanding at the airport. Something about a package of cocaine that was found in one of your bags."

Kelly began to stammer, "I—I don't know how it got there. I left my bag alone in the room for several hours. Maybe someone at the hotel planted it there."

"Of course," Venetti laughed as he approached her. She could smell the sweat and the odor of liquor on his breath. She turned her head in terror. "That happens all the time around here."

He reached down and grabbed her by the arms, lifting her off the bed and putting his face close to hers. "Now you listen to me, you little tramp," he hissed into her face, almost overpowering her with his breath. "You're going to do just what I say, just how I say it. You're going to be my little friend until I get tired of you, and then I'll decide if you deserve to be let go, free and clear. Otherwise you're going to prison, and let me tell you, someone who looks like you," he paused and carefully examined every curve of the body that pressed firmly against her tight dress, "will have her hands full between the guards and the lesbians. In our prison system you can even receive occasional visits from male inmates who pay for the privilege. You'll be a very busy girl."

Venetti didn't bother to hear her answer. He wrapped his arms around her and squeezed her tightly, covering her lips with a sloppy, wet kiss as his hands kneaded her buttocks. She tried to push away, but he held her easily with one strong arm as he reached up under her dress and began to pull down her pantyhose and underwear together. Kelly was gasping for air, but it was like a dream in which one wants to scream out and can't.

Guerrero waited until he could hear the sounds he had expected from the next room, and then acted quickly. With his fingertips he reached into one of his shoes and found the string to which was attached the handcuff key he had received from Venegas. Fortunately, all policemen used cuffs with interchangeable keys, and he soon had his open. He then dipped into his other shoe and pulled out a small pocket knife, with which he cut the ropes that bound him to the chair. He had hoped that, as he had been unconscious when he was brought to the Ministry, he would have been searched only lightly, and this was proving true. Watching the door, he slowly drew Venetti's revolver from its holster on the table and opened the cylinder. He checked carefully to see that it was loaded with live rounds, lest his tormentor should have left him a sucker's weapon. He then rose quietly and crossed to the doorway. No one was in the hall, and Venetti was obviously busy in the next room.

Venetti had succeeded in removing Kelly's undergarments, although she still had on her dress, now bunched up around her armpits. Venetti had doubled her over the rail of the bed, and as he was fumbling with his own pants he talked to her in a soothing voice. "I expect you'll be wanting to talk to your American Consul, won't you? Well, I wouldn't count too much on that. Right about now the Consul, like all the other American diplomats, is probably spreadeagled on the floor of his embassy with a man in a ski mask standing over him with an AK-47. Yes, terrorists are storming the American Embassy, right this minute. In fact, they should have the place well in hand by now. By the time that is all sorted out, the Americans won't have time to worry about what might have happened to a little American whore who decided to increase her income by doing a little drug trafficking on the side. Oh, yes, you're mine, sweet thing. You're mine until I tell you that you can go, and you're going to love it, just let me show you what a real man can—"

Venetti stopped when he heard the door click shut. He was about to scream abuse at whatever idiot officer had decided to get his jollies watching the old man at work when he heard the clear and distinctive sound of a revolver hammer being cocked.

"Excuse me," Guerrero said quietly in Spanish. "I don't believe we finished our little talk, and there was something I was just about to tell you, too."

Venetti turned slowly toward Guerrero, who was leaning up against the wall of the room, the pistol pointed steadily at Venetti's chest. Venetti reached down and began to try to pull up his pants, but Guerrero continued.

"What I wanted to tell you was: 'You're dead!'" The pistol barked once, and Venetti was flung back against the far wall, blood gushing from the wound in his heart.

Kelly's first impulse, although she had never before seen a dead man, much less seen one killed before her, was to pull her dress down to cover herself. Guerrero wasn't looking at her, he was peering through the small window in the door to see if anyone was coming.

"We have to get out of here," she said, not knowing who this man was or even whether he understood English. "They'll have heard the shot and will come to kill us both."

Guerrero turned his good eye toward her. "These rooms were made for torturing prisoners. Good acoustics was not something the architect was told to emphasize. With the door shut, you could fire a cannon in here and someone outside the door wouldn't notice. Who are you, anyway?"

"Kelly Slater," she said in a mousey voice. "I'm an American, and I was arrested at the airport. They accused me of having cocaine in my luggage."

"And did you?"

"Well, yes," she admitted, "but, please, you have to help me. You saw what that . . . man was going to do to me. And he said that terrorists were going to attack the American Embassy, or already had. We've got to get out of here."

"I know about the terrorists, and everything is being done about that that can be. Our concern is *how* we are to get out of here. There are about fifty armed men in and around this building, and I have exactly five bullets left. That's going to call for some mighty fancy shootin', ma'am," he added, using his best Texas drawl.

"Who are *you*?" she asked. "Why were they beating you? What did you do?"

"I'm what I guess you could call a political prisoner. I'm a naval officer, and, if things are going according to plan, my men are going to launch a coup in about four or five hours. The question is how we are going to survive down here until then."

Kelly could see that Guerrero's breath was coming hard and his face was covered with bluish bruises and drying blood. There was a small sink in the room with a dirty towel next to it. Forgetting her own pain and fear, she wet the towel, wrung it out, and began to dab gently at his wounds. Guerrero flinched at first, but then closed his eyes and let her finish.

"Thanks," he said when she had done. "Here, we'd better move him while we think of what to do." Together they dragged Venetti into a corner hidden from the window in the door. "It looks like he gave orders that he wanted each of us for himself, and since we have the last two rooms in this corridor, we have at least a few minutes before anyone dares come down here to investigate." Suddenly, Guerrero was overcome with fatigue and pain and slumped down to a sitting position, his back against the wall. Kelly sat next to him, resting her head on his shoulder, and cried.

Chapter Sixteen

Javier Nunez sat in the driver's seat of the blue Datsun parked in front of the La Paz City Hall, watching the front entrance of the American Embassy across the street. Earlier, a traffic cop had come by and gesticulated at him, indicating that parking there was prohibited, but Nunez had tossed onto the dashboard of the car a special pass with which he had been provided, and the cop had just touched the visor of his cap and gone on his way. This is almost too easy, Nunez thought.

He glanced at his watch. It was just after 4:30 P.M., about fifteen minutes to go. His leg muscles were still knotted up from spending most of the previous day jammed into the intercity bus that had brought him from Cuzco, Peru, to La Paz around the southern shore of Lake Titicaca. The trip had been bad enough, but what he had hated most was being in such close proximity to so many Indians for so long. Nunez had been a leading figure in the Peruvian Sendero Luminoso (SL) terrorist movement for over five years, and during that time he had been constantly living and fighting among the Indian populations of central and northern Peru, but he was of almost pure European stock himself. Like most of his fellow Senderistas, Nunez came from an upper-middle-class family, his father being a prominent lawyer, and he had joined the SL out of disgust with the corruption and gross inequities of the Peruvian political and economic system. He could not develop any affinity for the Indian peasants for whom he was allegedly fighting.

Nunez had spent most of the last two years systematically wiping out the Ashininka Indians of the upper Huallaga Valley in northern Peru. Village by village, he and his troops had massacred men, women, and children by the dozen, by the hundred. The fools had not only refused to abandon the cultivation of their traditional food crops to grow coca, but had insisted on joining the village self-defense forces organized by the Peruvian Army. But the soldiers could not be everywhere at once, and when they left Nunez and his experienced guerrillas would cut down these feeble defenders, armed usually with museum-piece weapons, and teach them a good lesson. The cocaine business meant money for his movement, and these primitives could not be allowed to stand in the way of progress. Anyway, these people, just out of the Stone Age, could hardly contribute to the new society that Nunez dreamed of.

The mission in La Paz was part of the same objective. Although it was superficially a contract hit on a large scale, paid for by the Bolivian drug mafia to get one of their number out of jail, that was only part of it. Certainly the five million dollars that would be paid would buy a lot of arms and would support the SL movement for months, but the real objective was political. The SL had bombed the American Embassy in Lima several times, along with other U.S. interests, like the Sheraton Hotel, in addition to their many assaults, bombings, and assassinations directed against the Peruvian government, army, and police, but this would really be something. To seize an American Embassy full of diplomats would be a propaganda coup of unprecedented proportions for the SL, even better than the seizure of dozens of diplomats, including the American ambassador, by the Colombian M19 some years before, which had made that group's name a household word. Of course they would demand the release of the trafficker, as they had been contracted to do, but there would be political demands, too. This would be bigger than Eden Pastora's seizure of the Nicaraguan Congress for the Sandinistas back in 1978. He could almost picture himself giving the V-for-victory salute from the doorway of the airliner that would fly them to safety.

The radio in his lap suddenly crackled to life, and Nunez heard two distinct clicks. He responded with one click. Across the street, in the gaps between the crowds of pedestrians already starting to fill the street at the end of the work day, he could see a man and a woman seated on the large circular cement planter that stood in front of the entrance to the embassy offices. Everything was ready, and it was almost time.

Bolivian Police Major Osorio rounded the corner onto Calle Colon from Calle Camacho and pushed his way impatiently through the mob of pedestrians on this very narrow portion of the sidewalk. A passing bus, scraping the curb with its tires, nearly took his head off with its side-view mirror, but he ducked and kept moving forward. When he finally broke clear into the broad portion of sidewalk in front of the

American Embassy he paused to straighten his dark olive-green uniform jacket and adjust his cap. Then he strode purposefully through the double glass doors of the embassy entrance.

Three policemen were standing in the small foyer that contained only the elevators and the stairway leading up to the embassy above. All three wore the same dark olive-green uniform as the major, but these men had steel helmets on and carried Italian Beretta 9mm submachineguns. All three snapped to attention as the major entered.

"How long have you men been on duty, Sergeant?" the major asked, knowing the answer in advance.

Sergeant Saavedra executed a crisp salute. "Since eight this morning, Major. Relief was due half an hour ago."

"Do you have any more men here?"

"Just these two, Major," Saavedra answered. "We normally have a fourth man, but he had to pick up his son from school, so I gave him permission to leave at the end of his shift. I hope that's all right, sir."

"Yes, yes," said Osorio condescendingly. One less to worry about, he thought. "In fact, it's almost five o'clock now. The embassy staff will all be leaving soon. Why don't the rest of you take off and go about your business? I'll stay here myself to wait for your relief and give them a piece of my mind when they do show up."

Saavedra's face brightened and he executed another salute. "Yes, my Major. Thank you, sir." His men happily picked up the small gym bags in which they normally carried refreshments for their long day's guard duty, and filed out the door.

Once they were outside, Saavedra spat on the sidewalk angrily. "Scumbag!" he said to himself. It had been just as Captain Venegas had told them. Some smart-ass officer would come and pull them off the embassy sometime during the day, and there would be no relief. Saavedra admitted that the act would have worked on normal cops, but his men were part of the special antiterrorist squad and a little smarter than most, especially when they knew where the enemy was coming from.

Saavedra nodded to one of his men, Mendez, who headed off in the other direction, crossed the street, and disappeared into a small door in the side of the City Hall building where minor art works were sometimes displayed. Saavedra took Carranza and headed up to the corner, to the main entrance of the Banco Popular del Peru building, and entered through the revolving doors.

Osorio waited for a moment after the guards left and then mounted the steps to the second-floor mezzanine. Normally another police guard would have been stationed here at the landing, where another set of steps led up to the embassy reception area. All that was here now, however, was a large pile of boxes of office supplies stacked in a corner of the landing, near the unused elevator doors. Satisfied, Osorio made his way back down the stairs and peeked out into the pedestrian traffic in both directions. The police guards were nowhere in sight. He glanced at his watch, waited another thirty seconds, and then quickly pushed his way out through the growing crowd. Twenty thousand dollars! he thought. All for five minutes' work. He rationalized that if the stupid Americans just cooperated no one would get hurt anyway, and it would all be over in just a few hours. Now he could afford to take his kids on that trip to Disneyworld that he had been promising them, and still have enough left over to buy a second car for his wife to use. And all for simply following the orders of the Minister of Interior himself!

From his position wedged in behind the boxes of office supplies on the second-floor landing, Police Private Villarroel had heard the three clear taps of a metal gun barrel on the metal of the stair's handrail, signaling that Saavedra and the others had been pulled off as expected. They wouldn't be far away, but he would be all alone now. Then he heard the single set of footsteps slowly mount the stairs, turn around, and go back down, again as Captain Venegas had speculated. Now he had to pay very close attention. If only a few persons came up the steps he was to let them pass. If a large number came running up he was to be ready for them and to fight for his life. He let out a long sigh and mopped his brow with a handkerchief.

In the embassy reception area, Police Lt. Mario Lopez paced nervously, never taking his eyes off the stairway door. He had not been surprised to learn that the elevator between reception and the ground floor had gone out of service. That would make sense. Only four or five people could fit in the elevator at a time, six at the outside. They would know that with the elevator out of commission the door to the stairs would remain open, and any number of people could come swarming up the stairwell. The video camera at the Marine's post would spot a large bunch, but if they came up a few at a time there would be no way to spot them among the normal flow of visitors to the embassy. He glanced at the clock over the elevator. In ten more minutes the embassy's office hours would be over and he could close the heavy metal door to the stairwell, opening it only to let the office personnel, who had already started to filter out, leave for the day. That would make him feel better.

Lopez was older than the usual police guard at this post, nearly forty. What the Marine who stood quietly behind his bulletproof glass shield did not know was that Lopez was also a member of the antiterrorist squad, as was his partner, Sgt. Anita Ruiz, and that both of them took medals regularly at international police competitions in combat shooting exercises. The Marine might have noticed that instead of the aged revolvers usually worn by the guards both Lopez and Ruiz carried modern Beretta 9mm automatics, and both had grips custom-designed for their hands. As an added measure of insurance, Lopez had a Beretta submachinegun in his gym bag under the small counter where Ruiz examined the contents of ladies' handbags before they went through the metal detector.

Back on the street, Nunez watched the police guards leave the building and disappear into the crowd. He watched for Major Osorio, who intentionally walked past the front of the City Hall and in front of Nunez' car with his cap in his right hand, as the final signal that all was ready. Nunez clicked his radio key twice and received an answering click, and he and the two men in the back seat climbed out of the car and made their way toward the embassy entrance. As they passed the man and woman seated on the concrete planter the couple rose and followed them in, leaving the packages that each had carried carefully wedged at the base of the planter.

Once inside the building the group stood aside to let a cluster of local Bolivian embassy employees come down the stairs before they began their own climb. Nunez stayed in the lobby, seated comfortably on the little bench normally used by the police guards and conveniently out of the line of sight of the video camera over his head. He closed his eyes, listened carefully, and heard the group reach the first landing and begin the second flight of stairs. He counted their steps, and when they had entered the reception area he withdrew a small radio transmitter from his pocket, extended the antenna, and pressed a red button.

The normal racket of the La Paz streets, with car horns blowing and newspaper vendors hawking the tabloids, was suddenly overwhelmed by a deafening blast as the two packages placed next to the concrete planter exploded, ripping the planter from its base and hurling it like a huge discus across the street. It knifed through the crowd, spreading death and crushing an elderly woman against the wall of the City Hall on the opposite side.

At the same instant the gears of a brightly painted yellow bus groaned into action, and the bus angled out into traffic from where it had been parked, blocking the sidewalk, at the top of the hill on Calle Colon just one block from the Embassy. The driver of the bus did not worry about the traffic, clipping the front fender of a taxi as he blocked the street, waiting a moment only for the cars ahead of him to move out of the way and for the stoplight at the bottom of the hill to turn green. He ignored the screams of the irate taxi driver and then put the bus in gear again and began to descend the hill, picking up speed. The passengers of the bus, three dozen veteran SL guerrillas, cocked their weapons and braced themselves, bending low in their seats.

In the Banco Popular, Sergeant Saavedra was stunned momentarily by the blast, which blew out all of the bank's windows on that side of the building. He rushed to the door with Carranza and saw the bus careening down the hill. "This is it!" he shouted, and grabbed one of the cowering bank guards by the collar, dragging him out the door with him. He shoved the guard to the right, up Calle Mercado, away from the embassy. "Go up to the corner and stop the traffic. Throw yourself in the street. Shoot their tires out if you have to, but stop the cars." The man took off running, only too happy to distance himself from the scene. "And if you see any police send them this way!" he shouted after him.

Saavedra and Carranza watched the bus tear by them, knocking down and running over pedestrians who were too slow to scatter, and bounce up on the curb, angling into the gap between the protective concrete planters that the explosion had created, and come to a jerking halt in front of the embassy entrance. The doors of the bus popped open and the terrorists began to pour out, but the nervous driver, instead of jamming the front fender of the bus against the building itself to provide a solid shield for the terrorists on one side, had actually stopped about a yard short, leaving a gap between the bus and the building.

It was into this gap that Saavedra, crouched in the bank's doorway, directed his first burst, cutting down one terrorist heavily laden with bandoliers of ammunition and other equipment, while Carranza, crouched next to him, swept the windows of the bus with submachinegun fire. On the other side of the street, Mendez had charged from the City Hall side door, slipping on the blood-covered cobblestones, and leaped onto another of the concrete planters to get a clear line of fire over the heads of the terrified civilians who had yet to escape the crossfire. His first short burst caught a terrorist full in the chest as he began to exit the bus, but as the heavy cough of a machinegun firing from the rear of the bus added to the din, Mendez caught a round in the forehead and flipped over backward, off the planter.

In the embassy reception area the large windows facing the street had been shattered by the force of the blast below, just as three men and a woman emerged from the stairwell, brandishing their small, boxlike Ingram submachineguns. They had not expected the quick reaction of the two police guards, usually the least experienced and intelligent men on a police force. As if in one of their competitions, Lopez and Ruiz drew their pistols and took two-handed grips in one smooth motion, each putting three rounds into their chosen targets, two in the chest, one in the head, just in case the target wore body armor.

Ruiz' man, however, had already pressed his trigger, and his wild burst ripped through the air, putting a chance round into Ruiz' neck just above the top of her bulletproof vest. She gasped and slumped back against the Marine's window. Lopez saw this out of the corner of his eye, but was too busy firing to mourn now. The other two terrorists had rolled to the ground and were spraying the room with wild automatic fire. Lopez had to dive to one side to avoid the fire, but the Marine guard, seemingly out of place in his dress blues, was laying down covering fire with his twelve-gauge shotgun, punctuating each shot with a high-pitched yell as his face grew red enough to match his short-cropped hair.

Lopez could hear heavy firing from the street outside, and he recognized the characteristic sound of the Beretta submachinegun, which told him Saavedra and his men were in the fight as well. He popped up and took two well-aimed shots, one of which caught one of the terrorists in the forehead. There were heavy footsteps pounding up the stairs. Two of the dead terrorists' bodies were blocking the doorway, and the fourth terrorist was still alive and firing. There was no way to get that door closed.

Villarroel had heard the four people go up the stairs. Then he had heard the explosion and the firing, both above and below. My turn! he thought, and he crawled quickly to the low cement wall connecting the stairs up from the lobby and those leading down from reception. There were people on the stairs now, running up. He paused a moment and then raised himself up, his submachinegun in firing position, paused another fraction of a second, just long enough to see that the people on the stairs were not police, and let rip a long burst, cutting down the first three or four men on the stairs. He then ducked back down behind the low wall as a hail of fire sent chips of paint and splinters of cement spraying in all directions. He changed position and fired again, unsure of his success, and wished he had a few hand grenades. No sooner had he thought this than several grenades came sailing up over the railing. He had just time to dive behind his wall of boxes before the grenades exploded.

On the ground floor, Nunez was pitching smoke grenades into the street to cover the entry of his men. It was just as well that the fool driver had been killed almost instantly, because Nunez would have killed him himself for his mistake. Only about a dozen of his men had managed to enter the embassy. He could see several dead on the street or in the bus, and from the firing above he could tell that all was not going well. Shit! he thought.

Saavedra and Carranza were firing wild through the smoke now, Carranza kneeling and Saavedra standing, taking as much advantage as possible of the cover provided by the corner of the bank's marble door frame. They were firing at the gun flashes that winked from all of the bus windows on their side, but Saavedra could tell that at least some of the terrorists had made their way into the building. Suddenly, several dark objects came flying from the bus in his direction. Grenades! He pressed against the bank door, but he saw that one of the bank guards had crawled to the door and slid home the bolt, locking them outside. Thanks! Saavedra thought, as he and Carranza flattened themselves on the ground. The explosions threw Carranza on top of Saavedra and both of them against the building. Saavedra could tell from the stillness of Carranza's body that he was dead, and there was a burning pain in Saavedra's left leg, but he could still move. He rolled Carranza's limp form off of him and picked up his gun again. A rumbling noise from behind him told him that he was no longer fighting alone.

Captain Venegas had borrowed the riot police water cannon truck for the "training exercise" he and his men were on, and the huge blue vehicle, the size of a school bus, was rolling down Calle Colon faster and faster. It was essentially a water tanker with a heavy bulldozer blade on the front and two large nozzles on the roof that could be directed from within the armored cab.

The terrorists who were still in the bus also heard the noise and then saw the truck heading for them. Some of them directed the fire of their heavy machinegun toward it while others tried to gather up the satchels of explosives with which they had planned to destroy the embassy, or threaten to. The truck came on, despite the bullets that pinged off its sides, and when it was within fifty yards the nozzles began to spray a powerful stream of water laced with tear gas through the broken windows of the bus, further disorienting the terrorists.

The dozer blade of the truck smashed into the bus just forward of the rear wheel and caught fast. The driver of the truck then twisted his wheel with all his might while gunning his engine, dragging the bus away from the building and into the street. Inside the bus one of the terrorists was frantically trying to make the electrical connections that would detonate the explosives with which the bus was filled. If he couldn't blow the embassy from the inside he would do it from out here. But the shock of the collision, the torrents of water that gushed through the windows, and the burning of his eyes slowed his work. He did not make the final connection until the bus was almost up against the abandoned old Tesla movie theater across the street from the embassy.

The force of the explosion flipped the water truck over on its back like a giant beetle, ruptured its tank, and sent hundreds of gallons of water flowing into the street. The bus, or at least its largest remaining piece, the chassis, was hurled through the two-story glass and steel windows of the Tesla, burning furiously.

In the reception area the Marine guard had come charging through the door to support Lopez, and Lopez had been lucky enough to get a clear shot at the remaining terrorist before he could cut the Marine down. The Marine stooped to examine Ruiz, but Lopez leaped up and grabbed him by the arm.

"Leave her. She's dead," he shouted in Spanish. The red-haired Marine just looked at him uncomprehendingly. The sound of more footsteps on the stairs ended their conversation, and Lopez pushed the Marine toward the door. "Get everyone upstairs. I'll hold them here as long as I can."

The Marine still didn't understand, so Lopez physically shoved him through the door, where Gunny Hanks had now appeared and was busily herding the screaming secretaries toward the stairway to the upper floors with one hand, carrying a shotgun in the other. The Marine protested, but Lopez wasn't in a mood to argue and closed the door behind him. Then he turned to pull his own submachinegun from his bag. As he took up his firing position he caught another glimpse of the Marine, as he paused in the doorway to the stairwell to the next floor. The Marine snapped him a salute, and Lopez smiled and touched his brow in response.

On the sixth floor the sound of firing had awakened Featherstone from the reverie he had fallen into as he composed his letter of resignation. He listened for a moment and then his hand went for the top drawer of his safe, from which he pulled a .45 automatic and several extra clips. He was shoving the clips into his pants pockets when Ambassador Lance Pearson suddenly appeared in his doorway, his face as white as a sheet of paper.

"Oh, my God!" Pearson screamed. "You were right. They're here. There are terrorists in the building! What are we going to do?"

"They're a long way from this floor yet, sir," Featherstone said calmly, "and, when diplomacy fails . . ." He jacked a round into the chamber of his pistol.

Just then Tom Evans came to the door, half out of breath. "Show time!" Evans said. Featherstone could see the barrel of Evans' Winchester pump protruding from behind the door.

"What's the situation?" Featherstone asked.

"Fighting in reception and in the street," Evans panted. "It looks like the cops didn't run out on us after all, but there's a whole busload of terrorists out there. The Marines are pushing everyone up to this floor. We'll make a fighting retreat up to here and hope help arrives before we run out of floors."

"How about personnel?"

"As we discussed, the section chiefs were discreetly letting people go early this afternoon, so we only have maybe a dozen locals and a few American secretaries in the building." Evans shot a quick glance at Pearson, half expecting a tirade about insubordination, but Pearson's eyes were glazed over and he was running his fingers through his normally carefully groomed hair. "We've got all eight Marines, about four military guys from DAO, three DEA agents, and four other staffers, including my people, all armed more or less. Oh! Hi, Ann!" he said brightly as he noticed Ann sitting quietly in a high-backed easy chair in the corner of Featherstone's office. Ann just smiled proudly and wiggled her fingers at him.

"Well, let's get downstairs and see what we can do," Featherstone said. "That *is* all right with you, isn't it dear?" he asked, turning to Ann.

"Oh, yes, love," she said cheerily. "I'll just stay here and keep Ambassador Pearson company." She walked over and put her arm comfortingly around the ambassador's shoulders and led him over to a couch. "We'll be just fine."

"Physically, we're pretty safe," Evans continued as the two men started down the stairs. "To get at us they're going to have to blow five or six heavy steel doors and shoot their way through us. We can also fill the stairwell between the reception floor and the USAID floor with tear gas. That'll slow 'em down some too. Our big worry is explosives. If they've got half the explosives their bus could carry they could take out this whole block, and they'll be able to tell us to put up or shut up. Either we surrender or they blow us and themselves up. Maybe they'll be bluffing, and maybe they won't, but that'll be a tough choice to make. I don't envy you."

"I'm not in charge here," Featherstone said peevishly.

"Come on, Bill," Evans argued. "You saw that jellyfish up there. I sure as hell wouldn't want my life to depend on his decisions on his *best* day. Right now he's lucky if he's got control of his bowels, much less this embassy. I'm afraid you're it, my friend."

Featherstone knew that, but he wasn't looking forward to the moment when the terrorists would put the decision before him. This wasn't exactly what he had gone into the Foreign Service for. Making life-and-death decisions in moments of extreme tension and danger was the stuff military officers were supposed to be good at. His forte was negotiating trade agreements and smoothing the feathers of the local worthies when Congress didn't pass the aid bill everyone had been hoping for. Damn!

The two men were nearly knocked off their feet by the force of the blast in the street outside. A cascade of plaster and dust fell on them from the ceiling, and Featherstone thought that the end had finally come. He held his breath and waited with his eyes closed tight. He opened them when he felt Evans' hand on his arm.

"What the hell was *that*?" both men asked together, and they hurried out of the stairwell to look down into the street through the shattered window on the fourth floor. Below them they could see the smoking wreckage of the bus hanging halfway out of the entrance to the Tesla and the police water truck lying on its back with its wheels spinning slowly in the air.

"Holy Mary, Mother of God!" shouted Evans, who was not normally very religious at all.

Featherstone shouldered his way past Evans and gazed down on the street. There were bodies everywhere, a couple of them in green police uniforms, some obviously innocent bystanders, and others in civilian clothes but with weapons by their sides. Featherstone could also now see a number of figures in the dark blue uniforms of the police antiterrorist squad darting from cover to cover toward the embassy.

"The cavalry's coming!" Featherstone shouted. "Let's just circle the wagons and hold on!"

Nunez left two men to hold the main entrance and led the rest of the twenty or so men remaining after the destruction of the bus in a final charge up the stairs. The first man to the mezzanine landing caught a burst of submachinegun fire in the face from Villarroel, who was badly wounded by the grenades but not dead yet, but the burst ended in a horrifying *click!* as his magazine ran empty. With bloody fingers Villarroel fumbled to reload, but Nunez strode up to him, kicked the gun from his hands, and smiled as he pulled the trigger of his pistol.

The other men were rushing up to the reception area, and Nunez could hear more firing. When he reached the reception floor he found two more of his men dead in addition to the original four. He also saw two dead policemen and his demolitions man, who was already fixing a plastic explosive charge to the security door. Through the bulletproof glass Nunez could see that this floor had already been evacuated. Shit! he cursed to himself. He had lost most of his explosives along with the bus, and his only hope now was to gain physical control of enough hostages to bargain with. His original plan had been to wire the building for destruction, even if the Americans holed up on the upper floors, thus making his position as strong as if he actually held them. Now he barely had enough explosives to force the many security doors he knew protected the building.

Suddenly the sound of firing from the street and a shout from one of his men at the window caught his attention. "Police, lots of them, working toward the building."

Nunez rushed to the window and saw the men in blue working their way forward, very professionally. This was not the way things were supposed to go! The police were not supposed to be involved at all, at least not for an hour or more, and then only to set up roadblocks and watch the drama unfold. These bastards meant to storm the embassy!

A couple of his men had begun firing from the window at the figures below. Nunez pushed them out of the way and drew a small bullhorn from his gym bag. He raised it to his mouth and screamed, "Stop where you are! We have this building wired to explode, and we will destroy it and everyone in it unless the police pull back!"

He was answered with a hail of bullets from the street, but when he raised his head to look he saw that the police had stopped in their positions. Someone in authority was going to have to decide. Good! he thought. He now had a few more precious minutes. He and his men ducked as the small charge on the security door was blown, and his men rushed through to cover the demolitions man as he went to work on the door to the stairwell to the next floor. This was going to be a tougher day's work than he had planned on, and it wasn't even six o'clock yet.

The charge on the second door blew and Nunez' men prepared for another charge, but the area was immediately filled with thick, choking clouds of tear gas. The men struggled to pull on the gas masks they all carried, but it would be minutes before their eyes stopped watering and their coughing fits stopped. Nunez knew that a counterattack by the Americans would catch them flat-footed, but it appeared that the Americans were in a totally defensive mode, hoping for salvation from outside. All the better!

When his men had recovered somewhat, they prepared to charge up the stairs to the next security door at the top of the flight, but no sooner had they begun than the first men up the stairs came crashing down in a heap on top of those behind. The Americans had poured some sort of soapy liquid down the stairs that made it practically impossible to climb them. Even when Nunez ordered his men to tear down the office curtains to throw onto the stairs, in order to provide some kind of traction, progress was painfully slow and required all of the men's attention. Then the first man reached the bend in the stairs and received the full force of a shotgun blast in the chest. It was a stand-off. The Americans couldn't get down and he couldn't get up. The only thing that was keeping the police from storming up from below was his bluff about the explosives, and it might not take them long to figure out that they wouldn't have had time to wire the building, even if they had the explosives. Nunez had to think fast!

Chapter Seventeen

Guerrero had nearly recovered his strength as he glanced up at the clock on the wall. Assuming that the Ministry of Interior types weren't slick enough to tamper with the clocks to make the prisoners lose track of time, it was nearly 7:30, and they couldn't expect the other SSE men to leave Venetti down here forever without checking on him. Guerrero checked his revolver again, as if more ammunition might have appeared. Then his eyes lit on Venetti's uniform jacket, hanging neatly on a wall hook.

"I suppose he didn't want to splatter blood all over it in the other room," Guerrero said as he painfully eased the jacket over his sore shoulders. It was several sizes too big for Guerrero's lean frame, and the pants they pulled off the corpse were worse, but it was all they had.

"I don't think so," said Kelly, wrinkling her nose and shaking her head.

"It'll have to do." He tried on Venetti's cap, and that turned out to be decidedly too small. "Oh, well," Guerrero sighed. "All we have to do is walk quickly down this hall, through the ready room, up the stairs, and out into the street. With luck, we might not even pass anyone. At least the uniform might give us an extra few meters head start. Even if we have to shoot our way out, once we get into the shadows outside we'll stand a chance. God! I hope it's dark enough now, but we can't wait to be discovered here." He turned toward Kelly. "You don't have to come with me, you know. If you stay here they'll know I did this, and if things work out for me and my people, I promise I'll come back for you later."

"No way," Kelly said defiantly. "I'd rather take my chances with a bullet than stay here with these . . . *pigs*."

* * *

Out on the sidewalk in front of the Ministry of Interior, the SSE duty officer was looking for the regular uniformed police guards who usually were posted at the entrance. No one was in sight. He could hear a lot of talking and noise coming from the police station on the other side of the broad Avenida Arce, and he suspected that the traditionally lazy and unreliable policemen had dismissed themselves to attend some sort of party at the police station. Well, he would just march inside and call up the colonel in charge and see what they had to say for themselves when he got through with them.

The officer never got to complete his thought, as something flashed across his field of vision and he instinctively raised his hand to brush away the fly, or whatever it was. He then felt the sharp constriction around his neck. His first reaction was to claw at the piano wire that already dug deeply into his flesh, but it was no use. When it occurred to him to draw his weapon and try to shoot his attacker he lacked the strength to do so, and his vision gradually went black.

A figure in a camouflage uniform released his victim, gave the limp corpse another hard kick just to make sure, and moved silently toward the entrance of the Ministry, where other figures, similarly clad, were already taking up covering positions. At his signal a tall man strode purposefully through the door and up to the desk, where a stocky young man was seated.

"I'm looking for a Commander Guerrero, I understand he's to be found here," Duarte said in a flat tone.

"I don't give a shit what you understand," the young man answered. "This is the Ministry of Interior, and no one gets to see a prisoner without the express, written permission of the minister himself."

The young man was about to go back to his paperwork when Duarte grabbed him by the shirt, pulled him to his feet, and shoved the barrel of his pistol into the man's mouth, knocking out two of his front teeth in the process. "Don't bother to tell me where he is, just point, thank you."

The man pointed toward a set of stairs to the right, and Duarte cuffed him on the side of the head with his gun. Duarte's men had already started to spread out through the building, and there was an occasional burst of automatic weapons fire where the SSE men were too quick to be taken captive quietly and not quick enough to get off the first shot.

Duarte bounded down the stairs two at a time and rounded a corner, smashing into an ill-dressed UMOPAR officer. Both men had their guns drawn and pointed in each other's faces before Duarte recognized Guerrero.

"Shit! What happened to you?" Duarte asked.

"Never mind that. What the hell are you doing here?" Guerrero growled. "The plan called for the coup to start at 2300 hours, and it's not even 2000 hours yet."

Duarte smiled. "I knew you'd be upset. An American named Featherstone called. The one who visited us during the drug raid. He said that his ambassador had tumbled to the possibility of your launching a coup and was going to inform the government. We thought it prudent to advance the kickoff time a little, as we figured you might be in a situation where a few hours would seem to you like a very long time. Oh, and what have we here? Good evening, Miss," Duarte tipped his cap gallantly.

"She was another guest of the late Colonel Venetti," Guerrero said. "She's coming with us."

"Of course!" said Duarte, offering Kelly his arm, but Kelly clung to Guerrero all the harder.

"Get serious, Lieutenant!" Guerrero snapped. "What's the situation?"

"We got everyone into La Paz and the other jump-off points without being detected, as far as we can tell. I don't expect the military police will have had much trouble at the Palacio Quemado and the Chamber of Deputies, and the 'Colorados' and the cadets are moving on the army headquarters now. That's where we're heading. I haven't heard from the president's residence yet or the airport, but the story is that there's a lot of fighting going on at the American Embassy."

"That's tough for them. We've got problems enough of our own. We'll have to leave that to Venegas to handle on his own."

As Duarte and Guerrero escorted Kelly from the building the remaining commandos continued their sweep of the ground floor and the basement, and then prepared to assault the upper stories. In the basement they had found several prisoners, all badly beaten, and they released them without further formalities on the assumption that if they had earned the animosity of Huerta's Ministry of Interior they couldn't be all bad.

In his office on the third floor Huerta had heard the initial shooting and leaped up from his desk shouting a curse, pulling a pistol from the drawer as he did so. He could hardly believe that the coup was actually coming off, even with its chief plotter already a bloody pulp in the basement of this very building. This was not the way things were supposed to be done. If you wanted a coup, you sized up your forces, and if you had a majority you were the new president. If not, you had the courtesy to pack your bags and get the Hell out of the country. He rushed out of his office to find one of his aides frantically handing out automatic weapons from a rack on the guard room wall to security men crowding the corridor.

"We only have to hold out for a few minutes, men," Huerta said unconvincingly. "The 'Ingavi' and the 'Tarapaca' are probably already on their way here, and they'll clean out this rabble in no time." Huerta did not feel this kind of confidence within himself. He had little doubt how long his men, in their clean white shirts and ties, would last against regular troops. His men had much more experience in beating bound men with rubber hoses than in urban warfare tactics.

There was a shout from the stairwell and a flurry of firing, and several of the security men rushed in the direction of the noise. A second later, however, there was a series of deafening explosions as hand grenades came arcing up the stairway, scattering the defenders and covering the walls and floor of the hallway with blood.

Huerta and his remaining men fell back to his spacious office and pulled the heavy wooden doors shut. He saw one of his aides desperately pressing the button on the cradle of the telephone, as if by his insistence he could undo the damage the commandos' wire cutters had done to the phone lines outside. Two of the men dragged a heavy serving table against the doors, knocking bottles of whiskey and glasses onto the floor. Others tipped his desk over and pulled a large sofa in front of it to provide some added protection, and then Huerta and the six or seven men with him crouched behind it, their gun barrels trembling as they pointed them in the direction of the doors.

There was a slow, heavy pounding on the door, and one of Huerta's men let off a burst of automatic fire that tore into the expensive panelling of the door. There was a laugh from outside.

"You'll have to do better than that," a voice said. "Minister Huerta, you are under arrest. Throw down your weapons and surrender, and you and your men will not be harmed."

"Right!" Huerta snarled sarcastically. "Am I supposed to believe that?"

"Have it your own way," the voice said. There was a scraping sound, and then the sound of scuffling feet moving back down the corridor. Suddenly, the room was filled with the roar of an explosion. The heavy doors were ripped from their hinges and hurled into the room. The serving table was toppled over and tossed along the floor like a dry leaf. One of the defenders screamed and rolled over, a large splinter of wood protruding from his chest and blood pouring down the front of his white shirt.

A dark figure appeared in the smoke-filled doorway, but a burst of fire from a security man cut it down. There was a wild shout from the hallway, a kind of primeval battle cry. Another figure appeared in the doorway, but only for a fraction of a second. It fired a short, tubular device, which only made a quiet "pop," and Huerta thought for an instant that whatever it had been had been a dud. Then the 40mm grenade exploded in the corner of the office behind the desk barricade, showering the defenders with shrapnel. This was followed by a number of other grenades that flew into the room, shredding walls and furniture and flesh indiscriminately. A commando dove into the room while two others sprayed the interior with automatic fire. They moved systematically forward, raking every form with fire, until they were convinced that none of the defenders survived.

The compound of the army high command was surrounded by a wall nearly twenty feet high and topped at intervals of one hundred meters with watchtowers that hung out over the lip of the wall, giving the guards a view of the base of the wall along its entire length. On the west face of the compound ran a broad, well-lit avenue, and the southeast face fronted a steep drop into a canyon. On the northeast, however, retired military officers had been allowed to build their homes to within a few meters of the wall, and it was over the roofs of these houses that dark shapes now raced and leaped to the top of the wall. Because of complaints from the influential residents of the neighborhood the bright spotlights that covered the rest of the perimeter had been dimmed and turned inward toward the large central courtyard, around which the barracks of the "Ingavi" Regiment and the offices of the high command were built.

In his office on the compound, General Morales sat with several young officers he had guided and promoted over the years, along with several noncommissioned officers whose families he had helped out from time to time with loans or access to medicines from the officers' military hospital stores. They were all wearing combat kit and carrying German G-3 automatic rifles. Col. Lorenzo Trujillo, commander of the "Ingavi," knocked sharply on the office door, and it was quickly opened to him.

"The orderly told me that you wanted to see me, General," Trujillo said in a displeased tone of voice. It was already long after normal office hours, and Trujillo had wanted to leave for the day and cruise by the American Embassy to rubberneck at the gunfight that was reportedly going on there. He stopped talking when he felt the cold metal of a gun barrel pressed against his head and saw the room filled with armed men.

"You are relieved of command, Colonel," Morales announced.

"Bullshit!" Trujillo spat. "I don't know what kind of support you've got, but I *know* that you don't have any of the five regiments. The 'Tarapaca' alone will run over you like you weren't there. I'm sorry about the death of your son, but I don't think the officer corps will forgive you this insanity, sir."

"Just be quiet and sit down, Colonel," Morales said calmly. "Whatever happens tonight, you're just a spectator from here on."

Trujillo raised his hands in surrender, but as he did so he swung at the man behind him, knocking his gun to the floor, and bolted from the room screaming for the guard.

"Kill him!" one of the officers in the room shouted, and an NCO cooly stepped into the hall and let go a burst from the automatic rifle slung from his shoulder. They heard Trujillo yelp and then the sound of something heavy falling down the stairs.

"Damn!" Morales cursed. "Let's spread out and try to clear the building and hold it."

At the main gate of the compound the officer of the guard heard the shooting just as he was about to examine the orders of the driver of an army Mercedes truck that had appeared unexpectedly with a delivery of new uniforms, or so the driver said. When the officer turned, the driver kicked his door open, slamming the officer in the back of the head, and the men of the "Colorados" Regiment who had been hidden in the back of the truck piled out and overwhelmed the men in the guard shack without firing a shot.

However, another guard, in one of the towers on the wall across the central parade ground from the gate, saw the commotion and swivelled his machinegun around. Just then the crack of a single rifle shot sounded, and the guard doubled over his gun, a neat round hole in his temple. But now confused firing was coming from the building where Morales had his offices, and more and more men were pouring out of the barracks, most of them armed. The ones who had been foolish enough to run into the center of the parade ground were cut down by carefully aimed fire from the commandos who had jumped onto the compound's northeast wall and by the fire of a machinegun that had been set up in the bed of the truck in the gateway. Some "Ingavi" officers had now taken command of their men and were returning fire from the barracks buildings.

One of the "Ingavi" officers called out, "Fernandez, get a platoon over to the armory. We're going to need more ammunition than what we've got in the ready lockers."

A young man carrying a pistol gestured to a group of infantrymen around him and led them under the cover of some storage sheds toward the compound armory. He set up a defensive perimeter around the building and ducked down the few steps leading to the heavy metal door of the weapons vault. He fumbled with some keys in his pocket and tried them on the door. After a moment he kicked the door viciously in rage, turned around, and led his men back to the barracks.

"Ha!" cheered a young NCO watching the scene from the window of Morales' office. "They just realized that you can't open a lock if the keyhole has been filled with solder!" He let off a burst of fire in the general direction of the retreating troops.

The wall towers along the avenue on the west side of the compound were now under fire from two directions: from the commandos on the northeast wall, who had taken the towers on that side, and from dozens of cadets, who had now arrived and positioned themselves among the buildings on the other side of the avenue. One by one the defenders surrendered, and the fire of those who continued to resist dwindled to single shots as their ammunition ran low.

Campos now arrived with the bulk of his regiment, and directed an infantryman to fire a rifle grenade through an upper window of the barracks where the rest of the "Ingavi" was still holding out. As the smoke grenade detonated, Campos picked up a bullhorn and called across the parade ground, "Throw down your weapons and come out, or the next ones will be high explosives, and we'll bring you the mortars." There was silence for a moment across the bare field, where the harsh spotlights on the walls cast eerie shadows. Then the silence was broken by shouted words, then a shot, then another. In ones and twos at first, then in larger clusters, infantrymen began to emerge from the barracks with their hands held high. The men from the "Colorados" and the cadets herded them into the motor pool area, while assault teams moved forward to check out the buildings.

It was then that Guerrero and Duarte arrived in an open jeep, with Kelly sitting in the back, shivering in an Army field jacket over her slight dress. Guerrero jumped from the vehicle before it came completely to a halt. "How goes the war?" he called to Campos, who was talking with some of his staff.

"All quiet here now. It looks like some of the officers wanted to hold out longer than their men did, and the men issued some less-than-honorable discharges of their own from the barrels of their guns. We've got the prisoners over there for now," Campos reported.

"How about casualties?" Guerrero asked.

"Other than yourself?" Campos grinned. "What did you do, walk in front of a bus?"

"There was a slight difference of opinion," Guerrero said. "Get on with it."

"Not too bad. About a dozen of my men, mostly wounded. A couple of yours over by the wall, and maybe one or two cadets. The 'Ingavi' took it a lot harder. We figure at least fifty killed alone, and over four hundred prisoners. It doesn't look like many, if any, got away."

"Good," Guerrero said solemnly. "Keep the prisoners under a minimum guard, and let the conscripts go as soon as it gets light. Have them change into civilian clothes, if they have them, and tell them that their military obligation has ended, permanently."

"You sure you want to do that?" Campos frowned. "Eighty percent of my men are conscripts, and they're not going to want to be far behind."

"We've already discussed that, Colonel," General Morales announced as he came striding up, accompanied by his small knot of men. Both Guerrero and Campos snapped to attention and saluted the older man. "Just follow the orders, and I'll leave it to you to keep control of your men. I don't really think they'll mind seeing that much less opposition in uniform for the moment. Now, what's the rest of the situation look like?"

"I've had reports from the Palacio Quemado," Campos continued, "the Chamber of Deputies, all of the police barracks, the radio and television stations and newspaper offices, the telephone exchange, and you know about the Ministry of Interior, of course," he added to Guerrero. "All of those have been taken without problems. No word yet from El Alto, but it will take them some time yet there anyway. I've dispatched half my effectives to back up your team on the highway, and as soon as we can get the 'Ingavi' APC gassed up and armed we'll send those up that way too, although they won't be able to do much to help against the 'Tarapaca' Cascavels.

"As for the American Embassy, Venegas' men have the place sealed off. We have no communication with the interior, but it looks like the Americans are holding out on the fourth through seventh floors, and the terrorists, or what's left of them, hold the bottom ones. Venegas' men really whittled them down, but the terrorists claim to have wired the building to blow. Maybe they're bluffing, and maybe they're not. Got a coin?" Campos shrugged his shoulders.

"General," Guerrero said, turning to Morales, "you'd better get over to the Palacio Quemado and prepare to make that statement we discussed before my little visit to the Ministry of Interior. I'll go with Campos up to the highway to help get ready to receive our visitors from Viacha." The general nodded, climbed into Campos' jeep, and sped off.

"Where's the president?" Guerrero asked after a short pause. Campos shrugged again.

One of Sergeant Robles' men hit the button that opened the heavy iron gates of the driveway entrance as two military police jeeps roared across the street from the MP battalion headquarters. Both jeeps were loaded with troops wearing flak jackets and carrying automatic rifles, and one mounted a .50-caliber machinegun. As soon as the jeeps cleared the gate the guards there closed the gate again and sprinted toward the residence to join them.

Inside the presidential residence an SSE bodyguard in civilian clothes saw the jeeps fishtail to a halt in front of the house and reached to draw the pistol from his rear waistband. His hand was seized behind him, however, and Robles shoved the barrel of his G-3 rifle into the man's ear.

"Let's go talk to the president," he hissed as he led the man toward Boca's office.

By this time the other MPs had entered the house and braced themselves on either side of the double doors leading to the study, where Boca had been working on a speech. "You open it," Robles ordered the bodyguard, stepping to the side as the man carefully turned the knob and pulled both doors outward.

The MPs glanced quickly into the room and then rushed inside, weapons at the ready, but there was no shooting. Boca sat behind his desk, stiffly erect, wearing the dark formal suit he usually wore on official occasions, with the red, yellow, and green presidential sash draped from his right shoulder to left hip.

"I've been expecting you," he said calmly. "I was talking with General Escobar at the Ministry of Defense on the phone, and the call was suddenly cut off. I assumed that this was the reason. I hope you men all know that you can be shot for what you are doing, whether you were ordered to or not," he added coldly.

"I didn't need any orders to do this," Robles growled, "just the opportunity. You're a disgrace to this office. How much money do they pay you, your friend Manco and his thugs?"

Boca flinched momentarily at the mention of the nickname of Benitez he had used so often and so obsequiously in this very building. He swallowed hard, then straightened again and said, "Well, you've got me. Now what are you going to do? Do you think that the other democratic nations are going to sit by and just let you overthrow a freely elected government based on your feeble charges? They'll know that if you care about corruption at all it's just that you weren't getting a cut. They'll stop all foreign aid. They'll withdraw their ambassadors. Your junta won't be able to borrow a dime anywhere in the world. Your government won't last a week." He smiled slyly at Robles' simple soldier face.

"That'll be for wiser heads than mine to figure out," Robles answered. "One thing's for certain, though. If you're still alive twenty-four hours from now it'll be because they didn't turn you over to me for handling. Now get the hell out of that chair and take off that sash so that we can send it out and have it fumigated." With that, he marched around the desk and pulled Boca from his seat, tearing the sash from his grasping hands.

A line of five large civilian cargo trucks sat in the gathering darkness alongside the dirt road that branched off the main La Paz–Oruro highway and ran parallel to the chain-link security fence of the El Alto

Airport. From his seat in the cab of one of the trucks, Lt. Agusto Martinez could see clearly the lights of the airport terminal building across the perfectly flat expanse of scrubland, over two kilometers wide, that separated him from the edge of the main runway and, beyond, the terminal itself. Past the civilian terminal and off to the left, he could also make out the hangars of the adjacent military airfield.

As the battalion's support group commander and an expert in engineering and demolition, Martinez relished his difficult assignment of disabling the entire airport complex, even though he only had one commando team of fourteen men, plus another ten men of his own 60mm mortar section, to accomplish it. If Martinez had had heavy artillery or aircraft at his disposal he could have shelled or bombed the airfields, but his unit's tiny mortar bombs would barely scratch the concrete, and his men could hardly stand about in the middle of the runways digging away with jackhammers to make craters that would make the runways unusable to any aircraft that might escape from Santa Cruz or fly there from here to load up with reinforcements for the units opposing the coup.

Martinez was aware that because of the thinness of the atmosphere at over thirteen thousand feet of altitude the runway of El Alto Airport was the longest in the world. Due to the lesser air friction the flaps of large aircraft had difficulty in slowing them on landing, and the same held true for takeoffs, as aircraft had to get an even longer running start in order to build sufficient speed and lift to get off the ground. He himself had experienced this, as had all other travellers passing through here. It always seemed that the pilot of a departing plane had decided to drive to his destination rather than fly, as the aircraft would bump along for an agonizingly long time before finally angling skyward.

In a sense, however, this made Martinez' task easier. He calculated that if he could crater the main runway at only two points, the adjacent taxiway at one, and the military airstrip at two more (to account for the shorter takeoff distances of most military aircraft), the field would effectively be out of action for the duration. The only problem was how he and his handful of men, without the benefit of heavy construction equipment, could make holes in the solid concrete of the runways big enough to prevent their repair during, say, a twenty-four-hour period.

Martinez was pleased with his solution. He and his men had commandeered the five civilian trucks and loaded their beds with high explosives. Fortunately, in a country with a large mining industry, explosives were relatively easy to come by for men with automatic weapons. Around and on top of the explosives they had piled sacks of potatoes, sand, rice, whatever they could find that would provide the necessary bulk and weight to direct the force of the explosion downward, through the chassis of the truck, thus turning each vehicle into a massive shaped charge. All that remained was to drive the vehicles to the designated spots on the runways and set off the charges. He calculated that the resulting craters would be over a meter deep and would extend nearly from one side of the runway to the other. As Martinez looked over to the young commando who was to drive the truck in which he sat now, he could see the man's knuckles turn white as his hands gripped the steering wheel, and Martinez wondered idly why anyone would be nervous about driving a truck loaded with explosives into what might turn out to be a serious firefight.

The rest of his force would deal with the aircraft themselves. One mortar team would take up a position near the main highway, from which they could work over the dozen or so aged cargo planes parked in the ramshackle hangars next to the civilian terminal. The other two mortar teams, plus about five commandos to provide cover, had already penetrated the perimeter wire and were moving into position near the air force base, in order to fire on the air force planes there and to provide cover for the two explosives trucks, Martinez' and one other, that would deal with the military airstrip. This would be the most ticklish part of the job. These trucks had the farthest to go and, as the vehicles reached the civilian terminal, the security troops there, who belonged to the air force, would undoubtedly open fire, thus alerting the men at the air base. With the small number of men available to him Martinez could only hope that there would be enough of a delay while the lowly airport guards checked with their superiors and wondered what was happening for his two vehicles to race the additional kilometer to their positions and to blow their charges.

Martinez raised his watch and saw the luminous second hand sweeping around to the twelve as the appointed time approached. He picked up his radio and gave three quick clicks on the transmitter button. It was answered a moment later by a single click followed by two more, as the two other sections acknowledged his transmission.

"Let's go," he told his driver, tapping him gently on the shoulder. The motor of the truck roared to life, and the vehicle jerked forward as the gears engaged. The other trucks, parked side by side, also moved out toward the distant airport lights, their own headlights extinguished. Martinez' truck reached the fence first and plowed through it without slowing. It was pitch dark now, and he was counting on the brightness of the airfield lights to blind the security guards there to what was happening out in the dark of the Altiplano.

The trucks bumped along at a brisk walking pace and soon reached the main runway without being discovered. The move had been timed so that no scheduled flights were due in or out, not hard to do in an airport as little frequented as El Alto, but Martinez was still worried about some private plane smashing into the side of one of his trucks before he was ready to spring his trap. The two trucks at opposite ends of the line peeled off to their positions on the runway and stopped, waiting for Martinez to get the other trucks into position.

The third truck pulled up on the taxiway and stopped as Martinez drove past it. This truck was clearly visible from the terminal, and as Martinez continued on, tearing through a second fence that separated the civilian and military airports, he could see two air force security policemen in their blue uniforms and white helmets walking curiously over from their guard post. A burst of fire from the truck's cab sent them scurrying for cover. Well, Martinez thought, that's done it. His driver involuntarily picked up speed.

The perimeter of the air base was rather more secure than that of the civilian airport, and there were twenty-foot guard towers every two or three hundred meters along the edge. However, because of the unpleasantness of the cold Altiplano nights and the eternal need of senior officers for the services of enlisted men as drivers, janitors, and cooks, only half of these towers were ever manned, and then not with very alert soldiers. Martinez' earlier reconnaissance had identified one of the vacant towers, and his two trucks stayed as close as possible to it. He saw a flash of gunfire from one of the flanking towers, but it was answered immediately by a burst of fire from somewhere in the darkness as one of the covering force commandos silenced it. Martinez could now see dark shapes running back and forth, silhouetted against the lights of the air base hangars ahead. He picked up his radio again and keyed the mike. "That's it. Detonate numbers one, two, and three. Mortars open fire."

He was answered almost immediately by a series of terrific explosions behind him as the trucks at the airport were blown by their crews, who had run spools of detonator wire to safe distances and had been awaiting his word. There were other explosions now as the single mortar began to lob rounds into the civilian cargo hangars, setting off secondary blasts of aviation fuel. Their only restriction was not to fire on the terminal itself, which was filled with passengers awaiting boarding on a Lloyd Aereo Boliviano Boeing 707 and an Eastern 727 parked on the apron. Martinez knew that his was essentially a back-up operation. Other than destroying the two A-37B Dragonfly fighter/trainer aircraft at the air base, his operation would have a major impact only if the teams in Santa Cruz failed to close that airport, something he thought rather unlikely. In any event, because of this, Martinez was determined to cause as little bloodshed among his fellow countrymen as possible. He regretted that he didn't have just a few more men, which would have permitted him to dispatch men to capture any sentries alive, thus limiting the losses even more, but he had to work with what he had.

In the shadows ahead of Martinez' bouncing trucks the two other mortar teams heard the detonation of the first truck bombs and dropped their first rounds down the tubes of their mortars. The weapons had been set up about fifty yards apart in some low scrub bushes just beyond the range of the floodlights around the hangars, and had been sighted in on the aircraft parked in front of them. Before the first rounds had impacted the gunners had dropped two more down each tube. As the bombs began to hit the gunners changed their aiming points to fresh targets, as their assistants passed them new rounds from the small pile next to each mortar. They had only about two dozen bombs per tube, what they and the handful of commandos now spread out to their flanks under cover could carry on their backs, although one innovative commando had bought a child's wagon from a boy they had met on the road and had used it to drag a few extra rounds as they crept through the bush to their firing positions. The single mortar crew at the civilian airfield had been able to drive to its position in a commandeered taxi and had plenty of ammunition on hand, but these men quickly fired off their remaining rounds, kicked the mortars into holes previously dug for them, and shovelled dirt on top of them. The now-useless tubes would be recovered later, if possible. The hangars and fuel tanks were ablaze already, and the mortar men took up their personal weapons and formed a skirmish line, firing occasionally to distract the confused defenders from Martinez and his trucks.

The two vehicles had angled away from each other, moving toward their positions on the runway, which was only about a hundred yards ahead, when there was a snarling, ripping noise and tongues of flame reached out into the shadows from the hangar area. A 20mm Oerlikon antiaircraft gun was firing blindly in the direction from which the attack seemed to be coming, using a flat trajectory about one meter above the ground. Suddenly, Martinez' truck was rocked by an explosion, and he could see flaming wreckage from his other truck raining down on the airfield, its charge set off by one of the Oerlikon's tracer rounds.

Martinez didn't have time to worry about the men in the other truck. His only thoughts were that his own vehicle was now plainly visible in the light of the burning wreck, and that the Oerlikon was still firing. His driver gunned the engine and the truck bounced onto the runway, but they were too near one end to accomplish their task. If only one crater was to be made, it would have to be near the middle of the runway, and the driver swung the wheel to the left, racing to get into position. Martinez was firing his assault rifle out his window, aware that at over five hundred meters range from a moving platform, he couldn't hope to hit anything. But he hoped that his firing coupled with that of his other men in the bush, who had all concentrated on the same target, might spoil the gunners' aim for just a few seconds more.

Then he saw a fresh stream of tracers mark out a line of red-and-yellow fire ahead of the truck, and they were heading straight for it! "Jump!" he screamed as he dove out of the cab. The driver did the same, and the truck continued rolling, but the wheel twisted by itself and the truck swerved sharply off the runway just as the antiaircraft gun found its mark. Martinez covered his head with his arms and pressed his body flat to the tarmac as he felt himself lifted off the ground and flung violently down again. It took a moment before he could breathe again, and he looked up cautiously. His driver lay a few yards away, a large chunk of the truck's engine block resting where his head should have been. A part of the chassis sat on the low berm at the edge of the runway, burning furiously, and by its light he could see a huge crater in the dirt. About four or five feet of runway paving had been ripped up by the blast, but there was still more than enough room for aircraft to land and take off. It would be up to the men in Santa Cruz to keep the "Manchego" Ranger Regiment out of the battle now.

Chapter Eighteen

Lieutenant Vasquez was grateful that sunset occurred so abruptly in the tropics as he examined the air force hangars in Santa Cruz through field glasses from a shallow ditch that ran just outside the chain-link perimeter fence. The hangars themselves and the tarmac around them were brightly lit, but the airstrip and the broad expanses of flat meadow that bordered it were plunged into even deeper darkness by the contrast. There was a makeshift watchtower about two hundred meters to his right and another three hundred meters to his left, but his team had had no trouble cutting the fence without being detected, and the fourteen men now lay spread out in the grass at the edge of the airstrip itself.

There was no way to the hangars without crossing the well-lit pavement, so Vasquez would wait for the several dozen Marines to open fire and storm the main entrance to the air base on the far side. With this distraction, most of his men should be able to rush in among the aircraft to do their dirty work, while others quickly dealt with the guards in the towers. Vasquez and a team of five men would have to see to disabling the airstrip itself.

At first blush this had not seemed like such a difficult task to Vasquez, but then he had begun to fear what a few armed men could do in the space of just a few moments to the group of men now rushing forward heading for the hangar buildings, laden with bags of grenades and explosives. When they had made a fair start, he turned to his own tasks with relief. Just then the battalion logistics officer, Ochoa, came up behind him with a group of eight or ten men, who were dressed in civilian clothes.

"Whatever you do, don't touch those four helicopters over there," Ochoa said, pointing to some large helicopters parked away from the others. "There's been a slight change in plans. When your men have finished, have them rally there, and we'll just fly out of here."

"You'd better get over there and see that someone doesn't toss a bomb at them then," Vasquez answered. "What's the plan?"

"Those are French Llama copters, the only ones around here capable of operating at high altitude. Once we're done here and all of the teams meet at the rally point, we have orders to fly three of the teams, plus some of the 'special passengers,' straight to La Paz, just in case the old man needs us there."

"You got it. Just get word to the other men," Vasquez replied, and Ochoa and the men with him scuttled off toward the copters, in a low crouch.

Once Ochoa had gone, Vasquez could check the progress of his other men. They had split up into two groups of four men each, starting at opposite ends of the line of hangars. In each group one man covered the other three with a light machinegun, and an occasional burst of fire was heard when the odd mechanic or ground crewman stumbled on the group and did not turn in headlong flight fast enough. The other men in each group ran from plane to plane, tossing in small, home-made pipe bombs prepared by the demolitions engineers with the battalion, each containing a small quantity of C-4 explosive and a detonator with a five-minute fuse. They tossed one into the cockpit or air intake of each aircraft, whether it was one of the air force's venerable Korean War-vintage F-86 Super Sabre jet fighters, a transport aircraft, or helicopter. As they progressed they shifted to devices with three-minute and then ninety-second fuses. These devices would not be enough to destroy the aircraft totally, but the damage to the engines or the cockpit controls would render them useless for days at least.

Once Vasquez saw that the hangar teams had made a good start, he dashed across to where some heavy construction equipment had been parked. Each of the men carried, besides his personal weapon, a small bag of gear and a twelve-liter can. Vasquez had noticed during his reconnaissance of the two Santa Cruz airfields that major construction work was underway at both. Here, at the military field, were parked a large bulldozer, a grader, and an earth-mover, and he had found men within the battalion who knew enough to get these metal monsters moving.

Vasquez hoisted himself into the cab of the giant earth-mover, next to the soldier whose father drove one for a living. The man adjusted some levers and pushed a button on the dash, and the engine coughed to life, as did those of the other two machines. Slowly, the man eased out another lever, and the earth mover began to roll forward as the engine roared. Their progress seemed agonizingly slow as they moved down the long runway, and Vasquez could see, although the racket of the engine drowned out the noise of the battle, that the Marines were being driven away from the base, and he knew that it would not take the security troops long to realize that they had been duped. Just then the first of the hangar explosives went off, blowing out the windshield of an Israeli-built Arava transport aircraft and starting a small fire in the cockpit. Then, at the other end of the flight line, an F-86 disappeared in a ball of flame, as the small explosive charge seemed to have touched off the fuel tanks. That would distract the guards for a while longer, Vasquez thought.

He looked over the rear of the earth-mover, which was now rumbling along at a brisk walking speed. He could see that the bulldozer was already in position, about three hundred meters from one end of the runway. Since it was the slowest of the vehicles it had been given the closest position. The two men on it had begun to pour the contents of their cans over the vehicle. Vasquez calculated that if they could permanently disable these huge hunks of metal at key points on the single runway it would close down take-off and landing operations even more effectively than the best cratering they could possibly achieve. As the construction equipment here and at the civilian airport at Viru Viru on the other side of town represented virtually all of the heavy plant in Santa Cruz at the time, there would be nothing available big enough to move the hulks out of the way for days. As he watched, he saw the thermite grenade explode and the bulldozer become engulfed in flames.

The grader had now pulled up even with the earth-mover, on the side away from the hangars, as they rolled down the runway in a race of tortoises. A bullet pinged off the front fender of the earth-mover in a shower of sparks, and Vasquez could see gun flashes now winking from beyond the hangars. The security guards were counterattacking. As plane after plane was hit by its explosion, the demolition teams, now finished with their task, opened a covering fire on the guards, buying Vasquez some more time.

As they reached midfield Vasquez signalled to the grader driver, who wheeled his vehicle, blocking the axis of the runway. Then the two men aboard the grader set about their work of sabotage. Vasquez leaned across the driver of the earth-mover and opened fire with his own weapon at the dark forms that began to appear off to his left, and which, terrifyingly, moved substantially faster than his lumbering vehicle. More bullets struck the earth-mover, but it kept rolling. Then the driver suddenly grabbed his neck, turned to Vasquez with wide eyes, and tumbled from the cab. Vasquez reached over and grabbed the wheel, pressing the gas pedal with the wrong foot, and made a silent prayer that the man had died quickly, before the giant wheels of the earth-mover crushed his body into the tarmac.

They were still several hundred meters from the end of the runway, but it would have to be good enough. Not knowing how to brake the thing, he cut the engine and skewed the wheel, nearly dumping himself out of the cab as the machine jackknifed in the middle of the runway, almost tipping over. When it had ground to a halt he quickly uncapped the driver's can of gasoline and turned it upside down on the seat, letting the liquid run all over the cab's floor. With his own can, his rifle slung over his back, he climbed up on top of the engine compartment, ducking low as the bullets continued to whistle past him, and began pouring out gasoline, while he furiously unscrewed the gas cap of the vehicle's own gas reservoir with one hand. Out of the corner of his eye he saw a glint of flame and instantly hurled himself off the machine, almost seven meters to the hard runway below.

The fire spread almost instantly, and he scrambled away on his bruised knees as fast as he could. Out of the darkness two figures emerged, and strong hands grasped him under his arms and propelled him away from the earth-mover just as it was consumed in a tower of flame and smoke. The three men threw themselves flat in the ditch along the edge of the runway, and it was not until Vasquez had recovered his breath that he realized that it had probably been the heat of the engine itself that had ignited the fuel too early; either that or a spark from a stray round. Either way, the earth-mover was now the third bonfire burning brightly on the runway, along with several lesser ones burning in the hangars. The commandos who had saved him helped him to his feet once more, and together they sprinted through the skirmish line set up by his other men to where Ochoa already had the rotors turning on the large helicopters.

The attack on the military airfield had been in progress only a few minutes when the "Manchego" Ranger Regiment received the alert. However, it had taken time to assemble the men, issue ammunition, and mount them on their trucks for the forty-five-minute ride to the airfield. The officers of the regiment had been chosen for their political reliability and their willingness to cooperate with the narcotics traffickers who had given the town of Montero, where the regiment was garrisoned, the nickname "the White City," a name that had nothing to do with the whitewashed walls of the smart homes of which it was justly proud. They took no time to obtain information about the nature of attack on the airfield, but from the fact that the television and radio stations had gone off the air about the same time they correctly assumed that a coup was in progress. They also correctly assumed that their proper place was at the airfield, to be in position to move by air to intervene wherever the army high command ordered.

Consequently, as soon as several deuce-and-a-half trucks had been loaded with troops assembled hodgepodge from various companies, several officers climbed into a jeep, formed them in column, and led the way out of the brightly lit compound toward the highway to Santa Cruz.

In the darkness of the grassy fields lining the road outside the main gate of the garrison a team of fourteen commandos lay hidden. They were armed only with their automatic rifles and two light machineguns in addition to four old American-made LAW antitank weapons of Vietnam War vintage. Since the team leader could not be certain if the single-shot weapons would fire after years of storage, he set them in pairs within a hundred meters of where the trucks would turn onto the hard surface road, the optimal range for the weapon and the point at which the trucks would have to slow down considerably. Each pair would fire at one of the lead trucks, one of the machineguns would take out the jeep, and the other weapons would work the rest of the column until he blew the whistle to signal their withdrawal.

The commandos watched as the gate barrier was raised and the jeep leaped forward, fishtailing in the gravel as it turned onto the road, then picking up speed. The trucks followed as best they could, their gears grinding in protest as the inexpert drivers urged them onward. As the first truck reached a cement milestone marker on the road there was a flash from the roadside grasses and a small rocket, trailing white smoke and fire, raced toward the engine griHe. Before it hit, a second rocket was fired and flew toward the truck, striking just above the fuel tank. As the two rockets exploded the entire truck was swallowed up in an orange-and-black fireball. Another rocket did similar damage to the second truck, and bullets were tearing through the tarps on the backs of the other trucks in the column.

When the first explosion hit, the lead jeep screeched to a halt, causing the machinegunner aiming at it to overshoot, but he quickly corrected and the four officers in the vehicle were torn to shreds before they could dismount. One of the LAWs had apparently misfired, but the two lead trucks were burning furiously and the others were stopped in their tracks. Men were leaping from them, some of them being caught by the murderously accurate small-arms fire as they were silhouetted against the bright lights of the base behind them. Other men were running from the base now, and a machinegun mounted in one of the base watchtowers was firing blindly into the darkness along the road. When the commando team leader had emptied two clips of his own into the column, he calmly took a metal whistle from his shirt pocket and blew a series of long, loud notes. His men began to fall back from the base by section, half of them moving back fifty yards and then providing cover for the remainder. In five minutes they had broken contact, re-formed at the rally point, and were jogging off to where their HUMMER vehicles were hidden.

Santa Cruz is a city with an air of wealth. Although the streets have been paved only since the late 1960s it has the look of a boom town. First it was a gathering place for the well-heeled cattle ranchers of the lowlands. They were followed by the oil boom of the early 1970s, as Bolivia's modest oil deposits, nearby, attracted considerable investment when the price of oil rose to forty dollars a barrel. By the time the price of oil began to drop cocaine had come into its own as the export of choice for the region, and a new breed of wealthy entrepreneur moved into town.

It was obvious there was money in town. There were none of the slums one would find surrounding a city of two hundred thousand elsewhere in Latin America. In fact, most of the city looked like an upscale residential neighborhood of Los Angeles. The houses were broad and spacious, unlike the cramped apartment rows in much of La Paz. They were not usually surrounded with the typical Latin American brick walls, but displayed their beauty to the passerby over low hedges or mere flower beds, as is more common in the United States. Even the brand new airport of Viru Viru was far fancier than the airport at La Paz and generally saw rather more international airline traffic.

The Soares house in Santa Cruz occupied a full city block, and it *was* surrounded by a ten-foot stone wall. It was a rambling Spanish colonial structure with a broad circular driveway and several outbuildings for servants' quarters and for the cars. There was a pool and tennis court out back, and its crowning feature was a four-story tower that rose above the two-story main house and looked out over the city. At the top of the tower was a small terrace, topped with a red tile roof, that was suitable for taking an after-dinner drink in the cool evening breezes above the treetops. Of course their house in Cochabamba was much larger, but this one served to give the family a place to stay when they came to Santa Cruz on business. Paolo Soares was here now for a series of meetings with Benitez and a number of other drug lords on a major joint shipment of cocaine to Europe using a new technique: dissolving the drug in solution and soaking cotton cloth in it, then shipping the cloth by container ship out of Argentina to Amsterdam. It sounded very promising.

The tower's terrace had the added advantage of providing a clear view of the whole grounds to the two guards posted there. Below them, video cameras maintained surveillance both outside and inside the walls of the compound, guards stood at the gate, and others patrolled the grounds with alert Dobermans.

The older of the two guards in the tower sat on the cool tile floor of the terrace, his back against the low wall, his Austrian assault rifle cradled in his lap, as his younger, bigger partner stood staring out into the night, eating fried chicken from a paper plate he held in his hand. Nighttime sentry duty was a job rather below what the older man had come to consider his due, but after his failure to prevent the fiasco with young Soares at the disco where the soldier was killed he was lucky the boss hadn't had him taken out for a ride in the jungle of the one-way variety. Of course he hadn't done anything wrong that night, but the man had long ago learned that justice isn't something someone in his line of work had any real right to expect out of life. If the young puppy hadn't gotten off in court, he was sure that the father's anger would have snuffed him like a candle, and his younger friend too.

All things considered, he really couldn't complain. He was forever grateful that things in Bolivia had never reached the point they had in Colombia during the big drug wars of the late 1980s. Sure, the mafia there had made some big scores, assassinating cops and judges by the dozen and even bombing the headquarters of the local equivalent of the FBI, with tremendous loss of life, but they had also had their losses.

He had read the press reports of the killings of some of the major drug bosses, usually accompanied by a dozen or more of their bodyguards, with none taken prisoner, and it made the hairs stand up on the back of his neck. Here all they had to worry about was an occasional raid by some competing trafficker, and right now most of the major hitters were working in very close harmony. Naturally, you sometimes saw some Young Turk trying to carve out a piece of turf for himself, but they didn't often have the muscle to pose a real threat. Of course the only risk presented by the police was knowing beforehand where and when the police would run an operation, and being somewhere else at the time. Soares himself never touched an ounce of coke, so no one could ever pin anything on him. Thus the defenses of the house were a matter of simple prudence, not outright necessity. The guard's hours were easy, his pay generous. Life was good.

The older man was about to stand up to stretch his legs when his partner turned toward him with his eyes showing their whites all the way around. He was making a hacking noise, and the older man thought for a moment that he was choking on a chicken bone and reached toward him to help. Then he saw the younger man's fingers groping feebly at the shaft of a crossbow quarrel protruding from his neck about an inch. A thin trickle of dark blood ran from the hole down onto the man's bright yellow guayabera shirt. He dropped stiffly to his knees and then toppled over through the hole in the floor where the stairs came up from below.

The older man was frozen in terror. Then he heard an explosion and peeked over the lip of the wall. A gaping hole had been blown in the compound wall and dark shapes were racing through it. He could see gun flashes as the attackers shot out the surveillance cameras and cut down the patrolling guards and their dogs. This wasn't the police, the man thought. There was no reason. And it wasn't another trafficker. These guys were too good. He assumed that it was Guerrero's commandos, come to exact their personal revenge for the death of that young officer. He raised his rifle but then stopped. He had a wife and family. If he just minded his own business it was likely the soldiers would assume that his late partner was the only man up in the tower, and they would hardly bother to climb the stairs to find out. He sank back down to the floor, aimed his rifle at the rafters of the roof overhead and let off a long burst, just so his gun would not be unfired if he had to explain things later to his employers and had to prove his contribution to the battle. Then he lay his gun down and remained very, very still.

Down below, the commandos, backed by half a dozen Marines, had charged across the garden and into the main house. An overweight bodyguard came rushing out of one of the back bedrooms, a .357 magnum in his hand. One of the commandos cut him down with a burst of automatic fire, and they moved on to the large living room, where Soares stood calmly, his wife and a young daughter cowering at his feet, covering their ears with their hands and crying. One of the commandos produced a pair of handcuffs, spun Soares around roughly, and cinched them tight. With his wife still wailing and screaming abuse at the attackers, they led Soares out into the night.

When Vasquez' helicopter touched down at the reassembly point, several miles west of Santa Cruz' suburbs, he found the team from the civilian airport raid already there, trading stories with the two from the special assignment in town, who were standing guard over several civilian delivery vans they had commandeered. The battalion intelligence officer, Daniel Rivera, greeted Vasquez on his arrival.

"We've been monitoring the enemy radio transmissions," he shouted over the noise of the helicopter blades. "From the sound of it, you closed them down for good at the military field, and they say it will take days to clear the runway at Viru Viru. The team from Montero hit the Rangers hard too. We expect them here in about half an hour."

"What about casualties?" Vasquez asked, still shaken by the fact that his left shirt sleeve was soaked in the blood, already stiffening, of the man who had been driving the earth-mover. Vasquez had never been in combat before, and Lieutenant Morales' funeral was the closest he had really come to death in his life.

Rivera became suddenly much more serious. "The Marines lost four men killed and about a dozen wounded at the air force base, nearly half the men they took in. The TV station and radio transmitters were taken without a problem, and there was no shooting at all over at Viru Viru. After the security guards saw they were up against real troops they just went home. No word from the Montero team yet. And not a single man hurt on the special teams." Rivera smiled again. "It was just like the old man said it would be. When our men went in to capture the traffickers, they just weren't expecting it. They knew that the government didn't have any evidence on them, so the only thing they had to worry about was a hit by one of their competitors. Those big, beefy bodyguards they've got. They're good for breaking some kid's legs if he doesn't pay them what he owes them, and they can shoot up someone as he drives to church with his family, but they aren't shit against real infantry."

"I was a little worried," Vasquez said absently, looking at the delivery vans. "You know, all the stories you hear about them hiring Israeli mercenaries and all that."

"It was just like Coco said. They can do that for some offensive job, pay them a million dollars or something, but how can they hire a force like that, of any size, on a permanent basis? Even the traffickers would run out of money, or the mercenaries would get bored and kill them themselves and take over the operation. No, we ran into some shooting, of course. I took one of the teams myself, and this guy Benitez had a little army of former street kids who would fight to the death for him. In fact they did." Vasquez saw a cold, hard look come over Rivera's face as he said it. "But how often do those thugs go to the firing range, or clean their weapons? Where do they learn their small-unit tactics? We just snuck into his compound by cutting the power to the whole neighborhood. So much for his surveillance equipment until he could crank his generator up, and then it was too late. Once we opened up they just kept charging us. We must have killed twenty of them. When they were all dead, of course, Benitez just gave himself up, very peaceful and civilized."

The two men began to walk toward the vans. "You'll be especially pleased at seeing these other gentlemen who happened to be in town," Rivera teased, his hand on the door handle of the nearest van. He slid open the cargo door of the van. Among the dozen men hog-tied on the floor of the van, Vasquez could see several faces he had learned to recognize from the photographs that Captain Venegas had obtained for them before the operation. All were major narcotics traffickers, but Vasquez' gaze immediately focused on two of them. The elder of the two, with his bald head and scruffy beard, was Paolo Soares, and next to him, trembling and with tear-filled eyes, was his son Kiko.

"Get that one out here now!" Vasquez shouted, and two commandos standing near the van reached in and dragged the younger Soares from the vehicle, writhing and screaming.

"Hey, 'Nardo," Rivera stammered. "You know that the old man ordered them all brought up to La Paz unharmed."

"I'm the senior officer here, and I'll take responsibility," Vasquez said in a low voice. "Unless *you* want to try and stop me."

He turned toward Rivera, and Rivera shrank back from the look of black hatred in Vasquez' eyes.

"Gather around, men!" Vasquez called out, and the commandos clustered close to where the two officers were standing. "This . . . man killed Lieutenant Morales. The civilian court freed him. I want to hear the verdict of a court-martial."

The men crowded closer, calling for his blood. One of the men holding Kiko pulled his head back by the hair, and Kiko screamed again.

"Let my son go, and I'll make you all rich men!" a feeble voice called from inside the van. The commandos stopped for a moment and all turned to look at the older Soares, who was trying to raise himself on one elbow. "I mean it. A hundred thousand dollars for each of you, if you just let him live. . . . He's my son," the man said beseechingly after a short pause.

Several of the soldiers spat contemptuously on the ground, and they all turned their backs on the van.

"It seems the verdict has been delivered," Vasquez said grimly, cocking his automatic rifle and raising it to his shoulder. Then he turned away from the crowd of men, jerked his head toward the open field beyond and yelled to the guards, *"Pull!"*

The two men holding Soares hesitated a moment, and then ghoulish grins spread across their faces as they drew Soares back and then shoved him toward the open field. His scream was cut short by a rippling burst of rifle fire.

Ochoa walked over and touched Vasquez on the shoulder. "We have to go. These civilian helicopter pilots I rounded up were goosey enough about helping us more or less of their own free will, but all this shooting is making them nervous. I sent a fuel truck on up the road toward Cochabamba over two hours ago. We'll rendezvous with it later and top off the tanks to get us to La Paz. We've had a report over the radio that the 'Tarapaca' has started to roll, and the old man might need us."

"Let's go," Vasquez said calmly, loading a fresh magazine into his weapon. "I'm finished here."

It had only recently grown dark at the base of the "Calama" Armored Regiment in Patacamaya, about halfway between La Paz and Oruro, and two of the regimental staff officers were about to head off-base to share a few beers after a day's work. As they strolled past the barracks they saw a ragged double column of soldiers shuffling dejectedly toward the motor park, hauling heavy packs and escorted by a short, stocky captain.

"A little late for training, isn't it?" one of the officers called.

"These imbeciles have all shown deficiencies in their maintenance of the vehicles, so I'm going to take them on a little hike to clear their minds, and then we're going back to the motor park and see that the deficiencies are corrected," the escorting officer answered.

"Who's getting punished, them or you?" the other staff officer asked, and the two men walked off laughing. They had noticed that all of the men in the fatigue detail were of virtually pure Indian stock, and it was only fitting that Capt. Quispe Mamani, one of their own kind, spend a little of his free time trying to bring them up to twentieth-century standards. After all, he was one of the oldest captains in the army and his career certainly wasn't going anywhere, so putting in a few extra hours of work might actually impress someone and get him promoted. Although it probably wouldn't.

As the two officers rounded a corner, Quispe grinned. "Kiss my ass," he said in a stage whisper, and the men of his "fatigue detail" smiled and picked up the pace a bit.

Quispe had found only twenty men whom he could really trust, most of them coming from his home village on the Altiplano or nearby. He knew their families and they knew his. He had done his best to look out for them, and for their brothers before them, as they did their compulsory military service while the sons of the wealthier European-blooded families in the cities went off to college and managed to get out of the draft. Still, he had enough to crew three of the Austrian tank destroyers, mainly because, counting himself, he had only three qualified gunners for the 105mm high-velocity main guns, but he could also man two of the small four-wheeled Cadillac-Gage armored cars and still have four infantry to put in each of those to give him a little "meat" on the ground if he needed it.

It had all really been quite easy, once his old friend Guerrero had visited him with his plan. Quispe had had no trouble drawing live ammunition for the vehicles he wanted and the thermite grenades that stuffed the "punishment" backpacks his men now carried. After all, he was the regimental supply officer, a very unglamorous side of soldiering, the details of which the more dashing of his colleagues preferred to remain blissfully unaware of.

As his small column approached the rows of parked vehicles, one of the sentries came to a sleepy sort of attention and saluted languidly.

"We're going to be working on the vehicles for several hours at least," he said to the sentry. "Why don't you round up your partner out here and go back to the barracks for a little shut-eye. Just be sure you're back before midnight." At this news the sentry immediately snapped to attention again, executed a much sharper salute, and ran off to find his colleague, knowing that when facing an uneventful twelve-hour guard shift after a full day's work, having a few extra hours of sleep given as a present was not to be sneezed at. "And don't make me come looking for you!" Quispe shouted after the man for good measure. His men giggled quietly to themselves. They stood watching the two guards trot off toward the barracks for a moment, and then Quispe sent a couple of the men to run a quick check for other unwanted company while the rest of the group began to open their backpacks, remove the grenades, and lay them out on the ground.

Once the area had been checked and two lookouts posted, Quispe had the drivers of the vehicles he had chosen start the engines and move them off to one side, leaving the motors running. The other men ran from vehicle to vehicle, opening their engine compartment access panels. There were 33 of the tracked tank destroyers, really lightly armored tanks themselves, the most powerful weapons in the Bolivian inventory. There were also three other Cadillac-Gages and nine Swiss MOWAG armored cars, armed only with machineguns. Each of the men, including Quispe, who was not driving one of the selected vehicles grabbed up three or four of the AN-Ml4 TH3 incendiary grenades, pulled the pin on the first one, and placed it on top of the engine block of the nearest vehicle, moving quickly to the next vehicle and the next.

Before any of the men had finished his assigned number of vehicles the first grenades began to hiss and give off an intense white light as they ignited. With all of the grenades placed, Quispe and his men dashed toward the rumbling vehicles at the edge of the motor park. Inside each engine compartment the grenade quickly generated heat of 2200 degrees centigrade, which rapidly began to melt through the engine block, disintegrating the electrical wiring and igniting the oil.

As he stood in the turret of his Steyr SK-105 tank destroyer, Quispe could see that one of the grenades placed in a similar tank destroyer had been a dud. With a mild oath, he spoke into his headset mike, and his loader rammed a HEAT (high-explosive, antitank) round into the gun. He sighted carefully on the rear of the tank destroyer's chassis, checked to see that the loader was in his position, pressed back against the side of the turret, and fired. The gun recoiled sharply, spitting the expended shell casing on the turret floor. The round slammed into the parked vehicle with a loud bang.

In his office the regimental commander, Col. Alejandro Calderon, had seen the television stations go off the air one after another, and he had been unable to raise any radio stations but the local ones in Oruro. A young aide had then rushed in from the radio shack with a report of confused transmissions coming from the La Paz garrisons about attacks at the army headquarters and the El Alto airport. It had just dawned on Calderon that a coup was in progress when the sound of explosions from his own base began to shake the windows of his office.

He bounded out of the headquarters building, several staff officers and office workers at his heels. He could see the vehicles in the motor park burning hellishly, but not all of them. At first Calderon was relieved, and then he saw a tank destroyer, one of *his* tank destroyers, begin to pump high-explosive rounds into the aboveground reserve fuel tanks while another fired a round into the radio shack, blowing the structure to smithereens. Several other vehicles were raking the regiment's truck park with heavy-machinegun fire, causing some of the trucks to explode as their fuel tanks were hit.

He stood there helpless, trembling with rage, as the vehicles then formed a neat column and headed off toward the highway south to Oruro, tearing a gaping hole in his perimeter fence on the way.

Chapter Nineteen

Captain Venegas crouched behind a stone fountain in front of the La Paz City Hall, across the street from the American Embassy. It was fully dark now, and there had been no shooting at the embassy for several hours. He had heard the much heavier firing from the army headquarters finally die down, and had now received reports of the seizure of all of the key targets in La Paz. The coup was well and truly started, but that was almost a sideshow to him now. His problem was how to get the terrorists out of the American Embassy without them blowing the place to bits. Of course, thus far he had only their claim that they had the place wired to explode, and he was of the opinion that, as the terrorists' bus had gone up with such a tremendous bang most of their explosives had still been on board when it did. That was a huge assumption to make, however.

He had been in direct communication with the trapped Americans, who occupied the fourth through seventh floors of the building, by the simple expedient of hurling weighted bags with notes inside from the upper floors of an office building, located across a narrow alley from the back of the embassy, to the corresponding floor of the embassy itself, and he knew that they had about forty-five men and a dozen women there, none of them hurt and quite a few of them armed. He also knew that nearly a dozen policemen from his own antiterrorist unit had already been killed or seriously wounded, but he could add that they had eliminated at least that many terrorists. From the fragmentary and often contradictory reports of eyewitnesses, he guessed that there might be as many as two dozen terrorists alive inside the building, well armed with automatic weapons, but that they were blocked by the steel security door at the top of the stairwell to the fourth floor. The terrorists had given their list of demands by bullhorn from the third floor window and had given him until four hours from now to comply. The demands had included the release from jail in Bolivia of Murillo and several other lesser traffickers and in Peru of over fifty specified Sendero Luminoso members. They also wanted ten million dollars and a large bus to take them to the airport, where they wanted a jetliner to fly them to Cuba. It had been with great pleasure that Venegas had announced that there was a war on up at the airport and that the runway had been blown up, so that they would have to wait. The terrorists were still thinking about that one.

Venegas had concluded that if the terrorists just held on where they were, they probably did have enough explosives, if carefully placed, to bring the building down. However, if they made another serious attempt to assault the upper floors, that would mean that they didn't have the explosives. On the other hand, he thought, if they didn't assault, it might also mean that they were too weak, his men having definitely confirmed only five or six of them alive, or that they couldn't figure out how to get past the fourth floor and were playing their bomb bluff as the only card left to them. Shit! he concluded.

The darkness inside the embassy was broken only by the light of the few battery-powered emergency lamps that still functioned and by the pale light of the city, which filtered in through the shattered windows. Nunez watched impatiently as two of his men lay on their backs on a makeshift scaffolding comprised of three office desks stacked one on top of the next. They had removed the drop ceiling and placed explosive charges in a rough circle on the ceiling above. There was no light in the stairwell, the emergency lamp having fallen prey to a stray round or a grenade, but Nunez had already lost a man there as he tried to sneak up to place a charge on the door. Although Nunez suspected that the Americans were firing randomly at noises in the dark, he could not rule out the possibility that they had night vision devices.

Time was running out for Nunez. Sooner or later the police outside would try to call his bluff on the explosives in the building, and it wouldn't take them long to push past the few men he had assigned to cover the stairwell below. Because of the other buildings on the block, he couldn't even prevent the police from working their way up along the sides of the neighboring buildings right to the entrance itself. The only thing he had been able to do was to prevent the police from installing a cable-car affair from a neighboring building to the upper floors of the embassy, apparently with the intention of shuttling the Americans out or more police in. One of his men had fortunately seen the cable, and a few bursts of gunfire had dissuaded them from continuing. Nunez knew that with a little effort the police could have massed enough fire to cover such an operation. He had just been lucky that they had not tried, or perhaps they still really believed the bluff about the bomb.

In any case, he saw his men now clambering down from their work platform and running a set of wires across the office to a small storage room, from which they would touch off the blast. His plan was to blow a hole in the floor above, at the far end of the building, at the same time a couple of his men made a noisy demonstration at the staircase. He would launch his assault through the hole and, he hoped, catch at least some of the Americans from behind. From the information the Minister of Interior had provided, he knew that the security door to the fifth floor had been removed to permit repairs to its warped door frame, so he could gain two floors at least, and if the remaining Americans above delayed in sealing the door to the sixth floor while waiting for their rearguard he might be able to rush the whole distance.

As added insurance, once the assault started two of his men would pry open the elevator shaft door and haul themselves up the cables to the seventh floor. With the elevators right next to the stairwell, the Americans would undoubtedly hear them if they tried now, and would simply open their own doors and gun them down. In the confusion of the fighting, however, he might be able to introduce a shock force behind the defenders at the crucial moment. It was a long shot, but Nunez had no choice.

His demolitions man gave him the thumbs-up signal, and Nunez was about to order the charges blown when one of his other men called to him to wait. "I've rigged something which might be able to get us past this damned door," the man announced. He showed Nunez how he had affixed a charge of C-4 plastic explosive to the end of a broomstick. Without going all the way up to the door, staying mostly behind cover, he could press the charge against the lock of the door. It was worth a try, Nunez thought, and it would certainly help to keep the Americans' attention focused on the stairs.

All was in readiness. The men at the stairs had eased the small charge on the end of its pole up against the door and wedged it in place. A couple of random blasts of a shotgun through the firing slit, which hit no one, told Nunez that the Americans apparently didn't have night vision devices. The charge on the ceiling at the other end of the building was ready, and a dozen of his men were poised to scramble up over the piled desks if a breach were opened. Two other men braced themselves at the elevator doors, one with a crowbar, one with a fire ax.

Enrique Contreras sat on the floor, his back up against the small breastwork of desks and couches that had been constructed facing the stairway door. He, one other DEA man from his office, three of the Marines, and an NCO from the defense attache's office were the front-line guard. Featherstone had instituted a system of shifts in case the siege turned into an epic, and the rest of the armed men were mostly on the fifth floor, with the noncombatants huddling together somewhere up on the sixth. One of the Marines was poised at the firing slit with a Remington pump shotgun, while the other DEA man pressed the end of a stethoscope borrowed from the nurse's office against the door, listening for the faintest sound.

Suddenly there was a tremendous thunder in the room, and the DEA man and the Marine by the door were thrown backwards as the door sagged off its hinges. The DEA man was holding his ears and moaning. The other Marines and Contreras opened fire into the darkness of the stairwell, from which wild yells and bursts of automatic weapons fire were coming. At the same moment another blast shook the building from somewhere behind them, but men were now coming up the stairs, firing, and Contreras was fully occupied. The NCO raced back through the shadowy offices to investigate, armed with a hunting rifle. There was a flurry of firing, and he reappeared an instant later, without the rifle and holding his bleeding arm.

"They're comin' up through the fucking floor," he shouted over the din. "Run for it!"

That was enough for Contreras. He and the other men formed a tight knot as they backed around the corner toward the stairs to the fifth floor. Contreras was holding his .357 with both hands, firing at the dark shadows that darted among the scattered office furniture. The other DEA man was at his side, firing his automatic with one hand and still holding his ear with the other. A gun flashed in the gloom and a trail of dark splotches appeared across the man's white shirt. He groaned and doubled over.

"Get going! Up the stairs!" Contreras shouted, and the men rushed upward, Contreras pausing to fire off his last couple of rounds. Then he, too, turned and ran, bullets chipping off plaster from the corner of the wall next to him. At the top of the stairs he tumbled over another low barricade of desks where a couple of Marines and a CIA man lay in ambush for his pursuers. "Give them a volley," he said. "Then bug out to the sixth floor. They'll make mincemeat of you with grenades without a door to protect you." Contreras continued up the stairs, reloading his gun as he went.

In the street, Venegas was distracted from the radio report he was making to Guerrero by the sound of explosions and gunfire coming from within the embassy. "This is it!" he screamed. "There are *no* explosives. Attack! Let's go!" He grabbed up his own submachinegun and charged across the street himself.

Several of his men had been braced against the wall of the embassy on each side of the entrance. At Venegas' words, two of them armed grenades and pitched them through the door, rushing in as soon as they had exploded, firing furiously. In the Banco Nacional building diagonally across from the embassy a police sniper peered through his telescopic sight and saw the figure of a man on the second floor of the embassy, aiming a weapon over the stair's bannister. The sniper fired, and the figure in the embassy jerked and fell from view.

The terrorist almost landed on top of Venegas, who leaped over the crumpled body and kept climbing. His mind was working as fast as his legs. If the terrorists were attacking the Americans, then it was because they hoped to get physical control of them. If he and his men moved fast enough he could avoid another stand-off with the terrorists and finish with them once and for all.

As he ran his eyes swept from side to side, looking for strange packages or telltale wires, but all he saw were bodies, lots of them. He saw young Villarroel lying dead on the first landing, but he also saw that he had taken at least half a dozen of the attackers with him.

"Grenade!" someone ahead of him yelled, and a round object bounced down the stairs past him. Venegas stared at it with wide eyes as one of his men caught it with his free hand and almost casually pitched it into the little alcove under the curve of the stairs in the ground floor lobby before diving for the ground. There was a sharp explosion, but the policemen were out into the reception area now. There were more bodies here, including those of Lopez and Ruiz, and his point men were engaged in a hot fire-fight with a couple of terrorists who were holed up in a corner office. Venegas pulled a concussion grenade from his jacket pocket and hurled it into the room. His men charged in behind it, firing from the hip. Their blood was up and there was no stopping them now.

Up on the sixth floor, the women and the handful of wounded had been crowded into Ambassador Pearson's office at the farthest point from the stairwell. Lieutenant Colonel Polsby and the last of the defenders from the fifth floor had just come through the last security door on the stairs, dragging with them the body of one of the Marines. The door was slammed and barred behind them.

"The police are storming the building," Featherstone said as Polsby leaned heavily against the wall. "I saw them from the window. If we can just hold them here for a few more minutes it'll be all over."

"I don't know, Coach," Polsby sighed. "They're coming fast. I think we got one or two on the fifth floor, but they just plastered us with grenades and automatic fire. We just couldn't fight them toe to toe. This door doesn't even have a firing slit, so whenever they get a charge wired they'll blow it, and then all we'll have is the central hall leading to the ambassador's office and the other offices feeding off the hall."

"That may be time enough, Andy," Featherstone said. "That corridor is nearly fifty yards long, and we've set up a little desk fort at the far end. I've hung drapes from the ceiling to within about two feet of the floor, so the only way they can toss grenades is by skittering them along the rug. They won't be able to reach us that way without coming down the hall, and they won't do that without thinking about it. I've also put a couple of men in each of three of the offices at random. If the terrorists don't stop to check out each office they'll get hit from behind as well. If they try to do all of the offices, that'll hold them in our field of fire in the corridor all the longer. Actually, this is Tom Evans' plan. I'm just the administrator."

"You're doing pretty well for an amateur," Polsby said, smiling.

Just as he said this the elevator doors, which the two were facing, popped open. The next few seconds, or minutes, Featherstone was never sure which, passed as if in slow motion. There were two terrorists in the elevator shaft, dangling by ropes tied around their waists, rigged to the overhead braces of the shaft above. Both held submachineguns and were grinning. At the same instant there was an explosion and the security door buckled and flew open, and more terrorists could be seen below, charging up the stairs.

Featherstone saw the two Marines to his right yelling and firing their shotguns into the stairwell. Polsby was also yelling something as he brought the long barrel of his hunting rifle up level, but he lurched backward, grabbing his shoulder, before he could fire. When Featherstone looked forward again, his own .45 was already pointing at the terrorists in the elevator shaft and his brain was calmly reminding him, like one of those recorded voices at the airport that tell you "the white zone is for the immediate loading and unloading of passengers only," that he should make sure the safety was off. It was, and the next thing he knew the face of one of the terrorists had disappeared in a burst of red pulp. The other terrorist was firing, and Featherstone felt a strange, cold-burning sensation in his left leg, but he kept firing, aiming for mid-torso as he had been taught when he accompanied the Marines for pistol practice on occasion.

When Gunny Hanks grabbed his arm and began to drag Featherstone down the hall it was almost as if he were waking from a dream. He came to quickly and began to move under his own power. He turned to see one of the CIA men blazing away with two pistols at the entrance of the small reception room where the elevators and stairwell were. Then a burst of automatic weapons fire caught the CIA man in the chest and hurled him against the corridor wall. Featherstone dove head-first over the desk barricade and lay panting on the floor of the ambassador's secretary's office.

Nunez leaned on the wall next to the sixth-floor elevators, gasping for air. Despite his long service in the Andes of Peru, he was still unaccustomed to this altitude, and fighting his way up several flights of stairs had worn him out. He could see his two men twisting slowly as they hung dead in the elevator shaft, and he could count only six men with him now. From the sound of firing below it was apparent that the two or three men of his rear guard weren't more than a floor behind him, with the police hot on their heels. If he was going to do something it would have to be now.

He had seen the drapes in the hallway and had cursed, as they took away his one significant advantage over the Americans, his hand grenades. He had his men load full magazines in their weapons and prepare for the final assault. He and another man pitched grenades as far as they could down the corridor, one fragmentation, the other smoke. When they exploded the seven men charged, doubled almost in half to pass under the curtains and firing as they went.

Nunez had just cleared the last curtain and was about to pull the pin on another grenade when he saw a dozen shotgun barrels appear over the top of the ridiculous fortress of desks and chairs, spitting fire. His legs went out from under him and another of his men crashed down on top of him, dead. Then doors along the hall were thrown open and there was more shooting behind him. His men were caught in a death trap. He struggled to free his weapon from under the body of the man on top of him, but then he felt the cold pressure of a gun barrel against his forehead.

A red-haired Marine in a fancy uniform was scowling at him from above. "Hi," was all he said.

Venegas' men overwhelmed the last terrorists on the fifth floor, and he led the way to the last level himself. There was no more shooting, and he peered into the reception area. There was a dead American in what appeared to be green uniform pants and shirt. An officer probably. There was another one in civilian clothes in the hall to the right. There were also several dead terrorists on the stairs and two in the elevator shaft. When had the Americans had the time to hang them? he wondered. Another of his men took the lead and peeked into the hallway.

"My God!" the man exclaimed. "Look at this!"

Venegas called ahead that it was the police and received permission to advance and be recognized. He moved down the hallway, pushing aside the shredded and bloodstained curtains, stepping over the tangle of terrorist bodies in the middle of the hallway. He smiled and shook the hands of the very relieved and very proud Marines and other embassy men, their faces blackened with smoke and their weapons still in their hands.

A tall, middle-aged American with graying hair and a neat beard was leaning up against one wall, his left pant leg darkened with blood. An attractive blonde woman was helping to hold the man up, a warm smile on her face. Venegas could tell at a glance that this was the man in charge. As Venegas approached, his hand outstretched, another man suddenly came striding out of the office beyond them. This man was wearing a nicely tailored and very clean suit. His hair was carefully combed. Venegas recognized him from his pictures in the newspapers.

"Ambassador Pearson, at your service, sir," the man said as he brushed past the man and woman, almost knocking them down. "I welcome you and your men to the American Embassy, and I thank you on behalf of my government for the blood you have shed in our defense." He grabbed Venegas' hand in a two-fisted handshake. "Of course, as you can see," he continued, making a sweeping gesture with his arm, "I think we had matters pretty well in hand ourselves." Pearson laughed alone at his own wit.

Featherstone squeezed Ann's shoulders and turned to look at Enrique Contreras, who was sitting on the secretary's desk, wrapping a wounded hand in a bandage. Contreras smiled benignly, made a fist with his good hand, and made an in-and-out pumping motion at waist level.

Chapter Twenty

Electrical power had been restored to the embassy quickly, but it was nearly midnight before someone in the ambassador's office called out that there was an announcement being broadcast on the television. Pearson was seated at his desk, and the other members of the embassy staff, those who had not been taken to the hospital for their wounds, filtered in and either sat on the floor or leaned against the walls, most of the furniture in the office having been pressed into service for the barricades outside.

After a few minutes of martial music and the Bolivian national anthem, there appeared a view of a conference table at which were seated three military officers. General Morales and Admiral Barco were readily identifiable, and, after some discussion among the defense attache office staff and Tom Evans' people, it was determined that the young, unknown, air force colonel had been pressed into service to sit on the triumvirate to present the image of total unity of the armed forces. Evans remarked that since Morales was in the center, where the microphone was, he was probably the force behind the coup.

Morales cleared his throat and spoke, reading in part from a stack of papers in front of him. "My Bolivian brothers and sisters," he began, "I speak to you as the head of the military junta which has just taken power in a coup. We of the armed forces regret that this move has been necessary, but we could no longer sit idly by while our country was being destroyed by evil interests. Our movement has taken control of the capital and most of the rest of the nation, although there are still some isolated pockets of opposition. We call upon those Bolivians who are in arms against us to join us in our holy task."

Tom Evans had begun a running commentary on the speech. "This is pretty standard. The translation is that they're holding on by their teeth in La Paz, and they're hoping that the breakdown in communications will let them convince other units around the country that the game is up and get them to come over. That would start a sort of bandwagon process and eventually reunite the military. It's been done before . . . usually works, too."

"Because of the fighting which may continue, a dusk-to-dawn curfew has been placed in effect . . ."

"This too is standard," Evans broke in. "At the first outbreak of firing everyone in town is glued to their TVs or transistor radios, like people planning a picnic listening for the weather report. Of course, only a fool would go roaming around in the middle of a fire-fight, but the exact hours of the curfew are good to know."

". . . free elections will be held within six months from today in which all political parties will be able to participate."

"That's what they all say," Evans said. "Of course, sometimes they mean it."

"As of next week, the armed forces of Bolivia will cease to exist as a separate entity. . . ."

Now Evans and the others leaned forward with renewed interest. "This is definitely new stuff," he commented.

"It is time that we realized that Bolivia simply cannot afford to maintain a military establishment which would not provide any protection whatsoever against the armed forces of any of our neighbors. There is no reason to maintain a military force equipped with jet aircraft and armored vehicles which can only be used, and have only ever been used, against the Bolivian people themselves. For this reason, we will create a new self-defense force of between two and three thousand volunteers. All other military personnel will be released from duty. All conscripts currently in the armed forces will be released from duty starting Monday. The remainder of the defense budget will be turned over to the Ministry of Health and Social Welfare. As most military bases will no longer be needed, their installations will be converted into low-cost housing and schools, and their lands will be turned over to neighboring agricultural cooperatives."

"Now this is dynamite!" Evans declared, slapping his knee. "They did this in Costa Rica back in 1948," he explained for the benefit of Pearson, whose ignorance of Latin American history was nearly perfect. "Just did away with the army altogether. That might have something to do with the fact that Costa Rica has the only working democracy in a region plagued with coups, revolution, and civil war. It's a neat trick—if you can pull it off," he added.

"While we will continue to welcome the support offered us by other nations in our fight against the narcotics traffickers who have been undermining the social fabric of our society, there will be no more extraditions of any individuals found guilty of violating Bolivian laws until they have served their sentences here."

"There it is!" Pearson announced triumphantly. "It's a trafficker coup if I ever heard one!" He uncharacteristically stopped talking when Evans shushed him curtly.

". . . however, the new Bolivian law will be that any conviction of involvement in drug trafficking will require the immediate imposition of the death penalty. This crime will include possession of more than one kilogram of cocaine hydrochloride or its equivalent, the possession of equipment or chemicals used for the preparation of narcotics, or the possession of funds connected with the narcotics trade. Cases of this type will be tried by a self-defense-force tribunal supervised by Supreme Court Justice Linares. This law will apply equally to Bolivians and to foreigners on our soil. It should also be noted that all of the property and assets of anyone guilty of such crimes will immediately be confiscated and become the property of the state." The studio shot faded to a standard picture of the Bolivian flag, accompanied by the national anthem.

"Doesn't sound so much like a trafficker coup now, I guess," Evans commented without turning away from the screen.

"I'm still not convinced," Pearson grumbled. "I'm still half of a mind that this entire terrorist thing was put up by the men behind the coup, by the traffickers themselves."

"I really don't think that's the case," Evans said. "I suppose I should tell you now that just before the police dragged that terrorist character, Nunez, off to the clink, I found this in his shirt pocket." Evans pulled a wrinkled piece of paper from his own shirt pocket and waved it in the air. "It identifies the bearer as being on a special mission for Minister of Interior Huerta and encourages any member of the police or military to extend him every courtesy. I'm not exactly a graphologist, but I would be willing to bet a lot of money that this is Huerta's signature. Of course, we'll send a copy to Washington to have the experts make sure."

"This might also help convince you," Contreras said, walking in escorting a young woman by the arm. Her short brown hair was a tangled mess, and over her scandalously short dress she wore a Bolivian Army field jacket. Her eyes were red-rimmed. "This is Miss Kelly Slater, and she was a 'guest' of the Ministry of Interior late yesterday afternoon—*before* the terrorist attack—and she heard our old nemesis at UMOPAR, Colonel Venetti, talking about what the terrorists were going to do with us."

Pearson stuck out his lower lip and slid further down in his chair. Suddenly his eyes brightened and he nearly leapt out of the chair. "So now we're going to take the word of some snot-nosed hippie drug runner as the basis for U.S. government policy?" he shouted, waving an accusing finger in the direction of Kelly. "I really don't know what sort of ax you people have to grind, taking the side of these coup plotters against a democratically elected government, which, I might add, has been *very* cooperative in supporting *my* antinarcotics campaign."

Contreras kept his face expressionless and added, "The young lady would also appreciate being able to make a phone call to the States, to let her relatives know that she's all right."

Pearson laughed out loud. "Sure! Why not? And let's take her out to dinner while we're at it. That's what we're here for, isn't it?"

Pearson kept on grumbling, but turned his back to his audience, and was examining the damage to his office rug as Contreras continued, simply talking over the ambassador's complaints.

"Of course she would like to call her parents," he said, matter-of-factly, "but she would also like to make a call to Washington to talk to her uncle. I believe it's someone you might know, sir, from your visits there, Sen. Ogden Slater, Chairman of the Senate Appropriations Committee."

At the sound of the senator's name Pearson suddenly stopped talking, and by the time Contreras had finished his sentence, the ambassador had spun around, his former grimace replaced by an angelic smile.

"Certainly I know the senator," he beamed, reaching out and taking both of Kelly's trembling hands in his own soft, pink ones. "Why didn't someone tell me this earlier?" He glanced around with a look of mock displeasure on his face as if about to castigate some delinquent aide, but most of his staff was either already on the way to the hospital or busy treating the wounded who remained in the embassy. "Well, come right this way."

Pearson virtually dragged Kelly by the arm into his office and then perched cutely on the corner of his large desk, which was still in place, as he had refused to allow it to be used for the barricade in the hallway. He picked up the telephone receiver, listened for a moment, and tapped the cradle button several times before huffing and hanging up again.

"Oh, bother," he sighed. "I suppose the telephone lines were knocked out during the fighting." He leaned closer to Kelly and smiled in a confidential way. "You may have noticed that we have had quite a day of it ourselves here. But no matter, the ENTEL offices are only a block from here, and we can make the calls from there."

He sprang lightly off the desk and propelled Kelly quickly toward the door.

"I don't want to go back down those stairs," Kelly said, trying to pull her arm away from Pearson's grasp. "They're full of dead people."

"She's right," Contreras added. "Maybe I could go and make the calls, just to send the word that she's safe, and she can call herself later. Besides that, sir," he added, making the "sir" sound like a slap, "perhaps you'd rather stay here and look after your people."

"Nonsense," Pearson spat. "I'm sure that the local authorities and our own Admin people have the situation under control here and could spare me for a few moments."

Or the rest of your fucking life, Contreras thought.

"Now, you just trust me, my dear," Pearson oozed, turning to Kelly. "Everything will be just fine, you just lean on me."

With that, he whisked her off down the hallway. There they encountered Captain Venegas, who assured them that the facilities of ENTEL, the Bolivian National Telecommunications Corporation, were functioning and at their disposal, and the group continued on with Venegas leading the way and Contreras reluctantly bringing up the rear.

At the head of the stairs, Contreras could see that Pearson's confident expression was rapidly fading, along with his color. There was a tangle of bodies there, at least five, four of which were apparently terrorists and one a Marine, but the limbs were so intertwined and covered with blood that it was hard to tell for sure. They had to step carefully as they descended the stairs. Although the slippery liquid had largely drained away by now, its place had been taken by a thick layer of blood, and Contreras saw that Pearson was holding onto Kelly now more to support himself than to comfort her.

There were more bodies in the reception area, and Contreras recognized the solid face of Lt. Mario Lopez, with whom Contreras had gone shooting on more than one occasion at the police range, propped on his forearm as if he were merely taking a nap on the floor. Medical orderlies were already starting to clear the bodies from this floor, and he saw two men carefully lift a young woman in a dark blue police guard uniform onto a stretcher. Contreras reached over and gently closed her sightless eyes as he passed, and he noticed that her pistol was still firmly clenched in her cold fingers.

There were still more bodies on the stairway leading up to the first landing, although Contreras was gratified to see that all of these were apparently terrorists. When the small group finally reached the street entrance they found ambulances parked all around the building and firemen hosing down the smouldering remains of the terrorist bus across the way. As they exited the building Pearson lost his footing on the slick cobblestones and fell to his knees, but then he lost what remained of his self-control. He remained on all fours, retching into the gutter and sobbing. Kelly and Venegas finally got him back on his feet and the group continued on its way.

Contreras paused as two medics pushed a gurney past him. He thought at first that the man on it was dead. His clothing was shredded by grenade shrapnel and there were streaks of blood on his flak vest, but Sergeant Saavedra's eyes opened and he flashed a toothy grin at Contreras, whom he recognized from his occasional assignments backing up DEA raids in La Paz. Saavedra's hand lay limply across his chest, but he raised his thumb skyward and made a loose fist as the stretcher was loaded into a waiting ambulance. Contreras snapped a salute as the ambulance doors closed.

They crossed in front of the City Hall, unknowingly passing next to the car Nunez had driven to the scene, and walked past the church next door. As they did so, Contreras was amazed to watch the rapid transformation of Pearson. From a quivering mass of jelly a few moments before, he had quickly returned to his normal swaggering self. He stood straight and picked up the pace, and Contreras could see the color rapidly coming back to his cheeks. What a recovery, he thought. He found no new respect for the man, but he did have to recognize that Pearson had a reserve of energy that he could tap when the occasion called for it.

When they reached the ENTEL building Venegas quickly made the normally haughty employees there understand that they were dealing with someone of authority, and they virtually jumped to put Kelly's call through to the States. Kelly stepped into a glass booth when the call to her parents came through and Pearson stood guard outside the door, while Contreras and Venegas gratefully slumped onto a couch a few feet away. She spoke with her parents only for a few moments, making an obvious effort to control herself so as not to worry them, and then signalled that she was ready for the call to Washington.

Pearson now took an intense interest in the conversation and frequently opened the booth door to suggest a point Kelly should make to the senator. Contreras could see that Kelly was reaching her breaking point, as the senator was apparently plying her with questions. The tears were beginning to flow and her hand gestures in the air became more and more frantic. When she had finished Kelly opened the door of the booth and beckoned to Pearson, who confidently swung the door wide and entered, gently shoving Kelly out of the way and giving a smug smile in Contreras' direction. Great, Contreras thought. He's going to come out of this smelling like a rose and will probably get a hero's welcome back in Washington. He rolled his eyes skyward as soon as Pearson's back was turned.

The voice on the other end of the line was a little gravelly, but clear enough. Pearson recognized the folksy Midwestern accent he had heard on the television news often enough, and he instinctively put on his best "photo op" smile, even though he was only staring at a white acoustic board at the back of the booth.

"Ambassador Pearson," the voice began. "This is Ogden Slater, Kelly's uncle."

"Yes, sir, Senator Slater, and that's *Lance*, by the way," Pearson bubbled. "It's a great pleasure to hear from you, sir. And let me assure you that your niece is perfectly safe now and that I'm taking personal care to see that she gets home as quickly as possible. I suppose Kelly told you of the little spot of trouble we've been having here today." Pearson chuckled at his affected British understatement, the sort of thing he always imagined diplomats were supposed to say when under heavy hostile fire.

"Yes, she did—Lance," the senator continued. "Actually, we have been following your activities here in Washington for some time, although especially in the last dozen hours or so."

Pearson twisted around in the narrow booth and flashed another award-winning smile at Contreras, who just stared back blankly.

"That's what I wanted to talk to you about before I swung over to the White House," the senator said. Pearson could feel his chest swelling, and he began to run through his mind what sort of position he'd really be shooting for when he got home. He had rather thought the House or the Senate, but now he wondered whether a Cabinet job wouldn't be more appropriate. He'd certainly get plenty of exposure there and he wouldn't have to bother with the formality and cost of an election campaign. With someone like Senator Slater in his corner the Senate confirmation hearings would be a cakewalk. As he daydreamed, he realized suddenly that the senator was still talking.

". . . just wanted to clear up a couple of points."

"Yes, sir," Pearson gushed. "Fire away."

"As I understood Kelly," the senator said, "as much as twenty-four hours ago you received information that there would be a terrorist attack on the embassy today, with the collusion of the Boca administration—a report, I might add, that Kelly herself was able to confirm to me just now."

"Well, yes," Pearson began to sputter. "Of course, when there is political instability you get all sorts of reports, some of them pretty wild."

"And yet your only action," the senator continued, "was to turn around and inform the Boca administration itself, thereby having the source of the information thrown into prison and tortured."

"Well, I didn't—" Pearson couldn't think fast enough. He had been lulled into a false sense of security by the senator's drawling tone, which had tripped up more than one witness during his younger days as a trial lawyer. Now the rising volume and quickening pace of the words had Pearson's head spinning as he sought to justify his actions.

"And you even failed to inform Washington or to take any kind of security measures in the embassy, resulting in the deaths of a number of American citizens and Bolivian policemen, and if it hadn't been for this coup by this Guerrero fellow, we'd either be shipping your sorry butt home in a box or acknowledging the release of a major drug trafficker and cop killer. Is that about right, *Lance*?" He made Pearson's name sound like a gunshot.

"Well, sir," Pearson stammered, aware that he had only seconds to get his side of the story out before the well would be poisoned forever. "We thought that this was some sort of ploy by the coup plotters to cover their own tails and to throw mud at the Boca government—"

"Don't give me this *we* stuff, Mr. Ambassador," the senator cut in.

"This is *your* embassy and *your* decision. I've seen reporting from the CIA and DEA already which implies that they took the information at face value and sought to warn Washington through their own channels when you refused to send anything up here yourself. And it certainly looks like it *wasn't* set up by Guerrero at all, as what Kelly overheard in the prison proved."

"I certainly don't want to cast aspersions on Kelly's perception of things, Senator," Pearson whined, "but she's been under tremendous pressure, and I don't know if we can expect her to have understood everything that happened, considering what she was going through at the time."

"Bullshit!" the senator shouted. "You screwed up big time, and there's a ton of evidence to prove it, but you won't do it again. You may think you're lucky to be alive right now, but you may wonder about that in the near future. I suggest you go home and pack your bags, *Mr. Ambassador*," he said, as if the title were an insult. "I'm going to have a talk with the president before the hour's up, and I see no point in your waiting for the official cable ordering your recall. You may have raised a few bucks for the president's election campaign, but *I'm* the boy who has to sign off on the federal budget, so you can see who the president would rather kiss up to. And I wouldn't bother stopping back through Washington on your way home either. After I get through talking with the president I'm going to have an intimate little drink with half a dozen columnists I know, and when their stories hit the press tomorrow you won't be able to do lunch with the men's room attendant at the Greyhound Bus Depot."

Contreras saw Pearson wince, obviously as the other party hung up the phone. He had watched the color drain again from Pearson's face and the whites begin to show all around his eyes as the conversation had progressed. It did not appear that things were going the way the ambassador had imagined, but Contreras couldn't be sure, so he smiled inwardly and maintained the stone-faced mask he always wore when winning large sums of money from Evans and Featherstone at their monthly poker games.

When Pearson had hung up, he silently opened the door and walked alone out into the street. Contreras rose to follow him, for security's sake.

He turned to Venegas. "Please see that Miss Slater gets installed at a hotel for the night, Captain."

"I'll take her to the Libertador, it's close," Venegas said, touching the bill of his cap. "I've called my wife to come over and sit with her this evening."

"Thank you," Contreras said. Then, before leaving, he turned to Kelly and shook her hand in both of his. "And thank you very, very much, Miss Slater." She smiled briefly, and Contreras left pretty certain that she would be all right in time.

In his hospital room Featherstone had been watching Morales on the small portable television he had brought from his office at the embassy. He turned to Ann, who was busy making up a sort of bed on the floor next to his, using cushions from the couch in the hallway.

"I'm looking forward to hearing the congressmen scream when some American pilot or trafficker gets dragged out to the wall of some stockade and gunned down," Featherstone commented.

"I expect Amnesty International will have something to say about all this as well," Ann added, without looking up from her work.

"But it's not my problem anymore," Featherstone sighed. "You know that I'd sort of like to retire to Kansas or Missouri, somewhere as far as possible from an international border."

"Oh, yes, dear," Ann soothed. "And we can take all our meals at McDonald's and Kentucky Fried Chicken."

"Sounds good," Featherstone said, as the sedative the doctor had given him finally took effect and he drifted off to sleep.

Padre Tomas hung his head as the sound of rapid small-arms fire echoed in the empty nave of the Don Bosco church on the Prado. He knelt there, listening, counting off the objectives that were apparently being captured around the city. The heaviest firing had come from the direction of the Estado Mayor in Miraflores, the headquarters of the "Ingavi" Regiment, but there had also been the sound of firing from nearer at hand, probably the Ministry of Interior, he thought. He had been confused by the sound of much gunfire and many explosions from somewhere uptown, and he feared that it came from the Palacio Quemado and the Chamber of Deputies at Plaza Murillo. This would have meant that something was going very wrong and that the death toll from the coup would likely be much higher than anyone had imagined. He had been relieved when a news report coming over his transistor radio, the earpiece of which he had secured tightly in his ear, with the wire running discreetly inside his jacket, announced the terrorist attack on the American Embassy. Then he hastily crossed himself and prayed for the killing to end.

In his pocket he had an official-looking document signed by General Morales that would serve as a safe conduct pass, permitting him to circulate after curfew, but he was counting much more on his priest's collar to get him through military checkpoints that might well be manned by young conscripts with only a rudimentary reading ability. He crossed himself and walked out to the door leading to the Prado. He buttoned his jacket against the brisk night air and stepped out into the street.

Looking up and down the avenue he could see the headlights of one or two cars, probably officials but possibly adventurous souls or people who hadn't gotten the word. There were no buses or taxis, a sure sign of political unrest.

First he walked a block or so downhill to the Plaza del Estudiante, from which he could see the tall yellow facade of the Universidad Mayor de San Andres. There were some lights on inside and a few students clustered around the main entrance under a huge placard calling for less government interference in the school's curriculum. The school administration had long since ceased trying to remove the posters, signs, and murals that appeared overnight on all of the university's walls protesting American involvement in Central America, the price of milk, or some government action, and each new group now simply painted or pasted over the previous message with their own, although this sometimes led to fights between opposing student political factions, led by the usual forty-five-year-old political "youth wing" chiefs. Padre Tomas wished that they spent half the time on education that they did on politics here. But right now he was looking for something in particular, which was not there.

There were no troops occupying the university, and this was a good sign. Normally, when a military coup was launched against a civilian government, the university would be closed and many of the students arrested to avoid protests. The fact that this had not occurred implied that Guerrero was keeping his word, at least so far.

He continued past the university to the Ministry of Interior. There were police on guard as usual, but also some army troops, possibly cadets from the Academy, which told him that the place had been taken. A pair of military ambulances parked at the side entrance told him that there had been casualties, and he crossed himself again, but he could find little pity in his heart for the men who normally worked there. On more than one occasion in his many years in Bolivia he had talked, cajoled, bullied, and bluffed his way into that sinister building in search of news about some relative of one of his parishioners who had "disappeared" under one of Bolivia's military governments. While the Bolivian Ministry of Interior did not have the reputation of bloodthirstiness of its Argentine or Chilean counterparts, it was bad enough.

He had descended those steps into the basement of the ministry building and heard the screams of the prisoners under interrogation. He had even encountered familiar faces there among the torturers, men he had known from his visits to the Panoptico Prison, common criminals who had been released from jail to lend their expertise to one disreputable military regime or another. It had sickened him to attempt to befriend these animals, but his goal had been simply to lay eyes on as many prisoners as possible, to get their names, and to be able, later, to testify that he had seen them alive on such-and-such a date in the ministry building, to make it less likely that they would "disappear" forever. With brutal gallows humor, the guards had often shown him "his" room, which they were keeping ready for him, a dank, dark closet with chains attached to the wall and suspicious dark reddish stains on the floor and walls. Fortunately the Church still had enough influence in this Catholic country to keep him safe, but he knew that he would not have been the first priest to be eliminated as a "Communist agitator" in Latin America. He turned quickly and headed back up toward the center of town.

Padre Tomas was a little concerned at the lack of the traditional military checkpoints in the city, and he suspected that this was due to a severe shortage of manpower on the part of Guerrero's forces. He swung off the main avenue at Calle Colon and passed the American Embassy. He was pleased that the fighting had ceased there, but the evidence of heavy casualties appalled him. He paused to give the last rites to a woman who lay motionless on the sidewalk about twenty yards from the embassy entrance as policemen and medical personnel scurried around him tending to the living.

He finally continued uphill and passed the Plaza Murillo, where regular and military police stood guard at the Palacio Quemado as always, but a few words with one of the NCOs reassured him that at least this portion of the coup had gone off without a hitch. Padre Tomas had to rest a moment after the steep climb to the plaza. His lungs had been expanded by years of hiking up to the working-class districts in the upper rim of the valley, but he had never fully acclimatized to La Paz' 12,000 feet of altitude.

When he had caught his breath again he continued north, rejoining the main avenue above the Plaza San Francisco and gratefully accepting the offer of a ride in a military police jeep to a small factory at the edge of the highway to El Alto, where Guerrero had set up his combat command post. He entered without being challenged, and inside he found junior officers rushing about, orders being shouted, radios crackling, and general pandemonium reigning. Someone shoved a styrofoam cup of coffee into his hand without his asking, and he strolled over to where Guerrero leaned over a large factory worktable, where maps of La Paz and of Bolivia had been spread out.

Without looking up Guerrero began to talk to him. "So far, so good," he said.

"From the look of your face, I'd ask you to define 'good'," Padre Tomas interjected, gesturing with his cup to the angry bruises on Guerrero's cheek, jaw, and eyes.

"Oh, that," Guerrero said, absent mindedly touching his cheek and wincing at the pain. "Just an honest difference of opinion between me and someone in the Ministry of Interior. He said I wouldn't live until sundown, and I said that he wouldn't. I won."

Neither man smiled at this, and Guerrero went on. He pointed to the map of Bolivia. "The blue flags are the military posts which have openly declared for us." Padre Tomas could see only a small cluster of blue flags in the area of La Paz itself, and a few more scattered from Sucre south to the Paraguayan border, although a sublieutenant came and placed two more blue flags in Potosi as he watched. "The red ones are those which have openly opposed us, mainly the 'Manchego' Regiment in Santa Cruz, 'Lanza' up by the lake, and the 'Calama' and 'Tarapaca' up on the Altiplano. The white flags," he said, indicating the vast majority of the flags on the map, "are the ones which are just biding their time. We've pretty much blocked out the 'Manchego' and 'Lanza,' and I think the 'Calama' will be neutralized, so it will be what happens when the 'Tarapaca' comes boiling down the hill in the next few hours which will decide things. We hold the city now, but if they get by us here the tankers will take it back in a hot minute. Then it won't matter what the other army units around the country decide. They'll go with the winner."

"So what do you figure our chances are?" Padre Tomas asked.

"*Our* chances," Guerrero emphasized, smiling at the priest's apparent declaration of involvement, "are about fifty-fifty now. That's not very impressive, except that I would have only given us one chance in ten this afternoon."

"That's not the impression I got when you first talked to me about this venture," the priest said, lowering one eyelid in mock suspicion.

"So sue me?"

Chapter Twenty-one

In his office overlooking the parade ground of the "Tarapaca" Regiment Col. Darius O'Higgins was stamping around his desk as he and his staff officers watched the announcement on the small black-and-white television on his desk. "Fucking Communist!" he screamed. "That Morales has turned into a fucking Communist! He thinks he's going to disband the armed forces? Well he's going to have a hard time doing that with a 90mm main gun round up his ass!"

O'Higgins' staff knew that his Irish blood had been up ever since they had received the report of the destruction of the "Calama" vehicles and then the report that the Rangers couldn't get to La Paz before another twenty-four hours had passed, as they would have to come by truck. Then there had been the report that a column from the "Lanza" had been ambushed on the way in from Guaqui, apparently by a mixed force of Marines and naval commandos, and had turned tail and limped back to its barracks. It was not that there was any doubt in the room that the "Tarapaca" alone could drive right through to the Plaza Murillo and finish this rebellion in short order. O'Higgins was apparently mostly irritated that, while all the commanders of regiments stationed around La Paz received a regular stipend for their loyalty, he alone would have to pull the government's chestnuts out of the fire. The other officers assumed that O'Higgins would claim a very large bonus for his support once this was over.

Since their firepower would be adequate but no longer overwhelming without the support of the "Calama" and the "Lanza," O'Higgins' men had spent the hours since the first attacks on the airport and in the city preparing their vehicles and outlining a plan of advance that would emphasize their strengths, speed, and shock power.

They had a total of seventy-two armored vehicles, all in running order. These included twenty-four Brazilian six-wheeled Cascavel armored cars, each armed with a 90mm gun with a coaxially mounted machinegun, and another machinegun for the commander on top of the turret. There were also twenty-four Brazilian Urutu armored personnel carriers, similar to the Cascavels, but without turrets, equipped to carry thirteen infantrymen and the driver, with roof-mounted .50-caliber machineguns. To round out the force were twenty-four four-wheeled Swiss MOWAG and Cadillac-Gage V-100 armored cars, each bearing a small turret with one or two machineguns and each capable of carrying several infantrymen.

O'Higgins' plan called for the battalion of MOWAGs and V-100s to secure the El Alto airport and air base, although the raid earlier that night by some commandos had rendered both unserviceable for bringing in reinforcements. That group would cover the left flank of the regiment's advance down the highway into the city, just in case the Marines from Lake Titicaca decided to move in that direction. The main advance would be led by a company of eight Urutus, with their infantry mounted for rapid movement. They would move as quickly as possible until serious resistance was encountered. Then a company of Cascavels, which would be providing overwatching fire, would engage at long range. Another company each of Cascavels and Urutus would flank the roadblock, if the terrain permitted, or would contribute their firepower to overwhelming the obstacle in a direct assault. In this case the infantry would advance dismounted, to provide cover for the vehicles from crew-served antitank weapons. Unfortunately the regiment did not possess any mortars or artillery with which to fire either support rounds or smoke, and the vehicles would have to rely on their own on-board smoke grenade projectors to cover their movement. Still, it did not seem likely that anything the rebels could muster would be able to withstand such an assault. It was one thing to take troops in their barracks unawares. It was quite another to deal with a fully alerted enemy advancing in skirmish order over familiar terrain.

The remaining company of Cascavels and Urutus would be O'Higgins' reserve, but he immediately detached a platoon of each to capture the television and radio repeater station at the rim of El Alto. After the initial announcement by General Morales the television and radio had continued to broadcast and had run a series of interviews with various police and military officers discussing the involvement of the Boca administration with narcotics traffickers and how Boca had actually authorized the entry into Bolivia of Sendero Luminoso guerrillas to attack the American Embassy. Although he was confident that the rebel movement would be crushed within a few hours, there was no point permitting these broadcasts to undermine the morale of the rest of the armed forces and the nation.

On the side of the coup supporters, the defense of the single two-story building that housed the equipment of the repeater station had been assigned to Lieutenant Kolkowicz. As the "Tarapaca" had not yet attacked along the highway, and Guerrero had arrived to take personal command along with most of the "Colorados" regiment, Kolkowicz had been given a dozen policemen from the riot squad as reinforcements and had worked his way through the upper, working-class districts of the city to the station, where one of his teams was hastily constructing defenses.

Kolkowicz chose to center his defense within the building itself, as the attackers would likely avoid using heavy weapons in hope of capturing the equipment intact. If the defense was overrun he would want to be close at hand to be able to destroy that equipment to prevent the enemy from broadcasting their own propaganda. The men had worked hard filling sandbags, with which they constructed protected firing positions on both floors, and they had laid out routes of retreat from the most exposed positions back to the interior stairs to the second floor. The biggest reinforcement that Kolkowicz brought with him, however, was a pair of LAW-80 antitank missiles, the only weapons the defenders had that were capable of penetrating the armor of the "Tarapaca" vehicles.

It was nearly two o'clock Saturday morning when the rumble of engines was first heard in the crisp night air. The six vehicles emerged from among the low brick buildings of the working-class residential area bordering the station with all headlights blazing and formed an arc just beyond the simple chain-link fence that was the station's only normal security measure. The floodlights around the station were shining, but none shone within the station itself, and the commander of the task force suspected for a moment that the rebels had abandoned the position at his approach. He shouted an order to his driver over his intercom set and his Cascavel lurched forward, ripping through the fence like tissue paper. A second Cascavel followed, and the Urutus began to disgorge their infantrymen to take possession of the place.

The task force commander heard what sounded like a rifle shot, along with a distinct ping on the side of his turret. If the fools thought they could stop him with rifle fire, they were badly mistaken. He dropped down inside the turret and slammed the hatch shut. Suddenly there was a flash off to his right, and another off to his left. The LAW-80 missiles streaked at the exposed flanks of the two Cascavels, both striking just above the turret ring. As the projectile was designed to defeat the frontal armor of modern Soviet tanks it had little trouble penetrating the aluminum-alloy armor of the Cascavels, sending a shower of red-hot metal into the turrets and igniting rounds of ammunition in the ready racks. Both vehicles exploded seconds later and burned brightly.

At the same time, the commandos and policemen inside the building opened up a murderous fire with automatic weapons and shotguns at the dismounted infantrymen now silhouetted against the headlights of their vehicles, thus covering the withdrawal of Kolkowicz's two antitank teams, which had fired from shallow foxholes off to the sides of the expected route of advance of the enemy.

The surviving vehicles retreated hurriedly, and one of the Urutus plowed into the side of a small building and became entangled in the rubble. The driver immediately abandoned the vehicle, its engine still running. The commander of the third Cascavel decided that he had better return to O'Higgins' command post and obtain fresh orders for this situation. It did not occur to him to use his radio.

From their first defensive position at the hairpin turn in the airport highway, Guerrero and Campos surveyed the deployments of their troops. With one commando team away facing the "Lanza," another at the repeater station, and a third busy rounding up traffickers in the city, Guerrero had a total of seven teams, plus his support group, and distributed among these teams he had a total of about twenty LAW-80s. He assigned one team with two LAW-80 crews and about 150 Academy cadets to Duarte, to reinforce the single team Kolkowicz had sent to cover the old airport road, in case the "Tarapaca" chose that route. Keeping a single team as a reserve, he deployed three teams in a rough arc around the hairpin turn, giving them a series of flank shot opportunities against any advancing force. The position was given depth by the presence of over three hundred men of the "Colorados," who were dug in in shallow trenches just off the highway and who had fortified several houses that had good fields of fire. They also had a number of M-113 armored personnel carriers taken from the "Ingavi" parked behind low walls, to give them some added protection, but these were intended primarily as mobile machinegun positions and for the rapid redeployment of troops if a retreat should be necessary.

As an added measure Guerrero had sent one team about half a kilometer farther up the highway toward the toll booths at the rim of the plateau, where they had blown down a pedestrian overpass. The cement rubble would not stop a Cascavel or an Urutu, but it would stop any trucks the enemy might be using to transport additional infantry, and it would force an advancing column to deploy and slow down. This would give the "Colorados" ' only antitank units, two 90mm recoilless-rifle teams, perfect flank shots at stationary targets from their positions well up a gully that ran off to the right of the highway. These gun crews would be covered by another platoon of infantry from the "Colorados." Lastly, Guerrero had positioned his three 60mm mortars and the half dozen 81mm mortars of the "Colorados" well down the highway, below his defensive position, to permit them to fire in support along the length of the highway above, mainly to cover the withdrawal of the delaying-position forces and to keep the tankers buttoned up, as the mortars could not knock out an armored vehicle alone except with an almost impossible direct hit on a vulnerable point.

At about 2:30 in the morning a policeman sitting in his parked car, wedged well back into a narrow alley but with a view of a portion of the highway near the airport, clicked his radio transmitter three times. At Guerrero's command post the radio operator monitoring the policeman's frequency called to Guerrero and said simply, "They're coming."

Guerrero climbed to the roof of his headquarters by a rickety ladder propped against the back wall outside. He could see dark shapes under the bright yellow glare of the highway lights, moving slowly past the small, decorative archway that welcomes visitors to La Paz.

Joaquin Leon watched his miners climbing into the backs of the large dump trucks in the dark streets of Oruro. The short, swarthy men all wore their mining helmets, each with its small light attached to the front, and were bundled against the cold of the night. Most of them carried old Mauser rifles that they kept hidden under their beds for just such an occasion, and a couple of the trucks boasted ancient light machineguns mounted on top of their cabs, weapons captured from the army during the revolution of 1952.

Leon and several other union leaders had seen the announcement by General Morales on a television in a small workers' bar. While they were still skeptical, they had to admit that Guerrero certainly appeared to be living up to his word. Some of the men were sincerely enthusiastic about the new era that seemed to be dawning, but Leon was more realistic. For years he had watched as the power the eighty thousand tin miners had once wielded in Bolivian politics had gradually waned. Twenty years before the miners were the only source of foreign exchange for the country, and the threat of a strike could bring any government to its knees. Of course this power had also brought its risks, and more than once the miners had been brutally repressed by the army for their independence. That was why they were always armed, always organized. Any thought of the miners coming to town continued to terrorize the middle-class inhabitants of La Paz, although there was no living memory of them ever having done so to loot and rape. They had come to fight in '52, and they had actually defeated the army.

But the high cost of extracting Bolivian tin had made the industry uncompetitive with the other tin producers, such as Malaysia, and it had become a vast social welfare organization, with the country actually losing money on each kilo of tin produced. Nevertheless, the industry kept thousands of men gainfully employed, so the government continued to subsidize it. Still, the threat of a strike was hardly valid anymore.

The power of the miners had now been taken over by the cocaine industry and the thousands of campesinos who grew coca leaf. It was these agricultural unions, sponsored by the mafia, that could really put the people in the streets now to protest any plan by the American government to spray unregistered coca plantings. Coca leaf was still a legal crop, but everyone knew that the new growing areas in the Chapare and the tropical lowlands produced many times more coca than could ever be put into herbal tea or chewed by all the men, women, and children in Bolivia together. It was the political and economic power of the drug mafia that pushed Bolivian politics one way and then another, and Joaquin Leon resented it. He resented that his beloved miners had become marginal players in the great game, and he resented perhaps even more the fact that he had become marginal with them. If this Guerrero really could cripple the mafia, although no one really believed that he could eliminate it, the relative power of the miners would have to increase, and if the miners made a significant contribution to this revolution, that power would increase even more, especially if Guerrero and Morales carried through on their promise to disband most of the army. For that reason Leon had called the miners together as soon as word of the coup reached him, and he was now dispatching dozens of truckloads of them toward the city. He, meanwhile, would remain here in Oruro, where he could better coordinate the operation, and whence he could more easily escape across the border into Chile if things went wrong.

The leading Urutus rolled at a steady pace down the highway. The vehicle commanders stood out of their hatches, manning their machineguns and scanning constantly for some sign of opposition. One group on each side of the highway divider, they moved in a diamond pattern, with one vehicle in front, one on either side, and one farther back. The leading vehicles spotted the downed pedestrian crossing and paused while the following Cascavels took up positions from which they could cover this stretch of road with fire. Several of the Urutus disgorged their infantrymen through small doors in the left sides of their hulls and sent them forward to check the obstacle for mines. When the infantry were in position the Urutus rolled forward.

The first Urutu reached the barrier and approached it at an angle, its large tires climbing up on top of the broken cement like giant feet, first one, then the other, using the extensive vertical range of movement allowed by the walking-beam suspension of the axles, and bouncing down the other side. As the second was just clearing the barrier and the third starting to mount, one suddenly shuddered, then the other, and smoke began to pour from their sides even before the two sharp reports of the recoilless rifles were heard. At the same instant the entire area was swept with deadly small-arms fire from dozens of hidden riflemen, cutting down the infantry preparing to move on down the road. The Cascavels began to open fire with high-explosive rounds, targeting buildings at random, and the remaining Urutus began to discharge smoke grenades to cover themselves.

O'Higgins was screaming into the radio to continue the advance, and the Urutus jerked forward, their commanders now buttoned up and firing their machineguns wildly. A third was hit as it crossed the barrier, but the position of the recoilless rifles had now been spotted, and the "Tarapaca" infantry began to work up the gully to drive them off, although they suffered under the fire of the commandos and the "Colorados," firing from concealed positions.

Then, as suddenly as it had begun, the firing ceased. The first of the Urutus was well past the barrier, and the Cascavels had reached it, taking turns covering each other as they slowly crossed. The infantry began jogging down the two borders of the highway, moving from cover to cover.

O'Higgins had also seen the hairpin bend of the highway as the logical place to make a stand, and he ordered up another company of Urutus to move ahead of the Cascavels, which would stay well back on the uphill leg of the highway and provide covering fire for the infantry as they moved around the bend and down the lower leg. His men passed the burning hulks of the Urutus at the barrier and saw several bodies sprawled on the highway. This was not how coups were supposed to work. Gunning down students in the street was one thing, but this was serious.

The Urutus moved cautiously around the bend in the highway and infantrymen spread out a little on either side of the road, although they did not dare to go far enough actually to reach the defensive positions laid out by Guerrero. The Cascavels had taken the precaution of shooting out the yellow street lamps in this section of the highway, realizing that they served the defenders more than they served the attackers, so the scene was now lit only by a pale full moon and the first fingers of dawn rising beyond the ridge of mountains to the east.

Then over the rumbling of the vehicles' engines the attackers heard the distinct thunk of mortar rounds being fired in the near distance. First a white flare blossomed in the night sky and hung, dangling from its parachute, and the scene was bathed in an eerie white light. Then the flashes of mortar shells began to appear all along the highway. The infantry dove into the roadside ditches or climbed into the nearest Urutus for protection as the fingers of machinegun tracers began to stitch up and down the open roadway. The machineguns on the Urutus answered blindly, and the Cascavels moved up to the edge of the upper highway to fire into the buildings from which the machineguns were operating. Then there was a flash, then another and another, and several Cascavels were bathed in flames.

In a narrow foxhole just above the bend in the road Lieutenant Martinez pulled the end covers off of one of his precious LAW-80s, making sure that the sight assembly popped up to the correct position. He laid the large tube on his right shoulder and sighted carefully on the rear grille of a Cascavel that was firing its main gun over the rim of the highway at unseen targets on the lower stretch of the road. At 350 meters, Martinez was well within the range of the LAW-80, and he pressed the trigger delicately, sending a single tracer bullet into the grille to verify his aim. He saw the bullet strike and switched the selector to fire his missile. There was a blinding flash and the tube rocked slightly in his hands as the rocket motor pushed the projectile out of the tube. The next thing he saw was a shower of sparks and flame as the rear deck of the Cascavel erupted before him. He grinned and discarded the now-useless tube, picked up his rifle, and rolled to a new position.

The accompanying infantry tried to drive off the antitank teams and the machinegunners on the armored vehicles fought for their lives, but they were now outnumbered by the defending infantrymen, who returned their fire. Five of the Cascavels were burning on the highway, and the others were backing and twisting in an effort to get out of the kill zone of the ambush. Another company of Cascavels had moved up in support, but a lone stay-behind team with a LAW-80 hit one of them, and the surviving vehicles of the entire column beat a hasty retreat, scrambling back over the barrier and leaving their infantry to catch up as best they could.

O'Higgins watched the debacle and raged at the defenders' brutality and his own men's cowardice. He had also by now learned of the failure to take the repeater station, but he had decided that this would have to wait. If he could crush the rebellion the repeater station would fall of its own.

He grabbed the commander of the reserve company of Cascavels, down to six vehicles with the losses at the repeater station, and gave him his assignment. "You take the other company of Urutus with you and head down the old airport road. Don't stop for anything. If a vehicle is hit, drive around it or push it out of the way. Keep your infantry mounted and firing from their vision slits. Just keep every gun firing all the way down the hill, and don't stop until you get to Plaza Murillo."

"What about all the civilians, sir?" the young captain asked nervously. "You know that that is a heavily built-up area, mostly apartments and houses."

"I know that better than you, you idiot!" O'Higgins screamed. "You're going to have to decide whether you're a soldier or some sort of fucking social worker. If you want to win this battle, that's what you're ordered to do. Now, are you going or not?"

"Yes, sir," the young man stammered. He saluted, hauled himself up over the front glacis of his Cascavel, and led the column to its assembly area, where he would issue his final orders.

Half an hour later the column, led by three Cascavels with the Urutus and the remaining Cascavels following, moved off in the blue light of dawn down the "old" airport road. This was really a simple two-lane street, lined along its entire length with small businesses and apartment buildings of the workers' neighborhoods, the route still used by most of the "popular" (meaning "of the common people") buses to get to the airport. It wound tortuously down the side of the valley, paralleling the highway for a short distance and then descending into the city itself, eventually rejoining the highway just above the Plaza San Francisco. From there it would be only a few blocks to the Plaza Murillo, where the Palacio Quemado and the Chamber of Deputies stood.

The column moved at a brisk twenty-five miles per hour, and the captain had assigned as commander of the lead vehicle a man whose family lived in this neighborhood, banking on his familiarity with the narrow side streets to enable them to bypass any possible obstruction if necessary. After a few minutes of uneventful driving the lead vehicle reported a barricade in the road ahead.

Duarte's men did not have the luxury of a concrete pedestrian overpass, conveniently made to measure, to block the road, but they had confiscated a couple of civilian buses, which they had placed nose to nose across the street at a particularly narrow point. Duarte set up one of his LAW-80 teams directly behind the barricade, and another was hidden in an upstairs room well above the obstruction, thus giving the men a shot at the rear of any vehicle trying to force its way through. His theory was that, even though the armored vehicles would have no trouble pushing past the buses, if he could manage to disable one or two of them in the same tangle the combined weight of inert metal might be enough to block the road effectively.

As an added precaution, Duarte had broken into a local store and, after some searching while his men held the enraged owner at bay, had finally found what he was looking for. His men carried out two cases of large earthenware dinner plates, for which he promptly paid double their value to the now obsequiously grateful owner. He then had his men lay these plates face down all along the road in front of the barricade, finally hanging two large, hand-painted signs on lamp posts farther up the road, declaring that the road had been mined. He hoped that the resemblance of the plates to antitank mines would deter the advancing column at least temporarily.

He had done his best to evacuate the area bordering the road, but even with the policemen who had been sent to help with this purpose, he did not have enough men to spare to enforce the evacuation. Some families either never left, or had filtered back when his patrols had moved on, more concerned with protecting their few possessions from looting than with saving their lives. Of course most of these people had lived through many coups before, and knew that the dead were mostly among the students and workers who took to the streets opposing or supporting one side or the other, along with the occasional bystander caught outside at the wrong place and the wrong time. Certainly, little could happen to one in the safety of one's own home, and, besides, it was apparent that the real battle was being fought on the highway itself, well above them.

The captain ordered the lead vehicle to ram one of the buses well behind the engine compartment and push it bodily out of the way. His first Cascavels were in a position to fire in support. When the driver of the Urutu stopped short upon reading Duarte's warning signs, the captain merely uttered a curse, swung his .50-caliber machinegun around, and traced a long burst up the road, disintegrating several of the plates. The captain knew plates when he saw them, and he also knew that there were no antitank mines available to any unit in La Paz, which was why the "Tarapaca" could always drive into the city at will and overthrow the government.

The lead vehicle then moved up, and with a grinding and screeching of metal began to push at the bus on the right, while firing off smoke cannisters to cover its position. Although the thick white smoke did obscure their vision, the crew of the LAW-80 in the apartment above the barrier could still see the Urutu clearly enough, and a finger of flame reached out to tear open its rear deck, sending clouds of black smoke to mingle with the white.

The Cascavels began firing with all guns. One in the rear of the column had identified the building from which the missile had come and began to fire high-explosive rounds into the ground floor of the structure. After several such rounds the fragile brick construction collapsed in a cloud of red dust. The leading Cascavels now roared ahead, firing. One pushed the bus on the left out of the way, popping smoke all the while. A LAW-80 round raced through the night, but it struck the bus engine instead of the Cascavel. The armored car tore free from the burning wreck and continued down the street at speed, followed by the others. Another LAW-80 caught a Cascavel in the side of the hull, and it exploded spectacularly as its ammunition cooked off, but the other vehicles in the column raced past the wreckage, all guns firing wildly, impervious to the hail of small-arms fire that rained down on them from the cadets along the road. One cadet dashed out into the street and hurled a satchel charge under the wheels of an Urutu as it passed, just before its machinegun cut him in two. Then the charge exploded, lifting the vehicle off the ground and hurling it on its side through the shuttered display window of a ladies' wear store. The charred mannequins mingled with the blackened bodies of the vehicle's crew. Still, Duarte had to make an urgent call to Guerrero that the column had gotten past him and that in any case he had no more LAWs to stop them with.

The sun was up over the surrounding mountains as the column of trucks on the road from Oruro pulled to a stop at the roadblock. Two armored cars were parked across the road, their machineguns trained on the trucks. As the miners examined the obstacle several tanks suddenly wheeled out from behind some buildings, their large cannon pointed menacingly at the trucks.

On board the lead truck Antonio Ticona, a thirty-eight-year-old miner, jacked a round into the chamber of his Mauser. He was too young to remember the revolution of 1952, although his wrinkled, leathery skin belied it, but he had fought as a young *miliciano* against the Banzer coup of 1971, which had overthrown the leftist government of Gen. J. J. Torres, so he was not afraid of the army. He also knew that, statistically speaking, he was due to die soon of black lung or one of the other mysterious diseases that kept the tin miners' lives unhappy and short, if not in a cave-in or some other disaster. In any case, this was as good a place to die as any. At least the air was fresh and the sun was shining.

As Ticona watched sullenly the hatch on one of the armored cars opened and a broad, smiling, Indian face emerged. The man was wearing an army uniform all right, but atop his head he wore a brightly colored *chulu*, the rather silly-looking but comfortably warm knit woolen caps with dangling ear flaps and tassles worn by the Indians of the Altiplano.

Quispe waved at the miners and called out in Aymara, "Good morning brothers! Let's go to town and kick some army butt!" As the miners stared in bewilderment the hatches of the other vehicles popped open and similar, smiling Indian faces rose out of them, each topped with its *chulu*. The miners raised their rifles above their heads and cheered as the armored vehicles took their place at the head of the column and headed off toward La Paz at the best speed the trucks could manage.

Although the sun was well up now, the streets of La Paz were still deserted. The surest indication of whether a coup or a particularly violent strike is afoot in La Paz has always been the presence of buses and taxis. The buses and taxis are privately owned, usually by the driver himself, and the last thing the owner-operator wants is for his tires to be punctured by nails strewn in the street by strikers or for his windshield to be smashed. In this case the sound of continued gunfire, where the main column of the "Tarapaca" was again hammering at Guerrero's blocking position, made the efficient *radio cocina,* the "kitchen radio," or grapevine, unnecessary to pass the word.

Consequently Lieutenant Vasquez had no trouble landing the Super Puma helicopters carrying his two commando teams directly in the broad Plaza San Francisco, the other helicopters carrying the prisoners having been diverted to land directly at the army general headquarters.

Martinez met Vasquez as soon as he landed, to pass on Guerrero's orders. The main threat as Guerrero saw it was that the column now rolling unopposed down the old airport road would reach the Plaza and send a force back up the main highway, taking Guerrero's men in the rear and opening the way for the rest of the "Tarapaca" to move directly into the city. It would be Vasquez' job to try to stop them, and Guerrero left it up to Vasquez' ingenuity as to how to do that with no antitank weapons. Martinez had brought with him a supply of Molotov cocktails and some more satchel charges his demolitions men had been working frantically to prepare, and Vasquez grimly moved his men half a kilometer up the old airport road to where they could at least take advantage of the constriction of movement provided by the buildings on either side of the street. Vasquez knew that the use of each of these homemade weapons would cost a life and that the chances of success were limited at best.

O'Higgins was not pleased with the losses his forces had suffered already. He had recalled the MOWAGs and the V-100s from the airport to join the main assault, but his primary force was down to these plus eight or nine Cascavels and less than a dozen Urutus, and he was still not through the first defensive position. He suspected that the enemy had a shortage of antitank missiles, but he could not be certain how many remained. Now he had massed his remaining vehicles for a Hell-for-leather charge down the highway, counting on speed and increased numbers to get them through to link up with the force already approaching the Plaza San Francisco by the other road. To supervise the assault he had taken over an Urutu as his command vehicle.

The roar of several dozen powerful engines was deafening and reassuring, but the sound of the explosion of the Cascavel next to O'Higgins' vehicle cut through the other noise like a knife. Pieces of deck plating flew past O'Higgins' head as he dropped down inside the hatch. Through the vision blocks he could see his headquarters troops being cut down in the open by the machineguns of some armored cars stopped farther up the highway. Three of the Austrian tank destroyers of the "Calama" were also there, hurling 105mm shells into the compact mass of his vehicles, and around them swirled hundreds of armed men in miner's helmets. Some of the Cascavels tried to turn their turrets and maneuver to return fire, but these were the preferred targets of the tank destroyers, and one after another they were blown apart. O'Higgins' first reaction was to try calling on the radio to get these fools to stop firing on friendly troops, but then he realized that this was no mistake at all.

The men at Guerrero's command post cheered themselves hoarse as they watched Quispe's gunners pump rounds into the remnants of the "Tarapaca." Guerrero quickly called his couple of remaining antitank missile teams and had them fire off their missiles as well, adding to the destruction. Then he waited by the radio for the call he was certain would come. It came in seconds later, with a stammering voice using the "Tarapaca" call sign. Guerrero accepted the offer of surrender and ordered all firing to cease.

Duarte's men crouched in their positions, tensed as they heard the armored cars rumbling down the street ahead of them. At first they thought that their position had been discovered somehow when the vehicles stopped. It was not until after the "Tarapaca" men began climbing out of their armored cars with their hands raised that Guerrero's message came over Duarte's radio. The fighting was over.

Chapter Twenty-two

That afternoon a small group of army officers and civilians were seated in the cramped meeting hall of the army general headquarters in Miraflores. The officers, most of them very young and still wearing their rumpled and dirty combat fatigue uniforms, were congratulating each other on their victory, and even Joaquin Leon was smiling, proud to see that his miners had been given the task of guarding the air force base and also of mounting a guard of honor here in the hall, alongside the soldiers of the "Colorados."

Padre Tomas was also there, talking with General Morales, making certain that the prisoners taken during the coup were being treated properly. Actually, all of the enlisted men had already been disarmed and released. The conscripts were freed to return to their families and the handful of professional NCOs were put on extended leave until they were either dismissed permanently or invited to join the new defense force. Most of the officers who had opposed the coup were under arrest, but once the demobilization of the old armed forces had been completed they would pose little risk to the new regime, having no troops to command, and Morales had promised them full retirement benefits in any case. Only the fate of the narcotics traffickers who had been arrested by Guerrero's men was still in question, and Morales refused to discuss the issue just yet. However, the priest was less than enthusiastic about intervening to defend their human rights.

A telex machine had been set up near the front of the hall along with some desks covered with ledgers and papers, about which studious young men and harried secretaries dragooned from the Central Bank were scurrying nervously. Guerrero had promised them that he would be revealing his national debt refinancing package to them in a few moments. While everyone thought this rather strange, they had all agreed that Guerrero had earned the right to do a little grandstanding and were willing to humor him for a few minutes.

Out in the bright afternoon sunshine a group of about thirty men in civilian clothes stood dejectedly in the parking area behind one of the "Ingavi" maintenance garages. Their hands were tied behind them, and some had blueish bruises on their faces or bloodstained shirts. They were surrounded by a cordon of grim-faced commandos. The men turned sullenly as Guerrero entered with Duarte, Campos, and Venegas in tow.

"Gentlemen," Guerrero began cheerily. "I am aware that you are all men of business, and I have an interesting business proposition for you. As you know, we have just overthrown the Boca government, and President Boca has been convicted of conspiracy to commit murder and sentenced to life imprisonment by a military tribunal. It has been confirmed that he facilitated the entry into this country of a group of armed foreigners for purposes of terrorism, an act which resulted in the deaths of more than a dozen Bolivians and a number of American diplomats. We have videotaped his confession, which was supervised by the Papal Nuncio and a number of other diplomats of unquestionable integrity to assure the public that no coercion was used. He also seems to have suffered something of a nervous breakdown, but his testimony is still valid." Some of the men's mouths dropped open, and they looked nervously from one to another.

"Oh, maybe you didn't know that," Guerrero continued. "Well, you do now. In any event, what that means is that my men and I are currently playing the role of God in your lives. If we so decide, you can leave this garage alive and go abroad and live comfortably forever. If we so decide, we will rip your fucking hearts out and make you eat them." Guerrero stared at them steadily, a pleasant smile still on his face.

"I suspect that I now have your full attention. My offer is this. A young accountant friend of mine has been doing some calculations, based on information provided by Captain Venegas here and from some documents we seized in your homes and from the files of UMOPAR, shortly after the untimely demise of Colonel Venetti. Consequently, we have a rough idea of how much each one of you is worth. Since the bulk of this money has never entered Bolivia, but is stashed safely away in numbered bank accounts in Switzerland or the Cayman Islands or elsewhere, we will request that each of you write down the amount of money you wish to have transferred to the Banco Central of Bolivia and whatever codes and instructions necessary to do so. If the amount compares favorably with the amount we have arrived at for you, you will go free, just as soon as the transfer has been completed and you have signed a document turning over ownership and title to all of your real property in Bolivia to the Bolivian government. Ownership of your personal property, such as cars and furniture, will also devolve on the government. Are there any questions?"

"Yes," shouted someone from the back of the crowd. "Are you fucking out of your mind? You can't do this to us. It's illegal. I demand to see my lawyer." There was a general murmur of approval among the prisoners.

"I see we have a misunderstanding here," Guerrero continued conversationally. "You see, whatever I say is legal, here and now, is legal. If I say it's illegal, it's illegal. If I order you all to convert to Judaism on pain of death, you still have your choice, of course, but it's totally legal. There are no lawyers involved here, no courts, no fucking legal tricks to get you out of the holes you've dug. You've had a very nice existence up to now, laughing at the legal system of the civilized world that was set up to protect the innocent while you murdered people by the dozen and filled the world's children full of your filthy drugs. It's just you and me now. I know what you've done, and you know what you've done, so let's cut to the chase. Now, who wants to go first?"

No one moved. By previous arrangement, one of the commandos grabbed Benitez and shoved him out in front of Guerrero. Guerrero grinned even more broadly.

"Well, Lazaro, it's been such a long time. I know that you have a certain reputation and prestige among this crowd, so I'm glad to see you step up and volunteer right away. So, what's it going to be?" Guerrero held out to him a pad of paper and a pencil. There was no need to untie his hands. Benitez just leaned forward and spat on the paper.

"I was hoping you'd do something like that," Guerrero said. He kicked Benitez in the back of the calves, dropping him to his knees. He tossed the paper and pencil on the ground and drew his pistol. "This is what we call a visual aid in military training courses."

He placed the barrel of the gun at the base of Benitez' skull and allowed him to scream, "No, wait!" before he pulled the trigger. There was total silence from the gathered men as the bark of the shot echoed faintly in the thin air of the valley.

"There, you see? He waited too long, and the offer was no longer open. Who wants to be next?"

Several of the men began to cry openly, sobbing about their families and the fact that they had never meant to harm anyone, or that they never had. The guards untied their hands and passed out writing materials, which they snatched up greedily, like drowning men grabbing for bits of driftwood. Some of the men knelt down, others used each other's backs to write. Occasionally, one of the men would look over to where Benitez' body lay still twitching on the ground, blood still oozing from the gaping wound at the top of his neck.

"I should warn you, gentlemen," Guerrero went on after they had had a few moments to write. "There will be no, shall we say, corrections permitted in the figures you give me. I am not much of a one for haggling. If your figure is significantly lower than the one I have noted for each of you, I will take it as a definite 'No' answer, and we will pass immediately to the phase Mr. Benitez just went through."

Some of the men looked up in horror from their papers, paused, began to erase furiously, and then started to write afresh.

Tom Evans was sitting in the back of the hall. His presence was not really necessary. There were men in the room who would provide full reports of the day's events to his men later, as they had already given him a rough idea of Guerrero's plan, but Evans wanted to see for himself for a change. The telex machine had been working constantly for over an hour, and a young army officer was putting up figures on a blackboard as the "returns" came in. The number had long since gone to ten figures in U.S. dollars, and the crowd had ceased to be as awed as they had been by the amount "donated" by the first trafficker. Not only would there be no more national debt, Evans calculated, but there would hardly be a need for foreign aid for some time to come. What generous, civic-minded people, he thought.

Of course, Evans' source had confided that Guerrero really had very little idea of how much money any of the traffickers might have abroad. There was, after all, no Chamber of Commerce for drug lords with a central repository of information on the amounts of cocaine they shipped or what they sold it for. Evans and Contreras of DEA had gladly provided Guerrero what information they had, unofficially, but even the U.S. government had only the faintest glimmering of information in this area. Guerrero was bluffing, but it was working. The traffickers could hardly take the chance that Guerrero might really know what each of them had, so they had to be very generous. It didn't matter if they were holding back even millions of their ill-gotten gains. What

Guerrero needed to make his gamble at taking over the government work was a tremendous infusion of cash, and he was getting it. Evans searched his own conscience for a trace of remorse that this money which was now flowing into the Bolivian Central Bank was the dirtiest kind of drug money, squeezed out of kids who stole from old people, even their own parents, to finance their drug habits, but there was none. That money had long been paid out, and the drugs had done their damage. Maybe now the money would at least serve some useful purpose and not just buy another Mercedes or villa in the south of France for some glorified thug.

Evans thought back to his days in Vietnam. There had always been talk then of letting the Vietnamese find their own solution to their problems. In effect, that was what had happened. The Americans had gotten out, and the North Vietnamese tanks had done the final negotiating. Well, here was a real home-grown solution, and Evans knew that he would find it far easier to live with this one than with the other.

That evening there was a knock at the door of Featherstone's hospital room. When Ann opened it Guerrero entered, cap in one hand, a small bouquet of flowers in the other. He smiled and nodded to Ann. "Good evening, Mrs. Featherstone," he mumbled shyly.

"Commander Guerrero," Ann said, making an exaggerated curtsey. "How rude of me not to have left the window open for you."

Guerrero laughed. "It took me a while to figure out how to work the door knob, but I think I've got the knack of it now." He paused uncomfortably. "I know that you've been through quite a bit lately, but I wonder if I might speak with your husband privately for a moment."

"Of course, Commander. I won't bother making coffee this time, since you'll probably slip out through the floor drain while I'm gone, but I'll just run and put these in some water." She plucked the flowers from his hand lightly and slipped out of the room, closing the door gently behind her.

"I'm glad to see that you weren't hurt too badly," Guerrero said. "That was quite a battle your people put up in the embassy. You should be proud. I'm only sorry we couldn't have done something to head it off altogether."

"Not as badly as I might have been if you hadn't risked your life to give us that warning. Thank you," he added warmly. "I've already been on the phone to Captain Venegas, thanking him for his men's sacrifices. It was a close run thing, as I think Wellington once said, and I don't think we would have made it if it hadn't been for what his men did."

Featherstone sighed and sat up a bit straighter. "I should also take this opportunity to say good-bye to you. I'll be leaving Bolivia soon, and I suspect that you'll be a pretty busy man, what with having your own country to run now."

"Wrong on both counts," Guerrero said. "First of all I am resigning my commission. Maybe I'm too concerned with appearances, but I really don't want it said that I did this for personal advancement. I'm thinking of getting a contract with the new self-defense force as a civilian instructor at the Academy. That'll give me something to do, but not too much. On the second matter, our Ministry of Foreign Affairs has just requested that your Ambassador Pearson be recalled, permanently. We've decided that he seems to have a medical problem, a tiny piece of brain lodged somewhere in his skull, and that this has affected his performance here. That makes you chargé d'affaires, and you can't leave."

"Well, I'm very . . . flattered, I guess, that you would want me to stay, but I'm not at all certain what the attitude of my government is going to be regarding your coup. You know that everyone was so pleased that Latin America was moving away from this sort of thing toward more democratic elections. I suspect that it would have been a photo finish anyway, whether you booted Pearson out of here or whether Washington withdrew him."

"I wouldn't worry too much about that. In fact I don't worry at all about it," Guerrero laughed. "Since we're leaving virtually all of the government in the hands of civilians, have called for new elections, and are actually disbanding the military, I think the various democracies will come around. We're also sending your government a present, a Boeing 707 nearly full of drug traffickers, many of whom are wanted by your Justice Department, and, believe it or not, they're very, very happy to be going. I'm sure Mr. Evans will explain all of that to you later. I'm sure that there will be a certain amount of pussing and moaning from the State Department, but we'll have to live with it."

"That's 'pissing and moaning'," Featherstone corrected him. "Although, for someone who's accomplished what you have, I suppose that a few liberties with old cliches isn't too much to ask."

"Let's not get too excited about what *I've* accomplished," Guerrero said, waving a finger in the air. "The drug trade isn't going to disappear just because we knocked a hole in the old mafia. We were able to wrap them up because they felt secure, no need to hide. They found out in Colombia during the big drug war of the late 1980s that a forewarned mafia is very difficult to dig out, and they can exact a terrible price if they want to go to the mat. The drug business is still there, and sooner or later others will come to pick up the pieces and re-form the trafficking nets, this time more clandestinely. All I've done is to give my country a breathing space, a chance to at least try to break the bond to the drug trade, which is as much of an addiction for a country as the drugs themselves are to the users. We'll see how they handle it."

Guerrero glanced at his watch. "Well, I really should be going." His face suddenly turned very serious. "I have some funerals to attend, hopefully the last before my own."

Featherstone nodded silently and extended his hand. The two men shook, and Guerrero bent to give Featherstone a firm *abrazo*, or hug.

In his office at army headquarters, or what now would be the office of the commander of the self-defense force, General Campos walked slowly across the thick carpet. It wasn't exactly luxurious, but it was a hundred times better than anything he had ever had before. There was real wood panelling on the walls, and the desk and chairs were of teak. As he rounded his new desk, he saw a piece of typing paper laid neatly on the blotter. At first he assumed that it had been left by the old army commander, General Escobar, but as he bent closer he saw that it had his name on it.

It read:

Dear General Campos:

Congratulations on your appointment as Commander of the Self-Defense Force of Bolivia. We are certain that your professional capacity will bring new honor to the Bolivian nation and people. We are a group of citizens concerned with the welfare of our country, and we believe that those who dedicate their lives to its service should not have to suffer financial hardship due to the scandalously low pay provided to the military, even with the new increases in salary. Consequently, we have deposited the sum of one million U.S. dollars in a discreet bank account in Europe for your use as partial compensation for your sacrifices and to help you perform your duties with greater dignity and efficiency.

We will be in contact with you in the near future to inform you of the administrative details for obtaining access to these funds.

Again, congratulations, and we look forward to working with you.

The letter was unsigned. Campos sat heavily in his new chair. One million dollars was more money than he could properly comprehend.